THE ROOSTER'S GARDEN

THE
ROOSTER'S
GARDEN

OLIVIA A. COLE

WHEN THE ROOSTER CROWS,
THE HIVE WILL BURN.

This one is for you, Fazha.

CHAPTER 1

The car dies in Iowa, right outside a private elementary school, covered in ivy and filled with small creatures who might once have been children, but whom the Chip has transformed into tiny, angry beasts. As she closes the car door, Tasha can see them at the windows, butting their heads against the glass like sea turtles in an aquarium. The glowing energy bar on the Chevy's dash had gone from green to yellow to orange. When it started to turn red, Tasha had steered the car off the interstate, and it had crawled to a stop in front of the school. The car hadn't made much noise, but something had drawn the mini-Minkers to the window: their yaps and snarls silenced by the glass. They could be an old silent movie. They are tiny Godzillas. Tasha hopes somewhere in the crowd of them is their teacher, also Chipped. Otherwise, she can imagine that morning's science lesson playing differently: the subject of human internal anatomy transforming from a conceptual discussion to a hands-on operation.

Z gets out of the car and stretches, rubbing the back of her right arm from where it had fallen asleep against the car door.

"So this is the Hawkeye State," she says, waving at the kids, who still strain against their windows.

"I've never been to Iowa," says Malakai as he steps out of the car, coaxing the poodle out too. It's been nine hours since the Apiary exploded like a massive crystal balloon. They'd stopped once to let the dog—and everyone else—pee, and now with the Chevy out of juice, they're stopped for good.

The dog doesn't seem to mind. It had spent the first hour of the trip shivering and whimpering inside the blanket Malakai wrapped it in. Tasha instructed him to open a can of SpaghettiOs from the backpack and he did so, feeding the dog with his fingers. After a few bites, it had roused itself enough to stick its whole muzzle into the can, polishing off the pseudo pasta in a flash. Malakai had dabbed the sauce from its slender snout daintily.

Now the poodle hops gingerly out of the car and sniffs around. Tasha wonders at her reasoning for bringing the dog. She thinks of how it had looked on that grooming table in Fetch Fetchers—beautifully clipped and all but dead. The dog really should be dead, Tasha thinks as it snuffs at a dandelion on the edge of the sidewalk. But here she is.

Ishmael is opening the trunk, where they had stowed the backpacks after their first stop.

"Anybody hungry?" he asks, extending a granola bar from one of the packs and munching on another as he looks around. Tasha holds her hands up in a diamond. He tosses her the bar. Z takes one too, but Malakai just watches the dog.

"So, uh…," Z says, chewing with her mouth slightly open and leaning against the car. "How are we gonna do this?"

Tasha has thought of nothing else since they sped out of Chicago, the sky behind them a sunset at noon as, somewhere miles back, what used to be the biggest shopping mall in the country smoldered like a campfire. And somewhere Dr. Rio is a marshmallow that had fallen off its roasting stick. Jumped, not fell—a marshmallow that wanted nothing to do with the graham cracker. Tasha puts this particular image out of her mind.

Dr. Rio had given them the maps: they know the route. Z has the single compass. They have food enough for a couple days, when they will have to stop somewhere to forage for supplies. Tasha looks at the poodle, which snaps at a passing butterfly. They'll need kibble too.

"Well, I guess we just...go."

No one says anything. They know she's right. What else is there to do but go?

Tasha thinks about this. What is "going"? Going now is different than a trip home to Kentucky on the high-speed train. She thinks of her last trip to her hometown, after her parents had died. For that hour-long journey, she had packed three snacks, two movies, and six changes of clothes, knowing she would only be there for three or four days. Now, faced with a trip across the country, on foot, with no train attendant bringing warm towels and low-fat unsalted peanuts—and certainly with no en-route movie—what does "going" mean? Going means being gone. Going means letting go.

The trunk already open, Tasha goes over and peers inside, still munching the granola bar. Their four backpacks sit there like stones. They could be full of drugs, body parts: they sit there suspiciously, black and gray. Except Tasha's, of course. Rio had offered her one of the dull military-grade packs, but she had kept her green canvas Prada. It's an odd duck here in the trunk—not necessarily a swan. Its stitching and delicacy look somewhat silly next to the sturdy usefulness of the other three: a former prom queen who showed up to boot camp with a French manicure and an up-do. Tasha rubs a finger over the canvas—it's been a little faded with dust and wear over the past weeks. Near one of the straps there's a sprinkling of blood. Whose? Tasha can think of many candidates, but she'd rather not.

Peering into the back of the trunk, she spies Dr. Rio's bag, a large beige nylon thing with many zippered pockets. He had left it in the car when they'd gone into the Apiary—he'd known he wouldn't need it again.

Z pops up over Tasha's shoulder like a meerkat.

"Is that Dr. Rio's bag? What's in it?"

Tasha shrugs, looking at it.

"Welllll, let's pop that puppy open!"

Tasha laughs and grips the edge of the hefty bag, pulling it to the front of the trunk. She finds that she's afraid of it, this decidedly unstylish khaki lump. Who knows what's inside? It could be another bomb. Perhaps Rio had rigged the bag to destroy any Minkers that got into the car. Tasha doesn't think this is likely—Rio had known Minkers are shit with doors.

Now Malakai has wandered over and is squinting into the trunk. He looks concerned, his brow furrowed. Tasha imagines he's a little traumatized. They haven't talked about Rio yet, or what had happened at the Apiary. The last nine hours in the car had been mostly quiet, everyone mining their thoughts and either carting out the diamonds or hiding the coals. All of them have coal.

Now Malakai, peering at Rio's bag, looks as if he might be ready to talk about how it came to pass that his mentor, the savior of old ladies and the Chipless citizens of Chicago, transformed into a lunatic on a suicide mission. But no. Tasha sees the boy's eyes wall off. Not yet. He's got more thinking to do. Instead, he just nods at the bag and says, "What's in it?"

"Might be a bomb," Z suggests.

Sometimes Tasha thinks of Z as a caterpillar munching through Tasha's thoughts, spitting them out for everyone to see.

"I thought the same thing," Tasha says, fingering the zipper on the bag. She thinks of Dr. Rio handing them all bags full of cyclonite, and the group accepting them, trusting his spectacles and his somber, well-trimmed beard.

She inhales through her nose, sniffing for the smell of cabbage. An odorizing taggant, he'd explained matter-of-factly. To disguise the smell of explosives from the seeking noses of dogs. She looks over at the poodle, who is sitting by the left rear tire, panting. The dog isn't very strong—after a week of starvation, trapped in a hangman's noose on the grooming table, a can of SpaghettiOs won't be enough to revive her. Tasha realizes they might be on foot from here on out, unless they can find a car someplace. That means the dog will either be on paw with them or left to fend for itself. Either way, it might die.

"Hey, dog," Tasha says, snapping her fingers.

The dog looks up. Tasha pulls Rio's bag from the trunk and tosses it to the poodle, who jumps, skittish. "Sniff this. Go on, sniff it."

Tasha points.

The poodle points its nose at the bag, pauses, then gives the material one slow lick.

Z raises her eyebrow.

"I don't know," Tasha mumbles, walking over and picking up the bag again. "I thought it might, like, know or something."

Z takes the bag from Tasha and arches her neck down, putting her ear alongside it.

"Well, it's not ticking or anything," she says with an air of drama. "Let's just open it."

She looks around. Ishmael nods. Malakai opens his mouth but doesn't say anything. Tasha shrugs. The dog pants.

The sound of the zipper is muted and the air remains still as Z digs her arm inside the pack. Nothing explodes. Nothing starts counting backwards from some terrifyingly low number. Tasha thinks of the elevator ride down from Cybranu's floor in the Apiary, Dr. Rio upstairs trembling above the clouds. She'll probably never ride an elevator again. She thinks of the Lift in the subways of Chicago—elevating sewer rats and underground Minkers to the upper street and the wind. The thirty-day power grid would die, and then maybe everything else would too.

Z withdraws a Glass and a compass, then one of the interactive maps. The second two objects are identical to the ones Z already has. The Glass she hands to Tasha, who turns it over looking for the power button. Z digs out a few more items: a flashlight; a hard case to carry eyeglasses, which is empty; a pair of woolen socks; a packet of sunflower seeds, salted. A canteen of water.

Tasha finds the power switch on the Glass and the screen glows to life. A box materializes in the center:

"This device is password protected," it reads. "Enter the password."

A little glowing gatekeeper. Tasha looks at Malakai and holds up the screen so he can see.

"Any ideas?"

He squints at it and shrugs.

"I don't know. Try *Cybranu*."

Tasha tries, tapping the touchscreen buttons, watching the asterisks appear in the blinking fields as she types in the word. She taps enter.

"So sorry," the machine reads. "That password is incorrect."

At least it's sorry, Tasha thinks.

Z shrugs.

"No biggie. I mean, I'm not really sure I give a shit what's in Rio's little diary anyway."

Tasha imagines that he only used the Glass to read inane drivel, his library filled with teen vampire romances instead of serious medical studies. Or something to soothe his tender, maniacal spirit: *Chicken Soup for the Mad Scientist's Soul*. Is that what he was? A mad scientist? He'd helped create the Chip, but he wasn't the man with the plan. Or so he said.

"Hey, look. One got out."

Tasha looks where Z is pointing. Through the gates around the private school—Whitlow Academy for Excellence, the ancientish placard reads—Tasha can see a kid (one of Whitlow's brainiacs) plodding around the corner of the school, her head swiveling, plaid skirt swishing around the stumbling knees. Tasha used to wear such a skirt. Her hips can remember the itchy wool; she wants to scratch herself just thinking about it.

"Should we, you know…do something?" Malakai asks. He's nervous, and his voice is soft. He moves closer to Ishmael, who is very still.

The girl in the skirt has a sixth sense for gossip—she turns her head in their direction, and even from fifty meters Tasha can hear her beginning to bark.

"No, don't worry," Tasha says, trying to sound the way she would have sounded in a time before, when a fourth-grader wouldn't have set her stomach clenching. "It's just the one. And she can't get around the fence, I don't think."

"Yeah, don't worry," Z echoes. "I'd feel bad killing a kid, especially all by herself."

She hasn't even closed her lips after delivering the words when a classroom of plaid-clad ankle-biters pours around the corner of the ivy-colored school, drawn by the first girl's barking. She must have been the class president, leading the pack. Tasha opens her mouth to say "Oh, shit," but someone's already saying it: they're all saying it, they're all looking around for possible missiles to launch, cannons to fire, gaps in the fence the little brats might fit through.

"What do we do? What do we do?"

It's Malakai's voice, small and thin. He might have said it a few more times but Tasha doesn't count. She does count the number of little Minkers that are swaying across the schoolyard.

"The fence looks strong," Ishmael says, nodding at the iron gates. "I don't think the gaps in the bars are big enough to squeeze through."

"That little runt might," Z points at a straggler in the herd, a skinny kid with a curtain of black hair over her face.

They stand staring at the oncoming mini-horde, the poodle standing behind Malakai's legs, Malakai standing behind

Ishmael's. They should all be running, Tasha knows, in case the herd manages to escape the schoolyard, but it's too much like *National Geographic*, the strange but strangely familiar predators on the prairie; Tasha and her group the naïve birdwatchers, ape observers. Minkers in the Mist, Tasha thinks, watching the kiddies' progress, but there is no mist. It's early evening and the air is clear, if darkening. The things they fear don't lurk in the shadows as monsters ought to—they're here, in collared shirts and neckties, the girls in plaid skirts. Are they girls anymore, or females? A girl, a woman, is human. A female is something else, something wild, something Other. The *National Geographic* voice in Tasha's head utters its muted testimony: "The female of the Minker species is smaller than its male counterpart, but equally vicious. Her thirst for blood is equally voracious, not lessened by the presence of a vagina."

"We should probably go," Z is tugging at the sleeve of Tasha's hoodie, her eyes fixed on the schoolchildren drawing near, their barks like boisterous crickets in the evening air. "It's getting dark and we don't have the car."

Tasha turns away from the private school's wildlife and nods, noting Malakai's grip on his brother's arm. The group heads down the empty street.

"We need to stay on the route though," Z says, patting her own ass. The map is folded into her pocket, half of it poking out the top. "We're already a little off."

Dr. Rio and his red lines, his path, his winding scribble across the country. Tasha thinks he might have just taken a pen and dragged it in swirls across the map—obviously he never had any intention of making the trip himself, so she doubts he really cared what conditions "the route" might pass through. She wonders how Utah will be. Aren't there deserts in Utah?

"It's getting dark," Malakai says quietly, to no one and everyone. His daemon of a dog lopes slowly beside him.

They've been hurrying away from the schoolyard and the dead Chevrolet, and the barks of the student body fade into the background. Tasha guesses the Minkerized children hadn't been able to fit through the bars, even the runt. She feels vaguely disappointed. She'd stowed the Wusthof in the backpack while they were driving, where it remains, which she suddenly realizes is very stupid. She swings the backpack off her shoulders and finds the knife.

"We need weapons," she says. Z still has her box cutter but Ishmael's hatchet had obliterated the queen bee at the Apiary and Malakai had lost his shovel somewhere around Cybranu. Maybe he'd left it with Dr. Rio, she thinks: one final offering from acolyte to priest.

So far the poodle is the only one who has looked around, so focused have they all been on first the hungry kids and then on getting away from the hungry kids. Tasha looks about her. They're in a town that the map orders them to pass through—Whitchapel, Z had said it was called when the car stopped; like everywhere in the world, it reminds Tasha of Louisville. A shorter, browner Louisville, its buildings and roads various shades of tans and camels, though no actual camels are present. Its silence is like a grasshopper's legs rubbing crispily together, the breaking apart of a locust's shell.

"It's like an old Wild West town from the movies," Z says, her voice low.

This isn't true, but Tasha knows what she means. There are no horses and no tumbleweeds—no cacti or cowboys either—but the dryness of the air bends the imagination.

"I haven't been this far from Lake Michigan since I was eighteen," Ishmael says.

"I'm thirsty," says Malakai.

Z passes the boy a canteen of water and they continue down the street, buildings on either side like bouncers ready to evict them from some snobby Iowa club. Or bodyguards to protect them, Tasha thinks, trying to be optimistic. But there's not much to encourage rainbows and sunshine, as neither rainbows nor sunshine are present. It's also almost night—not an optimal time for either.

"We need to find somewhere to sleep," Z says. She's holding the compass uselessly, as if she's making sure wherever they spend the night is facing exactly due west.

Tasha refers to her mental Rolodex of adventure movies for an idea of where they should rest. She imagines stripping trees of their more flexible branches, scooping mud from nearby trenches to patch together fronds for a roof. She'd be wearing a loincloth, of course. Unfortunately her version of survival applies only to a tropical disaster, and palm trees are as scarce here as cowboys. No trees at all, actually: just smallish city streets dotted with crashed and abandoned cars, trash, the random unidentifiable debris of disaster. And bodies. The usual clusters of bodies, indistinguishable from the many they'd driven past along the way.

"How about there?" Tasha points at a smaller building— what appears to be an antique store, rocking chairs and lamps in the windows, a painted doll propped up by a metal frame that appears to be skewering its wooden body. The store looks small and safe, its front windows unsmashed. There might be cushions in there too, old crocheted things, smelling of moths, but soft.

"Or, if you don't like the idea of splinters and old-lady smell, we could go there," Z points. It's getting dark, but Tasha can make out the once-illuminated sign of a Holiday Inn. In Chicago, its neon would likely have remained glowing, hooked to the city grid. No Whitchapel generators, she guesses.

"Maybe we can get some room service," Z grins, leading the way.

Ishmael laughs and follows her, holding onto Malakai's shoulder, steering him like a small, nervous ship. Only Tasha and the poodle, sniffing the fingers of a body wearing a worn striped shirt, hang back: Tasha nervously, the dog distractedly. The poodle's sniffing inspires Tasha to inhale through her nose; the smell of death is overwhelming, a clammy gray hand clamped over her face. Why is she only now noticing it? Surely that smell has been all around them, waiting to be noticed; the stench like steam-fingers in cartoons rising from the pie on the ledge—or, rather, the corpse—beckoning and beckoning. She suddenly feels nauseated, a sickness she has kept at bay since the morning of the Change, when, walking down Berwyn, she woke from her private thoughts to realize she was surrounded by torn and bloodied bodies.

She realizes now that she's been in a new kind of reverie, floating above the carnage, focused only on the knife in her hand and the necks needing stabbing; learning to keep her eyes level and avoid the death on the pavement. She takes them in now, the spell broken. She has traveled a few hundred miles in the blue Chevrolet, away from a city infested with the dead and the living-but-dead; arrived here in a small city, a town, a state, where she's never been before, only to find the same things. Death. Chipped. Blood. Broken windows. Empty streets. The stink of flesh rotting on warm pavement. The scuffling of crows over sockets picked clean of eyeball. She has traveled this distance, but is surrounded by sameness. She wants to cry, but the poodle is looking up at her, its deep brown eyes unblinking. She has a feeling the dog would tell someone.

"Are you coming?"

At first Tasha thinks it's the dog, but it's only Z, leaning out of the Holiday Inn entrance, holding the door open with the tips of her fingers. It's grown so dark that Tasha can barely make out Z's features.

"Come on, Tasha," she says. "You shouldn't be out here alone."

No, she shouldn't.

"Come on, dog," Tasha snaps her fingers, but the dog is already trotting toward Z, leaving Tasha behind. She follows its waving tail.

Inside the Holiday Inn it's darker and smells vaguely of burnt popcorn. Malakai is standing, as usual, beside and slightly behind his brother. Upon drawing Tasha into the lobby, Z fumbles around the door, something clattering against the handles.

"What are you doing?"

"Putting Rio's flashlight through the handles to lock it."

"We could use a flashlight right now."

"Power cell is dead."

"Oh."

"The automatic doors are dead since the power is out," she says, straightening up. "Nobody will get in this way, but there's probably other doors."

Tasha nods, but the light coming through the glass of the doors is so dim at this point that she doubts Z notices.

"Let's look behind the front desk for keys or a light or something."

They move slowly across the lobby. Tasha can feel her eyes focusing and refocusing like the lenses of two uncertain cameras, an aging owl straining its eyes to spy mice through the grass of the field. Likening herself to a predator is comforting. She feels less like prey.

But as quickly as she was owl, she is mouse again as her foot bumps against something soft. It's a body—she knows it: some name-tagged former night auditor caught in the lobby as guests and coworkers alike streamed down the stairs, snapping. It reminds Tasha of Brian, the doorman at her apartment on Foster. "On Foster" doesn't work now, she realizes, now that she's no longer in Chicago. It's no longer her apartment on Foster; it's her apartment in Chicago. In Illinois. It's no longer her apartment at all, really. She finds her hand wandering to the ring on her finger—reclaimed from the Apiary and back in its rightful place. It comforts her.

"Keys," Tasha says, fumbling around behind the desk whens she reaches it.

"To what?"

Tasha shrugs.

"To what?"

It's dark. She answers out loud, "I don't know. They're all scans though."

She assumes the room keys are all scans anyway—she can't really see them. They're key-shaped objects on a ring, but they don't jingle together in her hand, just click dully. Cute idea, she always thought: scan-card keys shaped like real keys, color-coded for different access points. A little old-fashioned—thumbprints have replaced almost everything, of course—but a two-story Holiday Inn in Iowa isn't exactly feeling the pressure to keep up with the times. Probably people came to establishments like this one to escape the techiness. Or to escape thumbprint detection, Tasha's inner 'noid whispers. Criminals. Rapists. Serial killers.

Suddenly there's a tiny moon, floating right before her eyes. It startles her. Already, in the five minutes that she's been creeping around the hotel lobby, she's grown used to the dark.

"Found a flashlight," Z grins, flicking it on and off like a strobe.

She flashes the beam over at Ishmael and Malakai. Malakai's eyes are huge, his mouth a flat line. His older brother looks grim.

"First floor or second?" Ishmael says.

"Are we going to stay here?" Malakai interrupts. His voice sounds the way Tasha feels: thin and tight, slightly unsteady.

"Might as well," Z says, sweeping the light across the lobby. It's just a basic flashlight so it doesn't do much, but its pale ray does reveal more dead than Tasha had first believed to be present. She continues breathing through her mouth, trying not to think about what might be floating in the air, wafting into her throat.

"Shouldn't we at least check it out first?" Tasha looks at Malakai, who's nodding as she says it, feeling slightly foolish for seeking an ally in an eleven-year-old boy. But Ishmael nods too and she feels less dumb.

"Okay, let's listen."

They're quiet. The lobby feels like a cave; Tasha expects to hear water dripping from some unseen stalactites, but there is nothing. Just the poodle, panting, a little farther from the door than the rest of the group. It's probably thirsty, Tasha thinks. Hungry too. Like her.

"I think everyone's dead." Any of them could have said it, but it's Malakai and that makes it worse. Tasha hears a rustle, which she assumes is Ishmael putting his arm around his younger brother. She's glad her parents are dead, that her sister is far away. How could she protect someone from all this? No wonder Ishmael has been so quiet.

"I think we should go to the second floor," Z says, "so we can look out a window and see what's going on out there."

"No," Tasha says, not wanting to argue but not wanting to die. "We should stay on the first floor. What if we have to run? What if they block the stairs?"

It's a lot like fire safety, she thinks. Stay low to the ground. Avoid stairs and areas with no windows. For god's sake, don't touch it. Tasha imagines the populations of the Minkers spreading across the country, burning up the States and leaving the land gray and brittle behind, crumbling.

"Okay, good idea." Z and the light move across the lobby, and Tasha and the guys follow after it like moths trailing a moving temptation. Somewhere nearby the poodle is snuffling— hopefully not lapping up anything toxic or biologically immoral—but Tasha doesn't snap her fingers or call for it. She doesn't even know why she told Malakai to bring the dog. Whether it stays with them or not isn't her concern.

They reach a hallway, darker still than the lobby. Tasha can feel her lungs get greedy as the gloom closes around her, and she tries to focus on Z's little shaft of light ahead, a beacon of hope, a miniature Olympic torch leading their procession. The smell is present, as it has been. It stirs a vague recollection in the memories of Tasha's nose—Kentucky, outdoors, grass, dirt, a dead bird under a tree, mauled by the neighbor's cat then left to rot. It's damp from dew, but its smell is stale, like a grave. Tasha thinks she remembers burying it. She must have been very young to have even considered touching it.

"Let's try this one." Z is stopped at a door on the left, a short distance down the hall.

"Listen at the door first," Tasha whispers.

Z presses her ear against the door, holding her breath, Tasha looking anxiously up and down the hall. She feels like she's breaking in: like the person she's afraid will apprehend them will be a police officer carrying a gun and plexicuffs instead of a random hotel maid with a mouthful of blood. Tasha wonders if the maids would have been eligible for the Chip. Hopefully they all got out alive.

"Tasha, did you bring the keys?"

"What?"

"The keys. The scans."

"Oh. Yeah. Shine the light."

Z reluctantly directs the light away from their surroundings and into Tasha's palm. The ring she holds is the home of about twenty key scans, little plasticky key-shaped objects. They remind her of a baby's teething ring. She considers for a moment that it actually *is* a teething ring, the keys look so ridiculously cartoonish, but no, she can see the small dotted barcode on the underside of a few of them. They're all marked with abbreviations: SR, SC, LC, RK, MK.

Tasha chooses RK, a pinkish key, thinking it might stand for "room key." She presses it against the black pad on the room's doorjamb, but she's not rewarded with a flash of a green light, or a click, or anything.

"Try the MK."

She jumps, not realizing how close Ishmael had been to her ear. His voice is very low like a purr.

"It might mean 'master key'," he adds.

Tasha tries the MK key, but nothing happens. She remembers her visit to the Post right after the Change—years ago, it seems—and feels stupid all over again.

"Guys," she whispers, "there's no power. These stupid scans won't work."

"Fuck," Z whispers, knowing Tasha's right.

"Language," says Ishmael. "What about for emergencies? One of the keys must work for emergencies."

"Only if they have a back-up generator, I think," says Tasha, pissed. They should have just broken into the antique store next door.

She hears a rustle and the sound of movement down the hall.

"What the fuck is that?"

The ray from the flashlight zooms away from the keys and down the hall where the sound came from. Its faint spot of illumination lands on the poodle's butt, which is disappearing into an open door a few rooms down.

"Good dog," Malakai whispers, and they silently move down the hall.

They stand in a cluster by the door while Z goes in with the flashlight, looking into the bathroom and behind the window curtains—the typical boogeyman hiding spots.

"Clear," she calls in a whisper, and they ease the door shut with a muted click, Ishmael tripping over the poodle, who has come to greet them as if they've just returned home and she'd been waiting.

"Two beds," Z says, already sitting on one. "Ladies with ladies, gents with gents."

With the door closed, the room smells less like a dead bird. The inexplicable stench of burnt popcorn is muted too. Z has set the flashlight on its end between the two beds, a tiny heatless campfire they gather around. The beam disperses into a soft glow on the ceiling.

Tasha had been hungry ten minutes before, but her appetite is gone now and she suspects the same for everyone else, as no one moves to open their backpacks. Except the dog, who sniffs at the half of a granola bar peeking out of Ishmael's pocket.

There's a little moonlight from the window. In her apartment on Foster—in Chicago, she corrects herself—Tasha had been able to see the moon only on the rare occasions when it was able to slip through the damask clouds that crouched above the city. Malakai had been the first to point out the clouds' absence as they drove farther and farther from Chicago.

"You can see the sky," he'd gaped. "There's the sun."

Tasha had imagined him as a small brown mole, emerging from his burrow for the first time to take in the world's entirety. Underground, peering at the sky from the depths, the sun was a dim, pebble-sized bulb. Its glare was a buzz, not a blast. Crossing from Illinois into Iowa in the car, Malakai witnessed its full glory and Tasha had to tell him not to stare straight at it—not for too long. He had learned in school that it would ruin his eyes, he'd said, but he never really believed it: the sun he'd known through the glaze of mottle over Chicago wasn't capable of such treachery. This new sun, though, the sun over Iowa—who knew the limit of its powers? Tasha worries what Colorado's sun will be like, the Utah sun. She imagines the air becoming drier, the overheard blaze more intense, with every step they take westward. Droughts had racked the whole country, but the West was always said to be worse.

"Can I give him some food?"

Malakai has his backpack in his lap, his hand half in it.

"What do you want to give him?" Ishmael asks.

They're talking about the dog. Tasha doesn't have the energy to tell them it's a girl.

"I have more SpaghettiOs."

"Give him those," Ishmael nods. "I don't want you eating too many of those anyway. Mom wouldn't like it."

"Why not?"

"It's not real food."

Tasha smiles, still looking out at the moon. She almost offers her can opener—carried with her all this way from Foster and Sheridan, Chicago, Illinois—but there's the sound of the can being opened, the tool taken from someone else's pack. The dog eats. Everyone else lies down.

In bed, Tasha stares through the darkness at the door, listening. They're safe here, she thinks. A closed door and a deadbolt are all they really need. They'll deal with getting out in the morning. She touches her mother's ring in the dark. Beside her, Z dozes on her stomach, her mouth muffled by a too-soft hotel pillow.

She murmurs something, the words swimming through the dark to Tasha's ear.

"Hmm?"

Z shifts slightly and says, half-sleeping, "We didn't even have to kill anyone tonight."

Tasha wonders how long that will stay true.

CHAPTER 2

Tasha wakes before anyone else, a hideous hotel painting greeting her from the end of the bed: a beach scene, all sunset and abandoned white chairs. The ripples in the water are poorly done—she knows enough about art to see that. Too obvious. Trying too hard to be water. Water just is, if you let it. The rest of the beach is convincing in its bare hauntedness, but Tasha suspects this was not the artist's intention. It was supposed to be romantic, probably: a view of the beach from a dreamy tryst in the bordering green, perhaps, the sky an erotic shade of red. She wonders briefly if any of the people who once slept in this same hotel bed saw the same thing she sees, or if their vantage was tinted by love; the contentment one feels when all is right with the world.

She looks at the sleeping figure of Z next to her, arches her neck a little to see Ishmael and Malakai on the other bed. Ishmael lies squarely on his back, his chest rising and falling. Malakai curls more, like a pup. From somewhere on the floor Tasha can hear the poodle breathing. Dogs have a breathier way of sleeping, less restrained. Their own snoring never wakes them.

It smells different here, she notes, shifting a little, trying not to wake Z. She'd noticed it as soon as the car had groaned to a stop. Stepping outside the car into Iowa air was like stepping from a time machine and emerging in another land. The world that blurred past them as they drove here hadn't seemed real. None of it had, really. The explosion at the Apiary was a surreal smudge of noise in her brain. Had that really happened? Had she been there?

Tasha hears the stir of cloth, a change in the pattern of breath that has created an ocean wave chamber in the hotel room. She turns from where she's propped up on her elbow surveying the room. It's Ishmael, sitting up, hair fuzzy from the pillow. The first thing he does is look down at his brother, his eyes serious. He looks at Malakai's face first, searching, and then gives him an up and down. *All is well*, Tasha thinks, smiling, but doesn't speak. The lives of men are so secret, she thinks. She enjoys this window.

After a moment he looks up, and they lock eyes.

"Hey," he says softly.

"Hey."

A moment of just looking.

"We should probably get going," she says.

They're ready in ten minutes. How things have changed. Only two weeks ago, Tasha can't help but think, she and Gina spent an hour trying on different colorful skins until they chose one. Tasha finishes tying her Nikes and sighs. This is all.

"Ready?" she says, standing.

Malakai is sitting on the floor with the dog between his knees, one ear in each hand. He scratches them sleepily and the dog groans, the sound muffled in the boy's lap.

"Have you ever had a dog, Kai?" Tasha asks.

"No. Mama is allergic."

"You know where to scratch," Tasha says, nodding down at the dog.

"Her ears are soft."

"Yeah," Tasha smiles.

Z is standing by the door with her ear against it.

"I can hear something outside. I think they're in the hall."

"Oh, great."

Malakai stops rubbing the dog's ears and she noses him encouragingly.

"Let me listen," Tasha crosses over to the door and Z stands to one side.

The door is cool against her cheek, cool and firm. How many times has she done this? How many more times will she? She thinks of the sounds on the other side of Dinah's door, that day of the storm, the thunder only barely concealing the screams. The sounds she hears now, hardly muted at all by the thin hotel door, aren't like that, but they're familiar. The shambling steps of purposeless feet. Those footsteps would change, she knows, if there were something killable in sight.

"Can you tell how many?" Ishmael has come over to the door as well, and now the small entranceway is crowded. Z steps back.

The peephole is empty. They're in the hall but at least they're not right outside the door.

"I'm going to look," says Tasha.

Z steps back over.

"Whoa, what? Look at what?"

"Just gonna stick my head out and see."

"Um…are you a walnut? No."

"We need to know what we're up against."

"Fuck that."

"Language," says Ishmael, tilting his head at Malakai, who is listening intently, his hands wrapped up in the poodle's fur.

"Sorry, Ish," says Z flatly. "And no, Tasha."

"She has a point," says Ishmael. "We can't just go out there expecting one or two and then run into a whole herd."

Tasha raises her eyebrow at Z.

"Christ. It's just such a bad fuck—freaking idea, guys. Come *on*."

"Well, *yeah*," says Tasha. "But we still gotta."

"Well, let *me* do it at least," Z groans. "I'm smaller than both of you."

"So?"

"Why does that matter?"

"Because," Z sighs. "I don't know. It just does, okay? Christ. Move."

She shoulders Tasha and Ishmael aside and withdraws the box cutter from her back pocket. She looks over her shoulder.

"Get your shit ready," she says sternly. "And get ready to block this door if we have to."

They nod.

Z's careful fingers find the deadbolt and rest on it, motionless, for a moment before slowly, slowly turning it, as if cracking a safe.

Tasha looks back into the room. Malakai is standing now and has moved back against the window, the dog sitting on his feet. They both stare at Tasha with large brown eyes, blinking.

Z has the deadbolt unlocked. Now for the chain. She uses both hands, holding the chain to keep it from rattling. That done, the door stands unlocked. The shambling outside is still audible. She leans forward to peer through the peephole one last time, then, box cutter in her right hand, she slowly, gently turns the door handle.

Then it's open and her neck is out in the hall, her head swiveling. The chorus of barks is almost instantaneous.

"Fuckfuckfuckfuck," she yelps, slamming the door.

Tasha leaps forward and throws herself against it while Z fumbles with the locks. Tasha presses her eye against the peephole. What had been an empty fishbowl is now filled with piranhas, their gaping mouths open and snapping, pushing against each other to get at the door, dead-eyed and irritated.

"Shit, there's like twenty of them," gasps Z. "The whole hall. Bellhops and maids and shit. Tons of them. Where were they last night?"

"It's like they just started the morning shift," Tasha says, disgusted. "Damn."

"Gotta use the window," Ishmael says without hesitation. "Now."

Tasha grabs her backpack and swings it onto her shoulders.

"Kai. Open the window."

The boy stares at her a moment, his mouth moving but with no words. Then he clamps it shut and spins around, shoving the heavy curtains out of the way. A layer of dust rises from them. The maid sure isn't getting a tip, Tasha thinks.

"There's...there's no latch. The window doesn't open."

"Wait, what?" Z sweeps over and hustles him to the side to inspect the window. She runs her palms over its edges, bends to look at the windowsill.

"Shit," she says under her breath.

"Move," says Ishmael.

He's already picked up the squat little chair that has been crouched under the room's desk until now. Tasha experiences a brief flash of a blush, for reasons she doesn't immediately understand. Not until she feels a butterfly flapping quietly in her stomach does she realize she has a crush on him. *Oh hell, Natasha*, she tells herself in her sister's voice.

The chair crashes through the window and Tasha winces at the din. If the entire hotel staff weren't already barking at the door, they certainly will be now, along with any outside Minkers in the area attracted by the noise. They've got to move fast. The window is like a serpent's mouth: open but rimmed with jagged glass teeth.

"Look out," says Tasha, and she snatches the hideous painting from the wall, its weird erotic sunset bending in the middle as the cheap backing breaks. Gripping it firmly, she shoves it into the window-mouth, scraping the remaining shards of glass out of the frame.

"After you," she says to Ishmael, motioning. He grabs Malakai and the two of them hop through like rabbits. Congratulating herself for the decision to stay on the first floor, Tasha tightens the straps on her backpack. Z is doing the same. Tasha looks down at the dog, which is standing there wagging dumbly. Still skinny. Tasha snaps her fingers at it and it blinks. Christ. She sighs and stoops to scoop it up. Its fluff is pressed against her nose. It's been awhile since she's done this: it brings back memories of her parents' kennel and also Fetch Fetchers, a swift flood of nostalgia and anger mixing in her mind. She gathers her strength and swoops the dog through the window. It struggles, its limbs splaying like an awkward lamb. She's used to it, even after so long, and deposits the dog neatly on the ground outside the window. The poodle barks once and runs to Malakai's side.

"Wanna pick me up too?" Z says. She hops through the window and Tasha follows suit. There's no real danger of the Minkers breaking down the door, she knows, but they still need to put as much distance between the hotel and themselves as possible. The staff may be keepers, she thinks, programmed or whatever to not leave their berth, but there may be seekers nearby, and depending on how big the herd, that could mean trouble.

"Too late," she says out loud as she steadies herself on the concrete. Already she hears barking that doesn't belong to the poodle. More are coming.

"Everyone okay to run?" It's Ishmael, looking around at them, his face serious. He has his hand on his brother's shoulder.

"Let's go," nods Tasha.

They jog. The Minkers in the hotel parking lot—six of them, Tasha estimates with a glance over her shoulder—haven't even crossed to the broken window yet, so Tasha and her group have a good start on them. The poodle gallops happily beside them with no concept of the danger nearby. She thinks it's just a fun game to play, she and her new humans. She's recuperating quickly, Tasha notes. The magic of SpaghettiOs.

"Are we looking for cover or a place to turn and fight?" says Z, jogging up alongside Tasha. She runs easily, her pack bouncing on her back. Tasha can feel Dr. Rio's Glass jostling around in her own. She needs to secure it better once they find a safe place to rest.

"Cover," says Tasha. She's hungry and has only been conscious for thirty minutes, tops. A bolt of longing for coffee flashes through her body, a vestige of an old life.

"Cover," Ishmael agrees, slowing his jog to fall back with Z and Tasha. Malakai trots ahead of them, the dog loping easily at his side.

"We'll need another car," Tasha says. "Better if we can find something old that takes a key. The anti-theft shit is nice on the new ones and that will make it harder to steal."

"We won't be lucky enough to have the owners' thumbs laying around for us this time," says Z, both panting and chuckling. "Man. I miss that Ferrari."

"Yeah," says Tasha. "But I'd take a hoopty right about now."

"There's a McDonald's," says Ishmael, pointing.

Z wrinkles her nose.

"I'd rather hide almost anywhere else."

"How about Chipotle?" calls Malakai.

He's already angling toward it, the dog arcing over to join him.

"Not perfect, but it'll do."

"It's smaller," says Tasha, following the kid. "That's good."

"Chipotle it is," says Ishmael, and they're all heading toward it, the pack of Minkers a hundred yards behind. The creatures seem slower now, Tasha thinks. Or maybe it's her fear that's lost its speed.

"We'll beat 'em," says Z. "Don't worry."

Tasha smiles.

Inside, Ishmael immediately snatches the abandoned mop from its lonely yellow bucket and rams it through the door handles. Not that the Minkers are much good with doors, Tasha thinks, but precautionary measures are what will help keep them alive. She feels a twinge of annoyance when she realizes this is something Dr. Rio would have said.

'We've got keepers," Ishmael says.

"Great," Tasha sighs. "Malakai, stay away from the door."

The two former burrito artists lumber from around the counter, their teeth snapping and their foreheads wrinkled. They could be brother and sister, Tasha thinks: sandy-haired and lightly freckled. Is this what Iowans look like, she wonders, or just the preferred face of this particular Chipotle? No nametags, she notes. Nameless drones, as she was in her blue Apiary dress. She wonders if they would have allowed Chipotle to pay for their Chip if they had known it would mean their eternal servitude, watchdogs of assembly-line tacos. Probably not.

"I've got the girl," Z says, who's closer. She drops her pack and clicks out the blade of her box cutter.

Ishmael, who hasn't replaced his axe, stays by his brother as Tasha steps toward the other Minker, who is snapping his jaws enthusiastically as he moves toward her. He can't be more than seventeen, Tasha thinks, eyeing his acne.

He lunges like a dog and Tasha blunders to get out of his way, slicing at his neck. In some ways she feels comfortable doing this—in other ways, the concept of stabbing a human in the neck with a knife feels like a nightmare. She slashes madly again, gritting her teeth at the idea of this boy as human.

First one thud and then another. Both burrito artists lie dead, the blood minimal as the Chip clotted it in its final efforts before succumbing.

"Any more?" Ishmael calls from the door. His voice is hushed.

"I don't think so," says Z, wiping her box cutter with the dead girl's apron. "Are the ones from the hotel parking lot outside?"

He nods.

Tasha motions for the guys to come away from the door.

"Maybe there's a back exit."

They step behind the counter. The smell of rot is stronger there: the prim buckets of seasoned chicken congealed and stinking. Tasha claps a hand over her nose and moves past the mess in a rush, pushing through the swinging door into the kitchen area with her shoulder. She walks directly into the arms of a Minker wearing a hair net. The man's mouth had already been open—barking, no doubt, but too stupid to get through the door—and it must have been surprised to find a shoulder placed so neatly in its jaws, because it doesn't bite right away. Tasha uses this moment of surprise to jerk herself away and swing her arm in a wide arc. The Wusthof severs a major artery, she knows, by the hot splash of blood that strikes her cheek. Chip or not, the sudden opening of the vein invites the blood to fly, eager for new rivers to flow to, before the skin patches itself with sticky, snaky membrane. Tasha destroys the Chip with one frantic stab before the repair is complete, and the hair-netted Minker topples to the floor, mouth still open to bite.

"Minty Christ," Tasha says, still gasping, swiping at the cooling blood on her face. "That was close."

"Minty?" Z chuckles and steps past her into the kitchen, looking around. They are alone. No more sanitized servants moaning around in back.

"Trash door," Ishmael says, pointing.

"Let's go outside," Malakai says to the dog, who trots happily over to the door, turning to look back at them expectantly.

"No window," Tasha says, following the dog to the door. "Do we want to assume there are more out back?"

"Hold on," says Z, ducking back into the front of the restaurant. The door swings a little in her wake, its round porthole window reflecting the light whitely. She returns a moment later, looking dubious.

"There's at least eight out front now," she says. "You know how they are. All buddied up."

"Damn," says Ishmael, forgetting his language.

"You need a weapon," says Tasha, eyeing him. "Who knows what we're about to walk into."

She turns her gaze to Malakai.

"You too, kid," she says more softly. "No more shovel, but I'm sure you can find something to make do."

Z is already at a prep table using her box cutter to sift through piles of muck that used to be lettuce and tomatoes.

"No knives, what the hell," says Z, annoyed. "This is what happens when they let machines do every damn thing."

"We need to hurry up," says Tasha, feeling impatient. "The longer we wait, the more time we give their herd to get bigger."

"They need *something*, Tasha."

"I know. Okay, everybody look. We need to hurry."

The four of them continue their search, sweeping food debris and shreds of vinyl sanitation gloves onto the floor as they look for anything that could be used as a weapon. The silence of the room, with only the sounds of their hasty work, reminds Tasha of the Apiary, her job in Fetch Fetchers where she'd listened to the endless drone of electric lights and the rustle of rich people's clothing swishing through the entrance. It had been like that here too, Tasha knows: this bright white room and all its moving parts, cameras in the corner to ensure that you didn't spit in the food, didn't slip any chicken up your sleeve to take home to your family after you clocked out from corporate watchery and minimum wage. Dogs, food: what does it matter what we sold, Tasha thinks as she swipes inside a refrigerated cabinet for sharp objects. We had the same orders, identical prime objectives: keep the machine running. She can almost hear those words in Cara's voice, from Cara's dead mouth: keep the machine running.

"There is nothing sharp in this fucking place," Z concludes, slapping her palm on a stainless steel countertop. "For fuck's sake, it's like they thought people would riot and didn't want them to be armed."

"Here's a pipe," says Malakai, hefting it so they can see.

"Not bad," says Tasha. "At least to slow them down."

Malakai hands the pipe to Ishmael, who hefts it easily.

"Well, I can use it as a club, at least," he says.

"If only the chef had that pipe before," Z jokes. "He could have led the revolution. Or at least got a raise."

"Give me that." Tasha has an idea.

Surprised, Ishmael hands over the length of pipe and accepts her knife in return, raising his eyebrow.

Tasha walks over to the machine on the back wall surrounded by piles of rotted meat. The smell is horrible, but she approaches and raises the pipe over her head, bringing it down with a clang on top of the machine.

A dent. Her fingers are tingling, almost unbearably, but she raises the pipe and does it again. A sound like a crunch. A tinkle of bolts and tiny metal pieces striking the floor.

"Why is she always smashing something?" Z says to Malakai with a smile. He doesn't smile back, just watches.

A third strike and the top of the machine is loose. Ishmael comes over.

"I know what you're after," he says, and takes the pipe from her vibrating hands, returning her knife.

He's stronger and the machine is in pieces two strikes later. Tasha steps up, moving the misshapen metal top to the side, revealing the guts of the machine. With its skin peeled back, its jagged bones are revealed. The blades that had sliced and diced the seasoned chicken while the employees stood idly by, feeding the whole parts in, are exposed: three rows of ultra-sharp wheels of teeth.

"Malakai, get the duct tape out of your pack."

Duct tape was one of the things Rio had insisted on, not allowing it to be replaced with mawkish items like picture frames or diaries or even an extra necessity like food. "It is primitive material," Tasha remembers him saying, "but extremely valuable." She knows he was right, reaching into the mouth of the machine to extract the monster's teeth. It's relatively easy with the casing cracked open. A lever marked "release." She remembers the glowing buttons at the Lincoln Park Zoo; the carnage that touching them had released. She hopes this one will not unleash similar carnage on her hand.

It doesn't. The wheels of teeth slide out one by one with a satisfying clunking sound, and Malakai extends the roll of duct tape like a surgical assistant.

The procedure itself is more difficult than she thought it would be, but with Z holding the pipe steady they force it through the center axle of the blades, empty now that it's been slid off its rod, and use the duct tape to affix one to the other. Voila: a modern reincarnation of the medieval mace. It looks evil, Tasha decides, wielding it: all metallic and spiny like a club from a hostile alien planet. She whacks it against the table, testing it. Its clang is obnoxious, reverberating off the many other metallic objects in the room.

"Gonna have to do," she says, handing it to Ishmael.

"It will," he says. He turns to his brother. "We don't have time to make you something so stay close. If you need to run, then run. And I mean run."

"Okay."

"I mean it, Kai."

"Okay."

"Ready?" Tasha is at the door again with the poodle, who is waving her grand tail, enjoying this adventure. Tasha guesses the Minkers have no taste for canine flesh or the dog would have been dead meat long ago, locked up with beastly Cara.

Everyone nods, everyone except Malakai, who only stares with his large brown puppy eyes. He doesn't look afraid, she thinks, as she opens the door, only sad. Just sad.

There are four Minkers waiting and Tasha runs at them before they get a chance to begin their chorus of barks. She takes one down immediately with a lucky strike across the neck that leaves the Chip a sparking lump on the pavement.

"Good one," says Z, who has leapt up to the rest of the crowd, a group of multi-colored Iowans who would all look entirely different if not for the crease between their eyebrows that makes them kin. Is this what Cybranu wanted from the Chip, Tasha wonders as she hacks at their necks, kicking madly at the fourth who got away from Ishmael and has come too close.

Out of the corner of her eye, Tasha can see Ishmael swinging the weapon they'd pieced together. His back is to her: all she can see are the muscles in his back growing and then stretching as he raises his arm and then drops it, striking one of the taller Minkers in the neck and face. He could be a cyborg warrior, with his gray t-shirt and his metal mace.

Malakai stands just beside Ishmael when the fourth and last Minker collapses to the ground. The boy's body is tight, ready to run as his brother instructed. The dog has been barking the entire time and still is. Tasha hadn't noticed with the noise of the now-dead Minkers.

"Malakai, make the dog be quiet," she says. "We don't need any more Minkers nosing around."

"Too late," says Z. "Hear 'em?"

Tasha can hear them: the rising sound of the strange barks, hurrying toward them from the front of the restaurant.

It's unanimous: "Fuck."

"Car," says Malakai. He's pointing and they all look. It's a Toyota. Old—very old—but not too rusty.

"Car," Tasha agrees and runs to it, hoping that an older model like this doesn't have the same fingerprint technology as the Ferrari in Chicago.

Malakai beats her to the car.

"It's open," he cries, swinging open the door.

"Malakai, wait!"

Too late. The Minker that had been in the backseat leaps out on top of the boy and has him on the ground. Malakai has managed to get his arm up in front of his face, the way they say you should with a dog, and the Minker tears at the sleeve of his hoodie with beautifully white teeth.

Ishmael is like a freight train. The force with which he tackles the Minker carries them both several feet beyond where Malakai sprawls. The Minker appears disoriented and hasn't yet realized that it's no longer on top of its prey. Its growling and spitting is brought abruptly to a halt as Ishmael caves in its face with the crown of the Chipotle mace. Another blow. Another.

"Ishmael, come on! We need to go!"

The Minkers from the front of the restaurant have rounded the corner and stand gaping at the edge of the parking lot, deciding what they need to attack.

"Ish!" Malakai is on his feet, clutching his arm. Ishmael swings the mace against the Minker's neck one more time before struggling up from the ground and dashing toward the car.

Z is pulling a dead body from the front seat. The smell is overwhelming, the car a tomb of murder.

"No key," says Tasha, who has bounded into the driver side. "His pockets! Check his fucking pockets!"

Z frantically pats the rotting corpse's hips. Behind her the pack has begun to bark, walking and then trotting toward the car.

"No keys! No keys!"

"We don't have time! Get in the car!"

Ishmael has already crammed his brother into the backseat. He's about to slam the door when the poodle jumps in after them. Cursing, Ishmael shoves it into the middle seat and yanks the door closed.

"In!" Tasha screams. "In!"

Z scrambles around to the passenger side, opening the door and throwing herself inside. The smell immediately swells as Tasha closes her door, the last one. They are locked in a box of stinking death: Tasha sitting where the dead man had been sitting, his throat an open husk and his eyelids—what was left of them—open. Or perhaps closed. Perhaps the flesh had thinned, disappeared in a mist of death.

"Jesus," Z breathes. "That smell."

They all jump as the Minkers arrive at the car, palms slapping the hood and windows as they eye their prey within the tin can of the Toyota.

"Tuna," says Tasha out loud. "We're tuna."

"We're what?" Z stares at her from across the car.

"Nothing. We need keys."

"Well, if this were a movie they'd be above the visor or whatever that thing was called."

"Yeah, well, we don't have visors anymore."

"Check the drug cup."

The drug cup—the compartment designated for the storage of legal drugs for easy declaration if cops ask to search the car—is closed. Tasha uses two fingers to slide its hatch open. A sprinkling of break in a clear plastic container is all that's inside.

A Minker slams its face against the driver's side window, smooshing its cheek against the glass and deforming its nose and lips. Tasha almost laughs. There are at least twenty of them now, surrounding the car like tourists at a wildlife exhibit. This is how the sharks felt, she thinks, when we came to ooh and ahh. Except she still feels less like a shark and more like a tuna.

The dog whimpers and Tasha looks into the backseat. Ishmael has pulled back Malakai's sleeve and Tasha is expecting blood, the elliptical connect-the-dots of human teeth marks. Instead there's only bruising: Malakai's brown skin is deeply black and purple just below the elbow. She remembers the day Mrs. Kerry attacked her in Fetch Fetchers. Cara had said that Tasha's complexion made her bruises invisible. What a bunch of shit. She reaches back and strokes the boy's wrist, feeling near tears. He doesn't look up, stares down at the car floor, his lip trembling. He thinks we're going to die, she thinks. Maybe she does too.

"Check everything," Ishmael urges.

"Right," says Tasha, and turns away.

Z is already flipping open compartments. The dashboard is like a fisherman's vest: a dozen or more little doors to boxes, some the size of a postage stamp. Most are empty. Some contain identicards, some house cubes of what looks sugar but Tasha knows is cocaine—which should be in the drug box, she thinks crabbily. But no keys. Maybe the tuna are fucked after all. The visitors to the aquarium all stand barking in a ring around the car, pressing against it. The woman smashed against Z's door is at least seventy years old. It's bizarre to see a granny snapping her dentures.

"No keys," she reports, trying not to let the panic color her voice.

"What kind of ignition is it?" Ishmael demands. The palms slapping on the windows almost drown out his voice. "I can look back here. Maybe the key got thrown around when his passenger changed."

"What kind…? Uh…"

Tasha inspects the area around the steering wheel, her heart pounding. She's only ever driven two cars in her life: an ancient Bronco in Kentucky and the equally ancient Chevrolet that had carried her and her friends here to Iowa, and both of them had the ignition of all pre-2040 electric cars: one that took keys. Some plastic, some metal: but keys. The Ferrari had taken fingerprints because it was a luxury car, she knows: more security because more people would want to steal it. The auto industry had done away with one-button ignitions after too many thefts. What the hell other kinds of ignition are there?

The area around the steering wheel doesn't have a keyhole. Tasha runs her fingers over all surfaces, her hands shaking. Nothing. All smooth, interrupted only by a thin slot with what seems to be the end of a credit card just barely protruding from it.

"Well?" Ishmael is brusque. His brother's pain has made him angry. Being a tuna has made him angry.

"I don't know!" Tasha says, raising her voice. "All I see is a smooth kind of slot thing. There's a raised part in the middle."

Suddenly Ishmael is halfway into the front seat, his body barely fitting between the two armrests. His hand reaches up to the steering wheel and frantically feels around the area Tasha described.

"For fuck's sake, Natasha, the key's already in!"

"What?" She's pissed, first at his tone, second at his use of her full name, and third at the fact that the fucking key might already be in the ignition. What fucking key? What fucking ignition?

"Move."

She leans farther to her left to give him more room. He presses on the edge of the thing that seems to be a credit card and it pops out. He pulls on it, withdrawing it from the slot. It's the size and shape of a MINK card but minus the gold material and the fancy engraved lettering. Instead it's plain white, each side printed with rows of text and numbers. Ishmael examines the card for a moment, then presses it back into the slot. There's a solid click and a keypad glows on the smooth area by the steering wheel that hadn't been there before.

"Brake," he says, one syllable but a syllable rushing to get out of his mouth.

She does, and he types in 4 numbers on the keyboard, which then disappears. The Toyota shifts a little underneath them, an animal that has suddenly began to breathe.

"Drive," he says.

She drives.

The Minkers are furious as they disappear under the tires of the car, their bodies remaining broken only for a moment until they rise again in Tasha's rearview. But she doesn't pay any more attention to them now. The tuna is loosed from the fish bowl, slipped back into the ocean to swim again.

No one says anything. Tasha quickly glances over her shoulder at Malakai. He still stares at the floor, unmoved by their escape. This is the second time he's been in a car surrounded by Minkers, she thinks, remembering Rio's brush with full-blown insanity as they'd cruised by the pack of rabid former cops. Is this traumatizing him for life, she wonders, turning her eyes back to the road, or just making him a man? She thinks maybe that's the same thing. She steers the car back onto the main road.

"We're going the wrong way," Z says.

"Huh?" Tasha looks around. Their surroundings look unfamiliar. How could new be wrong?

"The wrong way," says Z. "Right now we're going back in the direction of where the Chevy died. By the school."

"How do you know?"

Z points.

"That's the street we walked on last night when we found the hotel. We just looped back around."

"Oh." Tasha turns the wheel. One lost reindeer, she thinks, except this time Santa's heading west, not north. "Well, you're the navigator."

"Oh, right."

Z reaches down between her feet and rummages in her backpack. Tasha glances over and catches a glimpse of the photo she'd discovered in Z's pack at Ishmael's house, the one of Z and the handsome young man. Tasha feels a pang of jealousy, sharp in her stomach like a single green wasp. She still can't believe she'd left the photo of her parents at the apartment on Foster. She'll never see their faces again except in her mind's eye, where with time the details might blur and disintegrate, leaving only the dusty outline of a smile or the vague shape of a nose. Tasha sighs and shifts her grip on the steering wheel.

Z withdraws the map and unrolls its weird fleshy material on her lap. It's one of the better gadgets that Rio had stolen from his lab in Arizona, Tasha thinks. It even has GPS, a softly illuminated red dot in the middle of the mass that is the States. Although the car is moving, the red dot has not yet moved: the vantage point is too pulled back. Compared to the great distance they must travel, they haven't moved at all. If Z pulled her fingers apart on the map's surface, as if pulling something sticky between them, the map would zoom, and then maybe give their dot the illusion of progress.

"No getting lost with this thing," Z says, petting it almost affectionately. "We're going the right way."

"Funny how Rio said he hated technology but had all this stuff."

"He was a genius," Malakai says sullenly.

Tasha glances up in the rearview. The boy is still looking down at the floor, absently stroking the poodle's head. The dog gazes out the window.

"What are you going to name the dog?" Tasha asks him, anything to get off the topic of Dr. Rio. He needs to be discussed, but not now: not with Malakai.

"I don't know," says Malakai, finally looking up at her. "Something cool."

"Something *cool* like what?" Z says, turning around in her seat. The tickling voice. It always works on Malakai, man enough to care about cool but boy enough to be teased.

"Like…like…" he closes his eyes. "Spartaca. Or…or… Artemis."

"Nice names. Did you make those up?"

"No. They're comic book characters."

"Oh. Nice. They sound tough."

"They are. So is she," he says. He pets the dog's muzzle, who licks him distractedly.

A boy and his dog, Tasha thinks, smiling at the littered road.

"How far do we want to go today?" Ishmael has leaned forward and is peering at the map, which Z angles toward him.

"I dunno," says Tasha. "We should stop before dusk. Looking for a place to sleep in the dark last night wasn't fun. Let's not do that again."

Ishmael cranes his neck to see the energy meter of the Toyota.

"The car may not last that long anyway."

Tasha feels tension between them, a quivering rubber band pulled tight. He's angry because she hadn't known about the car key. Well, how the fuck would she know? She grips the steering wheel a little tighter.

"Can we pull over?" Malakai says softly.

"Give me a second, Kai," says Tasha. "I want to put some more distance between us and that herd."

A pause.

"I need to throw up," he says flatly.

"You need to throw up?" Tasha says, surprised.

"I need to throw up."

"Oh…I mean, oh. Okay."

She brakes, quickly pulling the car to the side of the wide road they've been driving on since Z directed them west with the map.

No sooner has the car come to a halt, somewhat abruptly, then Malakai's door pops open, his small body hopping urgently from the car, running a few steps away before bending over, his back heaving. The poodle had leaped out behind him and stands close to his legs, whining. Tasha looks away. She wouldn't want to puke and then turn to see she had an audience. Z and Ishmael silently do the same, busying themselves with their hands and studying the scenery on the opposite side of the car. Far away is the distant blue glow of the SkyDrive, stretching west to east, an almost intergalactic highway. Nearer, just ahead, is the town visitor center, a white official-looking building with brownish grass and a few shrubs, growing crookedly now with no one alive to tame them.

"There aren't very many here," Ishmael observes, almost to himself.

At first Tasha thinks he means the shrubs, but then realizes that he means Minkers.

"Chicago is a lot bigger," says Z, rubbing her eyes. None of them had slept well in the restless hotel.

"Yeah, but *some* people live here," he says. "I haven't even seen that many bodies. Not tons, I mean."

Z shrugs.

"Maybe the Minkers here eat them too. Clean-up crew."

Ishmael looks at her sharply and shakes his head slightly, glancing in Malakai's direction. The kid is out of earshot; otherwise Tasha thinks Ishmael might have had a few words to say to Z about curbing her urges to say the things she says.

Truth is, Tasha has wondered the same thing. The Minkers are predatory in the way they hunt, the way they kill. But not afterward. All the bodies Tasha has seen since the Change and none of them have been...devoured. Bite marks always: on limbs, shoulders, hands. Anything the killer could get a hold of before it managed to find the throat. Once that was torn, the victim dead, the Minker moved on. What kind of predator does that? Even Jaws ate the beach party it terrorized, bikinis and all.

"Maybe it's like the South Side," Tasha offers, trying to defuse the tension. "Maybe all the survivors shipped out."

"There's not that many Minkers either, though," Z says, serious now. Behind her, Malakai is straightening up and wiping his mouth. Ishmael opens his car door as if to get out, but stops.

"Maybe a bunch of them got fried when the Apiary blew up. Like Rio said."

Tasha shakes her head.

"He said it would only affect the ones in the radius of the Apiary in Chicago. I doubt the radius would be way out here."

Z shrugs as Ishmael gets out of the car and meets Malakai, who's walking back, trailed by the poodle.

"Yeah, I guess. I just felt like there used to be more people in the world. Where did everybody go?"

Ishmael returns with his brother.

"Keepers?" he suggests. "I mean, there could be 100 billion people on Earth, but if they all stayed inside nobody would ever know it."

Tasha imagines herself as an alien coming to Earth to scope out the infamous human race and finding nothing but shuttered windows and tall, silent condo buildings. "It seems the humans have vacated the planet," she, as a green scout, would report back to her many-eyed superiors. "There are many dwellings but no people."

Personally, the vacancy of the States doesn't shock her. Chicago had been bustling with tourists on Michigan Avenue and other high-traffic hot spots, but so many Chicagoans either worked from home or were slaves to their various occupations—the standard workweek increased from 40 hours to 60 in the Fifties—that the streets often had a ghostly quality. The only place she really encountered throngs of human beings was at the Apiary. Day or night, there were always people shopping.

"How far should we go?" she says eventually.

"I don't know. We've barely gotten away from the hotel," says Ishmael, and his hand flits to his pocket before stopping, almost of its own volition. Reaching for a Glass, Tasha thinks, or some other digital device to tell the time. Old habits.

"It seems like a lot longer," Z shrugs.

It does. Tasha remembers how the hours in the Apiary used to ooze by slowly, like sap sluggishly seeping from the bark of an old tree. Now time moves just as slowly, but in a different way. She is running, always running, leaping from one iceberg-moment to the next in frantic efforts not to sink, to evade the thing that's always behind her—but time doesn't keep up. It's on its own schedule, the sun slow and stubborn at the top of the sky. It might be noon, she thinks, blinking at it. They've been out of the hotel maybe two hours. She wonders if this is how their new lives will always be: rushing to stay alive and not really getting anywhere. Maybe she'll find a library, a museum, in this sleepy, deserted town. Go admire the artifacts she'll eventually become. She shivers.

"We should keep moving," Ishmael says. "It's the middle of the day. We have plenty of time to make some progress. Plus we have a car. If the people in the caravan ahead of us started walking when their cars died we might be able to catch up with them if we're driving."

"What if they found cars too? What if they're driving too?"

"I don't think they'd take cars."

"Why not?"

"Because Rio told them to walk."

Tasha considers this. Yes, Rio had said they would walk once the initial cars from Chicago died, but surely he didn't mean the whole way, not actually. When thinking about the journey ahead, Tasha had envisioned the ruined shoes, the sore feet, the long lines of footprints heading west that she would follow. She and Z had joked about it. For some reason the existence of all the cars that would be leftover—"leftover," like peas abandoned on a plate and not like remnants of a world destroyed—never entered her plan for the trip, or Rio's. She says this to Ishmael through the window.

"You know how he was about machines. Didn't trust them."

"Why?" says Z. She's not really listening. She's looking around, switching her box cutter from one hand to the other. Tasha smiles a little. The Web and its small, safe security room with all its watchful eyes still appeals to Z.

"Why do you think?" Ishmael snorts, handing Malakai a granola bar as he joins them. Malakai doesn't open it, just holds it limply in his hand. The poodle sniffs it.

"Yeah," says Z, "I guess if I worked for Cybranu and saw all the shit they were making in their labs, I'd be more of an all-natural type too."

"Nothing as natural as walking," Tasha says, moving back toward the car. "But we should get moving. Ishmael's right. Maybe we can catch the caravan."

"What if we've already passed it?" Malakai says quietly.

"How could that be?" says Z, patting the map on her lap. "They only had, like, six hours on us, and we're following the route on the map."

"What if they have a different map?" the boy says, looking down at the poodle, moving the granola bar in a circle so the dog's muzzle follows it like a wet black magnet.

"They don't. Tasha and I programmed them all the same when we were helping Rio get the caravan supplies ready."

"Okay," he says, walking toward the car. "I just thought we would have seen their cars by now."

The right corner of his mouth still shines a little from vomiting. Tasha feels a phantom muscle in her arm twitch, as if it thought about reaching out to wipe his face without consulting her first. She grips the steering wheel instead. Malakai and the poodle climb in. Ishmael follows suit.

"Am I going to drive the whole way?" Tasha says, fastening her seatbelt.

"I navigate, you steer," says Z.

Tasha half expects Ishmael to speak up, but he doesn't. He's settled in the backseat, gazing out the window, as if the ride has already begun, as if the view isn't the dusty visitor center, doubtless populated by pasty public officials ambling aimlessly around their former offices, maps of their meager city drying out on racks. Ishmael has been quiet, she notes, starting the car again now that she knows how and putting it in gear. She pulls back onto the road just as a Minker wobbles out behind them from beyond a line of shrubs. Close after him come two or three others.

Her friends don't see them. Z looks out the front window at the road, ready to point Tasha right and then straight, all the way to the west coast; Ishmael stares out the window as before; Malakai pats the poodle's puffy crest. Tasha open her mouth, ready to remark: "Oh hey, Ishmael, do you mind scooching over? A couple hitchhikers look like they'd appreciate a ride." But she closes it again. Why upset them? The dog's eyes are half-closed, Malakai scratching her ear, fingers buried deep in the squish of her coat. Peaceful. Tasha steers out onto the road, heading down the empty street, watching the small pack behind her shrinking in the rearview.

"Left up here," Z says, pointing.

Tasha turns left.

CHAPTER 3

Driving while the others sleep, Tasha feels more at ease than she has since they left Chicago smoldering in the rearview. Not just because she's traveling in this safe, moving box but because it's quiet: the hum of the world passing her—or rather her passing the world—is like the noise machine her mother had placed in Leona's bedroom when they were girls.

Leona had trouble falling asleep in silence. It scared her, she told Tasha when she'd sneak in for their past-bedtime conversations. The dark was quiet, and it could contain anything. The noise machine filled the blanks. Tasha remembers it looking like a shiny gray bowling ball; its buttons camouflaged in the faint marble pattern, buttons that when pressed would cause the machine to emit a variety of sounds: crickets, birds, wind, flutes, or, the most boring option, Tasha thought, but the one Leona always preferred: buzzing non-sound. A thrum of almost-static. "Why do you choose that one? It sounds like nothing."

"No," Leona would say in the dark. "It sounds like everything."

Tasha can hear it now: the everything. As she drives down the abandoned interstate, bright billboards glaring and flickering on either side of her, and beyond them towns and hills and sometimes trees and always dead bodies, the thrumming that vibrates vaguely through the car windows is everything. Here, out in the middle of Iowa or wherever they are, away from the artificial hum of the Volamus in the city, the hum of everything is more noticeable. Even the stillness of death weaves its way into the hum: the slow crawl of maggots through the flesh of the dead, the brittling of bones in sun. She can hear it all. The rhythm of the tires turning is just one heartbeat of a million heartbeats.

There's a Buick in the road ahead and Tasha slows a little, peering at it as she goes by: its windows are stained red from the inside, splashes of someone's last struggle. The passenger door hangs limply open like a broken wing, the killer nowhere in sight. A Minker, Tasha can only assume, drawn off by another herd, or perhaps pulled by the call of a place like the Apiary. Tasha thinks of the long line of them she and Ishmael had seen outside Rio's house, filing off toward downtown, docile and orderly. Soldiers called by a drum. But who beat the rhythm?

There's a rest stop ahead, its enormous sign dark, the neon dead. Local then, she surmises, as all the big national corps' signage she's passed is still lit, hooked to unseen power sources. Not the sun, she guesses. The corps still resisted solar. She can almost read the sign from a mile back, it's so big. Big and dead, she thinks—the only stop on this five-mile stretch. What's the point of a sign that huge? It's not like anyone could possibly miss it. Proof, she thinks. Proof of worth. "I'm big, therefore I am," like anything else. Cars. Breasts. A breast cannot be merely a breast. It must be a *big* breast. McDonald's doctrine, she thinks from high on her mental soapbox. Big Mac Philosophy. Dollar Menu Values.

She slows anyway as she draws closer. Without the neon the sign is hard to read, but up close she can see "DeGrazie's Heaven" in large curving letters, and in smaller font underneath: "Plug In. Get the Fuck Out." Tasha peers. The stop has 20-30 docks to enable electric cars to juice up; the building at the center of the lot appears to be a web café, with charging stations and many screens of varying sizes. Pointless, Tasha thinks, when pretty much anyone who's driving charges their devices in their car. She's surprised that weeklong batteries haven't put DeGrazie's out of business. But the place looks as if it's been around awhile.

She finds herself letting the car slow more and more, curious to catch the swaying silhouettes of Minker keepers. She feels pity for them, if they're there: they'll never see any action, not like their bloody-mouthed buddies in Chicago; urban ranks eating up all the fun for themselves. Being stationed way out here: tough break.

"Need to check your mail?" Z says, stirring.

Tasha almost jumps. Not quite.

"Be nothing but bills anyway," she shrugs, accelerating again.

"It's only a big bill if it's on paper. They mail it when they really want the money."

"Oh, I know. Columbia was hounding me for money to the very end. The day I got Leona's letter from the Post? The only other thing in the box was a collection notice on behalf of the school."

Z laughs quietly. Like Tasha, she doesn't want to wake the guys, still snoozing in the backseat. The dog, on the other hand, is awake. Tasha sees, looking in the rearview, that she sits up silent and alert between Malakai and Ishmael. Just us girls, Tasha thinks, returning her eyes to the road.

"How's the drive been?" Z says, stretching awkwardly in the cramped seat. "You haven't had to get out and fight any battles while I've been napping, have you?"

"Just one or two. You were snoring, so I figured I'd get out and do some slaying 'til you stopped."

"Ha. That must have been the dog. Not me."

The poodle whines a small whine. As if to either acknowledge that she is, in fact, "the dog," or as if to say, "I do not snore, assholes."

Tasha's back at 80mph, the deserted web café vanished behind them. At first she'd driven at a steady 45, the only speed she's ever gone, with the exception of when they'd fled Chicago. She supposes it doesn't count: she'd been fleeing a massive bomb, after all. Speeding while fleeing a massive bomb is in a category all its own. No cop could've ticketed her for that, she thinks. She doesn't know how she became the designated driver of this trip, but she doesn't mind. Not really. Once she'd gotten used to the feeling of a car, she'd felt her foot pressing more and more on the pedal. 60. 70. 80. What's the difference? The goal is to get to California, where the idea of Leona hangs like a bright orange carrot dangling from a string. Tasha lunges toward it.

"We're on course, right?" asks Z, reaching for the map.

"Yes, Miss Navigator. Once you got us on the interstate after the town, I stayed on it. I will not deviate from the route," she says robotically.

Z leaves the map folded but holds it on her lap.

"How much battery do we have left?"

"Woke up with questions, huh?"

"Always!"

"We have 45% left. At least that's what the dash says."

"Better battery than the Ferrari."

"Nothing about a Ferrari is meant to last," Tasha shrugs.

"True. What's that up ahead?"

Tasha sees it too. A few miles back it had looked like a mountain, or a large random hill. Now Tasha can see the faint crackle of neon lights, a man-made shape emerging through the clouds.

"I can't tell."

"It's a stadium."

Now Tasha does jump, not expecting the vibration of Ishmael's voice. She hears the thump of the poodle's tail against the seat, greeting him. Tasha feels her mental tail wag a little too.

"A stadium?" she repeats.

"Yeah. Basketball. You know that's all these middle states have going for 'em."

It's the size of a planet: a massive shiny palace with its own triple-decker shuttle train that Ishmael tells them connects to the SkyDrive and various airports. The stadium rears up on the right, its neon panels flashing obscenely in the afternoon light. Decades ago there would have been a parking lot circling it like a massive ring of Saturn, but now the stadium extends up instead of out, fifty or sixty stories high, the circumference fanning out at the top so from a long distance one could almost mistake it for a neon tornado, a funnel of steel. Tornadoes are actually common in this region, Tasha knows—twisters known to travel miles before dissipating. She guesses the stadium is built to withstand them.

"What's that?" Z gasps, a little too loud. Tasha jerks her head to look—afraid, suddenly, that a tornado is actually upon them.

Looming out of the top of the stadium, a figure moves: enormous, colossal, a giant person moving through the clouds, shoulders hulking, arms raised. Tasha instinctively presses the brake, fear trumping logic as she tries to understand what she's seeing.

"It's a hologram," Ishmael says, his voice even and unafraid. "An advertisement."

"It looks so real," Z breathes. They watch the giant person walk back and forth, everything below his chest hidden inside the stadium. He jerks his arms upward several times, as if ordering the audience out of their seats.

"Don't stop," says Ishmael from the backseat.

Tasha had no intention of stopping, but asks why anyway.

"There's gotta be tons of them in there, right?" he says.

"It happened in the morning," Z says. "How many games are going on at that time of day?"

"It's basketball season," Ishmael says flatly, as if no further explanation is needed.

"So?"

"Yeah, so?" Tasha echoes. She's slowed down a little, despite his warning. The curiosity of a cat on its eighth life is sweet and heady, a shadow beckoning from just on the other side of a rickety bridge.

"*So*," he says, a little annoyed, but a little loftily too, the air of all people who know something someone else does not. "*So* there are games back to back during basketball season. All night. All day. You know how NBA fans are: they are *going* to the game. Especially now that they include beer and lodging in the ticket prices."

"Lodging?"

He nods out the window at the monstrosity, closer now.

"Yeah, half of those floors are hotels. People come and watch game after game for three days straight. Some of the games are just holograms like that guy, but nobody cares."

"Okay, but nobody wants to watch basketball at four in the morning," Z scoffs.

"Some people do," Ishmael says, and Tasha smirks, hearing his own fandom in his voice.

He leans over to Malakai and nudges him gently. When his eyes crack open, Ishmael says softly, "Want to see something dope?"

The boy nods and Ishmael points.

"Coool," Malakai says, waking up immediately when he sees the gigantic stadium they're approaching. "Is that Roger Mandela?" he points at the pacing holographic figure, who looks across the miles between their car and the stadium like a god standing in the clouds.

"Yep."

"Awesome," he mutters, hands gripping the car door. "I wish we could go in."

Then he pauses.

"Do you think Mandela is a Minker?"

"No," Ishmael says quickly.

But of course he is, Tasha thinks. Of course he is. The NBA—and the NFL, before they were banned—would have made sure all their prized roosters got the Chip: protect their investments; take care of their livestock. Professional athletes were just as owned as the armed forces, she knows: highly trained bodies that now sway around in circles until something edible catches their eye. She wouldn't want to run from that Minker, she thinks. Or what about Olympians? Sprinters? Were they Chipped too? She hopes they had been on a train or something, she thinks darkly. Or in some training center with locked gates. The last thing any survivors need is to have to escape from a human cheetah. So far she's been quick but she'll never be that quick.

"It looks so quiet," Malakai says, and she hears the tones of longing in his voice. He wants to go in: he wants to smell the lacquer of the polished floor, let the flashing neon wash his skin and widen his eyes. He wants to stand under the sky-high hoop—raised six inches in '52 when players just kept getting bigger and bigger—and breathe in the smell of sweat sweated by titans. True titans, Tasha thinks bitterly: Mandela is like the kraken now. Opening a single door of that stadium could unleash not only the giants of the Iowa Energy, but their thousands of fans that had been Chipped, equal with the pros for the first time.

Tasha does slow the car a little more, giving Malakai time to let the stadium soak in. It's impressive, she thinks. The massive triple-decker trains branch out from two sides of it like shining metal wings: the metallic ferries that shuttle game-goers in like immigrants to the New World. It would seem like a new world, given all the flatness of Iowa that they've cruised through: rearing up like a volcano, a dinosaur's head breaking through the crust of the earth, opening a portal to a dimension below. One side is glass—the hotels and their spectacular view of nothing—and the other side a thick skin of neon screen, glittering and transforming from images of players into the thonged asses of multicolored cheerleaders, to the roaring faces of ecstatic fans, their mania captured and immortalized, face paint rendering them wild and raw. The fans' mouths are wide open in howling cheers, their teeth starkly white against their blue-painted skin. Tasha wonders if they're still blue, swaying around inside the stadium.

She accelerates. Malakai watches the stadium until it grows small behind them, mountain turned molehill.

"We should probably stop," Ishmael says, and for a moment Tasha thinks he means stopping for the stadium: going back and letting loose Mandela and his horde of bloodthirsty worshippers. But when she looks into the rearview he's not staring back at the stadium but over at the sun. It's getting low, she notices immediately. It's strange, relying on it for something other than warmth or light. The clock in the car said 1:02 when they got in, and it hasn't changed.

"Did you ever wear a watch?" Tasha asks him. "Like, before."

"No, not really. I had a Glass, you know. Didn't need a watch. Now I wish I had."

"Same."

"Girls wear watches?"

"What? Yes."

"Celebrities wore watches but they didn't actually tell time," Z adds. "They had hands and stuff but they never actually moved. A fashion thing."

Wealth makes time stand still, Tasha thinks. She looks at 1:02, glowing on the dashboard. Unless you're this old-ass car. That doesn't count.

"Seen any signs for hotels?" Ishmael says, leaning up between the two front seats. He's close. If Tasha turned her face to the right, her lips might brush his ear. She looks straight ahead.

"Best Western in eight miles," she says. "Maybe it said 10. I don't remember. It was on an ad a few miles back."

"Are we sure we wanna do the hotel thing again?" Z interjects, looking at the map laid out across her lap.

"Why not?" Ishmael and Tasha say in unison.

Z looks exasperated. "Am I the only one who remembers the fiasco this morning? That was only like seven hours ago and you don't remember? We almost got mobbed!"

Tasha nods. She had kind of forgotten. One escape blends into the next. One crowd of snapping Minkers barely differs from another. Days are just long stretches of survival: the inevitability of Minkers has soaked into her skin and left a film of indifference.

"True," she admits. "But where else are we going to stay? We can't sleep in the car. I think I'll lose my mind if I have to be cramped up night *and* day."

"We could…I dunno. We could use someone's house."

"Someone's house?"

"Yeah. I mean, a deserted house. Where everybody is…you know—gone."

"Gone like dead. You wanna sleep in somebody dead's house."

"No," says Z slowly. "Just somewhere smaller, where there's not a million employees waiting to mob us. Or, like a furniture store even. Beds."

"No bathrooms at a furniture store," says Ishmael. "At least not with a shower. Plus, furniture stores are usually all glass. No cover."

"Good point," Tasha says, surprised. She wouldn't have thought of that.

"Okay, true. Well, a house then," Z continues.

"I don't know if I wanna sleep in some dead person's house," says Tasha. She steers the car around something dead on the highway. Too small to be human. *For once,* she thinks.

"I mean, everywhere is going to be somebody dead's *something,*" Z insists. "We're driving somebody's car, ya know. Or did you think they just left it because they were ready to walk?"

"Also true," Tasha says reluctantly. She glances down at the steering wheel, feeling uneasy. "Damn."

"This area isn't exactly residential," Ishmael says.

They all look around. Beyond the thickets of billboards that line the highway the land is fairly empty, with the exception of corporate parks and clusters of restaurants.

"Wal-Mart country," Tasha says.

"Yeah, exactly." Ishmael's voice is so close to her ear that her lobe tickles. "I don't even know where the people who work in these places live."

"We could look around a little bit," Z insists. "I'm sure there's a way to get this map to access that kind of display..." She trails off, rumpling the map this way and that.

"I thought you said we should stay on course?" Tasha teases and then regrets it when she realizes that Z is scared.

"How about this?" Tasha says when Z doesn't respond, just sits there caressing the map. "How about we stay at the Best Western tonight, and then tomorrow we'll stop based on what we see that's residential? We'll find a nice condo. Or a cabin."

"Cabins are creepy," Z smiles, folding the map. There's still a little furrow on her forehead, but Tasha thinks she's satisfied. "Haven't you seen any scary movies?"

"More than you can imagine," Tasha says, thinking of the weeks spent in college dissecting films as old as the year 2000. God, those movies sucked. People talked so much. The screenwriters always had so much they wanted to say. What's the point in having actors? Just put words on the screen in empty space."

"Next exit," Malakai says, and the dog whines.

It probably has to pee, thinks Tasha. So does she. The car's time still says 1:02. It's probably closer to 7.

"Are we still in Iowa?" she asks Z.

"Yeah. Getting closer to Nebraska though."

"Nebraska." It's a real place, but it's not anyplace Tasha ever thought she'd actually visit.

"Yeah. It's going a lot faster than Rio expected."

"What, cuz we're driving?"

"Yeah. He really imagined us walking the whole way."

"So did I."

She doesn't know why she hadn't considered cars. Some would be unusable, she knows, either because they were dead and there was no power source nearby to charge them or because they were damaged. But there are plenty of others to choose from, like this aged Toyota. Everything in the world had seemed Changed at first. Primitive. No web, no Glass, no time because there was no Glass. With those staples absent, everything else seems to have decayed as well. *Exactly how Rio liked it*, Tasha thinks, thinking again of his distaste for machines. Even the unsophisticated keycards of the Apiary—which had barely seemed like technology to Tasha, in their simplicity—had annoyed him. She had gone along with his plans like a stupid child. *Fuck that guy*, she thinks, gripping the steering wheel a little tighter. *I drive.*

She slows down on the ramp, feeling the tires shift a little on the loose gravel. She had thought the roads in Chicago were bad, but Iowa's are like deer paths in comparison. There are more abandoned cars here, though, than in Chicago, scattered still and dull in the lanes as if their hearts just gave out: no skidding black trails indicating accidents or scorch marks telling a tale of disaster. Just stopped. Cold. Dry. Their cabs either empty or bloody. Tasha has stopped looking: the cars have stopped being eerie museum exhibits, distant horror behind glass, and have started being what they always were—tombs. Glass boxes with blood indicate the end of one small life, but also tell of a whole era, ended in a sudden lessening of pressure on the accelerator. A slowing, then the grinding halt. Tasha drives through the catacombs, picking the Toyota's path carefully, quietly.

"I see it," says Malakai, pointing. He seems eager to reach the hotel. He can't be tired, Tasha thinks: he's slept for hours in the car. It's not exhaustion that breeds the eagerness: it's fear. Tasha feels it too: the pull toward a closed space, the stillness of four walls. They are rabbits seeking shelter: a burrow away from the glare of a world of predators. Tasha tries to imagine herself as something else, but some of the power she'd felt rocketing out of Chicago has drained into her feet and all she wants to do is run.

There are several hotels. The Best Western hunkers on their left on a wide street called Greenleaf, but behind it is another Holiday Inn and an Airport Inn, despite the fact that there's not an airport for 100 miles. The Airport Inn is the shabbiest and the Best Western doesn't look much better. The Holiday Inn might have caught fire at some point; the entrance looks as if someone held a barbecue on the roof and then let the pork chops burn, along with the building.

"Nice options," Tasha says.

"I can still smell the smoke," says Z.

Tasha sniffs. She smells it too: the char of campfire settling in her nose hairs. At the thought of nose hairs, her eyes dart up at the rearview mirror. Does she have any? Are they sticking out of her nostrils like curious spiders? Nose hairs are worse than armpit hair, Tasha decides: not as easily hidden or as easily trimmed, unless you have a H-Airless. Tasha thinks of hers, the abandoned plastic wand sitting on her now-dusty sink, hundreds of miles behind. Another artifact in a museum of forgotten, useless tools.

"I think Best Western is still our best bet," Ishmael offers, and Tasha looks away from her hypothetical nose hairs and into his face. He's watching her, and she wonders for how long. He doesn't seem to have been reading her mind, thankfully, or she thinks his face would be less mild curiosity and more *what the hell*.

"Echoed," Tasha says, looking away. The Best Western is scruffy, the windows small and not lined with solar panels like newer hotels, but at least it has some impressive potted plants on either side of the entrance like leafy palace guards, unmolested by the Change. Minkers would have no reason to bother them. Now if the Minkers were herbivorous, Tasha thinks, they'd have a very different problem on their hands: decorative plants razed, BioBubbles raided of GMO vegetables, retirement home flower patches uprooted. The Minkers would be like mutant rabbits, burrowing under picket fences.

Halted but not parked on Greenleaf, the hotels on either side of them like the walls of a canyon.

"It'll do," says Z, folding her map into the backpack at her feet. She doesn't look up and Tasha senses her doubt, stiff and gray.

"Alright."

Tasha steers over to the entrance of the Best Western, almost expecting the two guardian plants to jump forward to take their bags. There are no other cars around. In Chicago this wouldn't have been a big surprise, with the masses of scooters and sprinkling of Pumapods taking their place on the barely-used roads. But in Iowa there have been more cars, though now that they're off the interstate, Tasha has noticed a few bus stops. Few Pumapods, though: the one crashed outside this Best Western is the first she's seen.

The Pumapod is a year or two old, slumped on its side in the shrubs lining the circular drive at the hotel's entrance, its owner nowhere to be seen. Tasha imagines her or him as a small-town rebel: enough money to blow on a Pumapod but not enough for MINK premiums. Perhaps she dreamed of straddling the hovering machine all the way to Chicago, or even farther to the towering roost of New York, leaving no tracks behind that the pallidness of Iowa could sniff along to bring her back. Too late now, Tasha thinks, suddenly very sad. No one expects to die, and then they do—all the plans they made and dreams they dreamed crumpling into wrinkled laundry hanging forgotten on the line. And here's Tasha—who hasn't made a single plan since her parents died, aside from leaving college and never going back—who has survived. In the span of these weeks, though, she has made plan after plan, the goal of every single one the same: survival. And she has survived. Now here she is outside the drooping Best Western, without any money but not needing it. She supposes in that way that she's just like every other person who ever wandered out toward Los Angeles in the last 150 years: broke and lost.

"I hope they still let us check in," says Z, opening the car door and dragging her backpack out after her. Tasha hears the clunk of canned goods inside it, and the sound has the effect that kibble striking a metal bowl has on a dog: hunger stirs suddenly, like a bear rustling out of the leaves after winter hibernation.

The poodle shoves her aside, eager, jumping from the back seat into the front and leaping out through Z's still-open door. She goes immediately over to the shrubs where the Pumapod lies on its side and pees in the weeds sprouting rudely up through the dry mulch. She squats in the way Tasha has always thought awkward, but she leans too, oddly, peering into the bushes, ears pinned back. Tasha knows that posture; she'd seen it enough in the kennel as a child: a sign of fear tempered by interest, but neither enough to make her stop peeing and run. Tasha shuts off the ignition and opens her door.

"Dog," she calls. "Hey."

The poodle finishes peeing, arching her body toward the bushes, her muscles taut and long like stretched springs.

Tasha walks quickly toward the bushes, knife in hand. Something is in the leaves: wild animal, Minker, she doesn't know. Something. She can't call off the dog as she would have at the kennel because she doesn't know its name. It doesn't answer to "dog" the way Tasha wouldn't have answered to "woman": what you are isn't always who you are.

"Tasha, what's the deal?" Ishmael calls, and she waves him off. She approaches the bushes with long, careful steps, snapping her fingers softly for the dog in case it decides to obey. But the poodle is as intent on whatever's in the bushes with the Pumapod as Tasha is, and her hackles ripple almost imperceptibly, her black lips flickering in the birth of a snarl.

Tasha leaps, knife raised, her jaw tight and her ears ringing, ready to stab, slash, take out whatever it is. But nothing attacks, nothing roars: it's a boy, a Minker boy, trapped under the weight of the Pumapod, squirming and writhing with new energy now that Tasha is in his sights. It's only his legs that are pinned: they would almost certainly be broken if it weren't for the Chip, knitting his broken bones like Rumpelstiltskin at his devilish sewing machine. But fixed or not, he's stuck: a fish on a line, thrashing.

Tasha pauses, knife still raised. All the adrenaline she'd mustered for the attack drains suddenly, leaving her feeling droopy, a wet dandelion. The kid's blood around the base of the Pumapod looks like oil: dark and not quite right. He's been here since the Change, she knows: he certainly wouldn't have been riding a Pumapod as a Minker. He looks too young to have been operating the machine by himself: no more than 10 or 11. Perhaps he changed while riding behind a reckless big brother, a crazy uncle; what had began as a thrilling morning ride—a dangerous "don't tell mom"—had become a disaster: he'd gone for the driver's neck, sending the Pumapod crashing into the hedge. Perhaps the older brother, the uncle, had disentangled himself from the wreckage, reluctantly leaving the boy pinned and squirming.

Scenarios, Tasha thinks sadly. An encyclopedia of them. She walks around to the other side of the bushes where the kid's head is most accessible. From here she can see that Z and the others are standing and watching, arms loose at their sides. Tasha kneels down and sighs before thrusting her knife into the part of the neck glowing a faint, flickering red. The snapping stops, the fish flailing on the line is still in the water. Tasha stands up after wiping the blade on the grass and snaps her fingers at the dog, who perks her ears and then follows after a pause.

"Dead?" says Z, gesturing at the bushes.

"Minker." She pauses, almost adding "kid," but looks at Malakai, his expression like a fawn, and closes her mouth. "I took care of it."

Ishmael extends her backpack to her as she rejoins them by the car.

"Thanks," she says, taking it, swinging it over her shoulder in one smooth swoop. It feels heavier than it did in Chicago, with all the extra shit Rio had insisted they pack. He had been like a mother in that way, but creepy and paunched, hovering over maps and canned goods, the magical water-testing canteens. She can hear the canteen clanking against her back. It's tighter inside her backpack than in Z's or Ishmael's: she'd refused swapping her Prada for the shapeless grunts that Rio offered. Less efficient, she knows: she's sacrificing space for style, which is especially stupid considering the new meaninglessness of style. But everyone does it, one way or another, she thinks. She hasn't asked Ishmael what thing he carries that is wasteful, stupid, dangerously nostalgic.

"We won't have the sun for much longer," says Z, clutching the map and looking at the sky. Tasha hides her smile. Z is a proper Girl Scout with the map.

"I guess we better get in there then," Tasha says, pulling the second strap of her backpack over her shoulder. "Ready?" She looks at the group. The dog waves its tail. Good enough.

The entrance to the Best Western is marked with a large symbol: an inverted triangle with squiggles inside it, the words "Tornado Safe" printed in red underneath. The glass does seem thicker than usual, Tasha notes as they enter the lobby, but it's still glass.

Inside, the lobby is quiet—as quiet as the Holiday Inn had been the night before—but at least now she can see. Last night her toes had collided blindly against corpses; now, in the fading daylight, it's all too easy to see the many bodies clogging the dusty tile floor, most of them in uniform. At the counter, though, smartly-dressed concierge and desk attendants slump either across the counter or on the floor: one man lies fully on the desk, as if he tried to climb over but hadn't quite made it. Farther into the lobby by the elevators are two maids, one male and one female, their aprons stained amber with furniture polish and red with the blood that pools around them.

No one says anything, gazing blankly at the carnage. There are guests too, of course: bodies of both. But Tasha can't imagine the hotel being packed to the gills with guests, situated as it was so randomly in Iowa, a state most travelers would've chosen to fly over instead of travel through in the time Before. They won't see many Minkers here, she guesses. She hopes.

"How many floors?" Z calls to Ishmael, who's crossed the lobby with Malakai and stands by the bank of elevators. Looking at the elevators, Tasha feels a sudden stab of panic. Phantom fear. The sight of the elevators has plunged her suddenly back into the Apiary, slamming her hand on the button over and over, waiting for the ride down that would save their lives, the seconds pulsing and swelling like a bruise bellowing across her chest, pressing against her heart until it stutters. The feeling passes quickly. She shakes her head, a small quick twitch to cast off the idea of sweat, the idea of her pulse in her ears pounding like the hammers in a feverishly played piano.

"Seven," Ishmael says, not turning. He looks up and down the halls that extend from either side of the elevator bank. He peers at the directory engraved between the elevators. "There's a pool," he adds.

Z is already walking toward Ishmael, short quick steps, her ponytail swinging. She reaches Ishmael and stands nearby, looking up and down the halls as he did. They're all silent, the dog standing near Tasha, not panting. The air in the hotel is thick, and Tasha reminds herself not to breathe through her nose: the stench of the dead is a cloud around them. She wonders if the dog's nose registers its putridity or if it's merely just one more smell, interesting in the same way as flowers or dirt.

"Seems okay," Z says, her voice echoing.

"There have to be some somewhere," Tasha says. She feels cautious and reluctant; as if declaring the area safe too soon is a trap laid by the Minkers, lulling them into a sense of calm by hiding in supply closets and IT rooms until Tasha sighs in relief, then bursting from behind curtains, snarling. They haven't been smart enough to lay traps so far, she thinks, trying to be reasonable, but what if they became smarter? Some system upgrade in the Chip's tiny red brain to make them more efficient killers. Do they learn?

"There must be, right?" Z answers, remaining where she is by the elevators. "All these dead people. Somebody had to have killed them."

"Maybe somebody was already here," says Malakai, standing close to his brother. "People like us. Maybe they killed the Minkers already."

"Or survivors let them out when they escaped. Maybe there's a door opened somewhere."

"Maybe," says Tasha quietly, to herself.

"What do you think?" Ishmael says to Z. They're all placating Z, her nervousness.

Z shrugs.

"Let's find a room. Tasha, look for keys?"

Tasha is closest to the front desk. She nods and picks her way through the dead bodies between her and the counter and peers over the top. She'd rather get them from here, if she can, instead of walking around behind the desk. It feels too much like a dead-end: the door to the office behind it open a crack, the space beyond it dark. She doesn't see any keys: only various Glass devices, some broken, littering the desk. She nearly picks one up. She can almost remember what it felt like. Her Glass had been a permanent fixture in her hand, glued to her palm the way her knife is now. She thinks of this nostalgically, seeing these dead relatives of her device: it's like a gallery of ancient ancestors, dead faces looking out through antique frames. But no keys.

Tasha slowly walks around to the edge of the counter, peers around the corner like a deer. Listening. Everything seems so quiet. *Too quiet*, a century of corny movies whispers in her head. She can't ever remember being somewhere so quiet: no humming Volamu, no buzzing ReVolve, no whisper of elevators rising and falling: certainly no tinny pop music, nasally vocals. It's like being in space—the silence. She can almost feel her feet lifting off the ground.

The mats behind the counter are sticky, the red of the residue invisible on the blackness of the rubber. It shines a little, the dried blood, in the light filtering in from the front windows. Where's the janitor, she thinks. Can you train a Minker to mop?

Keys. The same colorful Plasti-Keys as the Holiday Inn.

"No good," Tasha calls to Z and the others, who are watching from the elevator bank. "Plasti-Keys. Same deal. No power, the keys won't work."

"Ugh, so stupid," snaps Z. "Do none of these places have back-up generators? Fucking hicks."

"They might have, but I doubt it would have lasted two weeks," says Ishmael.

"Let's see if we can find another open room."

Tasha comes out from behind the desk, hearing the squick of her shoes attaching than separating from the blood-sticky mats. She feels Z's panic from across the room, stronger as she crosses the lobby and sees the lines on her face, the creases above her eyebrows. It climbs into her lungs like exhaled smoke from a stranger's cigarette. She almost coughs.

"Maybe the dog will find us another room," she says, trying to joke but sounding flat. Z stares back at her. Her usually expressive eyebrows tell Tasha nothing, which in turn tells her everything.

"Should we split up?" Z says, turning away. Tasha and Ishmael exchange knowing looks.

"No," they say together, and Tasha feels her face gets slightly hot. He smiles. She looks away.

Z looks at them, narrowing her eyes.

"Okay. Which hallway first?"

Tasha looks, scoping out the corridors stretching ahead and behind.

"Either," she shrugs. "This one. Come on."

The hallway is darker than the lobby. Tasha clutches her knife, wishing it glowed or something like Frodo's dagger. Wouldn't that be something! If only.

They eventually settle on room 111. Unlike the Holiday Inn, the first floor of the Best Western has many open doors, rooms either hastily evacuated or raided by maids, using their key cards to find money and valuables left behind. Tasha doesn't really blame them, those maids, now gone, making off with watches, cash, whatever else. Get it while you can. It was that kind of world before the Change—no reason it would be any different after.

They'd chosen 111 because there was no blood. 112 was empty and had lots of nice toiletries left behind in the bathroom, but the massive bloodstain marring the pristine white surface of one of the beds put them off. There was no body: just a huge red ink blot of blood, wavy and irregular at its sides like a horrific continent on an empty white map.

117 was also open, but its window was smashed, a jagged gaping mouth that someone might have escaped from. What was someone else's escape route had now become a trap, so at last they settled on 111; despite the pairs of shoes lined up beside one of the beds—orderly and ordinary as if someone would be back in a moment to claim them—they decided it was decent enough, plopping their bags down on the beds as if they'd carried them all the way from Chicago.

"Try the water," Tasha calls to Z, who is inspecting the bathroom.

The plasticky sound of the cheap shower curtain being slid to the side. The clank of the old-fashioned knob. A pause, then the hesitant spurt of water, hissing, growing stronger.

"It works," Z calls. "It was orange at first but it seems okay now."

A shower, Tasha thinks blankly. At first it's only a word, barely a concept, but it grows. The last time she had bathed, or anything close to it, was at the Web, days ago. Since then she had used bottled water from Ishmael's kitchen with a washrag. His mother's stove had worked, but not the pipes.

"I'll be right back," she says quickly, and ducks out into the hall.

"Where are you going?" She hears Z's voice follow her, tight and nervous, but doesn't answer. They left the door to 112 swinging open, and she darts in, angling into the bathroom where all the fancy bottles and tubes and paper-wrapped rectangles still sit, arranged like tiny plastic tombstones. She pulls the front of her hoodie out like a pouch, squats down a little, and scoops everything on the counter into her sweatshirt. A tube of toothpaste clatters to the floor. She doesn't retrieve it:

they have that. But soap they do not have—for all the planning and plotting and packing for a trip none of them were really sure they would be taking, no one thought to bring soap. And this is the good stuff, not the generic hotel brands that smelled vaguely of chemicals and left the skin ashy or with a film. Wrapping it all in her hoodie, she waddles back across the hall to 111, where Z is standing in the doorway looking annoyed. Tasha brushes past her.

"You could have just *said* 'hey, going across the hall, be back in a jiffy,'" Z says, closing and triple-locking the door.

"I wouldn't say jiffy," Tasha says, dumping all the spoils onto the bed nearest to the door. "Who wants a shower?"

Tasha goes last. She doesn't want to be rushed. While the others sit on the beds talking in hushed tones, the world beyond the hideously-patterned curtains growing dark, Tasha stands in the shower letting the water run over her body, barely warm. But the soap, thick and rich, is enough. She covers herself in it, squeezed from the bottle like cream, and stands away from the water, looking at herself. The soap has a pretty peach tint and over the brown of her shining wet body, she feels like a rare reptile, a magic snake with a sheen of pearly scales. In the water again, she lets it all rinse off.

She's admiring the largest bottle, a teal container of shampoo—probably not made with black girls in mind, but beautiful with tiny circular specks throughout it like caviar—when a tremendous *boom* shakes the bathroom, so powerfully that she feels the reverberation crackle through her feet up to her kneecaps.

"Holy fuck!" she cries, grabbing the towel bar as her knees buckle. Then everything is still again, but she can hear the *boom* tapering off into a long, low growl. She snatches her towel and is just finishing wrapping it around herself, half in and half out of the shower, when the door flies open, revealing Z, standing there wide-eyed like a specter. She's in her T-shirt, her hoodie discarded in the den of their hotel room.

"Did you hear that?" she says, demanding a yes.

"Of course I did," Tasha snaps. "What the hell is going on?"

Her fear compounds at the sight of Z. Alone, she can be practical, tactical. Wrap self in towel. Investigate. Act. With Z here in the bathroom—or anyone else—fear is first: they are clucking chickens, smelling fox.

"I don't know I don't know," Z says, her voice skipping pauses and punctuation. "It sounded like a bomb."

Tasha tucks the towel tighter and moves toward the door, grateful she hadn't gotten her hair wet yet. Z doesn't move out of the way at first, fear settling into her limbs like paralysis, but then she does and Tasha squeezes by her, clutching her towel, and makes a beeline for her backpack, ignoring the stares of Ishmael and Malakai, who suddenly seemed to be more afraid of her in a towel than the *boom* that had shaken the hotel.

"Let me get dressed," she says to no one, and has no idea what she'll do after that, but the words sound like a promise. She throws on clothes in the bathroom, jerking her bra-straps up her shoulders and cursing when they drag on her still damp skin. The back of her hair must have gotten under the showerhead when she was rinsing—it dangles in heavy wet curls, dripping and dripping like branches in a rain forest. She throws the towel over her head, squeezing her hair in her toweled fist. She opens the bathroom door again to another enormous boom, the lock on the door handle rattling with its force. For one insane moment she believes someone is trying to get in, but when the boom subsides so does the rattling.

"It's a storm," she hears Ishmael say, and rejoins them in the bedroom. He's at the window, his body missing a head, which he has stuck through the curtains. Dark has almost completely fallen, but she can see the sickly yellowish tint of the skies mixed in with the dusk. It's different than in Chicago, where the marbled mammatus clouds hid so much of the sky's mood. When it had color, it was mottled purple, or black and muted. This sky looks ill: as if it's holding on to some angry plague, a venomous fever it has plans to spread.

"Do they have superstorms out here too?" Z says, peering.

"Everyone does," says Tasha, echoing what she's heard said on the web. "I heard the only place that doesn't is Maine."

"Maine," Z repeats, staring out the window with a crinkle between her eyes. Ishmael has parted the curtains for them like an MC giving the audience a peek backstage. The show to come is nothing nice, Tasha thinks, and she remembers looking out her window on Foster in Chicago—the crackling strikes of lightning and their thunderous accompaniment drawing out the sound of Dinah's last struggle with Dale. Tasha's stomach clenches, her throat going raw at the memory. Perhaps that's how memory is, she thinks. A storm, any storm, will now carry the suggestion of her throat, ragged from screaming Dinah's name. Every storm bears her memory.

"Is the storm going to be bad?" Malakai says, standing away from the window. The dog crouches by the boy's feet. She doesn't tremble. Her body is as stiff and unmoving as a statue: she could be a stone memorial to some famous dog, the Balto of her generation, but with better fur. Even her eyes are marble: unblinking, bare with fear. Tasha remembers the sound of the kennel when she was a child: the keening at first, then the howls tapering off into silence as the storm bore down on them. She wants to keen herself.

"I don't know," Ishmael says, rubbing his neck. "I've never seen an Iowa storm before."

They all watch in silence, the sky roiling, some unseen force stirring it with a spoon. Eventually the dog does whimper and Tasha sees Malakai scratch her ear, but the sound doesn't stop.

"It's okay, girl," Malakai says, and he sounds a little like Tasha's father, coaxing a dog onto the table for grooming or nail trimming. *It's okay.* He'd spoken in that same voice to Tasha and Leona, a whispered guarantee.

"No more thunder," Ishmael says after a few moments of silence. "Maybe that's a good thing."

"Maybe," Tasha says, but the sky's ugliness disagrees. The clouds look even more diseased, their movement like an upset stomach, churning.

"The clouds look like they're going in circles," Malakai says. He points, as if they're not all looking at the same sky.

"They kind of are," says Z. She points too. Everyone wants to be sure they are seeing the same thing; that they have witnesses in their worry, someone to confirm or deny the thing they're afraid of. Preferably deny.

"They definitely are," says Tasha, and she points too, like an idiot, one of three scared people gesturing at the sky like cavemen naming clouds for the first time. [Yeah!] "They're going in circles. Like they're spinning."

And then it occurs to her, slowly, like she's been slapped and the sting settling in is delayed.

"We need to move," she says, turning on her heel. "Like, now."

"What? What?" Z turns too, quickly as if to catch Tasha, as if Tasha might run away and leave her with the spinning clouds.

"It's a tornado. Like, fuck, there's about to be a tornado. We need to go."

"Shit," says Ishmael, snatching the curtains closed, as if that will keep the storm out, as if to hide their plan from the sky, to keep it from following. "She's right."

"A tornado?" Malakai says, not moving. He wants more, he needs to know what's going on, too much is happening at once.

"Yes," says Tasha, jamming her feet into her shoes. "Grab your stuff. We have to go, come on."

"Where?" says Z, scrambling, dropping things, still catching up with the situation, too afraid.

"Basement. Maintenance room. Something."

"Is there a basement here?" Malakai says. He wants her to know everything.

"I hope so. I don't know. I hope so."

She has her backpack in her hands. Outside, the wind is becoming more clamorous, growing from whistle to howl, stretching its legs, getting confident. She considers for an instant going into the bathroom to rescue the toiletries from the shower, re-wrapping them in their fine paper packages. This is ridiculous. Instead she reaches in and snatches one of the still-wrapped soaps from the counter, stuffing it in her pocket as she yanks open the door to the hallway. Her knife points ahead like a compass needle.

The dog darts ahead of her into the hall and leads the way down the corridor, whining. The hallways are much darker now, with dusk (and the storm) fallen. Tasha can see a little, but finds herself relying on the swishing of the dog's furry legs as a sound to follow. The hallway opening up into the lobby lends more light, with the big windows just enough to make out the front desk and the opposite hallway, leading ahead to more rooms. Tasha hesitates.

"What do you think?" she says over her shoulder. She needs someone else to help make a decision. The thunder is gone, but the whole building still seems to be vibrating, as if balancing on a thrumming wire. The wind is not merely wind but a great yawning vacuum, making gravity less certain.

"I wish there was electricity," Z says, moaning slightly, and Tasha resists telling her that wishing there was electricity isn't an answer, and that wishing there was electricity doesn't help find a basement. She'd heard of some hotels, clubs, casinos having bomb shelters on the West Coast before the secession. If only.

"I don't see any signs," Tasha says out loud, still hoping someone will step up. No one does—Ishmael clutches his brother's shoulder, looking hard at Tasha—except the dog, who stands ahead of Tasha, looking back, waiting.

"Maybe there's a closet behind the desk," she tells them, and heads that way. Not perfect, but it's closer to the center of the building than their room had been. "Watch out for...the guy," Tasha adds, stepping over the body, feeling again the stickiness of soles on old blood.

With the weak yellow light from the lobby windows, Tasha can still make out the dim outline of the door behind the desk, slightly open. The dog rushes ahead of her into the room.

A flurry of barking follows and Tasha reels backwards away from the door. Into the light looms a Minker, hulking and poor-postured, the sound coming out of his mouth savage and strange. Behind him snarls the poodle—Tasha can hear her teeth clicking with each canine exclamation.

"Fuck!" Tasha yelps, running into the counter behind her. She bumps into Z, who staggers in the dark. Tasha hears her box cutter clatter against something—she can't tell if it's the counter or the floor.

"Shit shit SHIT!" Z cries, her words almost muted by a rumble of thunder from outside. Is it thunder? Or is it the building already being torn apart by the tornado? Tasha can't tell: it could be anything.

"Move!" Ishmael shouts. In the dark, he too is a shadow. But with better posture. Tasha sweeps Z back with her arm. It's too dark. Barking from the Minker and the poodle fill the stagnant air of the lobby. Tasha can't tell if she's choking on fear or the smell.

Ishmael bulls past Tasha and Z, the Chipotle axe raised high. Almost all light that filters in through the lobby windows has been wrung out by the storm. The little that remains glances off the twisted metal of the axe. It sweeps like a bolt from Zeus, laying the Minker low. He must be guessing, Tasha thinks, panting. He can't see. No way to aim for the neck. Ishmael smashes every part of the shadow that moves. Tasha feels something wet splash onto her cheek and nose. She sputters, clawing at the air and swiping at her face. It's hot. Blood. She knows it's blood without needing to see the sharp red of it.

"Ishmael!" she screams. All she sees are shapes moving in the dark. She can't tell which are real and which are her eyes deceiving her, groping for vision.

In the dark, a spark. And while the poodle's barking still echoes in the lobby, the roar of wind outside clamoring to get in, the barking of the Minker is cut short.

"I got it," she hears Ishmael, his voice ragged from breathlessness. "It's done, it's dead."

Tasha leaps forward in the dark, her hip slamming against the counter. She grits her teeth but keeps moving. The storm is above and around and everywhere.

"I can't see," she mutters. Her hands grope the dark ahead of her, hoping they don't run into anything living. Then she has an idea. Flipping one strap of her backpack off, she snatches open the top and rummages blindly inside until she finds Rio's Glass. Grasping it tightly, she pulls it from the pack, then presses the button along the top firmly.

The screen illuminates, asking for a password she doesn't have. But she doesn't need the contents of Rio's Glass: she just needs its light. Using it as a torch, she brandishes it at the room around her.

Blood everywhere. It makes her stomach quake. A desk. A shelf. A chair, turned on its side, a wheel broken off. Perhaps the Minker had been sitting right there, just waiting. Even here, the air rumbles with the squalling wind. On the wall opposite the desk is a door, open wide to reveal nothing but blackness. Tasha steps closer, afraid, holding the Glass ahead of her like a talisman. The poodle bounds ahead. No barking. A step closer, and the silverish light illuminates a large metal safe, dead monitors and screens all around it. A security room.

Behind her, Z almost yelps, leaping in, pulling on Ishmael, who in turn pulls on Malakai. Tasha follows, yanking the door closed after them, closing out the last spiderwebs of light offered by the bruised sky. When the Glass returns to sleep mode, their silver campfire goes out. It's dark, entirely, and silent.

"A security room," Tasha says after a while. "You must feel right at home, Z."

"Fuck you," says Z, and Tasha can hear the faintest of a smile in her voice.

"Language," comes Ishmael's voice from the other corner, and they lapse into listening. Tasha rests her head against the wall, feeling the pulse of the storm outside traveling through the stone and into her skull. If she closes her eyes, it sounds like a purr, and she focuses on imagining the storm as a large cat, slouching across the sky gently, the tornado just breath passing over the ground, there and then gone.

CHAPTER 4

When she wakes, she sees how wrong she was. The storm was not a cat, it was a wolf: not mere breath, but a seizure. When they open the security room door, she's shocked at first by the brightness, the heat. She thinks for a moment that someone had been in the hotel after all: well-hidden maids and bellboys who have now turned on every light in the place and cranked the heat as well. But the light is too sharp to be fluorescent; the immediate baking she feels on her skin, her cheekbones, tells her this is sunlight. It is.

"Oh," she says out loud. The word—more like a sound— floats out into what used to be the hotel lobby. Now it's just… Iowa.

None of them had slept. For bits and pieces at a time, perhaps: moments stolen in between the fury of the storm. In the night it had alternated between sounding like a thunderous motorcycle and a motorcycle being wrenched apart: the screaming metal, the rending apart of materials too strong to be bent by anything but disaster. Tasha had awoken from one instant of sleep to find the dog curled under her bent legs, shaking violently. Not whining, just shaking. Tasha had stroked the dog's head, wondering why it hadn't crawled over to find Malakai in the dark. But she buried her fingers in the dog's curly ruff, digging her fingertips deep until she reached the skin, and scratched. It soothed them both.

Now the five of them stand in Iowa, surrounded by stones and siding of the Best Western, whose sign had landed right in the middle of what had been the lobby, advertising vacancy even in its death. The storm, so exacting in its rage, was random in what it picked up: a refrigerator from god knows where, a dumpster. Where the front desk used to be is an armchair, green and plush, a spring piercing out through the seat cushion like an alien baby bursting from its host. And ahead, where they had entered so quietly the night before, is their Toyota, floating above them in an embrace of concrete, lodged in the destroyed front ceiling of the Best Western, half in and half out of the lobby.

"Oh shit," Tasha says, and moves slowly toward it, the dog at her heels.

The car hadn't really been theirs, but its destruction feels personal. Even in a world where she has almost nothing, the storm had managed to take something. Keeping a safe distance, Tasha eyes the car, angling her neck to look up at it. It's almost art, the car suspended above her like a chandelier of ruin.

"Of course," Z says, coming over. She stands looking up at the car too. It adds to the artistic quality. They could be in a museum. The Museum of Natural Destruction, she thinks.

She turns away, looking around. No one. No maids, no bellhops, dead or otherwise. The bodies they'd seen by the elevator must have been picked up, the corpse of the Minker outside the security room carried off and deposited elsewhere. No one else mills about—the hotel really had been abandoned. Sometimes the rules of the Chip confuse her. Why were they swarming at the Holiday Inn and not the Best Western? Different programming perhaps: the Best Western Minkers designed to wander larger territory, killing as many unChipped as possible. Or perhaps, Tasha thinks, an Iowa Apiary had summoned them home, and they're filing across the state at this very moment, swaying in a single line to wherever they called their hive. It's chilling to imagine: the States swarming with their kind, mindless and bloodthirsty. And it makes the loss of the car even worse.

"We need another car," she says. She feels anxious, exposed. This is how Z must have felt when Tasha plucked her from the Web: animal, afraid in the open. The cracked hull of the hotel—built to withstand storms like last night's—seems only to heighten her panic. She is a pit inside a peach, protected only by soft flesh, the hotel's and her own. Part of her dreads walking outside and witnessing whatever other destruction there is to be found out there. But if they're going to find a car, she has to start by leaving this spot.

Exiting through the door under the car seems too much like tempting fate, Tasha decides. It hangs above them like the head of some massive beast hung on a wall, threatening to come to life at any moment. Tasha looks up at its headlights—dead eyes—as she passes through the entranceway not threatened by the hanging corpse of a car. *We didn't know each other well,* she says to it silently, *but goodbye.* She imagines herself as a lover leaving behind yet another spurned romantic: the string of cars she's left behind: the Ferrari, the Chevrolet, evidence of her cold heart. *It's not you, it's me,* she thinks, moving out into the Iowa sun.

Outside, there other objects the storm has picked up and then tossed aside like discarded dolls. A fickle child, the tornado has moved on to new land to toy with new things to pick up and put down, or else gone back up into the sky to sulk. The roundabout in front of the hotel is littered with miscellaneous wreckage: another refrigerator, a smashed decorative fountain. Someone's bicycle, old and bent, snatched from the shed where it had been languishing for half a century. Although broken, perhaps it's also a blessing: free from forgottenness at last. The young Minker that had been in the bushes under the Pumapod the day before is gone, swept up and carried away, but somehow the Pumapod remains—maybe it's not even the same one. Tasha inhales deeply, smells on herself the soap from her shower just hours ago. Right now it's barely dawn.

"Looky here," says Z, pointing with a box cutter, already pulled from her pocket like a cigarette.

Z is pointing at a person, 20 or 30 feet away, wandering in circles, arms flapping, head twitching from side to side.

"What's he doing?" Malakai says. He peers at the person thoughtfully, and Tasha remembers how young he is.

"I don't know," Tasha says. She doesn't want to know. The person makes her nervous, as if it's a mad dog. Not frothing at the mouth, she can see, but the jerking movements...the man wears madness like a shirt.

"Hey," Z calls to the guy, and her voice makes Tasha jump. She grabs Z's arm, as if to tell her to hush, but doesn't say it. Nothing happens. The man doesn't look at them, doesn't pause in his circling or his arm-flapping. Had he not heard her? But his strangeness is familiar; his mechanical erraticness is like a dream she's had that she can't quite remember.

"I think it's a Minker," she says, still gripping Z's arm, but the fear she felt a moment before has melted out of her muscles. A Minker isn't crazy, it just...is. At this point she is somehow better equipped to deal with the lack of humanity in the Chipped population than with the dysfunction of the unChipped. She goes toward the Minker, her friends watching silently. The poodle tags after her, its step peppy, glad to be out of the dark security room and outside, where it can pee and frolic and do other dog things.

Nearing the man, Tasha can see that she's right: he is a Minker. His neck under his right ear flashes constantly red in a mechanical pattern, but faster than the red she's grown accustomed to seeing in the necks of the enemy. His pattern is erratic, panicked: rather than a steady drumbeat, the thump of robotic human heart, the light flickers incessantly, sometimes growing dim. The rest of him is out of sorts as well: his eyes are rolled up into his skull, all his fingers flexed and clawed, swiping at the air with every turn he makes. The dust under his feet is stirred, a cloud around him, his own miniature tornado.

"He's malfunctioning," Tasha calls.

The others join her by the circling Minker, watching him cautiously.

"He acts just like the ones in Chicago," Ishmael says, his eyes watching the Minker seriously. Tasha hasn't seen him really smile since his mother's house. The knowledge makes her wilt a little.

But he's right. The malfunction in this spinning Minker is just like those on the streets of Chicago after the explosion of the Apiary—and Cybranu within.

"Something must have fried his circuit board," Z says, walking in a wide circle around the Minker. She says it in a doctor voice, as if she should be writing notes on a clipboard, entering them into a MediGlass.

"The storm, maybe," Ishmael says. He looks up, as if the storm will answer, award him with an affirming roll of thunder.

He's right, Tasha thinks. It makes sense. Somewhere in the un-manicured jungle of her brain, she remembers learning about storms: the obvious electricity of lightning, but the positive and negative charges of thunderclouds. Entire areas of study were built around climate change at her almost-alma mater. Superstorms had captured everyone's attention when they started unleashing themselves several decades ago, but by then it was far too late, or so Tasha's professor had said.

Malakai is standing nearer to the Minker than the rest of them. He moves his head left and right, trying to keep the man's face in his view.

"Kai, don't," Tasha says, reaching for him with one arm, calling him. At this point the Minker doesn't really worry her, but the face isn't something one should memorize. The whites of the eyes, tinting red at the bottom edges, the veins usually hidden—looking at them is like watching something floating in a bilious liquid, a murky test tube discovered in a secret lair. Just because monsters are among us doesn't mean they need to be inside us, she thinks.

Malakai comes to stand by her without saying anything. The poodle wags her tail faintly, pointing her nose up at Malakai's backpack, dangling down from his thin shoulders. The dog may have chosen Tasha as her cuddle buddy for the storm, but Malakai is still the keeper of the food.

"The dog's hungry," Tasha says, nodding.

Clearly the dog knows the word "hungry"; her ears perk up like large movable plants. The Minker rotates on his access nearby. Some of the dust settles on Tasha's Nikes. It's time to move.

"Do we kill it?" she asks. She already knows Z will say yes, Ishmael no.

"Yeah," says Z.

"We don't have to," says Ishmael.

They don't look at each other. Just at Tasha.

"Kill it," she says, and Z does, a swift slice across the side of the neck that leaves a trail of bluish sparks. Tasha can almost hear the Chip sizzle as the Minker collapses to the ground. As the dust settles, they all stand there looking down at the body, circling no more. Tasha feels a flash of pity for the former person. She wonders if it's still inside somewhere: the person they had been before they became a Minker—somewhere behind the madness, their consciousness watching helplessly as their body does what the Chip orders, handcuffed to the wheel of a car they're no longer driving.

Z turns away first, extracting the map from her backpack. "California really isn't that far," she says, shading her eyes to see the red path. "Rio acted like it was this never-ending journey because he assumed we'd be walking, but by car it's only 36 hours, and we knocked out 12 of those already."

"So we could really be there in 3 to 4 days," Tasha says. "We just need to find another car."

"Yep," says Z. She looks pleased, the shadow of a smile in the corners of her eyes. The idea of being done with all this excites her.

"First we need a car," Ishmael says. "And I don't see one."

They all look around as if following an order. He's right, Tasha sees. No cars, other than their own, lodged through the Best Western lobby windows like a rocket fallen from space. Across the way in the shoddy Holiday Inn parking lot is nothing but wreckage: the building had claimed to be able to withstand tornadoes, but it was older than the Best Western, not built for new age superstorms. It's a wonder it had stood this long, Tasha thinks, or perhaps it had been knocked over time and again, like an arrangement of bowling pins in a particularly long and devastating game of bowling that the owners masochistically continued playing.

"We can't all fit on the Pumapod," Tasha says, imagining them all teetering on top of it like clowns or stacked elephants, the poodle on the bottom pedaling frantically with her paws. They'd roll into Leona's town just like that and be shot on sight, assumed to be lunatics. She'd said it as a joke but they all just look at her and she feels stupid, so she says briskly, shrugging, "So I guess we walk! We got feet, right?"

She sets off down the road, obscured by dust and debris, stepping around an ATM that might have been in the Holiday Inn lobby, conveniently relocated by the storm.

"Okay, we walk for now," says Z, and Tasha can hear her tucking the map back into her backpack. "But let's go this way. You're walking south."

"Oh."

They eat and walk, Malakai stopping every 10 steps to offer scoops of SpaghettiOs to the poodle, who follows eagerly, her tail waving like a brown banner at the head of the parade. Tasha likes Malakai out front where she can see him. She wonders if that feeling counts as maternal, but isn't convinced. Not wanting a kid to get attacked and devoured by monsters isn't quite the same as wanting a kid, period. It doesn't necessarily indicate the presence of some Mommy Bone buried deep within her. She gets the feeling that Ishmael likes it too: Malakai out front with the dog, with the rest of them trailing leisurely behind. His gait is relaxed. It feels like a stroll: their backpacks aren't too heavy and the sun isn't too hot. They should be more afraid, Tasha knows: their human genes are inferior to animals' genes in the fear department. Fear is what keeps squirrels in manic motion when down from the trees and on open ground. Humans? They turn it into a parade, a nice stroll through the park. Tasha has caught herself admiring the scenery on more than one occasion. *Stop it,* she told herself before actually commenting on a particularly pretty bush of yellow flowers. *You should be trembling. You should have your knife up in front of you like a dueling sword!* But she doesn't. It hangs down by her side, limp and relaxed.

"You guys ever heard of Michael Jackson?" Ishmael asks. They're passing the entrance to a gated neighborhood of mid-rise condos, gorgeous pink flowers overgrown and clotting the walkways.

The gate is firmly closed, white and metal, beside a small guard hut, inside which Tasha can see the back of a man in a white collared shirt slumped over the desk. She can't see any blood from here, but he's dead, of course. She can smell him—and probably others—from where she walks ten feet away. The big sign in front of the tidy neighborhood reads "Michael Jackson Luxury Condominiums" in big carved letters, painted white. There's a copper statue of a man grabbing his crotch, his face obscured by a hat, a microphone in his other hand.

"No," she says.

"Me neither," says Z, turning her head to continue looking at the statue of the man as they pass by.

"Missing out," says Ishmael.

"Who was he?"

"He was a star," he says. He scratches his ear. Tasha thinks that men are more inclined to scratch than women. Not because women itch less, but because they don't scratch. An itch on a man's ear is an itch on an ear. An itch on a woman's ear might mean she hasn't washed her ear, which means somehow that she hasn't washed anything else. *Dirty women are different than dirty men*, she thinks, and feels annoyed, feels a bit like rolling in mud.

"I'm surprised you haven't heard of him," he says a moment later. "Mad famous."

No one says anything. They've passed the Michael Jackson neighborhood and are approaching the next gated community, which they can see has another bronzed statue posed right out front, stiff like a castle guard. The walking—only ten or so miles so far—has already reached a level of monotony, perhaps because of the scenery. The hotels were the last buildings they had seen for five miles, and then it was just road. Scrubby trees on each side, and road. A burned-out car. Bushes. Road. Urban sprawl hadn't reached these Iowan guts: emptiness is just that. Empty.

Then Z had directed them onto another road, a fork whose lanes drifted subtly apart, at first seeming parallel. But the first road veered farther and farther south as they continued west and gradually faded out of sight. Now, mile eleven, the road has narrowed and become more residential. The trees are less scrubby. Tasha sees a bit of burlap poking out of the dirt at the base of one. Nursery trees, brought in to pretty up the dusty street.

"Rich people," she says suddenly. Of course. It had taken her a moment to recognize the signs: Iowa rich doesn't look like Chicago rich. But the guardhouses; the private white gates closing out the undesirables of the world; the imported potted trees. She looks around, seeing with new eyes. They're coming up on the next neighborhood: the sculpture is a statuesque woman, her hair made of stone but giving the impression of windblown-ness. She too holds a microphone. Tasha stops in front of her, but is distracted by the neighborhood beyond her, behind the white fence slats. She wanders past the statue. There's a parking lot in there, and a glowing Whole Foods. Private, the sign on the fence says, for the use of residents only. She can see a long row of charge cars too, all hooked to a glowing strip on the wall of the compound.

"It's glowing," Tasha says. "They've got power."

No one hears her. They're all crowded around the bronze statue.

"This one is Beyoncé Estates," says Z.

"You've heard of Beyoncé, right?" Ishmael says. She thinks he might be teasing her, but he's not.

"Everyone has heard of Beyoncé," Tasha says. "Even Malakai. Right, Kai?"

"Duh," the boy says, still studying the statue. "She was really pretty."

Tasha comes around to the front. The statue's face is surprisingly detailed. The woman's mouth is wide open in song, but the corners are still turned up into a smile. Her bronze eyes are full of life, her cheekbones sculpted. Tasha wouldn't have been able to name this face if she'd seen it on the street with no context, but knowing it is Beyoncé and seeing Beyoncé's face has the brain-jogging effect one experiences when being told something one already sort of knew. Yes, this face. Beyoncé, of course. She'd know the voice anywhere: it brings to mind Tasha's grandmother's kitchen, the big notes blasting out of a speaker older than Tasha, her grandma swaying at the counter. *Pretty hurts...* But the face before her, carved in stone, isn't as familiar, especially given the age of the face depicted here, young and undeniably Beyoncé, a shadow of the woman who became an ambassador at 66 years old.

"Do you know her as the ambassador or the singer?" Ishmael asks, giving her an intentional side-eye. He is teasing her but serious too, waiting to bestow judgment.

"Why does it matter?" Tasha says. She shrugs. "She was both."

"Moving on?" says Z, taking a step away.

"No, wait," Tasha says, remembering. Beyoncé, her face and life, had distracted her. "I think we should go in there."

"In where?"

Tasha points.

"Into Beyoncé Estates."

Z's smile fades.

"Why?"

"There's food. And, you know, it's a rich neighborhood. There's stuff."

"Stuff?"

"Yeah," Tasha says, but flounders a little. What does the gated community have, after all? They do need food, but not badly. It can wait until tomorrow. But the Whole Foods shines at her through the white gate like a glowing green oasis. She hasn't been in one since she first moved to Chicago: the last store had closed after the Clean Food riots ensured they were robbed weekly in produce heists. Now here's one a mere hundred yards away, locked away in a rich neighborhood where the residents didn't have to resort to violence to have access to safe food. The Whole Foods is guarded only by a statue of Beyoncé, a dead guy with a Taser, and a stupid white fence. No humans. Get the food. She suddenly wants it a little too much, and looks at Z helplessly.

"Um…they have cars. They look charged. Don't your feet hurt? We've been walking a long time…"

Z stares at her for a long moment, as if trying to make her admit something. Tasha isn't sure what she'd admit anyway: that she's a fatty, obsessed with the idea of food (good food) being free? That she hates the white fence and what it means? Finally Z breaks her gaze and looks down at her own feet, as if she can see through her shoes.

"I'm getting blisters," she admits.

"Me too," Tasha says quickly.

"Wait, what's happening?" says Ishmael, coming around to their side of Beyoncé. "Y'all want to hop the fence?"

"Yes," says Tasha at the same time that Z says "maybe."

"Why?"

"Food," Tasha says.

"Cars," Z says.

"Do we need food?" Malakai says, sounding worried. "Are we almost out?"

"No, no," says Tasha, feeling bad that she ignited anxiety in the boy. "We just…can get more. And, like, better food. And we can get dog food too," she adds, nodding at the poodle, who has wandered back toward Michael Jackson, but looks over at them.

"For Phaedra," says Malakai.

"Huh?"

"Phaedra. That's what I named her."

"Oh. That's a nice name," Tasha says, not really meaning it. "We could get Phaedra some dog food."

"Okay."

Good kid, Tasha thinks.

"What all do we have?" Ishmael says. He swings his backpack off his shoulders and lays it and the duct-taped Chipotle mace down on the road, unclasping the clip holding it closed.

Malakai and Z follow suit, so Tasha unslings the Prada backpack and flips open the flap.

Leona's letter. Rio's glass. A granola bar. A can of soup. A packet of dried apples. Her can opener from her apartment on Foster. A bandage, rolled up like a sock. Actual socks. Three pairs of underwear, which she keeps carefully sheltered in the pack. Water.

"A can of soup. Dried apples. As far as food goes."

"SpaghettiOs. A can of potatoes. Two granola bars." Ishmael has taken his items out and laid them on the pavement.

"Soup," says Malakai.

"Is that it? What happened to your SpaghettiOs?" Ishmael cranes his neck to see if his brother missed something.

"I gave them to Phaedra."

"Kai…ugh. Okay. Z?"

"Potatoes. Soup. Canned carrots. Dried apples. Five granola bars. Peaches. Tuna."

"What the fuck, Z," Tasha says.

"What?"

"Why do you have so much food?"

"Because I—what do you mean? I packed extra."

"No wonder your feet hurt. You're carrying too much."

"Didn't you listen to Dr. Rio?" Ishmael says. "Only pack food for one day. There's food everywhere. Wal-Mart, gas stations, all that. You have to travel light if you need to run."

"It's still light."

"Except not really," says Tasha, starting to laugh. "Okay, we don't really need food because of the hoarder over here. But the hoarder needs a ride, and those cars look like they're charging. Are we going in?"

"I don't know," says Ishmael. He's peering into the neighborhood. The Whole Foods is too far to reflect in his eyes, but Tasha can feel it reflecting in hers either way: a well-stocked paradise of whole-grain granola and organic snacks. The word "organic" is like Prada, almost: a thing you should want, a thing you need that will make you better.

"It seems quiet," she says, shrugging. She can't appear to want it too much.

"It seems quiet," Z repeats, almost mocking her but not quite daring to because as much as Tasha wants Whole Foods, Z wants a car. Tasha can feel "want" radiating off her like steam from a horse's coat. Z has never been one for being out in the open. Building to building. Car to building. Car to car. Building to car. That's okay. They'd been born into the Change in different contexts: their paths laid in unique patterns. Tasha is more like Ishmael: they don't mind open—not really—if it means getting where they're going: toward family, toward something. Or, in this case, merely getting what they want, which for Tasha is Whole Foods.

Ishmael looks at them, his forehead crinkled. Malakai stands neutrally to the side. The dog rejoins them, sniffing Beyoncé's knee. Tasha shoos her away. It feels sacrilegious.

"Well, since we're already here..." Ishmael trails off.

"Great," says Tasha, scooping up the Wusthof from the road, swinging her Prada backpack back onto her shoulders. "I'll get the gate."

She knows the controls will still work: the Whole Foods' glowing green sign and the illuminated panel for the charge cars both indicate power. These people were rich: they were on a generator. How does one get one of those generators, she wonders, sliding sideways into the hut to avoid brushing against the dead guard, a brown-skinned woman whose flesh is beginning to crumble around the fingernails. Are these residents on a federal power system? State? Private? How much? Could the South Side have gotten one? Two? Who sold them? Answers to questions that only rich people know to ask.

On the desk is an array of monitors, all but one or two still illuminated and showing various deserted staircases and backdoors. Tasha thinks of the head-banging girl in the Web, her crisscrossed tan, her egg head slowly cracking. Maybe she's still there. Or maybe the explosion of the Apiary was close enough to fry her Chip a little more thoroughly and she's crumpled to the fitting room floor, finally.

"Gate," Tasha reads out loud, and touches her finger to the digital pad. The gate button is square and orange and responds to the warmth of her index finger cooperatively. She hears the hum of the gate rising and is reminded of the cats in Lincoln Park Zoo, their eager springing through the opening onto prey. She gets it. She's about to spring onto some organic anything.

Outside the booth, the gate is swinging slowly up to give them access, and Ishmael ushers Z and Malakai underneath before it has a chance to change its mind. Tasha glances once more at the dead guard before hurrying to join her group, on the other side of the fence: inside Beyoncé Estates.

It's as tranquil inside as it appears to be from the outside. Behind them the gate hums slowly down again, which startles Tasha. It's on a timer, she thinks, unless the guard had reanimated just long enough to secure the perimeter, which sort of wouldn't have surprised Tasha.

"Food first?" Ishmael says, and she wants to high-five him, but doesn't. He is in caution-mode. Everyone is, even the dog: the serenity of Beyoncé Estates is suspicious. Little burbs like this always are: in every old horror movie she'd ever watched, the peaceful, deserted neighborhood was never peaceful or deserted. But Tasha doesn't feel the same caution that slows her companions. She feels loose, stupidly loose, looking at the large unbroken windows of Whole Foods, imagining the rows of undisturbed packaged goods, their expiration dates months and months away, eternities from now.

"Food first," she agrees, trying not to smile too much, and begins to cross the parking lot.

"Wait, wait," says Z, throwing an arm out to catch her before she takes a step. "Shouldn't we, like, check things out? You know, to see if there's any Minkers hanging out?"

Tasha looks around. Minkers are like germs, she knows: you don't really know they're floating around until they've already got a hold on you. At least Minkers bark and give that little bit of warning. She doesn't hear any barking.

"I feel like if we can get in and get out without them noticing, then that's our best bet. If we walk around the neighborhood poking around, we're more likely to, you know, rustle them up."

"Plus," says Ishmael, holding his Chipotle axe in both hands, "there might still be some folks left who aren't Minkers who wouldn't like the idea of a group of black folks traipsing around their gated community."

He grins and Tasha does too. When he smiles like that, it's like a sneeze: contagious. He smiles, you smile. One and two.

"I'm not black," says Z. She says it slowly, unsure.

"No, but we are," says Tasha.

"How do you know they don't like black people? They live in Beyoncé Estates and she was black, right?"

"Celebrities don't count. Especially dead ones," Ishmael says, waving his hand. "Everybody loves dead celebrities."

"Anyway," says Z, shrugging. "You're probably right. But let's hurry up, okay? Every time we've stopped there's been Minkers, so let's just get out of here."

There's a pile of bodies outside Whole Foods. She's so used to the sight of death that she barely notices them, their limbs tangled and stiff and jutting out at odd angles. She doesn't look at their faces, nor does she consider how they came to be piled here, their high-quality shirts bloodied in places by battles she doesn't care to imagine. Instead she leads the way past them, glancing at the charge cars lined up nearby. She doubts any keys will be left in the ignitions: they'll have to hope they can find a dead body in the ice cream aisle whose pockets they can pat. Either that or disturb the pile of stiffs.

There's no jingle when they open the door, and no music either, which surprises Tasha a little. She struggles to remember if that Jewel Osco so far away on the North Side of Chicago had its same old pop music playing the last time she'd raided its shelves before heading south. It must have: no one had lived to turn it off, and from what she knew, music in stores played endlessly and endlessly: the store never closed and the music never stopped. Even buying cauliflower is like going to the club: never stop feeling good, never stop the party.

Tasha has become accustomed to the constant disarray of the world. Crashed cars, with various broken-off parts scattered like Legos; bodies with limbs sometimes missing, like dolls mutilated by careless children: the world, it seems, is the room of a messy kid, the whole of it cluttered and coated in a layer of grime, forgotten under a dresser. And that's why the Whole Foods shocks her: its order is strange, otherworldly. The carts are pushed snugly together. The floors are clean of the debris, human or non, that usually clutters the floors of establishments like this post-Change.

"It's so quiet," says Malakai. He hangs back by the door, not trusting this quiet, orderly place. The poodle, on the other hand, has abandoned him and is at the end cap of Aisle 2 sniffing the display of organic Cheez-Nips.

"I think it's okay, Kai," she says, gesturing to him with her knife-hand. "It doesn't look like there are any Minkers here."

No sooner had the words left her mouth then a small shape emerges from the hidden tunnel of Aisle 2 and wraps its arms around the neck of the poodle, which jumps with a yelp. The scene plays out inside Tasha's eyes before it actually happens: the Minker, starved of human flesh, sates its appetite with the dog meat of the poodle, leaving the dog squirming on the ground in death throes before turning on the rest of them.

Tasha sprints to the dog, something like numbness dulling her senses. She feels slow and clumsy, like she's fumbling through mud, sliding on oil and not just her own fear. She feels the slight weight of the backpack on her back, the balance of the knife in her hand, ready to find the Minker's neck and pop out the Chip like an evil battery.

A woman appears in front of Tasha, her arms and mouth wide, blonde hair flying, fingers spread.

"No, no!" she screams. "No, don't hurt him, he's fine!"

Tasha almost stabs her, this waving, screaming creature that has appeared out of nowhere, like some kind of frantic guardian of organic goods. She pulls the knife back, her arm spring-loaded, but behind the woman, the poodle has her tongue out, her tail wagging; no blood, no open throat, no dying dog—just a toddler with its face buried in chocolate-brown fur. The knife falters.

"Who the fuck are you?" she says, feeling helpless. She looks at the woman now, actually looks at her, and sees that she's wearing mascara.

"I'm Amy," the woman says. "Amy."

She's pale, but paler currently from her fear. She has wide eyes, sky blue like an Australian Shepherd. To some they might have been striking. Her fair skin, her fair hair. But Tasha is only reminded of the restless spotted dogs in her parents' kennel: always barking, always jumping, never still. Neither is Amy.

"What are you doing in here?" Amy demands, gesturing at the store. Her fear is subsiding, slowly being rebuilt block by block with anger. "Who do you think you are? Just coming in here! And with a dog! Dogs bark, don't you know that! Then *they* come—"

"Hey, hey," says Z, swooping in. Wing woman. "Why don't you just freaking relax? We didn't make any noise when we came in, but now *you're* screaming and stuff!"

Amy jumps, looking at Z in shock. Then she looks beyond her, takes in Ishmael and Malakai, and jumps again. The fear is back, but the anger sticks around. Tasha can see it in the angle of her eyes, the tightness of her lips.

"Who...who are you?" She's addressing Ishmael.

"I'm Ishmael," he says, gently, as it coaxing a fawn out of the brush. Tasha doesn't think Amy looks like a fawn. She's not sure what exactly. Too frail for lynx. Too angry for a rabbit.

"Stay away from my children!" she spits, at all of them, but especially at Ishmael, who raises his eyebrows. Malakai stays silent, looking at the woman warily, the way one would regard a snarling dog.

"No one is near your kid, okay, lady?" Z says. She rolls her eyes. "You said 'kids'. Where's the other one? Or two? Or three, however many brats you have running around in here."

Amy whips around as if she'd been yanked. The toddler is still giggling into the poodle's neck, and Amy snatches him back, a boy of three or four with mouse-brown hair and squinty hazel eyes.

"Jacob, stay away from that dog!" Amy snaps, and then looks around frantically, her hair tossing over first one shoulder and then the other. "Cassie? Cassie!"

After a pause, Cassie emerges. She's over by the produce, and steps out from behind a table of blackened bananas, looking surly. She's fourteen, fifteen. Gaunt. Pale like her mother but with hair dyed dark, almost black. Her mother's blonde genes peek through at the roots.

"I'm here, mom." Her voice is flat and thick with dislike.

"Get out of the produce," her mother says forcefully. "There are bugs over there! Come here!"

The girl stands staring balefully for a moment and then walks toward Amy and Jacob, whose arm is still gripped tightly by his angry mother.

"Now," says Amy, glaring at Tasha, her children gathered around her, a tight horde. "I'm going to have to ask all of you to get out."

Tasha can feel Z revving up for a burst of annoyance, so she jumps in before she has a chance.

"Why?" The woman's intensity feels frail as wet cardboard. She knows this face. Thin and tight, the eyebrows arched, the upper lip puffy from injection or implant, the under eyes stretched and lineless. Her eyeliner is permanent, and so is her scowl. "Why do we have to leave?"

"Because you don't belong here!" the woman says, sputtering like a used car.

"No?" Tasha feels her heart thumping, her throat tightening. She's so angry. Her anger feels full and red in her stomach, as if she might spit it out in a ball of flame.

"I don't need to tell you why!" Amy insists, raising her chin. Tasha sees the chinks in her armor, the gaps in her bravery: no one has ever told her *no* before. One more *no* and she might crumble.

"I don't see your name on the door," says Tasha.

"Unless your name is Whole," smirks Z. "Last name Foods?"

Corny, Tasha thinks. *Corny as hell.* But it also feels good. This isn't Fetch Fetchers. This isn't Amy's world. Amy's pale face has gone red.

"Mama, puppy," little Jacob says.

"Shh," says Amy.

They're all just staring at each other. Cassie looks afraid now, and Tasha supposes she can't blame her much. Four strangers, three of them with weapons. Perhaps Malakai, young and nervous, is a comfort to Cassie, though he certainly isn't to Amy, who acts as if she hasn't even noticed there's a child with them.

Tasha and Amy lock eyes. Tasha notices her eyebrows, still perfectly trimmed into too-thin crescents. Not a stray hair to be seen. Perma Derma Wax, Tasha guesses: serum applied by a doctor to kill the hair follicles for good. No plucking, no waxing ever again. The eyebrows were obtained by brute force, thin shadows of their former selves. Tasha thinks her own brows must surely have returned to the wild: emboldened by the absence of wax, they've crept back out of their roots to emerge into the light.

"What do you want?" Amy says. Her pale blue eyes are squinted, suspicious. They dart down to the knife in Tasha's hand. Tasha wishes she could put it away, wishing again for a medieval scabbard where she could sheath it and show that she means no harm. Then again, the idea of setting Amy at ease doesn't feel high on her list of priorities.

Then she sees the scar. Under Amy's ear, a thick pink scar, large and square. Its edges are almost perfect, as if a stamp had branded her. The scar itself is raised, the tissue indicating the wound had not healed well.

"What happened to your neck?"

Amy's hand rises slowly as if through water, cupping itself protectively over the ugly pink patch. Her lips move, but either she's not saying anything or she's saying it so softly that Tasha can't hear.

"What happened to your neck?" Tasha says again, not softly.

Amy stares at her long and hard.

"My husband. My husband…he took my Chip."

"He took it?" Z says.

"Yes."

"In the divorce," says Cassie, harshly. The word *divorce* falls out of her mouth like a curse, and Tasha thinks it must be fresh: the wound, the word.

"They can do that?" Z says, and Tasha isn't sure who "they" is: men, MINK, or doctors. Anyway, it doesn't really matter. They is they. There is always a they.

"Yes."

"He took mine too," says Cassie. "He would have taken Jacob's but he was too young to get it to begin with."

"Quiet, Cassie."

Cassie is quiet. They all are. Tasha's anger settles down into her stomach, turning from angry red to purple, transformed into pity. Not sympathy, but pity.

"Look," says Tasha, still unwilling to be kind. "We don't want to hurt you. We just wanted to get some food and a car and be on our way."

"A car?" Amy says shrilly. "You mean one of the cars outside? Those cars don't belong to you. They belong to the people who live in this neighborhood!"

"Lived," says Z, the annoyance dripping from her voice like acid. "Lived. In case you didn't know, all those people are dead."

"You...you don't know that."

"Really? We don't?" Z raises her eyebrow.

"Who killed all those Minkers outside?" says Tasha.

"All the...the what?"

"The Minkers," she snaps. "The people that have probably been trying to eat you for the past, like, three weeks. Did you kill them?"

"No...no. I didn't kill anyone. I came down here when... when the property manager lost his mind. I just grabbed Jacob and Cassie and...and we ran, and we came in here and there were...there were dead people everywhere and people were running and shouting and I took the kids into the bathroom and locked the door until it was all quiet."

The poodle has found her way over to Jacob again and sniffs his shirt, wagging. Amy yanks Jacob to stand on her other side. Tasha snaps her fingers at the poodle, who comes over and stands in front of Tasha, waiting. Tasha wishes briefly that the poodle were an attack dog so she could sic her on Amy, even if just on her ankle.

"You moved their bodies outside?"

Amy nods.

"I didn't want the children to see."

Tasha raises an eyebrow and turns to look at the front door. Through the glass, the pile of bodies is readily visible. One stares dead-eyed through the doorway into the store.

"I keep the children away from the door," Amy says, with a trace of *duh* in her tone.

"So you've been here for over two weeks and you think that your friends in the neighborhood committee are just magically okay, huh?" Z clicks her box cutter in and out.

"I'm waiting for the police. The army," says Amy, raising her chin.

Tasha is suddenly out of patience: the last drop of it trickles out of her and evaporates into *fuck it.*

"Whatever, lady," she says. "We are getting food and then we'll be out of your hair. If you want to stay here and wait for the cops, that's on you."

Tasha moves toward the aisle of food, but Amy moves too, standing firmly in her way. She's let go of Jacob's arm and puts her hands on her hips.

"Nothing in this store belongs to you!" she says, loudly. "I will not sit here and watch you steal."

"Move, Amy," Tasha says. She feels her fingers tighten around the handle of the Wusthof. Her teeth grind against each other.

Tasha sidesteps and moves toward the aisle again, intent on obtaining some fig bars, some canned pineapple. She realizes that since they saw the Whole Foods, a vision has been rolling out in her mind. Food—good food, not the terrible SpaghettiOs she's been slowly getting used to—and a car. Maybe even a minivan so they all have a little more room. Z and Tasha and Malakai and Ishmael and the poodle all loaded up with groceries and hurtling across the miles toward California and Leona. Rio had insisted they go on foot, but in a car they can make the trip shorter, safer. They can get to the end of the route and either find Ishmael's mom or wait for her.

It all starts with canned pineapple. "Canned fruit" is on Aisle 3's marquee, and she moves in that direction.

But here's Amy again. Pale blue eyes like the gaze of a cavefish, piercing into Tasha like two empty mirrors. Tasha wonders how a woman like this came to be living in a place called Beyoncé Estates.

"You're a thief!" says Amy, her voice shrill with rage. "You're a looter!"

"We're not taking TVs, lady," says Z from somewhere behind Tasha. "We're just getting food."

"Which doesn't belong to you!" Amy snaps. Her eyes have widened in her outrage. The skin looks stretched so tight that it might tear. Tasha hopes it does.

"Move, Amy." She tries to get around her again.

Amy curls her arms and shoves Tasha. A pathetic shove. She's slight and trim from aerobics classes, weak from not lifting weights. Either way, the contact of her hands against Tasha's shoulders extinguishes the purple pity in her stomach, throws gasoline on the embers of her anger, and suddenly her stomach is in flames, the fire exploding higher. She drops the knife—the clang is loud and slow, it seems—and uses both arms to shove Amy as hard as she can.

The woman hurtles backwards, arms shot out in front of her, legs limp. She flies several feet, nothing behind her to stop her trajectory, before crashing heavily to the tile floor, her hair a mess of ruffled blond feathers.

Tasha doesn't look at her, doesn't speak to her. She stoops, picks up her knife, and proceeds to Aisle 3, plucking a basket from the end cap as she goes. She's already putting canned pineapple into the basket when she hears, "You thug! You black bitch!"

Amy is screeching and Jacob is crying and Tasha is putting pineapple in her basket. Z joins her a minute later, also with a basket. She silently adds food to hers.

"What's she doing?" Tasha says after a moment.

"Nothing, really. Flipping out. Just sitting there on the floor."

"Hmm."

"She's crazy," Z adds.

"Yeah."

They go to the end of the aisle, toward the back of the store. The meat counters are still lit and refrigerated, but Tasha can smell the bad meat. They gather granola bars and bottled water, packets of organic instant potatoes and other instafood. It's all they can take, really: organic and pesticide-free or not, this far into the game everything real is rotting. As they pass the produce section on the way back up front, the smell hits Tasha like a wave of putrid earth: the fruit has passed the stage of initial stink and blossomed into full-blown rot. The swarms of insects, born of the air, bask in it. Tasha breathes it in. It is unpleasant, but when it fills her nostrils she feels relief: better rotting kale than rotting bodies.

Ishmael and Malakai are standing where they were, appearing not to have moved a muscle. Malakai looks as if he might have cried. The poodle stands beside him, mouth slightly open. Tasha remembers dog food.

"Malakai, do you want to get some dog food?"

Malakai looks up at her, his eyes still wet. He seems a little angry at her. Tasha decides to ignore this.

"Yes," he says.

"Do you want to come find some with me?"

The boy looks from her to Amy, whom Tasha has not acknowledged. Out of the corner of her eye Tasha can see that Amy is still sitting where she'd fallen, Jacob now sitting with her, sniffling. Cassie stands several feet away, arms crossed over her stomach and looking small.

"Yes," says Malakai, and takes a step toward Tasha.

"Come on," she says, being gentle. She puts her arm around his shoulders, half expecting him to shrug her off, but he doesn't. Together they walk to Aisle 7, making a wide loop around the pile of Amy.

"How about this," says Tasha, pointing at a large bag of dry kibble. The dog on the packaging is a collie—the All-American dog, *Lassie,* Tasha thinks, remembering an entire class in college called Man's Best Friend: The Representation of Pets in American Cinema. The dog is as airbrushed as any supermodel, its eyes colored blue, though any idiot knows collies' eyes are brown.

"Yeah," says Malakai. "That looks okay." He's trying to sound tough, normal, but his voice still quavers a little.

"What about some good stuff too," says Tasha, picking up a can labeled Organic Turkey Dinner for Dogs. Her parents wouldn't have allowed it for the kennel, but it can't hurt as a treat.

"Yeah, I think she'll like that," she says, nodding at her own choice.

He squats down to get something from a lower shelf: a bowl, ceramic and engraved with the words Mutt Love.

"She needs a bowl," he says, standing up with it.

"Yeah, she does. We can keep it in the car for her."

"Tasha," he says, and she wonders if she's ever heard him say her name.

"Yeah?"

"Is this stealing? Like that lady said?"

"No," says Tasha, trying to sound like something he'll believe. "The rules have changed."

"What if the rules change back?"

"What do you mean?"

"What if things get…fixed? What if the cops come, like that lady says? They'll kill us."

"The cops wouldn't kill us for taking food, Kai. We would just go to jail. But that's not going to happen."

"Yes they would," he says, and he stands back a little so they can really look at each other. "They kill people all the time."

"Maybe, but not for taking groceries."

"They killed my dad and he didn't do anything. He was on his way to work," says Malakai, his voice breaking a little. He's still holding the bowl and it shakes in his hands. Tasha slowly reaches out and takes it, and his hands drop to his sides.

"The cops killed your dad?"

"They kill everybody's parents," he shrugs, looking down. She almost misses the tear dangling from his chin. Tasha touches the tear with her pointer finger, catches it. She suddenly feels like she's in too deep, up to her hips in something thick and heavy. He knows more than she does, carries something at 11 that she had not put on her shoulders until years later.

"The cops are dead now," she says, and wishes it meant something more. But maybe it does: not revenge, but relief.

They stand there together for a moment, holding the dog food, him looking at the floor, her looking at him.

"You ready?" she asks softly. Aside from Amy's scowl, they have no real reason to hurry, and Tasha doesn't feel the need to rush out on account of Amy's fury.

"Yeah. How are we going to find the keys to a car?"

"Well," she says, and stops. Should she say it? No real way around it. "I'm pretty sure one of the... bodies outside will have keys in their pocket."

"Oh," he says, blinking. "Yeah."

Tasha hefts the bag of dry food and Malakai fills his arms with canned. Together they walk back toward the front of the store, where Ishmael and Z stand with the two full baskets of food already gathered. Amy crouches by the end cap where her son first sprang out at the poodle. Her eyes are red but dry.

"That's looting," she says one more time, as if determined to shame Tasha into returning the food, can by can, bag by bag.

Tasha slowly lowers the dog food to the floor and sighs. She turns and walks toward Amy. Amy shrieks, cowering, as if Tasha is a grizzly bear hurtling through the brush, jaws slavering.

"And what do you think you've been doing?" Tasha says softly. "What have you been feeding your kids? What have you been eating to survive? I bet you haven't been putting money in the register. Have you?"

"That's different!" squawks Amy. "I have to feed my children...I..."

Tasha's finger flies in the direction of Malakai, straight like a weathervane.

"And him? You don't think I have to feed him? He's 11."

Amy's lip trembles, her eyes shining, hard.

"The police would understand," the woman says finally.

"Yeah, they would, wouldn't they?" Tasha says.

She turns on her heel, returning to the spot where she left the dog food, heaving it up on her shoulder. She feels heavy and light at the same time: as if she could float up into the ceiling but slowly, reluctantly, like a stone tied to a cluster of balloons.

"We need a cart," she says to Ishmael, who looks at her with eyes brown and sad. He nods.

They put everything in the cart. It's an impressive amount of food. They look at it, planning their next move, the hard part: the car.

"I'll go," Z says. Tasha hears eagerness in her voice: she wants to do something for Tasha.

"I can help," says Ishmael, raising his hand slightly as if in a crowd. "They'll be heavier than you think. Moving them around will take two."

He means the bodies. Tasha remembers her first night in his mother's house, how he and Mr. Jackson had gone into the street to kill the Minkers. She wonders where Mr. Jackson is: had he eventually joined one of the caravans? Or was he still huddled in his home on the South Side, uselessly guarding his valuables?

"Okay," says Tasha. "But I might as well help. Malakai, stay in here with the dog and sit tight."

"Why?" he asks. He doesn't want to be alone with Amy; Amy and her silent, staring children.

"Don't worry about her," Tasha says softly. "We'll be right on the other side of the glass."

He pauses, looks halfway over his shoulder at Amy, who watches, a pale hawk.

"Okay," he says at last, like it was dragged from him.

"Okay," she says, nodding, satisfied. "Try to keep the dog quiet. We don't want to attract any attention."

"You will," calls Amy. Tasha ignores her.

"Alright," says Z. "So Ish and I move them, you check the pockets?"

"Works for me," says Tasha: Move the bodies. Check the pockets. It doesn't feel like a real conversation, even now, even after all this.

They open the door cautiously: more cautiously than when they'd come in. They have more to lose now. They haven't seen a single Minker coming in, but this is when bad things always happen in every story: she'd watched enough films in college (analyzing their plots until every twist was laid flat in every film thereafter) to know that it's when you have the most to lose that the monsters come crawling out from beneath the beds.

"Quiet," she says, and almost adds "slow," but clamps her mouth on it, knowing it will remind everyone of the Apiary, those last nerve-ruining moments. No one needs to be thinking about the Apiary right now.

Ish grasps under the arms of a dead man wearing a checkered shirt. The smell is serious and Ishmael turns his face away, grimacing.

"Fuck, he stinks," says Z, holding the guy's ankles.

"They all do," says Tasha, patting the guy's pockets.

"Do you guys remember when keys would jingle? So much easier to find." Ishmael grunts under the man's weight. "I don't like thumbprints for everything."

"We're in a rich neighborhood," Z says. "A lot of the cars in here might be thumbprint ignition."

"Not that rich," Tasha says, glancing around. "They're Lexus rich, not Ferrari rich."

"Check their wallets," says Ishmael, struggling with the next man, a fat guy in a pink shirt, the front hugely stained with blood. "Remember that card key from our last car."

Tasha does remember, still a little embarrassed, but hadn't thought to check wallets, so she does.

The third body, a slim older man with what had been a stylish haircut, silver and white, has a card key. Three etched ovals decorate the surface. Tasha presses her finger to one. She hears a chirp, like an electric sparrow, behind her in the line of cars. She looks, just as the glow of headlights against the Whole Foods wall fades.

"We're in luck," Tasha says, standing.

"Hold on," says Ishmael, rising from where he'd been kneeling next to the bodies.

He jogs over to the line of cars and then turns.

"Do it again."

She does it again.

The chirp, light illuminating the wall once more, comes from what must be the third or fourth car in the row.

"No good," he calls, softly, trying to be quiet. "It's a Corvette. Two-seater."

Z makes a sound of disgust.

"These guys and their mid-life crises."

Tasha smiles. The word "crises" sounds so strange. Like Pisces. Like crystal. It sounds like something valuable. No wonder rich white men have them.

"We'll keep trying," she says.

"Look for women," Ishmael says, returning. "There's a couple minivan-type things over there."

"Way to stereotype," Tasha says, smiling, searching the pockets of a woman who had been soft-bodied, now stiff with death. Nothing. Women carried purses, not wallets. No purses here. Amy was probably hoarding them in the back of Whole Foods someplace, she thinks nastily, shooting a look through the window. Malakai and the poodle stand there watching them, Malakai with fear and the dog with interest, her ears alert. That haircut really is ridiculous, Tasha thinks admiringly.

"This one has something in her pocket," Z says hopefully, nodding down at the woman she and Ishmael have just uncovered by removing another body from the pile.

Tasha returns to the job at hand. The woman is slim, gray-haired, and in shape. Her face looks horrible. Over two weeks dead. But Tasha thinks she had been beautiful once. She reaches into the woman's pocket, which bulges. It's not a wallet, Tasha knows right away: it's something rolled up. She pulls it out: a nylon shopping bag. No key.

"Check her bra," Ishmael says.

Z and Tasha's heads snap with the same shocked elasticity.

"Check her what?" they chorus.

He looks bashful, and shrugs.

"My mom never carried her purse in the grocery store," he says. Tasha half expects him to scuff the toe of his shoe. "She always puts her wallet in her bra."

Tasha stares at him.

"It was a small wallet," he adds.

"Tasha," says Z grandly. "Would you like to do the honors?"

"Fuck no," Tasha says, jerking her neck. "What the hell do I look like putting my hand in a dead lady's bra?"

They both look at Ishmael, who looks back with his eyebrows raised.

"What? Me? Nope. Nope." He shakes his head. "Noope."

"It was your idea," Tasha says, putting her hands on her hips. She's flirting with him. She can't believe she's flirting with him over the prospect of putting a hand in a dead woman's bra. This is life.

"Yeah," Z echoes, and Tasha wonders, light-greenly, if she's flirting with him too.

"Do…not…care," Ishmael says. He's not flirting.

Tasha looks back at Z, who puts her hands up as if in surrender.

"Tasha…no," she says, giggling, but Tasha sees the nausea, the almost-panic.

Tasha sighs.

"If there's no key in her bra, one of you guys owes me…I don't know, something. You owe me something."

"How about a backrub?" Ishmael says.

Her spine tingles at the prospect of his hands on it.

"That'll work," she says shortly and kneels down.

The woman's skin is spotty and mottled, bulging out in random places that Tasha guesses it didn't before death. The flesh of her chest is gray, but not in the dignified way of her hair: it's the color of bone covered in ash, the trap of the crematorium emptied onto skin. Tasha wishes she had a glove. She could deal with putting her hand down that shirt if only she didn't have to feel the skin.

It feels like the skin of an apple left to rot on the table: stiff, still soft in a way that's not quite right. The bra underneath is beige lace. Just beneath the left cup, between the beige and the dead-apple skin, Tasha's trembling fingers find leather.

"I think I found it," she says. Ishmael and Z look on, grave and vaguely repulsed, as if watching a particularly gory surgery through glass.

Tasha grips the corner of the wallet with two fingers, drawing it out slowly. The last thing she wants is to drop it and have it loose in the woman's shirt. The longer the fishing expedition, the more likely she'll vomit.

She extracts it: a simple leather square with little folds for various things. It's an antique, Tasha can tell. Real leather. Most people carried only a digital device that would unlock their car or house, but as hackers got more sophisticated, it was found to be safer to revert to old wallets for the highest possible security – you can't a hack a piece of leather. Everything has its cycle, Tasha thinks.

Tasha pulls out the first item that catches her eye in the wallet, glittering gold: the woman's MINK card. Tasha holds it, looking, remembering Gina's, remembering the one she'd held on Michigan Avenue, what feels like years ago. "The Few," the card's familiar engraving reads. Reading it before, she had thought it referred to the people bearing the Chips, which had never seemed few to her: the mobs of them stalking the streets of Chicago, the horde in the Apiary, the packs of them guarding stores and restaurants. But now she wonders if the Few refers to someone else: the people Dr. Rio had cursed on the 107th floor of the Apiary. Cybranu, the invisible boardroom of creators, toasting each other above the mottled clouds of Chicago. Maybe MINK didn't protect the people with the Chip, but someone else less obvious. She thinks of Rio's Glass buried deep in her backpack and wonders what secrets it contains.

Tasha slides the heavy gold card back into its leather groove and pulls out the next item, a transparent card the same size and shape as the MINK card but lighter. It's an identigram: a card that, when tilted in one direction displays the cardholder's photo and identification information and when tilted in the other direction reveals bank information for payment and withdrawal. Sometimes there's a stereogram too, which one has to blur one's eyes to see. A simple sort of encryption, but unscannable by remote hackers. Tasha tilts the card toward her and the woman's face appears like a ghost out of the mist: she *had* been beautiful, her cheekbones prominent and her skin even, wrinkled around the eyes. Her eyes had been green. Now Tasha wonders if she still has eyes at all. "Monica Potter" the name reads.

"Any key?" Z says, hushed. She doesn't look around, not with her eyes, but her body is a suit of eyes: twitchy, wary. Being out here without cover has her nervous.

Behind the identigram is another card, light red. Printed in almost invisible font is the word Honda, and again Monica Potter. Tasha presses the faint circle in the corner. A flash of lights over in the row of charge cars answers.

Ishmael goes over to look, walking quickly but not running. He peers, then returns immediately.

"It's an SUV," he says, not smiling but giving off a feeling like a smile. "It's good. Let's go."

He turns back toward Whole Foods, where Malakai and the poodle still stand, both looking wide-eyed and hopeful. Behind them, Tasha can see Amy and her two children have moved closer, presumably to watch. *So much for not letting her kids see the bodies*, Tasha thinks.

Ishmael motions to Malakai, who immediately pushes open the door and pokes his head out.

"Bring the cart," Ishmael calls quietly. "It's time to go."

The boy rushes over to the cart, tripping on the poodle, who's underfoot, and swings it around hurriedly toward the door. Tasha sees Amy's body twitch, a full body spasm, as if Malakai taking the cart outside is pulling her spirit from her body, as if the cart leaving the store will kill her. Tasha watches her closely until Malakai and the dog are safely outside, the door closed firmly behind them.

"Okay," she says, her hand on the front of the cart, guiding it toward Monica Potter's SUV, the chariot that will take them out of Beyoncé Estates and on to California.

Loading the groceries is easy. With Malakai holding the dog, who kept climbing in and out, and Tasha, Z, and Ishmael loading, the back of the SUV is full in minutes. Tasha looks at it: the towers of cans inside the plastic Whole Foods baskets, the bagged goods stacked neatly, the sack of dog food leaning. The sight of it all puts a lump in her throat. Excess. Packed in a car. They could be going camping, they could be going home. She hasn't put groceries in a car since she was a child, shopping with her father.

"Ready?" says Ishmael. He's looking at it too, the food, perhaps having memories of his own. Z, on the other hand, stands with her back to the open hatch, surveying the estates. All quiet, Tasha thinks. Maybe the Change had happened later here, when everyone was at work.

"Ready," says Tasha. "Am I driving?"

"If it ain't broke, don't fix it," Ishmael says, shrugging.

Tasha looks down at the key card in her hand. *Sorry, Monica*, she thinks. *We'll take good care of it.*

"Roomy," Z says as they climb into the SUV.

It is. A seven-seater, with floor space for the dog to sprawl. Ishmael stretches out his legs from one of the middle seats. Tasha glances back, wondering if he ever wears shorts. She thinks men should wear shorts more often.

"All buckled up?" she says. The weight she's been feeling is gone. She looks over at Whole Foods, where Amy and her two children stand near the front door. Tasha waves cheerfully, suburban soccer mom greeting other passive-aggressive suburban soccer mom.

Ishmael gives her a double thumbs-up. He feels it too: this small return to normalcy, getting in a car with groceries, buckling seatbelts as if the only way to die is a car accident. Tasha starts to put the car in reverse.

"Wait, wait," Z says and for a moment the panic wells up into a bubble. But Z just says, "We have to unplug," pointing ahead at the charge rack the vehicle is still affixed to.

"Oh," says Tasha.

"I got it," says Z, and she's climbing out of the car, box cutter in hand, moving to the front of the vehicle to disengage the Honda from the glowing blue wall of power. Tasha watches. Z fiddles for a moment, half obscured by the hood of the car, and then there's a soft melodic ding, two notes Tasha hears from the dashboard, and a green power cell appears in the glassy display. "Power is at 100%," a soothing male voice says from somewhere, and Tasha feels as if it's measuring her energy as well: topped up, green, ready to roll.

But suddenly Amy is at the hood of the car, grappling with Z, snatching at her arm, and Tasha sees a stripe of red appear on Z's bicep, a long ragged scratch from Amy's fingernails. Even through the car windows, Tasha can hear Amy's screeching. Tasha yanks open the car door.

"Amy, what the fuck are you doing? Get your ass back inside and leave us the fuck alone!"

But Amy's not listening; she's screaming: incoherent sentences punctuated with words like "won't let you," "call the police," and "thugs." Z is grabbing Amy's hands, trying to break her grip, the box cutter fallen to the flawless pavement of Beyoncé Estates. Tasha has seen Z break a Minker's arm for less. She's being gentle. Tasha's sick of it.

She leans back in the car and snatches her knife from the middle console, Ishmael looking alarmed. She ignores him, slamming the car door and blitzing toward Amy and Z. Wielding the knife, she points it at Amy's face.

"Amy," she says as quietly as she can. "Go back inside before I cut your fucking throat. Dead serious. Leave us alone."

Amy stumbles backwards.

"You're thieves!" she screams. "I won't let you just steal!"

Z just shakes her head, rubbing her neck where Amy had grabbed her. Tasha shakes the knife.

"Do you see this? I will cut you. Go…away. Shouldn't you be watching your kids?"

"Thugs!" Amy screeches.

"Shut *up!*" Tasha hisses. "Are you an idiot? Do you *want* all your ex-neighbors swarming around?"

"Too late," says Z.

"What?" Tasha freezes, listening.

At first nothing. Z is a statue at the front of the car, half-bent to pick up her box cutter. At first nothing but the gentle electric hum of Monica Potter's Honda, the liquid chirping of a bird in one of the few trees dotting the estates. And then a bark, so soft Tasha thinks it might be the poodle, but the dog's face is in the windshield, looking intently at them, tail waving and mouth closed. When Tasha hears the bark again, she hears the human in it: the raspiness of the syllable, the irritation. She realizes in that moment that if it weren't for the Chip in the throat, regulating, militarizing the sound, the barks might sound like screams.

"Z, get in the car," she says, pointing the knife, a long straight finger, a sharp bone, demanding.

Z does, tripping on the curb. They can hear more now: the sounds rising, growing. They're coming. From where, Tasha doesn't know: a neighborhood watch convening by a dumpster, chatting in growls about how trespassers will be dealt with. They're coming to protect their neighborhood: Chipped versions of Amy.

Tasha turns on her heel. She's reaching for the car door when she feels her head jerked backward, the feeling of claws knotted in her hair sending an icy chill up her spine. The memory of a Minker's teeth sinking into her bicep so far away in the Web comes pulsing back through her brain like small icy earthquakes. She tries to turn, fend off the toothed attack that must surely be coming, to keep those square white teeth from taking her life. But the face she sees is not the strangeness of a Minker with eyes glazed and breath foul. It's Amy: eyes wide, angry, and human, nostrils flared wide like pink trumpets, teeth gritted. Tasha grips the Wusthof tightly, but her arm won't do it: it won't whip around to hack at the fingers wrapped in her hair, the arms they're attached to, two peach sticks with subtle pudge. This isn't a Minker. As much as she wants to hurt this woman, she isn't a Minker. What would happen to her kids if Tasha killed her? The panic throbs along with her scalp, and she can hear the chorus of barks, louder and nearer. She has to kill her.

And then there's Ishmael, out of the car and squeezing Amy in a bear hug from behind, pinning her arms like the wings of a stringy raw turkey. He heaves her away from Tasha, hauling her feet off the pavement with his strength, and Tasha feels Amy's fingers release her hair, tugging a little as poorly-cared-for cuticles catch on Tasha's curls. She's free.

She whips around to watch Ishmael moving to the doors of Whole Foods, where he drops Amy like a bag of refuse, not ensuring that she finds her feet before he lets her go. She topples to the ground, its surface perfect and black and recently paved, right on her ass, limbs sprawled like a strange frog.

"Don't touch my hair, you crazy bitch!" Tasha spits, but she doesn't even want to see Amy's reaction. No time. The barks are closer and louder and when Tasha climbs back into the driver's seat, Ishmael slamming the door as he reenters, she sees a pack of them rambling around the corner, like a pack of joggers, heads swiveling.

She puts the car in reverse just as the Minkers stumble into the parking lot. The windows are up, but Tasha hears Amy scream, not yet moving, but screaming.

"Go, Tasha. Go go go," says Z, her voice rising. *Go's* in groups of three are always the most urgent. Tasha whips the wheel around, backing out of the line of charge cars as fast as the dares. She hears the whine of metal as her rear scrapes the side of the car next to them, the green Corvette. It's not enough to impede their progress, but Tasha feels herself wince, apologizing to Monica Potter for scratching the car so soon after promising to take care of it.

She throws the car into drive, the Minkers now behind her, their faces flashing in her rearview mirror. They've set their sights on Amy, who's scrambling up, her legs appearing to be malfunctioning. She's reaching for the door backwards, not wanting to turn away. The bodies she'd moved out of the store onto the pavement lie still and lumpy like battlefield sandbags, but they won't keep out the Minkers.

"The gate—" Z starts to say, fingers outstretched as if casting a spell.

"No time," Tasha says, and she presses hard on the gas of Monica Potter's SUV, squinting her eyes as if the windshield might explode.

But it doesn't. The gate blows apart with the impact, the metal pieces bent and flying like gnarled black driftwood. Tasha expects the sound to attract the Minkers—perhaps it does; she doesn't look—and some small part of her hopes it draws them away from Amy. On the road—Z frantically pointing right: west—Tasha cranes her neck, looking back into Beyoncé Estates, searching for Amy's pale figure. The glass doors of Whole Foods are open, or at least one. Amy nowhere, Minkers everywhere. Then nothing but road, trees, and the statue of Beyoncé growing smaller, singing Tasha away.

CHAPTER 5

"Should we sleep in the car?"

The dashboard of Monica Potter's SUV says 7pm, but Tasha isn't sure if it's correct. Either way, the daylight is starting to fade, the sun simmering almost directly ahead, the arch of its yellow skull sinking. They haven't seen a hotel in hours. Nothing but skin clubs, bars, and restaurants, devoid of their garish neon lights, leaving long stretches dim and empty like the husks of locusts. No Minkers here: only the high-end skin clubs would have offered MINK and nothing here is high-end. It's a knockoff Vegas where gambling still wasn't legal and the women were limp and deflated. Middle America in all its glory: dry before and now brittle in neglect. No hotels, except one or two by-the-hour establishments that Tasha wouldn't sleep in even if they contained the last beds on the planet. Tasha had driven past them without comment, and no one else said anything either. Even Malakai had kept his mouth shut, as if they could all sense the mist of scum radiating from the buildings.

"Negative," says Z. "I'm not sleeping in the car unless we absolutely have to. The dog stinks."

"She does not," says Malakai, reaching out to pat the poodle's head, who pants happily.

Z darts a glance back at them.

"Yes, she does. Sorry."

"We might have to," says Ishmael. He hasn't said much since they left the Whole Foods. He's done a lot of looking out the window. Tasha hadn't thanked him for yanking Amy off of her; maybe he wants her to. It would feel awkward to do it now, hours later. Besides, it's Amy who should thank him: it was *her* life he'd really saved, not Tasha's. If she even lived. Tasha didn't kill her, but the glass door swinging open, the Minkers swarming...

"How come some stores stay lit up and some don't?" says Malakai. His eyes take in each depressing storefront they zip past, the suggestive outlines of women's bodies dark and almost invisible, their breasts like ghosts. Tasha thinks a ghost boob must be a fairly unthreatening specter, but you never know.

"I think it's about who they paid off," says Z. She isn't listening fully; she's looking at the map and squinting, willing something to appear, as if the map will suddenly start glowing and guide them to shelter.

"It's not even that secret," says Ishmael. He's petting the dog, who leans her head against his knee, sighing. "The big corps are on the city power grids, at least in Chicago. Out here there may not be a city near enough to be on their grid in the first place, so they may be federal. The federal grid is a whole different thing. I just know that there's all kind of lobbying and political trade-offs that let different places be connected to city and federal power."

"How do you know all that?" Tasha asks.

He shrugs.

"My mom. Lawyer stuff."

"Oh. Yeah, that makes sense."

"It doesn't really," he says. "Why should those big corps be allowed to keep power when even residences can't?"

"Oh, no, I meant it makes sense that you know. With your mom being a lawyer and stuff."

"Oh. Yeah."

He's angry. Tasha can feel the force of it spreading out from his silence like ripples.

"Are you okay?" She feels she shouldn't be asking this here in the car, with Z and Malakai such obvious audiences. But they may not be stopping for awhile. And when are they ever alone anyway? Alone. Together. The idea of it clouds her mind for a moment. What if they were alone together? She doesn't think they'd go on a date: where would they go? She imagines them going to a movie complex, all the silent rows of seats, the viewing helmets tilted back, empty. They could sit in that film graveyard and stare up into the empty black dome; they could wear the helmets and bask in nothing. That could be their date. Or perhaps to a restaurant: the service would be bad, the hostess murderous. The bar would be closed, the floor would be sticky. No, not a date. Even a walk in the park would be tricky. Carrying weapons instead of flowers, listening for barks instead of crickets. So much dies with the world as it was known.

"I'm fine," Ishmael is saying, and she tunes in to listen, tuning out all the thoughts of bad romance. "It's just bull, you know. People like Amy, thinking we're the bad guys when it's dudes like the ones that worked at Cybranu who are the real bad guys, the people who let this happen. Why doesn't she see that?"

"People like Rio," Z says in a voice that communicates disgust.

"Rio?" says Tasha, glancing across the car at her.

"Yeah," says Z. "He worked at Cybranu, didn't he? He admitted that he helped them design the Chip. He could've stopped it."

"He was just one guy," says Tasha. She's reluctant to call Rio a monster. It feels strange, like she's walking on the sticky floor of her imaginary dinner date with Ishmael, wondering what it was that clung to her Nikes.

"Yeah, well, so was what's his name. Gandhi."

"Who?"

"Gandhi. The peaceful guy. Wasn't he a boxer or something? Whatever, look, Rio almost let my head get chewed off by a bunch of Minker cops. He's a psycho. *Was* a psycho."

"Is Dr. Rio dead?" Malakai says, and Tasha darts her eyes at Ishmael in the rearview mirror, but he's already looking at his brother.

"Yes," says Ishmael carefully, as if his words are a scalpel, pressing against sensitive tissue, testing for numbness. "He was in the building when it blew up."

"Yeah," says Malakai, sighing. "I just wasn't sure. I thought maybe he got out somehow. Took a secret elevator or helicopter or something."

Tasha smiles at this, steering the car around an unidentifiable lump in the road ahead. If anyone were to find a secret elevator it would be Rio. She imagines him waiting until Tasha and the others had fled Cybranu before leaping to a closet and snatching a parachute from its shelves. But Tasha thinks back to Rio's resignation, his hopeless fury in the face of a faceless enemy, and knows he wouldn't have wanted to escape. He didn't want to survive.

"He wasn't crazy," Malakai says softly, looking out the window at the storefronts growing shadowy with dusk. "He was just really mad."

They find something that might be a hotel, six miles past the stretch of skin clubs, an eyesore called The Pentagon. It's a yellowing white building with a crumbled front awning, which may or may not have been decrepit before the Change. There are no cars or Pumapods in the patchy concrete surrounding it, and Tasha can tell with one glance that it wouldn't have supplied MINK to its employees. If it had any employees at all: its size tells Tasha that it couldn't have more than ten rooms.

"Is this even a hotel?" asks Malakai. He gets out of the backseat slowly, as if he isn't quite sure he'll go inside or not.

"I'm not sure actually," says Tasha. She had assumed it was a hotel because what else would it be? Its dead sign would have had plenty of cheesy pizazz before it lost power, and at least it isn't called The Smiling Yoni or some other lurid, unimaginative name like the by-the-hour places on the stretch behind them. Up close, though, it doesn't quite have a hotel feeling. It's just a building with a sign calling it The Pentagon, with no other indication of what it might be.

"It's getting dark," Z says, the familiar edge in her voice. Tasha wonders if that edge will always be there, a permanent deformity of her speech. She supposes it's like any other disaster survivor: she'd learned in school about survivors of things like September 11th never riding airplanes again; rape survivors never having sex again. Catastrophe changes you, sometimes forever. Maybe open territory will always be a wound for Z. Tasha wonders where her own wound is; if, like an unnoticed bruise, it will continue existing, small and purple, until the time comes when she presses it accidentally, catches it on a chair, when all the pain and horror will gather to her like seismic ripples before spreading out in a shattering boom.

"We'll have to take what we can get," says Tasha.

"Is there going to be another tornado?" says Malakai.

"I don't know," says Ishmael, who's opening the hatch of Monica Potter's SUV and pulling out their backpacks. The poodle pees by the entrance of The Pentagon.

"We'll be okay," says Tasha, taking her backpack from Ishmael. "We just have to be careful. We'll scout it out."

They stand there a moment, uneasy. It feels very much like the continuance of a very unpleasant pattern: walking into buildings of any kind has not gone well for them. But they don't have much of a choice, Tasha thinks. Driving straight through to California isn't an option with a car that needs to be charged. The horizon is dark: no city lights illuminate the sky in any direction, as far as she can tell. Driving out into the darkness with the possibility of the car dying in the middle of the night is stupid—even stupider than walking into The Pentagon.

"Well," says Tasha, gripping the Wusthof a little more firmly to reassure herself. She feels her mother's ring press against its handle. "Let's get this shit over with."

"Language," Ishmael says softly as they step cautiously through the front door.

The Pentagon is darker inside than Tasha had expected: no windows, it turns out. There had been what looked like windows on the outside of the structure, but inside nothing but smooth walls, the paint done in a marbled pattern to look like granite. But it's not granite: the space isn't cold enough, not echoey enough. From what Tasha can tell, the building doesn't have an open lobby like a hotel. It seems to be a modestly sized entranceway with two or three doors branching off to separate hallways. It feels like a small-town doctor's office, Tasha thinks. Maybe. Or a museum: the entrance to an art exhibit. Her skin crawls a little; the idea of a museum feels old, dusty, full of moths. She hopes there are no moths, their wings thick and feathery, brushing one's skin like the fingertips of ghosts. Especially in this place, which seriously calls for ghosts.

"What is this place?" Z murmurs. The building calls for murmuring the same way it calls for ghosts.

"I don't know. There's no signs or plaques or anything."

"Plaques?"

"Yeah. It seems like it would have plaques."

"Yeah, it does," Ishmael agrees, and Tasha feels a small, stupid thrill. He goes on to say, "Hold the dog this time, Malakai. We don't know what this place is. I don't want her to get lost."

In the gloom, Tasha looks down at the poodle, her tongue glistening, her teeth seeming to glow. The dog looks at no one, her tail still, mouth slightly open. Tasha gets the feeling she listens better this way: letting any dangerous smell float into her mouth as well as her nostrils.

"Good girl," Tasha whispers, and the poodle gives one short wag, acknowledging that she hears. Tasha knows this language, even if her fluency is rusty from her kennel days. The dog is not comfortable. Neither is Tasha.

"Let's go in the middle door," says Z, moving slowly forward, waiting to be contradicted.

"I don't know if this is such a good idea," says Tasha, and Z stops quickly. "We can barely see."

"What happened to that flashlight from the other hotel?"

"Left it there," says Ishmael. "That was stupid. I even thought about grabbing it, but since we were walking…"

"Another thing to carry," Tasha nods.

"It seems dumb to just walk into a dark room," says Z, and Tasha agrees. She's studied enough films to know this is true. Cinema or not, nothing good comes out of walking into dark rooms blind.

"What about the Glass?" says Malakai, pointing at Tasha's backpack. "Don't you still have it?"

Tasha looks at Z and shrugs, feeling stupid.

"That'll work."

With the Glass illuminated and held out in front of them like a beacon, they cluster into the middle hallway, which is much shorter than Tasha would have thought. They've only taken three or four steps when the glow of the Glass reveals what seems to be a thick black curtain, affixed close to the ceiling and falling all the way to the floor.

Tasha reaches her hand to touch it and finds that it's velvet, or something like velvet. She feels the shiver return to her spine: this really might be a museum. Old, dead things. Dry hallways. Glass tanks with the bodies of people and animals long deceased, their natural decay inhibited by chemicals so that they could go on being stared at. Tasha remembers walking the streets of Chicago in the time before the Change, the way eyes had moved over her body like insects, usually belonging to men but occasionally women; women like Cara, women like Amy: women who stared as if Tasha's body, her features, her hair—especially her hair—were things that didn't really belong to her in their eyes. Museums are like this: bodies owned by something or someone with no right to own them, the eyes glassy with death, and somehow resignation.

"Are we sure about this?" Tasha whispers, turning to look back at the rest of them, clustered close behind her. She's surprised to find Ishmael the closest: as she turns, some of the light from the Glass strays onto his face, and his lips are fully illuminated, the hair growing around them coarse and rugged. She can see his nose too, wide and strong. Above, his eyes fall into shadow, but she knows they're looking at her. The lips part to speak but it's Z's whisper she hears instead.

"Shh. I hear voices," she says. "Do you hear voices?"

Ishmael's lips close again, stunned into silence, and Tasha immediately turns back toward the curtain, her ears straining. She does hear something: not quite voices, but the rhythm of something human. Breath, maybe. Perhaps the smudge of whispers. Then she sees it: the palest light coming from the left edge of the curtain: so faint and yellow it might have been nothing, but she doesn't know how she didn't see it before. Perhaps the curtain had shifted, perhaps a hand had shifted it, a hand she hadn't seen in the dark. The whole place suddenly feels like a trap. Immediately she locks the Glass and hands it to Ishmael.

"Put it back in my backpack."

He takes it and complies without question. She grips her knife tightly and feels her heart accelerating. Adrenaline rising.

"Are you guys ready?"

"Ready for what?" comes Z's voice from somewhere in the darkness.

Tasha assumes that's a no.

"To, you know, go in. Handle it."

"I guess," Z says slowly. "But let's take it easy. We need to stay here tonight. Our options are this or the car."

"I'm fine with the car," Tasha mumbles, even if she's not really.

"Malakai," says Ishmael. "Stay behind everyone. Hold the dog."

"Okay."

"Okay," repeats Ishmael.

"Okay," says Tasha. She thinks maybe they can just continue saying "okay" if it means not going through the curtain. She can smell its musty mothiness. Scientists on the other side. Doctors. Museum curators running a creepy museum of murdered travelers. In the dark anything becomes possible, especially when a musty curtain is involved.

"I'm going to move the curtain," whispers Tasha.

"Okay."

"And then we'll go in," says Tasha.

"Okay, Tasha."

Tasha moves the curtain. Slowly. She can barely see her hand reaching out through the gloom, the contrast of her fingers against the backdrop of the black velvet. But her fingertips find the surface. She takes it between thumb and forefinger, gently pulls it to the side, waiting for a squeak, a creak, anything that might give them away and send the museum curators into a frenzy of pulled levers that will send Tasha and her friends into a containment pit where they will await experimentation and mummification. Had she always had these fears? Or did Cybranu give birth to them?

The curtain slides easily on a rod and the dark dissolves under the warm glow of a room full of candles. The arrangement is circular, but messy and with gaps, jars and things with low flickering flames in a mostly bare room scattered at the edges with a few couches, futons, armchairs. There are displays on the stone walls—still no windows—former digiboards for transcribing the lectures written upon them, but without power they are matte black surfaces, absent of words. The candles are dully reflected in the eyes of the screens, but most interesting are the people at the center of the lopsided candle circle.

At least ten of them, all facing the same direction, their heads bowed low, their arms stretched on the floor reaching past their ears. Their breath fills the room, a measured ocean wave of sigh. At the front of the group bows a figure set slightly apart; from his direction Tasha hears a murmured word or two, and the figures start to rise. Tasha grips her knife in a vise, her muscles twitching in an internal debate of fight or flight. There are nine, she counts now, including the front figure: nine religious zealots worshipping a fearsome god in a creepy old museum oddly called The Pentagon. They can't take nine of them: too many. If the wack-jobs decide to rush them, they're through.

"And back into downward dog," the voice at the front of the group murmurs, and Tasha does an aural double take.

"Did he say…?"

"Downward dog," Z murmurs, bemused.

Dumbfounded, they watch the group complete their sequence. They finish standing, their hands at their hearts.

"Namaste," the figure at the front says, who Tasha sees now is a man, and the group echoes it back in soft voices. Silence for a moment and then the man turns to face his group.

"Well done, everybody. Really nice. I think—"

He stops, his mouth slightly open, his eyes on Tasha, she thinks, from the distance. Tasha and her group, their weapons, their ridiculously puffy dog, standing there in the doorway watching them do yoga.

"Uh, hey," he says, letting his voice echo across the flickering room. One by one the heads of his group start looking back at them. One gasps.

Tasha waves with her knife, then realizes how it might look, stops, and waves with her empty hand.

"Hey," she says.

CHAPTER 6

They're dreamers, Tasha realizes quickly: activists who are both suspicious and optimistic, the kind of people who start sentences with "If the government didn't…." They remind Tasha of Leona, her conversations that made Tasha roll her eyes when she was a teenager. Leona in the kitchen with their father, helping to make dinner, the two of them prattling about presidents and protests. Tasha's mother had joined in sometimes, but never Tasha. It seemed pointless: to sit and talk about all these wrong things and have no means to change them. Still, Leona had wandered west with rage in her heart, her letters filled with *if only*s.

Roger is like that, Tasha learns. He's older than Tasha—close to thirty, a white guy with hair that might have been brown but is lightened in most places by the sun, and thickened at the root by its unwashedness, held back in a loose ponytail. Tasha watches him as he tells the group's story, and his own. His skin has the seasoned look white people get when they spend a lot of time in the sun. At his age it's not quite leather yet—just heavily freckled, lines around the eyes. But the leather will come, and Roger seems like the kind of guy who would wear its roughness proudly and without apology.

"I'm not from Nebraska originally," he starts, "and my name's not Roger. Well, it is, but it's my last name. First name's Nathaniel but no one's called me that since I was nine. I'm from Rhode Island, but I moved to Detroit. That's where I met LaBrenda," he gestures to a woman on his left, almost as tall as Ishmael and with long arms and legs like a deer or other long-limbed grazer. Tasha doesn't realize until she looks again that the woman's left arm is bionic, a smooth appendage identical in shape and size to her right arm, but made of smooth black metal. "But I didn't come out here 'til four or five years ago. Big weed market out here. First they legalize it, then they ban it. Back and forth. My granddad was one of the first farmers to manage a ten-acre farm of weed after one of the first national legalizations," he says proudly. "Glad he didn't live to see them take it all back."

The rest of Roger's group is a mix of men and women, black, brown, and white. One woman catches Tasha's eye, short and muscular, her hair cropped close to her skull. Her dark skin is like an atlas, white in some places, pigmentless patches around her eyes and mouth, pale shapes like clouds at her elbows. Vitiligo, Tasha knows it's called, although she hadn't known how beautiful it was. The woman catches her looking and smiles a close-lipped smile. Tasha looks quickly back at Roger, embarrassed.

"It's just nine of us," Roger is saying, and Tasha notices he arranges his mouth carefully when he speaks. A recovered lisp, perhaps, always paying attention to the movement of his tongue, listening with it, avoiding his teeth. "We lost Esperanza and Nolte in the first week. We're more careful now."

"Careful?" says Z. "We walked right in."

Roger blinks at her.

"Well, you guys are cool," he says, wide-eyed as if stating the painfully obvious. "I mean *them*. The Cybranu freaks. Chippers don't do doors."

Tasha smiles a little. She's heard so many names for them now, always prefaced by *them*. Minkers. Chippers. Biters. The Few. She still prefers Minkers. It's the most accurate, she thinks. Besides, Chippers sounds too cheerful. Like a bagged cheddar snack.

"You're not worried about the people who aren't Chipped who survived? Crazy people?"

Tasha knows Z is thinking of Amy. She is too, of course, though she imagines there must be worse than the likes of her wandering this new world. It's the first time she's thought of it and it makes her shiver, the idea of it dropped into the pit of her stomach like a seed in the earth. She steps on it quickly to keep it from growing. She doesn't need a tree sprouting there: the kind of fruit it bears is exactly the kind she can't help but gnaw.

"We haven't seen anybody else before you guys," Roger says, shrugging. His shoulders are thin and so is his t-shirt. "The Chippers aren't too good with doors, and they're the ones we've been worried about, so we haven't really bothered blocking doors and all that. Plus it's really inconvenient when we wanna go out."

"You go out?" Ishmael says, looking amused. His eyebrows rise on his forehead and drift a little farther apart.

"Sure."

Tasha supposes he's right. Here she is, after all: not cowering in her bunker on Foster Avenue waiting to die. Granted, it had taken prodding from Dinah to get her to go to the Post. If it hadn't been for Dinah, Tasha might never have found the letter from her sister in time, urging her to the South Side to find Dr. Rio. She might have been too late if she'd gone later— Rio already packed into a car headed west. Or perhaps he still would've found his way into the Apiary one way or another. Perhaps he was destined to explode.

"You folks hungry?" says one of Roger's group, an older man about Rio's age with dark, serious eyes.

"We have some supplies," Ishmael says. "But we can share if you're willing to share."

Tasha looks at him out of the corner of her eye. She thinks of their bounty from Whole Foods with some selfishness. They'd gone through a lot to get that stuff, and here he was ready to give it away to this raggedy group of activists. Her inner mongrel snarls a little.

The older man, though, smiles and says, "What do you have? I imagine you've been eating what you can find. Canned stuff."

Ishmael nods. Malakai says, "Yeah. It's getting really old."

They all laugh, including Tasha. She's a little surprised. The kid hasn't been one to pipe up on his own since they left Chicago. But he's not behind Ishmael, as he usually is. He's standing forward, looking unafraid. Something about Roger's group, their relaxed attitudes, lounging on futons, makes him feel a little braver.

"We've got something much better," the long-limbed LaBrenda smiles. "Come on, we'll show you."

LaBrenda leads them back to the front of the room, back to the dark passage they'd entered through. Some of the group join them, some remain lounging on the sofas and on the floor. Roger joins LaBrenda, and Tasha notices him trailing alongside Z, overhears him ask if she does yoga, if she liked bikram Before.

LaBrenda bends before they reach the dark entranceway, retrieving something from the floor before straightening up again. She holds it in front of her as she sweeps the black curtain aside, and it makes a clicking sound in her palm. The short hallway is illuminated, a cone of soft yellow light emanating from her hand.

"Sun disc," she says, holding it up for Tasha to see. It's a palm-sized white object the shape of a clamshell, and it glows strongly. "Solar powered. We charge them during the day and keep them down here with us at night."

Tasha nods. She wonders if they have any extra discs they'd be willing to part with. Or maybe trade for, she thinks, feeling like a pioneer. She doesn't say anything out loud. Something about LaBrenda's long-limbed grace, her hair luxuriously kinky, her skin deeply brown, makes Tasha shy. She feels short and clumsy beside her, has to speed up her step to keep up with the woman's long stride. Next to her, Tasha feels like a teenager, rough and unlearned.

As they reach the lobby, through the glass of the door she can see Monica Potter's SUV. She hopes it's okay out there on its own, feels a sudden pang for it, as if it might be lonely or scared in the new territory far from home.

"It will be fine. You're the first people we've seen that didn't have Chips," LaBrenda says in a voice that's full like a ripe melon and thick with something that could be humor. Tasha stops herself from looking at her sharply: had she read her thoughts? She decides she'll be careful with what she thinks around this woman. Her eyes see more than what's in front of her.

LaBrenda leads them to another of the three hallways, plunging into the dark of the left doorway.

"What's down the right hall?" Tasha asks.

"Just the bathroom," LaBrenda says, her voice floating back over her shoulder as if the light from the sun disc is speaking. "The toilet still flushes, but who knows for how long."

"Do you guys own this place?" Tasha says, stepping carefully once they enter the hallway. The sun disc is bright, but not that bright.

"We do now," LaBrenda says, looking back with a grin. Tasha smiles back. Where were women like LaBrenda before the Change? Tasha had been boxed in at the Apiary and taking lunch breaks with the likes of Gina. She hadn't known there were Dinahs and Vettes, Azaleas and LaBrendas. If she had known, she might have crawled out of the hive a lot sooner.

"We rented it before all this," LaBrenda adds. They've reached a narrow staircase and she seems to rise before Tasha's eyes before the stairs are illuminated by the sun disc. "Even with people running around eating each other we thought the owner might come to collect anyway. But he didn't. So we figure it's ours now."

Once Tasha starts climbing the stairs the poodle darts ahead, her nails click-clicking on the stone. She reaches the top before LaBrenda and stands waiting. When LaBrenda gets close enough with the light, Tasha can see the dog fully, standing at the top and looking over her shoulder at them. There's no lock: LaBrenda reaches out and twists a doorknob that squeaks and then they're outside again, on what must be the roof.

Tasha smells it before she sees it: life, green and brown. She smells dirt and plants, the spicy smell of ripe something. Her nose can't identify the smells, and she's not even sure she's smelled them before. Her senses spin in a deep Rolodex of memory, the scents prickling from between manila folders in a file cabinet heavy with dust. The folders crack open, only barely, enough to release a puff of pollen. Tasha inhales deeply, feeling it in her chest, and asks even while almost knowing the answer: "What's that smell?"

LaBrenda is a few feet away, fiddling with something Tasha can't make out. The daylight is almost entirely gone. The sun is only a thin orange arch peeping over the faraway edge of the earth. West, Tasha thinks: the sun will always tell. Here on the roof, Tasha feels much higher than she actually is: it had only been one or two flights, but with the cooling evening breeze wavering across the roof from someplace, she could be on the helm of a grand ship, floating across the desert that must be ahead on waves of sand.

"Here we go," says LaBrenda, her voice muffled. Tasha looks, and LaBrenda's face is illuminated brightly by the sun disc, which she clenches in her teeth. Her hands are obscured by dark, but Tasha hears a deep, solid *clunk* as whatever LaBrenda is working at shifts.

Light. From all around, light, and Tasha gasps, surprised, by the suddenness of it, surprised by her own surprise; surprised that she is shocked by bright light at night, as if light switches are a thing her ancestors knew and never her. It's so easy to forget, once one is used to night being unchangeably dark.

"It's solar-powered," LaBrenda says from behind Tasha. Tasha doesn't respond, but her mouth is open.

She's looking at the garden: six green, leafy rows, some with stakes rising from their midst, tomato vines crawling up their spines; small peppers dangling from stems like budding green bells. She can smell it all: the dirty purity of plant and vegetable and soil, illuminated every six feet by seven-foot pyramids of light.

"Why are the lights triangles?" Z asks, arriving on the roof.

Tasha barely listens to LaBrenda explaining the virtues of a triangular prism in capturing solar rays that bounce off the edges of rooftops. She's moving forward with a hand outstretched, her fingers like a magnet as they connect with the leaves of a plant. It's not quite smooth: bristles like a cat's tongue catch on her fingers. She finds herself smiling.

Ishmael appears beside her.

"I've never seen anything like this," he whispers. He hasn't said much since they came into the Pentagon: he's kept his hand on Malakai's shoulder and kept his mouth in a firm line. Now Malakai is turned loose, wandering down a row with the poodle close behind.

Tasha looks at his face, watches his brown eyes sweep over the sight of the garden. He's as in love with it as she is. She *is* in love with it, and isn't sure why. She looks away, back at the garden.

"It's so beautiful," she says softly.

"Did your parents have a garden?" he asks. He's curious about her awe, wants to find the root of it.

She laughs.

"No way. My parents couldn't keep a piece of grass alive if it was in a pot. All the energy went to the dogs."

"The dogs?"

"They owned a kennel."

"Oh, right. I think I heard you mention it to Z before."

"Yeah. It was beautiful too, but not like this. Nothing like this."

Roger and Z are in the next row across from them and Roger grins over the top of some beanstalks, his hair let down from its previous ponytail.

"What do you think?" he says, spreading his arms.

"It's amazing," Tasha says, and means it, makes sure he knows she means it.

"LaBrenda is the mastermind," he says, gesturing. LaBrenda smiles, a wide close-lipped smile that could have been ugly but isn't. Tasha feels a vague stir of jealousy, deep in a part of her stomach that hasn't moved in awhile. "She had a whole neighborhood of rooftop gardens in Detroit before I recruited her."

"Why'd you leave?" Tasha asks. "Or, you know, why'd you come?"

LaBrenda slides a look in Roger's direction, so quick and small that Tasha thinks she might have imagined it. But the way LaBrenda shrugs and says, "Oh, just ready for a change," tells Tasha she did not. She makes a mental note of it; she'd like to ask Z what she makes of it. Perhaps LaBrenda and Roger are in love. But LaBrenda seems to have zero qualms about Roger's obvious interest in Z, so it was either a fling or something else entirely. Tasha dog-ears the note.

"Have you ever done any gardening?" Roger says, directing the question at Z.

Z darts her eyes at Ishmael and Tasha before answering.

"I mean, yeah, a little. My dad used to have a little garden on his deck. I had a tomato plant in it. I named it Roxanne," she giggles.

Tasha raises her eyebrow. Did Z just giggle?

Malakai is suddenly at Tasha's side, tapping her.

"This place is really cool," he says softly.

"Yeah, it is."

"Are we going to stay here tonight?"

"Do you want to?"

He shrugs. "Yeah. Kinda."

Tasha looks at Ishmael, who also shrugs. Men.

"We might as well," she says, then adds, "If that's okay with you guys. LaBrenda?"

LaBrenda shrugs too. People.

"Fine with me," she says. "Roger? Guys?"

The handful of people who had come up to the roof with them murmur and nod. Roger is still talking to Z.

"Roger? Cool with you if they stay the night?"

"What's that?" he says. "Oh. Yes, sure, of course. As long as you want!"

He grins and Tasha half rolls her eyes and half smiles. Z giggles again. Bad-ass Z; foul-mouth Z. Giggling.

"We should probably go back in," LaBrenda says, motioning with her metal arm toward the door. "We try not to leave the lights on for too long at night. We haven't seen too many Chippers out here, but we don't want to flash a welcome sign."

"Of course," Tasha says, even though she's not really ready to say goodbye to the garden, even if goodbye is only goodnight. But she turns, however reluctantly, to follow Roger and the others.

"Malakai, is the dog with you?"

"Yes."

"Okay."

LaBrenda goes back over to the controls, which in the light, Tasha sees, are simple: a panel of ordinary sliding switches.

"Up for on and down for off?" Tasha asks as LaBrenda slides her finger over each one, the pyramids of light fading out one by one and returning the garden to darkness. Even when the last pyramid has gone out, the dark doesn't seem as it had before. Now she knows what it contains, and it still seems to glow.

"Yep," says LaBrenda, who slides a metal door down over the switches, concealing them. "The panels charge automatically when the switches are in the off position."

"Nice," says Tasha, but feels stupid saying it. As if she could contribute anything else to the conversation beyond this small, simple word. She has no idea how solar panels work, how different shapes are more efficient at collecting energy. She thinks her parents' kennel had solar panels but isn't sure. Her focus when she was living at home had always only been the dogs. As if on cue, the poodle rushes by their legs and pads down the stairs ahead of the group.

"She's beautiful," LaBrenda says. She's slightly behind Tasha on the stairs, the solar disc in her hand again, guiding their progress. Tasha hopes she's not looking at her hair, which needs a comb and has likely trapped any amount of debris throughout the day, lint or leaves clinging to its coils. "Is she yours?"

"No…well, yeah, I guess. She's ours. Like your building."

"Tasha rescued her," says Malakai from somewhere behind them both. "From the Apiary in Chicago."

"The Apiary?" says LaBrenda.

"It was a big shopping mall back home," Malakai says. Tasha doesn't think she's heard him sound so normal since they were in his mother's kitchen playing cards. A lot has happened since then. People change quickly. Especially kids, and especially in this world. "Tasha rescued her from a pet store before the mall blew up."

"The mall blew up?" LaBrenda says, sounding intrigued. "How?"

"A bomb," Malakai says simply, and Tasha is glad he doesn't elaborate. Everything that had happened in Chicago is more than a two-second topic of small talk. There's so much more to be said than "bomb." They've reached the bottom of the staircase anyway and Tasha steps aside to let LaBrenda lead the way back into the room where they'd found them doing yoga.

"So the garden," Tasha says as they enter the room again, rejoining the group that had stayed behind. They haven't moved. "That's where you get all your food?"

"Mostly, yes." LaBrenda returns the solar disc to the low shelf at the foot of the stairs. "We're still trying to figure out how to make bread without wheat. But we've been doing okay without bread, so maybe we shouldn't even bother, right?"

She laughs, a pleasant sound, almost like an instrument of some kind. Tasha wonders what her own laugh would sound like if part of an orchestra. A kazoo, perhaps, when she laughs unexpectedly and not in the presence of people she wants to impress. In front of LaBrenda, she'd be a clarinet, most likely. In front of Ishmael, a cello.

LaBrenda's looking at her expectantly, and Tasha realizes she's missed something.

"Sorry," she says. "Say it again?"

"No worries. I daydream too. I asked if you guys are staying here tonight for sure. It's dark now, so I'd recommend it."

Tasha looks around for her group. Ishmael has settled on a couch with his brother and is getting food out of his pack. Typical Ishmael: eating the food they have before breaking into the Whole Foods bounty. The poodle stands before them, hovering, ears alert to ensure her message of "feed me" is clear. Z is sitting on the floor between Roger and a light brown girl with hair that used to be bright pink and is now growing in black. The pink has faded. Z must be asking about the hair, because the girl is laughing and holding up a handful of it, pointing at the ends. Roger just watches, smiling, his eyes never leaving Z.

"Looks like my friends have decided on yes," Tasha says.

"I don't know if Roger would let her go anyway. He likes your girl."

"He does, doesn't he? You don't mind, do you?"

LaBrenda cocks her neck.

"Mind? Me? Please. Roger's a friend, and not even a close one."

"Oh," says Tasha, relieved. The last thing they need is a lovers' quarrel. "Upstairs I just thought it seemed like you guys were… you know, close."

LaBrenda has led her to an empty futon and sinks down onto it. Tasha follows suit. Her legs are tired. They've been driving for hours but her thighs feel as if they've walked the couple hundred miles.

LaBrenda reclines, digging her fingers into her hair and massaging her scalp.

"What a day," she says, eyes closed. "Sometimes I think the boredom will kill me."

Tasha is surprised. The yoga and the gardening, the aura of relaxation that the Pentagon effuses: she wouldn't have thought of boredom as a thing that would exist. LaBrenda and her crew seem too…pure for boredom. Tasha raises her eyebrow.

LaBrenda opens one eye, notices Tasha's brow.

"Seriously," she says, disentangling her fingers from her fro. "Before all this, we were busy keeping the drunks out of the building and watching the strip with binoculars on the roof. We'd take baskets of vegetables down to the hotels to sell to people passing through. We *did* shit. There was shit to do. Seeing you guys come through the door was the most exciting thing that's happened in weeks."

"Glad to entertain you," Tasha says, smiling. "But we've had our fair share of excitement."

"Yeah?"

"Yeah. Trust me."

"We're about to make dinner," calls Roger, raising his voice for the whole room. It echoes a bit in the cavernous space. Tasha wonders if the room had always been this empty. "Whoever feels like eating, let's drag some seating into a circle."

LaBrenda stands and jerks her head at Tasha.

"Come on. Let's drag this thing over."

"Oh. Okay." Tasha rises and grips the metal edge of the futon. "Do you guys do this every day?"

"Not every day," LaBrenda says. She grips her side of the futon, her bionic hand making a soft *clink* sound as it wraps around the edge. "But usually. We like to eat together."

The ragtag collection of futons and chairs forms a lopsided circle. Two or three of Roger's people don't join, instead stretching out on their sofas as if to sleep. One has a book: an actual paper one, which he holds high up over his face, like a mirror, looking into it with an expression of supreme concentration. Tasha wonders if he's actually reading or if he wants to give the impression of occupation, an excuse not to join the group. She decides that if she were him, she would be doing the same thing.

The rest of Roger and LaBrenda's group, however, is interested in Tasha and her friends. There are no children Malakai's age, but one young woman, maybe seventeen, sits with him and the dog, chatting and showing her teeth in a wide, generous smile. She pets the poodle enthusiastically, ruffling the soft ears constantly, which the dog seems to enjoy. Ishmael takes a seat on a chair instead of a futon, which Tasha surprises herself by appreciating. The pink-haired woman pulls a seat up nearby and Tasha watches their small talk from across the circle, so intently that she doesn't notice when Roger fires up what looks like a large gray washing machine. It only gets her attention when the smell of cooking food draws her senses away from Ishmael and the pink-haired woman and onto Roger.

"What's that?" she says to LaBrenda, tilting her head at the machine.

"A solar stove."

"You lug that thing upstairs every day?"

"No, no," LaBrenda laughs. "There's a cell that we charge up top and slide into the stove to give it power. The cell works on other machines too, like sharing a lightbulb between different lamps. But we only have the one stove."

"Wow. I didn't even know this stuff was out."

"Ah well, they don't make it easy to find. Or affordable. But we happened to have this one made for us personally."

Roger stands over the solar stove with a small smile on his face, his eyes on the surface of the grill. He wears a stained blue apron, an apocalyptic Betty Crocker.

"What are you making?" Tasha asks, but he doesn't hear her, lost in thought, until LaBrenda raises her voice.

"Roger! Tasha asked what you're making."

"Smells like asparagus," Z says, and Roger turns to beam at her.

"That's right," he says, turning back to Tasha. "Grilled asparagus and probably some charred tomatoes. Potatoes too. We grow those down here, along the back edge of the building."

"We can add some… SpaghettiOs to the table," Tasha says, only slightly embarrassed.

Roger laughs but it's LaBrenda who responds.

"Save it for now," she says. "Tonight you're our guests."

A few people around the circle murmur their agreement and Tasha can't help but wonder if she and her friends have wandered into the den of some fiendish cult. Gardeners who seem harmless enough on the surface, but whose soil is enriched with the crushed bones of trespassers, their grilled asparagus served with a side of travelers' entrails.

"So why is your building called The Pentagon?" Tasha asks, inching imperceptibly away from LaBrenda. Strangers being friendly and calling you their guests—sharing their food so willingly—is a sure sign of some evildoing, she thinks.

LaBrenda laughs.

"We lie about what we do here," she says. "Just like the real Pentagon."

Tasha hears the little alarm bells sounding in the long hallways of her brain.

"So you're not really gardeners?"

LaBrenda laughs again, shaking her head. Her hair swishes around her head a little.

"No, no, that's the true part. We lie about not being gardeners. Well, lied. We don't have to lie anymore."

"Before," Roger continues, using long metal tongs to turn the asparagus, bluish light from the solar stove creating a distortion in the area above its surface, "our front was interior design."

"Interior design?" Tasha says, laughing. "For what? People's houses?"

"Yep."

"Who would believe you did interior design?" she snorts, looking around the large room. With the exception of the futons and solar stove, there are only a few shelves that line the walls, plus some desks with lamps that now have no power source.

"Well, it looked better before," Roger shrugs. "The futons can be folded into these squareish benches and the solar stove folds into what looks like a big silver statue. Everything in here folds up into something else. Besides, minimalism was all the rage! Or at least, that's what we told our clients." He chuckles.

"Not that we had many," the pink-haired woman says, directing her answer at Ishmael. "We just needed a semi-believable front for when officials came knocking."

"Why cover up being gardeners?" Tasha says. "I mean, who cares?"

"It's illegal," says Z from where she sits behind Roger. She says it matter-of-factly, as if Tasha is the only one in the world who doesn't know this.

"Illegal?"

LaBrenda nods.

"Very illegal, actually. Private citizens in most states are only allowed one plant per household; depending on the state, your dirt patch has to be under a certain amount of square footage."

"Big fines," says a chubby man on the other side of Ishmael. He sits on a futon but his size takes up most of the space so he sits alone. His skin, Tasha notices, is almost perfect. Dark, almost purple, with not a single scar or flaw that she can spot. "They don't mess around. A friend of mine in Colorado got hit with a fine so big for illegal agriculture that he had to sell his house. All for a 6x6 backyard garden."

"Since when has that been illegal?" Tasha snorts. She's shocked. It seems so absurd. In Chicago, its jungle of concrete and iron, she hadn't known anyone with space or interest for planting anything. She'd seen artificial plants for sale everywhere, and that's what everyone usually bought.

"For a long time," says Z. She looks thoughtful. "My dad's garden I told you about…he planted that before the laws were passed. He didn't try to hide it, though. He just got rid of it."

"For six years, specifically," says LaBrenda. She sinks back into the futon and Tasha feels it creak under her own back. "They started cracking down right before California seceded."

Tasha thinks back to her sister's letters—she almost remembers this now. She shakes her head, still in disbelief.

"It's outrageous, I know," says Roger, using the tongs to take cooked asparagus from the solar stove onto a platter that Z is holding out.

"But why?" Tasha says. The poodle has left Malakai and pants in her face, hot dog breath fogging onto her skin. She leans back into the couch and pets the dog's muzzle with half her mind.

"To get all the money they can," Z says. "They're greedy."

"Yes," LaBrenda agrees. "But it's more than that. It's about control. They want to control the money being made but they also want to control citizens' independence."

"And put more people in jail, of course," says Ishmael, and the chubby man nods enthusiastically.

"Yup," he says, leaning forward in his seat. "That's right. We got more prisons than we do hospitals. More prisons than schools. They're always looking for more stuff to criminalize so they can lock more people up."

Tasha feels her mind sharpen with annoyance. She dislikes this "they" being thrown around. It puts her in mind of super-villains, faces smudged in shadow, headless suits at a long secret table, fingertips touching in a solemn oath of evil.

"That's what they did to my brother," Z says, looking at no one. Tasha thinks of the folded photo in Z's backpack, but it doesn't quite soften the irritation growing inside her.

"Who's *they*?" she says.

LaBrenda shrugs.

"You know who *they* is."

"Oh, I do?"

"Yes," says LaBrenda, turning to look her in the eyes. Nearby the solar stove hums in its gentle way, but everything in this moment seems to have teeth, everything seems to glow with the same heat as the blue light of the stove. "You do."

Tasha is silent. She breaks away from LaBrenda's endlessly brown eyes and looks across at Z, who once had to be dragged from her cocoon and now stands, bold butterfly, with Roger, looking at Tasha seriously. Even Ishmael has leveled his gaze at her, waiting. The "they" is present for them too. Only Malakai looks uncertain, looking the way Tasha must have looked when Leona and her father would stand at the sink talking about wars and conspiracies.

"Did you really think this was all just an accident?" LaBrenda says softly.

"Yes," Tasha says, forming the word hard in her mouth like a stone, but the stone is soft and changes shape in the air. She's never been sure.

"Let's eat," says Roger, holding the tongs up like a weapon, or maybe a white flag, and Tasha imagines her weak *yes* flattening into a puddle and dripping to the floor.

They eat. They tell stories. LaBrenda talks about Detroit, painting a picture that Tasha had never heard or seen. For as long as she can remember, the webnews had paraded slideshow after slideshow of warzone-type decay: bullet holes in school windows, unpatched; scorched patches of earth where homes had been burned in the night. Generations of neglect and violence, the web had said, meant a city unsalvageable. But LaBrenda tells a different story: one of rooftop gardens in the heart of slums, tended by supposed gang leaders whose warfare was waged on behalf of demanding running water. She speaks of poverty and desperation, but businesses being run on front porches, barter systems, and trading posts. Tasha watches her face in the dim light of the candles and solar torches, her eyes shiny, glazed over with remembering.

"My grandmother was twenty-three when the water crisis started," she says. "She's seen it all. But I'm glad she doesn't have to see this."

"Was there a lot of Minkers in Detroit?" Malakai says, chewing. He'd examined the asparagus carefully before eating it, squinting, but now he puts each spear into his mouth without care. Tasha eats quickly. The taste of asparagus releases something pleasant in her. It's harder to chew than the canned and bagged food she's been eating for weeks. Her jaws relish the work.

"I don't know," LaBrenda says. "I had already been gone for a couple years when this happened. Before, I wrote letters to people back home, but there's no telling now, with everything shut down. I can't imagine too many people inside Detroit itself got the Chip. No jobs, no money. Probably not many Cybranu implants, if any. Who knows, maybe Detroit is just fine, just going as usual. Might be better off, with no cops around to harass people."

Tasha listens, still chewing, her previous irritation melted down a little with the taste of food. She remembers her mother, how she'd always get a little red around the edges when she was hungry. The poodle comes up and snuffles at Tasha's knee. She offers her a piece of asparagus, which the dog sniffs and then snorts at. She whines.

"The dog is hungry," Tasha says and stands, setting her plate behind her on the futon cushion. "I'm going to go to the car and get her food."

"I don't know if that's a good idea," says Roger. He has a piece of asparagus between his fingers, halfway to his mouth, and pauses its trajectory.

"I'll go with you," Malakai says, half rising.

"No," says Ishmael, blunt and quick. "Eat your food, Kai. I'll go with Tasha."

Tasha bends to pick up her knife from where she placed it on the smooth floor. Holding asparagus instead of a weapon has been nice. She sighs.

Ishmael stands from his chair, wipes his hands on the front of his jeans. The pink-haired woman looks up after him with something like disappointment on her face. Tasha moves toward the door without looking at Ishmael, clicking her fingers at the poodle, who follows eagerly.

"Yell if you need me," Z calls after them. She has slouched into the couch a little, her eyes dull. She's tired. They all are.

Tasha brushes the curtain aside and doesn't wait to hold it for Ishmael. She realizes once she's in the hallway that she's blind: night has reclaimed the earth. If the hallway had been dark before, it's black now. She turns back to get a solar disc from LaBrenda's shelf, but the curtain is already being swept aside by Ishmael, his hand glowing.

"Need a light?" he says. She turns her face away and stumbles on the dog, who'd been on her heels. "Come on," she says.

"I am."

"Not you, the dog."

He doesn't answer. They move down the dark hall, finding themselves in the lobby after a few steps.

"Did you bring the key?"

"Yes."

"Now that you know what it looks like."

She thinks he might be flirting but she's annoyed, the prickliness returned to her mood like sharp insects flying and then landing before taking off again. They rest on her skin and make her bristle. One of the gnats looks like the pink-haired woman.

"Yes." She keeps her voice flat, reaches the front of the Pentagon, and turns the handle. She pushes out into the night air and is surprised by the chill. She pauses, letting it sink in, and Ishmael stops beside her. The solar disc creates a blue orb around them and she thinks they could be anywhere, on another planet even. The air so empty and cool, they could be spacewalking on the surface of Jupiter, or somewhere even more unimaginable, a parallel Earth, where maybe Cybranu hasn't ruined everything yet.

"Do you think the whole world is like this now?" she says.

"Like what? Quiet and dark?"

"Shut up."

"I don't think it matters what the rest of the world is like. This is our world. Until something shows me the rest of the world still exists, I'm going to pretend it doesn't."

"No Minkers tonight," she says.

"Nah. Probably are in that strip we passed, though. All those bars and hotels."

He descends the four steps to the ground and walks out into the night, the light around him like a halo. It falls on the car and Tasha is relieved to see it's still there, not picked up by a tornado, not torn apart by some other unknown force of evil. So many ways for things to go wrong, Tasha thinks, but that was true before the Change. She follows Ishmael to the car. She can't see the poodle but she can hear its quick steps, its gentle panting. It's not until this moment that she realizes how much the dog comforts her. A body with eyes and ears that can hear and see what she cannot, a nose that can smell danger or discord. She remembers sleeping just 400 meters from hundreds of dogs like the poodle, ready to rouse the alarm when needed—and sometimes when not. Out here on this dark plain on this dark planet, the poodle is something like a secret weapon.

"Key?" says Ishmael.

Tasha fishes it out from her back pocket where it's been stowed since they arrived. She'd considered putting it in her backpack but had liked the comfort of its edge against her butt: a reminder of their ability to flee. She wonders if the gardeners have a hookup they can use to charge the SUV. Can solar power be converted to power an electric car? She has no idea how that shit works.

The car tweets softly when she presses her thumb to the keycard, its lights blinking briefly in a kind of mechanical hello.

Ishmael opens the hatch. The light inside is powerful, brighter than she would have expected for a car. Together they dig out the dog bowl Malakai had chosen and the big bag of kibble. Tasha uses the Wusthof to open the top. The thick plasticky paper slices easily, though not as easily as flesh, she thinks without meaning to, and is disgusted with herself. Is this who she is now? Is this a symptom of disaster? A nation of people who compare the cutting of anything to the cutting of flesh? Will she never be able to slice cheese or open a box without accidentally imagining their severability compared to human skin? She dips the bowl into the bag to get kibble for the poodle.

"That's not very much," Ishmael remarks when she brings it out.

"Dogs really don't need to eat that much. People overfeed them all the time."

"Well, we overfeed ourselves," he says, shrugging. "Makes sense we'd try to make our dogs fat too."

She laughs without really wanting to.

"You say that like you're fat," she says, side-eyeing him.

"I was before the Change! I lost 50lbs in that soccer field!"

"What?" She looks at him, and he looks back, his eyes wide and serious.

"The apocalypse diet," he smirks. "I'm gonna make millions."

She shakes her head, laughing, and nods at the hatch.

"You wanna close that? I've got her food."

He reaches up to close it, his shirt sleeve sliding up to reveal his bicep. He catches her looking.

"What you looking at?"

She feels her face get warm.

"The results of the apocalypse diet," she sneers, and turns back toward The Pentagon, the poodle prancing next to her, sniffing eagerly.

"Lock it?" he calls after her, following.

She locks it. They're almost back to the steps when she stops and turns to him.

"Do you really think this is the apocalypse?"

He looks around, spreads his arms open wide.

"Seems like it, doesn't it? Catastrophe. This is a catastrophe and no one is coming to fix it."

"Yeah." She's had this conversation. With Dinah, with Z, with herself. But somehow out here in the dark, a rooftop garden above and grilled asparagus only steps away, she needs to be reminded. "But...I don't know."

"We blew up a mall, Tasha. A huge freaking mall in downtown Chicago. And the only thing that happened is that it burned."

"*We* didn't blow it up," she says, objecting.

"The bomb was on my back. I carried it up there."

"You know what I mean."

"Yeah, but does it really matter?"

"I just wish I knew why," she says, turning her back on the Pentagon and looking out at the dark. Stars. That's all. Nothing neon or glowing. Just stars. "Why did Rio want to blow up the Apiary? He wanted revenge on Cybranu but there wasn't even anybody there. What's the point?"

"I think there's probably a lot we don't know about him," Ishmael says, rubbing his forehead. "We'll never know. Maybe he was just crazy."

Tasha thinks about the word "just." Just crazy. Just crazy, like only? Or just crazy. Just-crazy. Justified.

They hear a creak and Tasha's knife springs up like a soldier caught napping at her post. She whips her head toward the source of the sound, but all she sees is Z's face, stuck between the small crack of the door.

"Oh, hi," Z says. "Just making sure you guys were okay and not being eaten alive while I flirted with Roger."

"At least you admit it!" Tasha says, and throws a piece of dog kibble at her.

Z blocks its trajectory with the door and then reappears again, grinning.

"Come on," she says. "Everybody is going to bed."

"Do they actually have beds?" Tasha says, climbing the stairs.

"Not exactly."

Inside, the large open room that had previously housed couches and the solar stove has been transformed into a dormitory. The futons are gone, replaced with at least a dozen bunk-style beds, their frames metal and their cots orange.

"Whoa," Ishmael says, following Tasha into the room. "When did all this happen?"

Malakai appears in front of them, smiling.

"While you were gone. Watch, they showed me how to do it. It's really cool."

He approaches one of the smooth bunk beds and grasps it by its frame, his smallish brown hands clutching it with fingers close together. Tasha sees the tendon at his wrist flex, his fingers squeezing some unseen apparatus, and she hears a sound like a click and a clang. Something about the frame changes, a subtle narrowing, a slight shift in dimension, then Malakai is slowly folding the outer frame in on itself, the top cot lowering, sinking down to obscure the bottom. Malakai settles the top cot into the frame and then slides his hands along to the sides, flat, gently pressuring two protruding panels flat. He steps back, breathing only a little harder, and looks at Ishmael with his eyes bright. The bed is now a couch, perhaps the very one Tasha had reclined on with LaBrenda.

"That's really cool," Tasha says to him, smiling. He's happy and relaxed and it makes her happy and relaxed. She ruffles his boy-dog ears with her words, wanting him to stay this way, wanting him to forget all that has passed.

"I think Andromeda wants to eat," he says, pointing. Tasha looks. The poodle is snuffling at her hip, tongue out and extended toward the bowl Tasha still carries.

"Oops, sorry, pooch," she says, and lowers the bowl to the ground. The poodle sticks her face into the food immediately.

"Andromeda?" says Ishmael, eyebrows amused. "I thought her name was Phaedra."

"Yeah!" says Tasha, but in truth she'd forgotten, instead calling the dog "dog" in her head.

"Yeah," says Malakai, turning to raise the couch back into a bed frame. "But it didn't really match her. Not really."

LaBrenda approaches their group. She's changed clothes, now wearing loose gray sweatpants and a fitted orange tank top. She isn't wearing a bra and Tasha glances down at her breasts, small but high. She wonders if LaBrenda needs a bra at all: perhaps she hadn't been wearing one this entire time and Tasha hadn't realized until now. She wonders momentarily if Ishmael has noticed and then realizes it's probably pretty apparent that she's having an inner dialogue about LaBrenda's breasts. It's always obvious when a man does it; surely it's no less obvious when the person staring is a woman. Tasha slaps her inner hand, but feels herself puff her chest out a little.

If LaBrenda notices Tasha's internal breast conflict she doesn't let on. Instead she gestures at the bunk bed Malakai popped up and the one beside it.

"These are for you guys," she says. "Malakai already converted them for you, as you can see."

"Several times," says Z, tickling.

Malakai shrugs, smiling.

"We have a few doubles if you two…" LaBrenda points her index and middle finger and Tasha and Ishmael, wiggling them, letting her voice trail off.

It takes Tasha a moment to grasp her meaning; when she does, she stutters.

"Us? Oh, no. No, we don't…we don't need…no thanks."

"The bunk beds are fine," says Ishmael, looking directly at LaBrenda, and a brief stab pierces Tasha's chest as she wonders if maybe he is communicating that a double isn't necessary for him and Tasha, but it could be for him and LaBrenda. Tasha turns away and places her knife on the top bunk of one of the frames.

"I'll take top, Z," she says. "You move around too much. You'd probably break your neck in the middle of the night."

"You'd catch me, wouldn't you, Malakai?"

"Yeah, right."

Later, when all the solar torches are switched off, the candles blown out, and Tasha lies on her back staring up at what must be the ceiling, existing somewhere up there behind and inside the darkness, she thinks of her sister. Her sister and her garden, somewhere out toward the sun that has already set. She probably started gardening just to piss off the mysterious *they*—she probably talked all about it with their father while Tasha sat at the table playing with one of the dogs, doodling, daydreaming. She'd always been the quiet one; she'd had her own private inner life. Leona was the sister whose mouth was always open where Tasha's was always closed. When their parents died, Leona had those conversations to build on. She went and lived the life their parents expected. Tasha was left floating, thinking her secret thoughts, quieter than ever, drawn into the Apiary where her silence was expected. She wonders how different she would be now if she'd joined Leona in the kitchen with her parents. Perhaps she'd have a garden now too, far away from Chicago bloodshed, the Chip's effect never touching her, far from the loss of the Dinahs and the Vettes. She sighs deeply, from her gut.

"Tasha." She hears her voice whispered from somewhere below. It's soft, not Ishmael's low rumble. It's Z, her whisper rising like a spark.

"Yeah?"

"I can hear you thinking. Shut up."

"I'm trying."

"Try harder."

"Okay."

A pause.

"Do you think my sister's okay?" Tasha whispers.

Z responds immediately.

"Absolutely."

"Okay."

And then sleep, sleep creeping into her nostrils, clouding her brain: sleep that smells like the garden on the roof, filling her dreams with clover and peppers and vines that mean no harm.

CHAPTER 7

A mechanical hum jolts Tasha from her sleep, a groaning of metal and machine that wakes her clawing and wild, searching for the Wusthof. Where is it? Where is she? For a moment she's back in the Apiary, in the lobby staring across the masses of Minkers at the cold insect eye of the crystal bee. The mechanical groan is the building coming down on top of her, the ashes of Dr. Rio fluttering down over her like gray, burning snowflakes. But when she's fully awake, her eyes wide open and looking madly about her, she remembers where she is—though it doesn't explain why the ceiling is cracking apart.

The groaning comes from above, and with each second that passes the light grows brighter, the sun pouring in and drenching the cavern of the Pentagon in fierce white sunshine.

"How—how…?"

The crack down the middle of the ceiling widens and widens, the surface of it parting like a massive eye opening its heavy metal lids. The two halves disappear into their respective sides, leaving a wide hole of sunshine, rows of a garden floating across it.

Z appears by her head.

"Oh good, you're awake."

Tasha looks for her, finds her standing, dressed in a fresh shirt, to the right of Tasha's bunk. Their faces are level and Z smiles.

"What the hell kind of way is that to wake people up?" Tasha says, flopping back down onto her cot. Her heart is still racing and she squints at Z while it slows down.

"The rest of us have been up for an hour," Z shrugs. "I'm surprised you didn't wake up before."

"I was tired," says Tasha, rubbing her eyes.

"Clearly. Are you hungry? Roger is cooking."

"Of course he is," Tasha says, her voice a little mean but she's not quite sure why. She wonders if Ishmael is already awake too. She looks up again at the ceiling, its seeming invisibility. Beyond the greenery is the sky, clear blue with clouds thin and unthreatening. After her years spent in Chicago with its oppressive mammatus clouds, this kind of sky is like stumbling out of the haunted forest of the Wicked Witch and into a meadow ruled by some benevolent sorceress.

Above, the poodle trots across open air, Tasha seeing only her belly and paws. She trails behind another figure's feet, who Tasha guesses is Malakai, smaller than the other people whose shoes have replaced their faces. It's like being trapped below ice and watching those on its surface going about their business as she drowns.

"Is everybody up there?"

"Not everybody. You're the only one still in bed, though."

"So? It's not like I'm going to be late for work."

"True."

"So what are they doing up there anyway?" Tasha says, sitting up again and clumsily swinging her legs over the edge of the bunk, letting them dangle. "Is that what gardeners do? Get up early and tend their crops?"

"You're an ass," Z says briskly, leaning down to the lower bunk to fold her blanket. The blankets they'd been provided with are thin, and Tasha was skeptical at first, but the night chill never crept in and she'd slept soundly.

"I'm not an ass," says Tasha, yawning.

"Oh, you are." Z straightens, using her chest as a surface to smooth the blanket. "Don't act like that asparagus wasn't good as hell last night."

"I'm not acting!"

"Maybe not, but don't bite the hand that feeds you. Or, like, don't piss in the garden that feeds you. Whatever."

Tasha shrugs.

"I'm not biting. Just wondering what they're doing."

Z looks up at the glass ceiling, where five or six pairs of feet— and one set of paws—mill around.

"LaBrenda is showing Malakai how to water the plants. They've got an irrigation system that pumps water up the sides of the building. Doesn't even need electricity."

"Let me guess, solar powered."

"Wind powered, actually."

"Ahh."

"Why are you being a dick?" Z laughs, swatting Tasha with the folded blanket.

Tasha hops down from the top bunk and stretches. She thinks about whether she's being a dick and what that means exactly. She can't really decide. A dick is a conundrum: both soft and hard, both impressive and not. Being a dick is to be in transition, perhaps: to be undecided. Maybe a dick is exactly what she is.

Tasha reaches into her backpack, groping for the self-foaming toothbrush she'd brought from Chicago. There is a moment of sudden, silly panic as her fingers can't locate it, but she finds it at the very bottom, wedged up underneath Dr. Rio's Glass. She pulls both out, laying the Glass on her cot where it's safe while she digs out her comb as well. It's a stupid flimsy thing she'd acquired at the Best Western: she hasn't tried using it yet. She scowls at it, knowing it won't work. Her curls will laugh and consume its fine teeth.

"You brought a Glass with you?" LaBrenda says, appearing beside them. "Some mail you need to check?" she smiles.

"It's not mine," Tasha says, embarrassed as if it were.

"Oh."

"An old friend's," Z says. "No longer with us."

"I see. Sorry."

"It's okay," Tasha says quickly. The words "old friend" make her uncomfortable. "Dr. Rio wasn't really a friend."

"Dr. Rio?"

"The guy who died," Z says.

"Right," LaBrenda says and turns back to Tasha. "So you kept his Glass? That's kind of a strange choice of keepsake."

Tasha shrugs.

"Not really a keepsake. I can't open it anyway."

"No?"

"Password."

"Ah. Yeah. I kept a password on mine too Before. No telling what people would have found if they went through it after I died." She laughs her throaty laugh and Tasha laughs too. "Now, want to come up top? We're going to eat outside before it gets too hot."

"Okay." Tasha slips the Glass back into her backpack. "I need to brush my teeth and I'll be up."

"So proper," LaBrenda says.

"You don't know the half of it," says Z, low, as if she's sharing a secret.

"Shut up." Tasha shoves her, laying her backpack on the floor so she can figure out how to fold the bunk back down into a futon. LaBrenda steps forward to help and Tasha finds herself staring at LaBrenda's metal arm again, its smooth luster almost as warm and shining as her dark skin. LaBrenda catches her looking this time as they fold the bunk into itself. She offers a small friendly shrug.

"You can ask," she says.

Tasha swallows. Artificial limbs had become common, she knows, but they didn't look like this anymore: mechanical, robotic. The commercials for Nulimbs were glamorous and sexy: women who looked like Cara seductively moving perfectly manicured fingers across their lips, caressing their blushing cheeks. You didn't know the caressing fingers were Nulimbs until the sultry model removed them to show the natural ease of on and off. Even disembodied the fingers were beautiful, sculpted perfectly with peachy tones of life-like skin. Tasha had heard rumors of people putting their second hand in blenders and ice chippers after losing their first: the Nulimbs were beautiful enough to want two.

But LaBrenda's arm isn't Nulimb: though smooth and shapely, it's not altogether human and certainly doesn't pretend to have skin. The metal is bright and hard, unapologetically black.

"How'd you lose it?"

"Shark attack," LaBrenda says, and waits for Tasha's eyes to widen before smiling and shaking her head. "Gardening accident. Fell from a rooftop garden in Detroit. Landed on top of a police car. Bones splintered: metal shards through it all. But I'm lucky it wasn't my head."

"They couldn't save it?" Tasha says. It's a stupid question: the arm is gone. Saving it sounds like they threw out a lifejacket that LaBrenda's arm just couldn't reach.

"My brother says they could have, but they prosecuted me for assault when I landed on the cop car, so I ended up in a prison hospital. They just chopped it off, ya know. They weren't going to waste taxpayers' money on a criminal's arm."

"You're kidding," says Z, who has been listening. "Right?"

"Nope," LaBrenda says, straightening up after tucking the futon's arms into place. Her metal fingers make their soft clinking sounds against it. "Claimed I tried to commit suicide and purposefully aimed myself at their car." She laughs, but it's not the musical laugh of before. It's harsh and thick. "Even our deaths are weapons to them."

"That's...so fucked up," Tasha says, nearly speechless.

"It is," LaBrenda nods. "I served two years before my aunt found footage that proved it was an accident. That was a stroke of luck. But two years with one arm in prison is a long time. Would've been fifteen without the video though."

Tasha's toothbrush hangs limply in her hand, forgotten.

"They didn't give you anything?" Z says. "No temporary prosthetic?"

"Nope." LaBrenda shakes her head, a smile starting to form. "But the day I got out, my mother picked me up with this one in her hands." She shrugs her left shoulder, the black arm flashing. "She made it." She looks down at her arm with a warm, sad smile, her eyes seeing more than metal.

"She made it?" Tasha repeats, her eyes wide again.

"Yes. She was an engineer at MIT for thirty years. Moved back to Detroit when we started gardening. She made all kinds of stuff. The sun disc I had last night? The little glowing thing? That's her design. So is the solar stove and its portable cell."

Tasha can hear her voice swelling, with pride and something else she recognizes easily. LaBrenda's mother is dead: Tasha doesn't need to ask to know it. The grief is laced in between every word, resting there like grout between tiles. It's resin holding the words together.

"Wow," Tasha says. "Your mom must have been really special."

LaBrenda looks straight at her, their eyes meeting and melding.

"Yes, she was."

The three of them walk toward the front door with its three hallways.

"You didn't want a Nulimb?" Z says as they push past the heavy curtain. "The skin on those looks so real."

LaBrenda shoots Tasha a look, a tight smile.

"Yeah, when somebody is your complexion or lighter," she says to Z.

Z looks puzzled but doesn't respond. LaBrenda continues.

"They don't have options for people with my complexion," she says, rubbing the fingers of her metal hand across the skin of her chest. "Nulimb's palette stops about a shade darker than you, Z."

"What?" says Tasha so Z doesn't have to.

LaBrenda stands to the side in the lobby when they clear the hallway. Tasha takes a step toward the hall that leads to the bathroom, still clutching her toothbrush, but pauses to look at LaBrenda.

"I'd look like a calico cat," LaBrenda says, shrugging. "I'm dark-skinned. Ever notice how they don't have anyone who looks like me on the commercials?"

"Yes," says Tasha.

Z says nothing.

"Well, they don't have skin for their products that matches me. That's all. Just shades of beige."

They stand looking at each other, Tasha holding her toothbrush and Z standing with her hands on her hips, her forehead wrinkled.

"Anyway, I'm going to go up top," LaBrenda says, pointing with the arm her mother made. That's both of them, Tasha realizes. "Meet you up there when you're done freshening up."

She flashes her easy smile and turns, disappearing up the steps hidden around the corner of the far hallway.

"Wow," Z says while Tasha is brushing her teeth. In the bathroom, which has a flushing toilet and running water as LaBrenda promised, Tasha looks at herself in the mirror in the grayish light. A little of the foam from the toothpaste has crept out onto her top lip. She swipes it away with her pinky finger.

"What?" she says, muffled.

"LaBrenda. Her arm. That's insane. Her mom made her arm. How awesome is that?"

"Yeah. But it's fucked up."

"Huh?"

Tasha spits in the sink.

"It's fucked up," she repeats, feeling the coolness of the toothpaste spreading through her mouth.

"What is?"

"Why she has a prosthetic to begin with."

"Oh. Yeah. Fucking cops. I hate cops."

"Says the wannabe cop," Tasha says with a smile. Z sticks out her tongue and Tasha bends to spit again, rinsing her mouth. She raps the toothbrush against the sink, knocking off the last of the water.

"Can I ask you something?" she says, turning to Z.

"Hmm? Yeah. What?"

"What happened to your brother?"

Z opens her mouth and closes it again, pursing her lips crookedly as if thinking.

"Why?" she says, barely a question. The word is a barb on a wire fence.

"You told me once that he's in jail," Tasha says, surprised by her friend's sudden defensiveness. "I just wondered what he did. Or…you know. Whatever. If that's why you hate cops. Or if that's why you became a security guard or…I don't know." She pauses, then adds, "You don't have to tell me."

Z looks at a spot above Tasha's head on the wall. Even with the sun up outside, the room is dark. The slitted windows make Tasha think even more of jails and prison.

"Let's go upstairs," Z says finally, avoiding Tasha's eyes. She gestures with her head and steps out of the bathroom into the hall.

Tasha says nothing, following her out into the hall and wedging the toothbrush into her back pocket.

"I can't keep sleeping in jeans," she says, determined not to let Z's awkwardness infect the rest of their day. "Next time we're on the road, we need to stop at a mall that's not too Minky and grab some sweatpants."

"And more underwear," Z says absently, moving toward the stairs. "Next time we're on the road. Are we not leaving today?"

Tasha shrugs. She hadn't really thought of it in concrete terms until now, but she feels the tug against nomadism pulling her.

"Malakai seems comfortable here. And it's safe. Plus...food. You know. It might be nice to chill for a day or so after the last few stops we've had."

"Good," Z says simply, continuing up the stairs. Tasha doesn't say anything else, just follows her. She'd expected Z to argue, eager to get on the road and to California. She wonders if she wants to linger because of Roger, or something else.

On the roof, the sun strikes Tasha's face in warm stripes, the smell of the garden rising up to greet her even before the gardeners do. Roger approaches, wearing thick green gloves, the fingers dark with soil.

"Good morning. LaBrenda said you'd probably be up soon. We're just doing some weeding before we eat. Want to pitch in?"

Tasha exchanges a look with Z, amused.

"Sure," she says. "But I've never weeded before. Someone should probably show me exactly what I'm supposed to be pulling up or I may uproot all your vegetables."

Roger throws back his head and laughs, and Tasha thinks it probably wasn't that funny. But Z laughs too, looking at Roger, and Tasha knows they're laughing for each other. *Look at how friendly I am, look at what a fun person I can be.* Tasha rolls her eyes.

Malakai has already learned how to weed, so when Tasha is assigned a little patch of earth by the tomatoes, he crouches with her and shows her which of the plants sprouting up through the dark soil need to be plucked and which are okay to stay. It's fairly obvious: the gardeners keep a clean garden and pretty much anything that looks out of place actually is.

Tasha focuses on the bed of soil so as not to look down through the transparent glass ceiling, through which she can see all the futons and chairs. She thinks she can spot her backpack too, leaned up against a bunk. She hasn't been this far from it, from her knife, in weeks. She looks around. Little metal trowels and tools are at hand everywhere: the one she holds currently resembles three metal fingers, curved into hooks for turning up the soil. It could be a weapon if it needed to be, and this comforts her.

Ishmael appears across from her, his hands hidden by red gloves. Tasha has only ever seen him in a white t-shirt, and the splash of color makes her stare. She feels silly. Since when did gardening gloves become a sexy accessory?

"Sleep well?" he says, looking at her over the tops of the tomato plants.

"Yes," she says. She plucks out a little green sprout and tosses it into the basket that Malakai has placed between them. He's quicker than she is, plucking and tossing easily. "Better than I thought I would in a room full of people."

"Same," he nods. "I think it's because it's safe."

"I like it here," Malakai says, his eyes on his work. "I wish Mom and Marcus were here."

Tasha doesn't respond but rubs his back with one hand. Her fingers leave a few crumbs of dirt on his shirt and she swipes them off. He smiles.

"I've been thinking about the caravan," Ishmael says.

Tasha waits, playing with the dirt but not really weeding. She hadn't been given any gloves—late riser—and the soil has begun to blacken the crescents under her fingernails. She doesn't mind, not really. She's more concerned about her hair, which she's mostly had to comb with her fingers. She wonders if LaBrenda has a big comb.

"What if we passed them?" Ishmael is saying. "I feel like we should have seen them by now, right? Or seen where their cars died? They'd be walking from there."

Tasha shrugs.

"They probably found new cars, like we did, after theirs died. We said we were going to walk because that was Rio's plan, but once you're out here it doesn't really make sense."

"Maybe they found a limo," Malakai says, still weeding. "And they're driving in that. All together."

Tasha holds out a hand and raises her eyebrow.

"See?"

"But their cars…"

"I've seen hundreds of dead cars. Maybe you would have recognized them when we passed, but when you guys are asleep I'm just driving."

"Or maybe they got on the SkyDrive," Z says. She crouches down on Ishmael's side of the soil bed. "It would have taken them off the route, but it would have gotten them a lot closer to California and then the drive would be short. They could be far, far ahead of us with that."

Tasha hadn't considered this. They'd seen the SkyDrive from a distance but she had just assumed it would be dead, powerless.

"Do you think it's still running?" she says.

Z shrugs, pulling at a weed or two. Malakai is the only one actually working; Tasha wonders if any of the gardeners notice.

"Probably," Z says. "It's a federal thing, right? Probably hooked up to the big grid."

"Hmm," Ishmael says. He looks not satisfied, but close. He takes a tomato leaf between his thumb and forefinger, rubbing it but not plucking it, his forehead thoughtful.

"Your mom is fine," Tasha says, her heart beating a little faster. Maybe that's not what he's thinking about and he'll scowl at her for saying it, but when he looks up from the tomato leaf she knows she was right.

"I hope so," he sighs.

"She is. She had several days' head start. She and Marcus are probably already there. They're just waiting on you."

Malakai has stopped weeding, but doesn't look up from the soil.

"Hear that?" Ishmael says to him, and his brother's eyes raise. "We just gotta get to her."

"Okay," the boy smiles, and Tasha feels warm in her chest.

"Let's eat," Roger calls.

They eat: more asparagus brought up from the solar stove downstairs, paired with tomatoes sliced from the vine and grilled with some potatoes and mushrooms. The smell of it had struck Tasha's nose with a force that filled her mouth with saliva, almost making her laugh. Who knew grilled vegetables would ever be so exciting?

"You came at a good time," says Roger, chewing. "All the good stuff is in season in June."

"It's June?" Malakai says, looking up from his plate, a pink ceramic thing that matches nothing.

"Yep."

"How do you know?" the boy asks, suspicious, his asparagus spear hovering near his mouth.

"We've kept a calendar," says LaBrenda. "We still need to, you know, keep track of important dates." Tasha hears something in her voice, but by the time she looks up, LaBrenda's face is already clear, if there was never anything there at all.

"What's today then?" Malakai says.

"June 3rd."

Malakai laughs sharply, his face lit up with boyish glee. He lowers his hand to his plate and looks at Ishmael, who is also grinning broadly.

"It's your birthday, Kai!" Ishmael says, laughing. He rests his green plate on his lap.

"Are you serious?" LaBrenda says, looking from one of them to the other.

"June 3rd! June 3rd is my birthday!" Malakai says, in cheerful disbelief. "I'm twelve!"

"You're twelve!" Ishmael echoes, and his face looks soft, a shade of blue under the gold.

"Let's sing Happy Birthday!" Tasha says quickly. The gold feels fleeting, an oasis like this garden. She hates singing, hates singing Happy Birthday especially, but she starts the song, hearing her voice slightly cracked, far from melodious. By herself, the words sound like crumpled paper rising on the wind, but by the time she gets to "to you," the others have joined in and the song floats easily over the tomato plants.

Malakai's face blooms, even as he lowers his eyes in embarrassment. He's too old for this, he'd say, maybe, in another lifetime. Everyone is smiling as they sing, and even the poodle joins in, barking from somewhere farther away: downstairs maybe. But then Tasha sees the dog by Ishmael, tail wagging but muzzle closed. It's not the dog. Tasha raises her voice even louder for the last few notes.

"And many moooore," she sings, almost yelling, obnoxiously, anything to keep the moment intact a breath longer, before everyone else hears it too and Malakai is jerked from the cloud he's floated up on.

LaBrenda hears it first. It's quiet, almost hidden by the breeze that's picked up and rustling the leaves of the plants. Her eyes dart over to Roger, who's laughing and hears nothing. Tasha catches her eye and holds it.

"I want to hear it in Spanish! Sofia!" LaBrenda says loudly, and the pink-haired girl looks up, smiling, slightly puzzled.

"You want me to sing it in Spanish?" she says.

"Yes!" LaBrenda insists. Tasha listens for the barking. She's can't hear it, but she can almost feel it: the throatiness hiding behind the wind. "Malakai, has anyone ever sung Happy Birthday to you in Spanish before?"

"No," he says, embarrassed but laughing. It wouldn't be as funny if Sofia weren't so pretty, and he likes the attention.

"Sing it!" LaBrenda says, still a little too loud. Ishmael is listening. Tasha can see the tenseness in his jaw, his eyes wandering to the edges of the roof as if the Minkers will come spidering over the brick.

As Sofia sings, LaBrenda motions to Tasha. They slip away from the group, sliding through the door and rushing down the stairway, lit halfway down by the sunshine from the roof. LaBrenda takes the steps two at a time and Tasha follows suit. Back in the cavernous common room, Tasha goes straight to her bunk and retrieves the Wusthof from where she'd left it resting on the futon. Her hand grips its contoured familiarity, comforted by its weight. LaBrenda appears at her side with a spade, its handle long and smooth, its blade shining. She grips it in her metal hand, smooth and vise-like, and nods at Tasha.

"Let's go."

At the front door to The Pentagon, LaBrenda pauses with her eye at the crack, peering out.

"Three," she says.

"Fine," says Tasha.

"Okay."

LaBrenda opens the door, blinking in the light. The Minkers cluster around the car, not barking anymore, just swaying, dead-eyed and agitated. She almost doesn't recognize them. The sanctuary of the garden creates amnesia; the memory of the Minkers floats back into her consciousness in a slow wave of annoyance. Fear too. She's afraid. Why do these things have to be real?

Tasha moves more quickly than LaBrenda, forcing herself over the obstacle of her fear; she approaches the small pack with her knife ready. They wheel on her, snarling, two of them lunging almost simultaneously.

She pierces one's stomach as the second one rushes her from the side, and she gasps, shouldering him hard, sending him solidly to the ground. The red light flashes from the neck of the one she stabbed as she holds him at arm's length, spitted on the knife. No matter how many times she does this, the panic still rises and floods her body. The flashing red light is a target, but it's also a warning—she wants to run from it, but makes herself stay.

In one motion, she yanks the knife out of the Minker's belly and arcs it up at the neck, hoping to get the Chip in one try. She does, slicing through the Chip with the usual feeble spark. She turns away as the body begins to topple, frantically kicking the other Minker rising from the ground in the chin. She scrambles down to him before he can rise again, slashing his Chip. More sparks. Tasha stands up, panting.

LaBrenda has to swing the spade a few times to get the Chip of the third. Her tool is strong but inaccurate. On the fourth swing the Minker—a blonde man in his forties with dirty Adidas untied on his feet—is nearly decapitated, the black tentacles doggedly attempting to patch the wound. The spade finally finds its mark and with a last spark the Minker lies dead, blood pooling around him, moving slowly toward the back left tire of Monica Potter's SUV.

LaBrenda, also panting, turns to Tasha and nods at her knife.
"I need one of those."

Tasha laughs, still catching her breath, and leans down to wipe the blade on a Minker's jeans.

"It's nice because it's precise."

"You just have to get closer to them. I hate getting close to them."

"Afraid they'll snatch you?"

"Yeah!"

"I got bit once."

"You're lying."

"Nope."

Tasha points to the now fading mark on her bicep.

"The day I met Z," she says. "She patched me up."

"Bad?"

"Not really."

"War wounds, huh?"

"Unfortunately."

They pause, looking down and around at what they've accomplished.

"Let's move them around to the side of the building."

"Yeah."

Tasha's reluctant to put the knife down, but she can't grip the Minker's ankle while clutching it, so she places it gingerly on the ground before bending to grasp the feet of the guy with the dirty Adidas. He was a real musclehead before the Change and weighs a ton, but between the two of them they lug his body around to the side of the Pentagon, stopping twice, before dumping him out of sight. They go back for the other two, and Tasha can't help but think of Brian, her doorman back at her apartment in Chicago; how she'd dragged him across the lobby after killing him, vomiting at the sight of his blood. How the times have changed, she thinks.

They lean against the car when they're finished—LaBrenda with the spade out in front of her like a cane and Tasha holding the Wusthof lightly.

"Thanks for what you did upstairs," Tasha says when they've been silent for awhile.

"It's okay."

"I just…I didn't want to ruin his birthday, you know?" She feels stupid, almost trembling.

"I know."

"I mean, it's his birthday, you know? It's his birthday."

"I know."

And suddenly Tasha is crying, as if a great metal gate has been raised, holding back the river that's in her heart, a crashing tidal wave of pain. She drops the knife, not caring if it lands on her foot, severs an artery. She covers her face in her empty hands, sobbing, the feeling like an earthquake expanding and collapsing her chest; like the tornado that picked up their car has picked it up again and sent it smashing through her lungs.

LaBrenda's arm slides around her shaking shoulders, the spade making a soft thudding sound on the ground as she lets it fall. And for a moment that's all there is: the tears and LaBrenda's arm, which doesn't move, just stays there, heavy and warm.

But eventually she stops crying and embarrassment sets in. She wipes the tears with the heel of her hand, carefully under her eyes.

LaBrenda laughs, withdrawing her arm smoothly.

"Did you wear mascara? You know, Before?"

Tasha waits for the thorns to crop up, the attitude that will defend her makeup, her Prada backpack, her spotless Nikes. But her Nikes aren't really spotless, she thinks, glancing down, and the thorns don't come. So she just says, "Oh yeah."

LaBrenda raises her eyebrows.

"Makeup? A lot?"

Tasha gives her a long look, dropping her chin.

"You have no idea."

LaBrenda laughs.

"You seem to have found your way okay."

Tasha snorts.

"I'll find my way once I find a real comb."

They push off the back of the SUV, bending to pick up their weapons, and wander back toward The Pentagon. Tasha is surprised no one has come looking for them. Z is busy flirting with Roger, and Ishmael tending to the birthday boy. Tasha wonders if they can make him a cake. No flour. No eggs. She wouldn't know how to make one even if she had those things.

"So you were a lot different before this, huh?" LaBrenda says, angling her head behind her, at the blood that stains the ground by the SUV.

"Wasn't everybody?" Tasha says. She looks down at the knife in her hands.

"I wasn't," LaBrenda shrugs, pausing at the steps and looking back, around. "Not much. I mean, I wasn't killing people. But in Detroit there were people in uniforms trying to kill us. Now it's just the who that's changed. We're used to this."

"Not even that has changed," Tasha says. "Cops have the Chip too. I dealt with a couple after the Change."

LaBrenda shrugs, gesturing as if to say "see?" But after a moment of looking out at the emptiness of the world, she says, "But yeah, I guess we all have changed in one way or another." She pauses. "Your friend Dr. Rio, you guys weren't close before he set off the bomb?"

"No, I barely knew him. Ishmael knew him better than I did. He was a little nuts at the end, and we're still trying to understand why he did what he did. Z thinks he was a lunatic and I guess she's right but…I don't know. I still feel like there's more to it than that."

"There usually is," LaBrenda says, turning back to The Pentagon, climbing the steps.

"How did you know it was Rio who set off the bomb?" Tasha says after her, her voice catching at her like a splinter on a sweater.

LaBrenda waits briefly, a half-pause before she says, "Malakai must have told me," and disappears inside.

Above, Tasha hears barking, her heart jolting once before she realizes that, this time, it's actually the dog. She follows LaBrenda inside, sealing the door behind her.

CHAPTER 8

They make Malakai a cake. It's a crumbly thing made of two Twinkies, held together by honey that the pink-haired girl, Sofia, admits to have been hoarding since long before the Change, but Malakai eats it happily, despite being a little shy, begging them not to sing again. He's spent the day in the sunshine pulling weeds and picking ripe vegetables. Looking at him, Tasha imagines him in Leona's garden, if she still has one. How will she find her sister once they make it to California? Or Ishmael's mother, for that matter? She had tried to soothe his worries, but she has her own doubts too.

She's sitting alone on one of the orange futons as she thinks, and looks up as Z sinks down beside her.

"Oh," says Tasha, "you've torn yourself away from Roger for a few minutes?"

"Ha ha," Z says, rolling her eyes but smiling. "It's not that serious. He's cute and all. Really it's just nice to have someone think I'm cute. I may never have another boyfriend again, you know?"

Tasha wants to dismiss this with a laugh, but she can't quite bring herself to do it. She'd only had one or two real boyfriends before the Change, one named Angelo shortly before her parents died. When she'd come back from Kentucky with her nails painted black and loss hanging from her like rags, he'd slowly faded away. He didn't need to return her notes because she'd never sent them. Now those notes on the screen of her Glass are as much a thing of the past as her parents—but is love?

"*You* don't have to worry about it," Z adds, interrupting her thoughts. She's teasing but her eyebrow arches.

"What?"

Z glances over at Ishmael, who sits with Malakai as he has all day. Malakai's happiness is a small candle Ishmael cups his hands around against the wind.

"Oh, stop," Tasha says when Z looks back at her grinning.

"*You* stop!" Z says. "Or, I mean, stop stopping. You guys could be great together. Mr. and Mrs. Apocalypse."

"Oh my god."

"Just saying."

"I'm thinking about my sister," Tasha says, leaning back into the couch. "That's all."

"See," Z insists, but she flops back into the futon too. "You're lucky. You have a guy and family."

"Not really."

"More than me. Everyone's dead."

"You don't know that," Tasha says weakly. She's so bad at this. But, she thinks, adding a little kindling to her hope, it's the same for Leona. "Your sister could be like my sister. Somewhere in New York, surviving. And your brother…"

"Dragon was in jail," Z says, the fun leaked out of her voice like air from a balloon. "It's been weeks since the Change. There's no way."

"You never know is all I'm saying. You keep that photo for a reason."

Z says nothing, watching Roger and the others eating grilled tomatoes and broccoli around the solar stove. Malakai has set his Twinkie cake aside for the moment and juggles a hot tomato from hand to hand, smiling. Nearby, the poodle waits anxiously, her ears cocked, ready to snap up anything that happens to fall.

"We really need to name that dog," Tasha says after awhile.

"I thought Malakai named her."

"He did. But he changed his mind."

"Ah well. The name's important. It'll come."

"Like Azalea? Snapdragon?"

Z allows herself to smile.

"Yes, exactly."

LaBrenda is approaching, something bright pink in her hands. She extends it to Tasha.

"You were wanting a comb?" she says.

Tasha's eyes widen. She accepts the comb, a large plastic thing with thick, wide-spaced teeth.

"Oh my god! Yes!"

She stands awkwardly, moves to hug LaBrenda. She pauses, hangs back, suddenly bashful. Does her excitement over something so small seem ridiculous? The hand not holding the comb wanders up to her hair, squeezing it. She doesn't even want to know what it looks like. Even with her blind hand she can feel the attention it must need.

"Do you want me to braid it for you?" LaBrenda says in a gentle voice. "It looks a little dry. I have oil. Bands too."

Tasha is taken aback. She hasn't had her hair braided since she was twelve. Her grandmother used to do it for her. Her parents were still living, and they'd all go to Chicago to visit. Leona would always go first, sitting quietly, wincing as Grandma's fingers worked deftly through her scalp. When it was Tasha's turn Leona would sit nearby and keep her company, patting her own new braids when they itched.

Tasha wants to say no, to politely turn her down and comb her hair alone, the usual private ritual. But the big comb in her hand is too pink, too friendly, and the soft memory of her grandmother's knees close and warm around her shoulders is too strong.

"Would...would you?" she says shyly.

LaBrenda's face brightens. She'd expected Tasha to refuse.

"Yes," she smiles, a wide smile that shows many of her straight white teeth, the incisors slightly pointed. She tilts her head left and right to take in Tasha's mane. "We better get started. You got a lot of hair."

They all sit in the lopsided circle of futons and chairs, the ceiling's shell still pulled back to reveal the early evening sky.

"What was this building before, do you think?" says Tasha, her head lolling against LaBrenda's left thigh as LaBrenda plants tight, neat cornrows along the right side of Tasha's head. The pressure and sting is almost hypnotic. "It's kind of weird, the ceiling."

"We thought maybe a planetarium," says Sofia. She sits across the circle, near Ishmael. This had made Tasha squint at first, but every time she glances over at him, he's staring back at Tasha. He looks away whenever she catches him. It makes her both nervous and pleased. Maybe she looks strange, with half her head lush with curls and the other half in braids. She decided she won't look at him anymore, as if by not seeing him, he won't see her.

"Or an art gallery," a man whose name Tasha has forgotten says. He says it wistfully, as if he truly hopes it was.

"Are you guys going to stay here?" Z says. She's sitting next to Roger on a futon and is leaned slightly into his shoulder. Tasha suddenly wonders if they'll have sex at some point before they leave this place.

"I don't know where else we'd go," says the art gallery man.

"I mean, you can't survive on what you grow up there forever, right?" Z says, pointing at the ceiling.

"We'll probably plant something other than potatoes outside at some point," says LaBrenda from above Tasha. Her fingers don't pause in their artful work on Tasha's head.

"Outside?"

"Yeah, in the ground, not planter beds. Corn, maybe. Or oats."

"Where would you get the seed?" Tasha says, curious.

"There's a small town about six miles from here we've gone to in the past. Seed and mulch and stuff before we had a compost pile. We'd probably go there."

"Six miles? On foot?"

"Yeah. We're not planning to do that anytime soon. But you know, eventually."

"What about you guys?" says Roger, nudging Z. "We haven't really talked about this. Where are you going? Somewhere? Or just…wandering?"

"Tasha's sister lives in California," Z says. "We're going there."

"Whoa," says Roger. He raises his eyebrows, surprised. "California!"

"Speaking of which," says Ishmael, leaning forward in the armchair he sits on. "You said you haven't seen anyone but us since the Change. But what about cars? From a distance maybe?"

Trapped by LaBrenda's hands, Tasha can't move her head, but she directs her eyes at Roger to learn his response. Roger just shakes his head.

"No one," he says. "Sorry. Got separated from friends? I never thought I'd say it, but I do miss having a Glass sometimes. Made things so much easier. Just had to pick up and then there's their face, telling you exactly where they are. And even if they don't know, they can show you."

"Couldn't agree more," Ishmael says. Although he stops short of sighing, Tasha can see his worry in the way he slumps back into the chair.

"We were supposed to be part of a caravan," Z says. "But we went on a little errand with our friend Dr. Rio and never caught up with them. We should've been following the same route, but we haven't seen a sign of them. Ishmael's mom left even earlier, so we don't think we'll catch up with her 'til California, but it'd be nice to know if she passed this way."

Z, leaning against Roger's shoulder, couldn't have seen Roger's eyes, but Tasha does. They dart in Tasha's direction, but not at Tasha: above her. At LaBrenda. Tasha wishes she weren't here on the floor so she could have glimpsed LaBrenda's face too. Had she caught his look? Had she returned it? Tasha glances at Ishmael but his eyes are on the floor, thinking of the caravan and his mother.

"Maybe they found a quicker route," LaBrenda says brightly. "The SkyDrive, maybe? They could be way ahead of you, especially if they didn't stop and waste time with weirdos like us."

Tasha feels relief bloom in her chest. Roger reaches up a hand and idly brushes a few wisps of hair off Z's forehead. *Nothing to worry about,* Tasha thinks, feeling the rhythmic tugging of LaBrenda's fingers in her hair.

"Or maybe you guys are off course?" Sofia says to Ishmael, her voice sweet. She sees his distress and wants to comfort him. Tasha snarls a little inside. "Are you using a digital map? Sometimes the programmed route can change and you don't even notice..."

"I'm sure their map is fine," Roger says quickly.

They all sit in silence until the poodle comes over to Malakai, stuffing her snout in his armpit and making him laugh.

"What are you gonna name that dog?" Tasha says.

He ruffles the dog's ears.

"I don't know. Something cool. She doesn't even really need a name so far because she follows us everywhere. I haven't had to call her."

"Everyone needs a name," LaBrenda says. "Maybe she'll choose it herself and show it to you. Those are the best names."

It's late when they move to go to bed. A few people had left the circle already to sleep; the remaining group tries to move quietly as they convert futons to bunks.

Tasha's head feels tight and slightly inflated, as if she can feel the blood pulsing rhythmically under her scalp. It's a pleasant, familiar soreness. She reaches up to touch the cornrows gently, counting seven of them, thick straight lines from forehead to nape. She thanks LaBrenda in a whisper as together they pop up the bunk that she and Z share.

"This will be so much easier until we get to California," she tells her. They'd finally closed the roof a few hours ago, hiding the moonlight. Only a few candles and solar lamps glow in the room. "We'll see if Leona remembers how to braid when I get there." Then she glances apologetically up at LaBrenda's hair, its proud puff a round shadow in the dark. "I wish I knew how. I could've returned the favor."

"It's alright," LaBrenda shrugs, reaching up to pat her hair gently. "I like picking it out every day. Like an appointment. Besides, you can owe me one."

"Yeah."

"I'll give you some oil before you leave to keep up with your edges."

"Thank you."

Z comes over from helping Malakai pop up his bunk. Tasha glances over and her eyes fall on Ishmael, pulling his shirt off over his head. It's as if she's unwittingly gripped an electric fence, her hand on the wire trying to pull away but fastened there by a hot current. She stares until he half turns, pulling on a new shirt, unaware of her gaze. She jerks herself away from the invisible wire and turns back to Z and LaBrenda, who are both grinning.

"Yikes," LaBrenda says, raising her eyebrows appreciatively.

"Oh hush," Tasha whispers.

"Tasha, if you don't just…" Z starts.

"Shut up, both of you!"

They giggle quietly, LaBrenda waving her hands in surrender, loping off to her own bed toward the back of the room. She doesn't pop it up into a bunk: rather she flops down on its couchness, pulling the blanket around her like the soft outer layer of a cocoon.

Tasha pulls herself up onto the top bunk, her backpack beside her on the bed. She digs around until she unearths the white tank top she'd worn a day or two ago. Stretching it, she carefully wraps it around her head, tying it in a clumsy knot in the back. Not perfect, but better than nothing. She can feel one of the straps of the shirt flop loosely by her ear. Not perfect at all.

"What are you doing?" Z says when she emerges from the bottom bunk after tucking in her sheets. She almost laughs.

"To keep my braids from getting fuzzy," Tasha sniffs. "Shut up."

"You look hilarious."

"Maybe we can find a scarf next time we stop."

"A scarf?"

"For my hair."

"Oh. Whatever you say. Anything to stay pretty for you know who." Z darts her eyes toward Ishmael, who is settling into his bunk as well.

"Oh my god, shut up!" Tasha hisses, looking too. "It's not for *him*! I want to keep my hair braided until we get to California so I don't have to deal with it."

"Sure thing, Tasha. Sure thing."

Tasha rolls her eyes, pats the makeshift wrap gently, and crawls under her cover. Something is weighing down the blanket. The backpack. She sits up again, takes it by the strap, and hangs it over the corner of the rail by her head.

"How long until we get to California?" she says softly to Z, lying on her side.

"Just a few days if we can keep getting lucky with cars."

"Wow."

"Yeah, I know. Have you thought about how we're going to find your sister?"

"No. I mean, yes, I've thought about it. But I don't know how."

"I mean, if California is still Chipless, it can't be too hard to find some people, right? We can just wander around."

"Yeah."

"What city does she live in? I don't think I've ever asked you that."

"Junot," says Tasha, picturing Leona's wispy handwriting on the yellowish paper of her envelopes. "Used to be Los Angeles."

"Okay. Well, even if everything is still all torn up from the secession, there's gotta be signs. If not for Junot, then old signs for Los Angeles, if it was big enough. We'll find her."

"Thanks, Z."

Across the room, Roger extinguishes the candles one by one, switching off solar discs. He leaves two glowing by the front entrance for anyone groping their way to the bathroom in the night, and slowly makes his way back to his own bed. Tasha can hear the rustle of his body in the dark. When he is still, she reaches under the cover and unbuttons her jeans, lowering her zipper and then slowly inching her way out of them. She never gets up to pee at night and she's sick of the too-tight claustrophobia of the pants. *This is how you get a yeast infection*, she thinks. Once off, she drapes the jeans over the rail beside her hanging backpack, enjoying the feeling of her skin against the covers for once. She considers reaching down to rub her legs, but cringes at the idea of unlasered body hair.

"Good idea," she hears Z whisper, and Tasha wonders how she knew. The frame of the bed trembles slightly as Z follows suit. Tasha hears the whisper of the covers and the gentle swish of Z's jeans sliding onto the polished concrete floor of the Pentagon. Tasha smiles a little as the idea of the two of them in the middle of nowhere, pantsless. She remembers the day she met Z, being naked in front of her as she dressed to fight the Minkers. *No telling where you're going to meet your friends*, she thinks as she drifts off to sleep.

Someone is breathing near Tasha's face. She wakes slowly, clumsily, at the gentle hush of breath, at first not remembering where she is. All is dark, the breath quieter than a whisper. She barely hears it, thinks maybe she hadn't heard it at all, a trick of dreams and sleeping in an unfamiliar place. But no, someone is nearby: they brush against the top of her pillow then freeze, waiting to see if they've awakened her. They have: she's fully awake now, her eyes wide open in the dark, focusing all of her stirring senses on the presence nearby, the breathing person hovering so near she can feel the heat emanating from their body.

Tasha's backpack shifts slowly, so slowly it's as if the backpack is coming alive thread by thread. She can hear its fabric whisper against itself, the muted jingle of the metal buckle as the breathing person opens it in the dark, reaching inside.

Tasha sits up quickly and twists, shooting her arm out in the dark, fingers snatching. Her hand hits the person's face first, accidentally, and she's pleased by their gasp of surprise before she gropes frantically for an arm, a hand. She fastens her grip on their wrist, shouting, "Z! Wake up! Ishmael! Hey! Hey!"

She hears others in the room stirring immediately, a call in the dark from someone—Roger—asking what the hell is going on.

The person whose arm she's holding struggles hard; their strength is surprising but she holds on doggedly. But her grip is slipping: their skin is too smooth, too hard, too difficult too squeeze.

"Z! Z!"

A sun disc pops to life across the room, a speck of glowing blue that Tasha sees only out of the corner of her eye. The last shreds of drowsiness evaporated, she feels her body vibrating with the same energy that fuels her when she comes face to face with a Minker. This is a person, she knows, not a Minker. It must be. But person or not, she wishes she slept with her knife the way she did when they had bunked in various hotels.

More lights come on. Z's head finally appears beside Tasha, swaying slightly with the effects of sleep.

"What's going on?" Tasha hears Roger call from across the hall.

Hearing Roger's voice again, Tasha realizes that she'd thought it was his wrist she's latched on to. But as another light comes on and then another, Tasha's fingers slipping on the bony, slippery wrist, she realizes she's wrong. It's LaBrenda. Tasha lets go.

"What the hell?" Tasha says when the light reveals LaBrenda's face. She's moved a few feet away from Tasha's bunk and stands there looking at her, half reproachful and half apologetic.

Tasha hops down from the top bunk, a little too quickly. She sways a little when she lands and holds on to the rail of the bed for balance. The rail feels too much like LaBrenda's bionic arm and she lets go again quickly.

"Tasha," says Z softly.

"What the hell, LaBrenda?" Tasha repeats, growing angrier as other gardeners rise from their beds to see what's going on. "Why are you going through my shit?"

"Tasha," Z says again, and nudges her.

Tasha looks. Z is extending a pair of pants to her. Seeing them, Tasha becomes aware of the chill on her bare legs. Bare.

She'd taken her pants off. She snatches the pants from Z, cursing, and tries to put them on while maintaining her lofty anger, refusing to break eye contact with LaBrenda again.

Roger pushes through the small crowd that has formed, including the poodle, who stands wagging. Tasha puts her hands on her hips as he approaches, ready for him to play mediator, gentle gardener calling for peace and love.

"Did you get it?" he says instead, brushing past Tasha and going to stand in front of LaBrenda.

"What?" Tasha shouts.

"Yes," says LaBrenda, ignoring her. She holds up the thing she'd taken from Tasha's bag, and Tasha jerks her head to the side to see around Roger's body.

It's Rio's Glass.

"What the fuck is going on?" Tasha says again, still shouting, still angry, still buttoning her jeans.

"Roger!" Z says shrilly when he ignores Tasha. He turns, finally, enraging Tasha even further. "What are you doing?"

Roger's face is smooth, the laugh lines and easy smile that Tasha has come to know over the course of the last day missing. But he softens a little looking at Z.

"I'm sorry, Azalea," he says. "But we had to."

"Had to *what*?" Tasha demands, stepping forward now that her jeans are secured. Her knife is behind her on the floor, beneath her bunk. She knows she can reach it quickly if she needs to.

"We needed this." Roger turns slightly, back to LaBrenda, taking the Glass from her hand and holding it up for them to see.

Tasha glances around, looking for Ishmael. She finds him, halfway from his bunk to her, paused. Behind him, Malakai sits up on the top bunk, eyes wide. Ishmael doesn't want to get too far away from him, she knows. Good. Keep him close. They might have to run.

"For what?" Tasha spits, looking straight at LaBrenda, who can't hold her gaze. "Check some mail? Isn't that what you said to me? Why do you need my shit?"

"It's not really yours," LaBrenda says. Her voice wavers, as if it had tried to be angry and couldn't quite pull it off. "Really, it's ours."

"Is this some gardener philosophy bullshit?" Tasha's almost laughing. She had known staying here was a bad idea. She had known something would go down. She had known.

"No," says Roger, the softness ironed out of his face when he transfers his eyes from Z to Tasha. He opens his mouth to continue, but LaBrenda interrupts him, stepping a little ahead, her arm crossing his chest.

"It's not what you think, Tasha. It's not bad like you think," she says.

"Taking my shit out of my backpack in the middle of the night? What am I supposed to think?" She becomes aware of something flopping against her neck. The tank top she had wrapped her braids with when she lay down. She reaches up and snatches it off her head, throwing it on the ground, glaring.

"It's not yours," LaBrenda says, sounding near exasperation. "It's Dr. Rio's. Which means it's ours. Because...because *he* was ours."

Roger makes a sighing sound that Tasha ignores, glaring hard at LaBrenda instead. Her mind races, scrambling to put the pieces together. Her teeth are clenched. She takes a step back, nearer to her bunk, nearer to her knife. LaBrenda doesn't seem overly hostile—even Roger seems more impatient than violent—but she's not willing to put any trust in either of them right now.

"What are you talking about?" says Z. "Roger, what's she talking about? Yours how?"

Around her, the gardeners who had gathered to watch shift a little. Tasha hears a few soft murmurs, expressions of disapproval. They're all in on it. Whatever this is, they're all in on it. She takes another step back to her bunk, bends quickly, and grabs the Wusthof. She flexes her fingers around it, making sure her grip is good.

"He was one of us," LaBrenda says slowly, the hand not holding the Glass held up at waist level, as if confronting a snarling dog. The only dog is the poodle, Tasha thinks, glancing at it. It stands dumbly, looking cheerful.

"What? A gardener?"

"No," says LaBrenda. "Dr. Rio wasn't a gardener. But we... had things in common."

"Like what?" Tasha squints at her, darting her eyes around the group, glancing at Roger to be sure his face isn't betraying some signal to attack.

"Like," LaBrenda pauses. A long silence. Someone standing nearby coughs. "Bombs."

CHAPTER 9

Bombs. Just like that. A word as short and blunt as "thumb," or "down," and spoken just as simply. Bombs. No flourish, no drama. LaBrenda could have said "knitting" or "jogging." These are things that people have in common—people have zodiac signs in common, films. People share interests like rowing and even, to the extreme, cosmetic surgery. Not bombs.

"Bombs," Tasha repeats, just in case she might have misheard.

"Yes."

Tasha almost laughs. She recalls the way Dr. Rio looked in Cybranu's minimum-security office on the 103rd floor of the Apiary. Stark, cold, ashen. The straightforwardness of his utterance of "bombs" had been something like an "amen" at the end of a particularly long and exhausting prayer. LaBrenda doesn't say it like that. "Bombs" falls out of her mouth like a shrug, or an apology from a child who isn't quite sorry but knows she should be.

"So you knew him," Tasha says. In spite of her distrust, she finds herself allowing her raised knife to droop to her side. She's tired. She doesn't have the strength to run, to save herself or anyone else. If The Pentagon is going to blow, then she's okay with being ashes fertilizing someone else's garden.

"Yes. He belongs to Red Rooster, same as we do."

"Who is Red Rooster?" Z says. Tasha had expected her voice to sound weak, but she doesn't sound changed at all. Maybe she's numb too.

"It's kind of a what and a who," says Roger.

"Then what? Who?" Z says. She does sound tired, Tasha decides. Not weak. Just tired.

"We couldn't say even if we knew. Rooster isn't his real name, just what we know him as." Roger looks smug, and Tasha feels her jaw clench again. He's a little shit, she decides once and for all.

"So it's a code name? For what? That's your boss or something?" Z says.

LaBrenda shrugs.

"Kind of. We don't really know why Rooster is the name. It was his screen name online. Apparently he has one eye?"

"So?"

"So I guess there was some old movie with a cowboy that had one eye. I don't know."

Tasha gives her collegiate memory a quick scan. It sounds vaguely familiar but she's too annoyed to think about it.

"But whatever, it's like a wake-up call, you know? A metaphor for a new morning."

Z looks skeptical.

"That sounds like bullshit," she says.

"Right," Tasha joins in. "Enough with the bullshit. Why did you take my—okay, *Dr. Rio*'s Glass out of my bag? In the middle of the fucking night, I might add."

LaBrenda doesn't answer right away, and neither does Roger. LaBrenda glances around the circle at the other gardeners and then even looks up at the ceiling, intensely, as if her eyes pierce through the closed roof to the very garden itself. Eventually she looks back at Tasha, and when she does Tasha knows she will hear the truth.

"Because we think it might contain intel about Red Rooster's next target. We've been told that this particular target is the key to finding all the others, and we want to have as much information as we can get before we go." She pauses. "Rio was supposed to come here after he evacuated Chicago. We've been waiting, but he never showed. Now we know why."

Tasha pauses, soaking this in. Rio's red line across the country had been drawn with a different purpose in mind than simply leading to California.

"But what do you mean, finding all the others? Finding the other what?" Tasha says after a moment.

"The other hubs. We know there's a lot of them: different places where Cybranu has placed a signal that controls the Chippers. If we can find all the hubs and take them all out…"

Roger stops and glances at LaBrenda, who shrugs.

"What?" says Z.

"If we took out every Cybranu hub, we would fry every Chip in its radius."

Someone coughs again. Tasha wonders if they actually have something in their throat or if it's a nervous tic. Leona used to do this, except it was a yawn. Whenever she was nervous or unsure, she would yawn. Their parents hated it, their dad in particular interpreting it as an act of defiance whenever she was in trouble. She wonders if Leona would be yawning now, or if she would be rolling her eyes at what must be a lie, what couldn't possibly be the truth. How could a raggedy bunch of gardeners happen to have the answer to what Tasha now sees is the apocalypse? She realizes it's a good question and decides to ask it.

"So you guys…a bunch of nobodies in a garden in the middle of Nebraska…*you guys* have the cure, huh?"

"It's not a cure. People won't…" LaBrenda pauses, almost biting her lip. "Tasha, everyone with the Chip will die when we destroy the hubs."

The enormity of it takes a moment to fully form in Tasha's mind. Millions. Countless people worked for a corporation of some kind, given the Chip for free. Others were cops or members of the armed forces, mandatorily Chipped. Everyone else paid out of pocket, desperate for the newest must-have bio-accessory. Only the poor and the cynical did without—and those whom MINK found unworthy, Tasha remembers, thinking of the Knox exam. Applicants' medical histories and voting records were all accessible by MINK when anyone applied for coverage. Race. Sex.

Tasha breathes out, a short hard breath. Imagining all the Brians and the Ginas of the States swaying to the invisible orchestra of the Chip one minute, and collapsing to the ground the next, lifeless.

"All of them?" Z says softly.

"Yes," LaBrenda replies, the emotion wrung out of her voice. Tasha looks at her face, studying it, searching for lies. She finds none: just a face that is unapologetic, but apologetic for its lack of apology. Tasha sits down on Z's bunk, her elbows on her knees. LaBrenda looks at her, waiting.

"What the fuck, LaBrenda," Tasha says finally, exhausted. She drops her knife with a clang on the smooth floor. She almost kicks it, but remembers she's barefoot. She smoothes her fresh braids with both hands. "What the fuck."

"I know. It's…a lot."

"You're fucking right it's a lot."

"You lied to us," says Z, her voice flat. Tasha glances up at her. She says "us" but she means "me." She's talking to Roger.

"I tried not to," Roger says. His tone is a blanket: soft, comforting. He wants to drape it around Z's shoulders, sit under it with her. He actually likes her, Tasha realizes, and she hates him a little less. A little.

"It's not something we would just tell strangers passing through," says one of the gardeners. Tasha looks. It's the chubby guy who guessed the Pentagon had been an art gallery. He's wearing a faded red shirt that doesn't quite cover the bottom of his belly. He runs a hand through his loose black curls. "We can't just tell people who we are. What we do. Even now."

"But when you heard us talk about Dr. Rio," Tasha argues, throwing a hand out at LaBrenda. "You could have told us then. We could have just given you the Glass. Simple."

"We couldn't be sure right away that you weren't spies," LaBrenda says. The apology in her voice is easier to hear now.

"Spies?" Tasha scoffs. She points at Malakai. He's sitting on the bottom bunk of his bed with Ishmael, leaning against his brother's shoulder. "Does the kid look like a spy to you?"

LaBrenda shrugs.

"We've seen some crazy shit under Rooster. Moles from some of the organizations we work against. Couldn't be too careful."

They sit in silence again. If thoughts were clocks the room would be full of ticking, rising to the metal eyelid of the ceiling. Tasha catches Ishmael's eye. His face is placid. Tasha sighs.

"Good luck getting the fucking Glass unlocked," she finally grumbles, nodding in LaBrenda's direction.

LaBrenda glances at Roger, who shrugs. LaBrenda brings the Glass up closer to her face, presses the side to wake it up, then taps in a code using the alphabet Tasha knows appeared on the screen. She hears nothing, but in the dim light of the room, the illumination on LaBrenda's face changes from white to blue. She looks up at Roger.

"I'm in," she says.

"What?" Tasha says, standing, nearly bumping her head on the top bunk. "How? What was the password?"

"Phoenix," LaBrenda says with a smile, holding up the screen toward Tasha.

"Phoenix? Why?"

"Because that's where the next target is."

With the exception of Malakai, none of them sleep.

"If you have questions, you can come watch," LaBrenda said, "but we have work to do. I'm sorry."

And she'd taken the Glass to the part of the common room where the gardeners had been doing yoga on the first night, her group following along, yawning but alert. Speechless, Tasha and Z go over to Ishmael's bunk where he still sits with Malakai.

"What do we do?" Tasha whispers, clutching her knife again.

Z shrugs.

"What *can* we do? They outnumber us: we can't just take the Glass back, not if they really want to keep it."

"They've got a point anyway," Ishmael says, low. "It isn't really ours. If they knew Dr. Rio, then let them have it. Who cares."

"And if they didn't actually know him and they're all full of shit," Z says, looking over her shoulder at the gardeners, who are crowding around what turns out to be a projector, "who cares? We don't need Rio's Glass to get where we're going. We have maps. Let's just go."

"Now?" Tasha says, looking at Malakai, already drifting off to sleep, his hand slowly scratching the poodle's ear.

"Okay, maybe not now," Tasha says, gazing at the boy. "But first thing in the morning."

Tasha looks at Ishmael, who nods.

"I don't think they mean us any harm, but if they're anything like Rio, we want to get away from them," Ishmael says, even lower now that Malakai is sleeping.

They look over at the gardeners, where the glowing blue light has become an orb at the center of their circle, the projector warming up. Z sighs.

"Let's at least go see what they're talking about."

Ishmael stays with Malakai. Worried that one of the gardeners might come and steal him too, Tasha thinks, glancing over her shoulder as she joins the circle. LaBrenda is already talking.

"There's not much here," she says, scanning the contents of the Glass, swiping the screen with her finger. The projector's blue sphere is empty for now.

"We knew there wouldn't be," says Roger, yawning, leaning back on the chair he'd pulled up with his arms behind his head. "All our intel says that Rio was careful. He didn't want to take too much and get caught."

"I'm surprised he even took files from the Box at all. Risky," says Alexis, the woman with vitiligo. "But I'm glad he did."

No one says anything. Z nudges Tasha. Tasha doesn't look at her.

"Wait, we have blueprints," LaBrenda says, a small smile cracking her lips. She taps the Glass.

The blue sphere of the projector is suddenly filled: a three-dimensional rendering of a square building of four or five stories, its hallways and rooms and doorways illuminated and transparent; the figure of it rotating so slowly Tasha almost doesn't notice. Still, the sight of it hanging there in space puts a chill down her spine. Another mall, she assumes. Smaller than the Apiary but just as sinister. She pulls her knees to her chest on the futon and watches.

"Rio mapped it pretty well, it looks like," says Roger, frowning. He has a tomato that Tasha hadn't seen him pull from anywhere. He bites it like an apple. "Does anyone see a control room? Cerebellum?"

Alexis stands and walks into the floating image, its light turning her face blue. She looks even more like a map now, Tasha observes: the pale parts of her skin blue oceans and the dark parts solid land. Tasha finds herself wanting skin like that, feels embarrassed at the thought. Life with skin like hers can't have been easy, and here's Tasha wanting it for pretty's sake. But still, she thinks, watching Alexis: beautiful.

"Here," Alexis says, pointing. Her arm is a blue branch reaching up through the rotating image to indicate a circular space on what looks to be the third floor. "I'd bet that's where we can get access to what we need. No windows. Core position."

She goes back to her seat, plops down.

"It won't be easy," she adds.

"What ever is?" says LaBrenda, staring at the image but looking through it, thinking.

"What exactly are you trying to do?" Tasha asks. She can feel Z look at her but doesn't look back.

LaBrenda looks at her for a long moment before she replies.

"Why?"

"Just curious."

Another long pause.

"This place will give us a map of Cybranu's hubs," LaBrenda says. "We need to get in and get that data. The sooner we know where all the locations are, the sooner we can put a stop to all this shit."

"And this is just the beginning," Roger chimes in. "You think the Chip is the only fucked-up thing that Cybranu is responsible for? Think again."

Tasha ignores him.

"How do you even know you can?"

"Can what?"

"Destroy the hubs."

LaBrenda laughs, not unkindly.

"Girl, what? We already have! Twice."

Tasha stares at her.

"You were there for one," LaBrenda says, a little more gently. "And the Mall of America? That was us too."

Tasha gapes at her, processing. She remembers when it happened. No one had known who was responsible for the blast or why. Now here she is staring at the people responsible. Her head is pounding.

"And we know it works," LaBrenda continues. "Did you see any of the Chipped people after the explosion in Chicago?"

Tasha feels flustered, remembering Rio's rambling above the clouds and realizing now that it hadn't been rambling but the truth.

"When we went over the bridge…" Z says, staring at LaBrenda. "We saw them acting weird. Rio said they would be fried…"

"They were acting weird," Tasha agrees.

"Yes, fried," says LaBrenda, nodding with satisfaction. "Anything with a Chip in a 50-mile radius got fried when the Apiary blew."

"Wait, so Chicago is…okay?" Z says, interrupting.

LaBrenda looks at her with the patience of a PR rep.

"Not exactly," she says. "It's a dead zone now. No power. Lots of bodies. There will be a lot of disease with that many corpses. Few places to grow new food in the city, and eventually that will be needed."

Tasha glances carefully at Z, afraid to see her face as she thinks about her father, fried in the city and left to become fossil. Her friend's face is blank, dry.

Ishmael sinks down next to Tasha on the futon and she jumps. She hadn't seen him coming or heard him approach. Packed between him and Z on the couch, she feels even more that she's reliving that day in Rio's car: before the Apiary, stuffed into Rio's backseat. Rio in the front seat strange and spooky…

"But why did Rio try to get people out of Chicago if he knew that the bomb would fry all the Chips?" Tasha says. Her mind returns to Rio's living room, all the South Siders packing up their belongings. Bianca, her picture frames and her diary. She was old. Surely it would have been better for her to stay in Chicago.

"The Apiary wasn't the only hub in the Midwest," LaBrenda says firmly. "And like I said, people need to go somewhere where there's a future. Moving people to California is still the best bet. It's the only place where there are no Chips. None."

"So that's true," Tasha says. In spite of the daze that has come over her, she feels hope swell in her chest. No Chips. Leona, Morris, and baby Amani; their sweet little orange house. They might all be okay.

"Definitely," says Roger.

"How?" says Z, and Tasha can hear the hope in her voice too—a small furred thing peeking out of its hole, looking for sunshine.

"The secession," Alexis says. She sits forward in her chair, staring at them intently. Tasha wonders who she was before all this. Probably a prodigy of some kind: she seems like the kind of woman who learned to code when she was two. "We've known this was coming for quite some time."

"The secession was planned with this Cybranu shit in mind?" says Ishmael, and Tasha's pulse spikes at the sound of his voice. Something about the way he says "shit" makes her spine tingle. She brushes the tingle away. *Stop it*, she warns herself, and her spine.

LaBrenda and Alexis exchange a look.

"Something like that," LaBrenda says. "There were a lot of people who wanted to secede for other reasons, but then Dr. Rio got in touch with Red Rooster with information about what the Chip had the potential to do, and we knew it had to happen. The secession, I mean. If we could control a definite portion of land and keep any hubs from being built, we knew we could have a hope at surviving."

"You couldn't have picked a better state?" Z says, leaning back into the couch. "California isn't exactly the most stable environment."

"Nowhere is," Alexis shrugs. "Climate change has fucked everything up. At least we have ways of keeping an eye on the parts of the coast falling into the Pacific. The superstorms of the Midwest are much more unpredictable."

"We thought they were bad in Chicago," says Ishmael, sighing. His arm grazes Tasha's as his chest expands, and she freezes. "We ran into a tornado in Iowa. Don't have those back home."

"You'll see those here too, unfortunately," Roger says. "Droughts too, like everywhere else. California has found some ways around that."

They're silent for awhile after that. Tasha watches LaBrenda's face, still staring at the glowing 3-D map of the building in Arizona. She wonders if this was always LaBrenda's dream: to grow up and fight invisible government entities in a post-apocalyptic wasteland. Tasha hates that word: apocalypse. Post-apocalyptic implies that the apocalypse is a definitive event, with time measured as before and after. But pieces of California had been falling into the ocean for years; fires had run rampant across the country for years: trees had died, tornadoes had raged, and the sky of Chicago had bruised and never healed. How different, really, was a Chip that made people murderers, Tasha thinks, remembering what Malakai had said about his father, when police had been killing children's parents for a century?

"We should look at the personnel," says Alexis after awhile.

"Yeah," LaBrenda sighs, rubbing the back of her neck with her metal hand. Tasha bets she gives a good massage. "We can look at the blueprints later."

"There's personnel?" Roger says, frowning.

"Yeah, it looks like it."

"How up to date can that be?" he says, scooching his chair closer to her.

She shrugs and looks down at Rio's Glass, tapping its screen with a flesh fingertip. In a blip, the blue layout of the building disappears, and the air between them all is dim again. The candles and solar discs, which had seemed bright enough a few minutes ago, now seem hazy and sinister, casting shadows from their bodies that only vaguely resemble humans. Tasha raises her hand to make a shadow puppet, but when LaBrenda glances at her, she pretends she was reaching up to pat her braids.

"We have quite a few personnel files here," LaBrenda says, tapping the screen, and the blue light floods the area again. This time there isn't a map of a building but a face: the shoulders and head of a man with a blank, bald face and large pale eyes.

"Michael Walker," LaBrenda says, but she doesn't need to, Tasha sees: the man's name is floating in the air near his cheek, along with other information Tasha doesn't understand.

"Clearance Level Falcon," Tasha reads, squinting at the neat glowing words. "What does that mean?"

"It means he's a boss," says Alexis evenly, staring up at Michael Walker's face. "Any relation to President Walker?"

"Probably," says LaBrenda, scanning the Glass in front of her. "It doesn't say."

"Ah, well. Safe to assume. The president was probably just his idiot brother. Who else do we got?"

LaBrenda swipes slowly through what must be a fairly large database of personnel. All of them have the same blank expression, their eyes seemingly soulless. Men and women of different ages and races, all of them with the same empty stare.

"I'm not sure how useful it is to review the personnel," Roger says. "I'd rather learn more about the security."

"In a minute," LaBrenda says, not taking her eyes off the projector's glow. "I'd like to learn more about who might be waiting for us when we go."

"It's doubtful they'll leave any personnel behind," Roger says, sounding annoyed. Tasha glances at him. *Eager*, she thinks. Eager to start blowing stuff up.

"In a minute," LaBrenda says again.

First one face and then another fills the air at the center of the dark circle, staring out at them. Beards, noses, mascara, pointy chins, a folded ear—the faces blend together in Tasha's drowsy eyes as LaBrenda swipes through. And then suddenly there's a face Tasha recognizes. She had been almost asleep during the endless parade of personnel, but now she's wide awake, gazing at the spectacles and neat goatee, the pleasing brown skin, wrinkled only slightly around the eyes. It's Dr. Rio.

"Wait," Tasha says, leaning forward on the sofa, her hand outstretched as if to reach LaBrenda's hand. Z too sits up, her mouth open slightly.

"Rio," Z says, shaking her head. Tasha can't tell if it's disgust or a strange fondness.

"This is Dr. Rio?" LaBrenda says, raising her eyebrows and giving the floating face a closer look. Rio's name is there beside him like a nod: yes, this is him. "He's older than I thought he'd be."

"Wait, you mean you didn't know him? I thought you said you knew him?" Tasha says, suspicious. The gardeners had been cautious in believing that Tasha and her group were merely travelers passing through, but now Tasha's caution rises as well. "I thought you were part of the same group? Reporting to Yellow Chicken or whatever."

"Red Rooster," LaBrenda corrects with a smile. "But we didn't know him, not really. None of us really know each other. We were told that after he handled the Apiary, he would follow the same route you guys took and end up here. Then we'd go to Phoenix together."

"So, what, you guys all meet up how? In a social network for, like, domestic terrorists or something?" Z says. Tasha smiles. Z can be so corny, but it's still funny.

"Not too far off, really," Roger says, smiling. Tasha knows he wouldn't be smiling if it had been Tasha who'd said it. "Rooster recruited some of us in person, some on the web. Like me. I was recruited on the web."

"We're not terrorists," Alexis adds.

Tasha looks back at Rio's face floating there, tinted slightly blue. He has the same blank expression as the rest of the stream of faces. But Tasha thinks she sees the faintest glimmer in his eyes. Maybe she's imagining it. She looks back over her shoulder to make sure Malakai is sleeping. He is. She hopes he stays that way at least for a moment longer: if he woke up he'd think he was seeing a ghost, last seen behind a closing door above the clouds of Chicago. He doesn't need to think about the Apiary.

"Wait," says Tasha, turning back. "So this hub or whatever in Phoenix isn't a mall?"

LaBrenda looks perplexed.

"A mall?"

"I mean, you guys, or the one-eyed Red Rooster or whatever, blew up the Apiary. And you said you blew up the Mall of America too."

"Oh," says LaBrenda. Then, understanding: "Oh! No, not a mall. Not all the hubs are malls. At least, well…" She turns to look at Alexis raising her eyebrow. "Maybe they are? Except this one?"

Alexis shrugs.

"We won't know until we get inside the Arizona hub. This is where they made the Chip: that's where we'll find our answers."

"Big plans," says Tasha, more to herself. The memory of Rio has begun to change form. His back seems a little straighter when she thinks of him now.

LaBrenda nods, smiling.

"Yes."

"Enough of the personnel files," says Roger. "Let's move on. What else is there?"

LaBrenda looks down again, frowning in concentration as her finger swipes.

"Some scientific shit that's just a little over my head: algorithms. Alexis can look at that later. Some of this stuff might make more sense once we access Arizona's database. This data is stale: some of it has probably changed since Rio left. What else…some of Rio's notes about the Cybranu board: nothing Rooster didn't show us already. Test subjects. Poor bastards."

She projects a new face up into the air between them, looking up at it to see it better. A man with yellowish-tan skin, his eyes opened wide for the photo. One of Cybranu's guinea pigs. LaBrenda swipes. A woman Tasha's complexion with her eyes narrowed, looking angry. A woman with the same thick natural as LaBrenda with forlorn creases across her forehead. LaBrenda keeps swiping. And Z screams.

It's a small scream—a cry, really: not even loud enough to wake Malakai, though the dog raises its head to look at them from the boy's bunk. But Tasha is near enough to be scared to death, jumping hard before turning to admonish Z, who has risen from the sofa and is standing there, almost swaying, pointing at the new face.

Tasha looks, and almost thinks it's an illusion, reflecting Z's face back to her like a bluish mirror. But it's not: it's a boy. A man. The features are similar, almost identical but not quite: the jaw squarer and the eyebrows heavier.

"Z…" Tasha begins, but Z is already whispering.

"Snapdragon," she says. She covers her mouth with two fingers. "That's my brother."

CHAPTER 10

"Your brother?" says LaBrenda. Her fingers pause over the surface of the Glass, poised to swipe but stopped, frozen. "You have a brother in Phoenix?"

Z doesn't answer. She stares at the face hovering there, her eyes shiny, a splash of blue reflected in each.

"He's so much older now," she whispers.

Tasha is dumbfounded. She'd known Z had a brother, of course. But seeing his face here in the midst of the gardeners… it's like knowing that the dodo is extinct only to run into one in a park.

"So wait, you said this place is where the Chip was made. But Z's brother was in prison. Dr. Rio worked in a prison?" Tasha says. She lays a hand on Z's shoulder, awkwardly, not knowing what her friend needs. Z doesn't brush her hand off, so she leaves it there.

"No," says Roger, looking quickly back and forth between Z and Tasha. Tasha can't tell if he's suspicious or concerned.

"Z's brother was in prison. Right, Z?"

Z just stares at her brother's face.

"I haven't seen him in five years," she says.

Tasha bites her lip.

"He was in prison," Tasha says a third time, looking up at LaBrenda.

LaBrenda looks at Alexis, then at Roger. Tasha studies each of their faces. Something's there: something like a surgeon who is deciding how to tell their patient about the grapefruit tumor found in their skull. Tasha says nothing, puts her whole arm around Z's shoulders the way LaBrenda had done with her. Part of her is steeled for rejection, ready for Z to move away, shove her off. She doesn't. Instead, Tasha feels the slightest give in Z's body, a melting, a slackening of muscles resulting in the slightest lean against her. Tasha looks back at LaBrenda, stares pointedly.

"The Arizona hub isn't a prison," LaBrenda says slowly. Her voice is a scalpel working tenderly at bad stitches. "It's…it's a test facility."

Tasha feels Z look at LaBrenda.

"A test facility," she repeats. Tasha thinks she sounds like a string strung tightly between two nails. Too tightly.

"For the Chip," Alexis says softly.

"A test facility for the Chip," Ishmael says. "What does that mean exactly?"

LaBrenda eyes Z carefully before answering. Next to her, Roger sits rapt, his bones turned to steel. Tasha wonders what he's thinking. Worried about his love interest, wanting to help; or his interest fading now that Z has become complicated. Problematic. Human.

"The target is the Neovison Research and Development Facility. It's Cybranu's parent company. Rooster refers to it as the Box."

"Creative," says Tasha, her voice dull. Z croaks a laugh. Tasha thinks she might snap if they're not careful.

"The Box is where Dr. Rio and his team developed the Chip for the federal military. They make a lot of things there and own lots of companies. Mostly focused on combat and military technology until they acquired Cybranu and started selling to civilians."

"So they make bombs," Ishmael says flatly.

"Other things too," Roger says. "Research."

Why is it always bombs, Tasha thinks.

"Cut the shit, okay," says Z suddenly when the room has been quiet for several minutes. Her voice is thick with tears Tasha knows won't fall. "What are you telling me? That my brother didn't actually go to prison? That he lied to me?"

"No," says LaBrenda quickly. "No, he didn't lie to you. He was lied to. You all were."

"This is something that's been happening a lot in the last ten years," Alexis says. She's sitting on the edge of her seat, leaned toward where Z and Tasha sit. The pattern of pigment on her face gives her an expression of curiosity—the lighter skin curving up over one eyebrow more than the other. But her eyes aren't curious: they're hard and bright. She can't be curious because she already knows.

"Prisons have become big business in the States," she goes on, her hands in fists with the knuckles pressed together. "They have been for a long time. They've been locking up black and brown kids in private prisons—some of them owned by companies like Cybranu and Neovison—and then spitting 'em back out as adults with no skills, no right to vote, no education. The ones they don't lock up they kill."

Tasha looks quickly at Malakai, breathing a sigh of relief to see him still sleeping. But the boy's father had another son too, and she moves her eyes to sneak a look at Ishmael beside her. His jaw set, he's staring intensely at the two women ahead of him. Tasha thinks they might just turn to stone under those eyes, but Alexis keeps talking.

"Now they've found another way to control them," she goes on. "Test facilities. Promising them reduced sentences if they agree to be guinea pigs."

The room is too dark and the lights are too dim. Tasha wonders if the sun might be rising. She wishes they had left the ceiling open to let the night sky in, so that she'd know when the dawn arrived. Right now she needs dawn. This room and all these words being spoken inside it are heavy with shadows. In another room, in another time, she might have called these words bullshit and got up to leave the conversation; maybe flip through her Glass. But her arm is around Z's shoulders, and Z is looking at the face of her brother, a face in the patient files of a test facility, when he was supposed to be in prison. She says nothing.

"So my brother is a guinea pig," Z says slowly. Tasha thinks she feels her trembling. "My brother is a lab rat."

Guinea pigs. Lab rats. Rodents plucked from one cage and deposited into another.

"I was a rat in Arizona," Tasha whispers. Pearls. Dark roots. Mole people. Ninja turtles. "Oh, shit."

"What?" Z tilts her head toward Tasha, not taking her eyes off the face of her brother, but listening.

"The Bean," Tasha says. "Remember? The woman we saw?"

"The walnut?"

"Go through the patient profiles," Tasha says, suddenly feeling urgent. She feels something hot pulsing through her veins, something frantic.

"What?" says LaBrenda, puzzled.

Tasha gets up quickly, closes the small gap between her and LaBrenda, takes Rio's Glass out of her unresisting hands. It feels strange to be holding it, this thing that at one point was so familiar. Its digital glow shines up on her face like sunshine, but not.

Strange or not, her fingers remember what to do. She swipes quickly, faces blurring by in the space inside the circle of people. Brown and black faces, both men and women: so many of them. Tasha doesn't rest on any of their faces, even though she wants to. They are a stream of dull eyes and blue shoulders, all suited in the same uniform gown. Tasha does occasionally pause on a face light-skinned enough to break the succession of darker faces, but none of them are the face she's looking for. Finally, after the face of a Latina woman with soft eyes like Dinah's and a spider tattoo, Tasha finds her. She actually skips her, her fingers lost in the rhythm of swiping. But when she swipes back, there she is.

"See?" Tasha says triumphantly, gesturing with the Glass.

Z stands, her feelings about her brother momentarily set aside.

"Shit," she says, taking in the floating face. "That *is* her."

It's the blonde woman from Chicago, who Tasha had first seen days before the Change, and then again next to the Bean, when it had been miraculously painted blood red. No pearls in this photo, Tasha knows. Who knows where she got the pearls?

"You know this woman?" Roger says, standing now too. He looks troubled, like Z might be a Trojan horse he let into his careful little kingdom.

"No," says Tasha, not looking to comfort him but not wanting him to misunderstand. "I saw her once in the subway before the Change and then we ran into her again afterward, on our way to the South Side. She mentioned Arizona but we just thought she was a walnut. Crazy."

"She's Chipped," Z adds, looking at the woman. Her face tells Tasha she's thinking of that encounter under the Bean as well: the strange swaying, the way the Minkers had left her alone even as she stood there among them.

"Yeah," says Tasha, glancing again at Z, glad to be steering the conversation away from her brother, at least for now. "It was weird. She was Chipped, but not a Minker. The Chipped people left her alone, but she could still talk to us. And she wasn't violent, not exactly. Just weird. Like she had a force-field protecting her from them."

"Like a hybrid," Alexis says, looking at the blonde woman's face. "Interesting."

"I wonder how she escaped," Z says softly, and Tasha winces. She's back on Dragon: wondering if he might have done the same. What if he's crazy too? Tasha thinks of her parents and wonders if it would be better if they stayed dead, or if they returned to her ranting about a secret lab, out of touch with the people they had been before. She thinks death is probably better, but she will not say this to Z.

"According to this file," LaBrenda says, peering at the Glass, " that woman is still in this facility. But we know Rio wouldn't have had the most recent data."

"Maybe he took her with him" Z says, gazing at the woman. "I don't know how she would have traveled to Chicago on her own."

"Figures Rio rescued the white woman," Ishmael mutters, and Tasha allows herself the smallest of smiles.

Z turns from the image of the blonde woman and stands facing Roger. Her arms hang at her sides, but her body is tight, rigid.

"So you're blowing the place up?" Z says, and Tasha looks at her out of the corner of her eye. "Is that what you're going to do? You're just going to walk in and blow it up?"

"Well…," Roger says slowly. Tasha can almost see him planning his steps through the landmines of Z's face. "The plan was to go in, extract some information, and then…well, yes. Blow it up."

"With all those people inside."

"It's highly doubtful that personnel will still be in the Box. They were all likely removed to a secure location like the rest of Cybranu."

"I'm talking about the prisoners," Z says.

The words seem to echo. They hang there, suspended, until they seem to clatter to the floor. Roger swallows.

"The patients…I mean, the prisoners…"

Tasha thinks he might keep trying, but he gives up, swallowing whatever words might have come next.

Z stares at him, dead-eyed. If her face were to float, blue-tinged, between them, she could be a prisoner at the Box. But she's not silent like the prisoner.

"But why?" Tasha feels goosebumps rise unsummoned on her arms at Z's words. "Why did this happen? They *knew* this was going to happen. But why?"

Tasha expects a pause, but there isn't one.

"We're still trying to figure that out," Alexis says quickly, flopping back into the couch as if exhausted. It reminds Tasha of how tired she is: she realizes her temples are throbbing. She should be sleeping but instead of dreams her mind is full of conspiracies. She sneaks a look at Z, feeling guilty for her own exhaustion. Grief is supposed to keep you awake, isn't it? She wonders how many nights Z has been sleepless, thinking of her father, her brother, her sister. Or maybe she's like Tasha, who had withdrawn into a cave after the death of her parents, the permanent departure of Leona. Tasha had slept and slept, wanting to do little else. She'd lost weight, and remembers Gina telling her how hot she looked, a funeral home advertisement personified.

LaBrenda powers off the Glass.

"I think that's enough for tonight," she says, glancing first at Alexis and then around the circle. "We should go to sleep. Unless," she adds, a hint of a smile in her eyes, "you don't feel comfortable sleeping under the same roof with a bunch of terrorists."

Tasha snorts, wanting to say something sarcastic but finding nothing suitable in her drained brain.

"It doesn't even matter at this point," she says, raising her shoulders and then letting them flop down. "Just don't let me wake up again tonight with you breathing on my head and rummaging through my shit."

LaBrenda smiles a crooked smile. Tasha shakes her head inwardly. First Rio, now this. Rio, the shepherd helping those struggling on the South Side. LaBrenda, gardener for the oppressed. Does one have to be a terrorist to do some good in this world?

Something wakes Tasha again, closer to dawn. She almost shouts when she becomes conscious, her fading dreams telling her Roger is elbow-deep in her backpack. But the sound that stirred her from sleep wasn't Roger, or any of the gardeners. It comes from beneath her, from Z's bunk. The sound of breath running away, too quivery to be caught. Fully awake, Tasha realizes the bed is shaking ever so slightly.

"Z...," she whispers in the dark. Her voice feels too soft, too weak. Baby bird wings that can't manage to flutter down to reach the ears for which they're intended. But they do.

"Yeah," Z says after a moment. Her voice is damp, spongy. Tasha pauses, deciding how to phrase it: Are you okay? Are you alright? Words that signal the willingness to comfort. But then the bed shakes again, one small solitary tremble, a muffled sob.

Tasha pushes the blanket down to her hips, uses her feet to push it all the way off. The shirt she'd rewrapped around her braids comes loose as she gets up, but she leaves it.

Z is curled into a ball and Tasha curls around her, a leaf around a small, quaking pod. They say nothing, leaf nor pod. Tasha holds her until her shoulders stop trembling, until the storm of her breathing settles to a whisper. When Tasha finally sleeps she is still curled around her friend, remembering what it had been like to have a sister this close.

CHAPTER 11

Ishmael's face is the first thing Tasha sees when she opens her eyes. In some way, she had expected to, and doesn't jump as she takes him in. Z is gone, Tasha stretched out on the bed alone, and he crouches at the edge of the bunk, watching her. His eyelashes are so long, she thinks. Like a deer. She knows a man would not appreciate being compared to a deer, but she can't see why. Deer are fast and strong. A deer will total your car. A shame that acknowledging something's ability to destroy is the only way to make it appear masculine. But she doesn't say these things, only stares into the brown deer eyes before she gradually realizes how close he is and how her breath must be stale, her eyes must be crusty. She sits up.

"Chill," he says.

"I'm the only one still in bed," she says, ignoring him. "Again."

He moves back and stands as she swings her legs over the edge of the bunk, places her feet on the floor. He's wearing a clean set of clothes, she notices. She looks down. The front of her shirt still has a few spots from where she'd dropped a piece of asparagus at lunch yesterday. The spot glares at her and she glares back, hating it.

"Where's Z?" she says, looking back up at Ishmael, trying not to glare.

"Up top." He points.

"Why isn't the ceiling open?"

"They didn't want to wake you or—"

Tasha's annoyance spikes.

"Why? I can wake up when everyone else does. I'm not a kid."

He smiles with half his mouth.

"But Malakai is. I was going to say they didn't want to wake you or Malakai. They wanted to let him sleep. After last night."

"Oh."

They look at each other, him studying her with a half smile. She glances at his chest, the muscles creating a pattern of rises and falls through the thin blue material. Back to his eyes, wondering if he noticed.

"Z's been up since before dawn," he says.

"Doesn't surprise me."

"Is she going to be okay?"

He asks the question as if her word will put all doubts to rest. Perhaps he thinks there is some type of telepathy between women, an ability to assess each other's wounds, diagnose them. Tasha wishes this were true.

"We'll just have to see," is all she can say.

"Yeah."

"I'm going to go up and check on her."

"I'll meet you up there. Malakai's getting dressed."

They're weeding again, Tasha sees as she emerges from the stairwell onto the roof. It surprises her for some reason. She'd expected them to give it up now that their secret is out: terrorists don't care about tomato plants and leaf-eating beetles. She looks for Z but finds LaBrenda, kneeling in one of the beds of soil as she gently ties back a vine that has grown too heavy with tomatoes. She handles each leaf like a baby bird, her knuckles rounded, never rigid. Even her metal hand is as delicate as a paintbrush.

She looks up as Tasha approaches, then stands, dusting her hands off on her gray leggings.

"You're up," she says, a tentative foot on ice, testing.

"I'm up," Tasha agrees.

"You're leaving today."

"Yes, we are. Where's Z?"

LaBrenda nods toward the back of the garden.

"With Roger. Talking."

Part of Tasha wants to go check on Z herself, make sure she's okay. But she knows it would be an annoying thing to do.

"Huh," she says eventually. "Probably trying to convince her to stay."

"Yeah, probably."

"Well, she isn't," Tasha says, too hard, as if to Roger himself. "And he's not coming with us."

"No," LaBrenda says, then looks down at her tomato plant. "But I am." She leans down and plucks a velvety leaf from the stalk.

"What?"

LaBrenda looks up, raises one eyebrow only slightly.

"What?" Tasha repeats.

"You've got room. I need a ride. And this is time-sensitive. I don't have time to walk ten miles east to the strip for my own car."

"What?" Tasha says again, determined to be pigheaded.

"Come on, Tasha," LaBrenda sighs, and Tasha winces a little. She sounds like Tasha's father. It's the voice of someone with X-ray vision.

"Come on what?" she demands.

"Why does this upset you?" LaBrenda says. Her calm finds its way into Tasha's veins. Now LaBrenda is some soothing combination of Tasha's father and Dr. Rio: doctor voice, tranquil and probing.

"Because we have things to do," Tasha insists. "We're going somewhere. We have a route to follow."

"You think I don't know the route?" LaBrenda says, looking at her frankly.

"It's not whether you know it. Oh, you mean like *that*. Ha. Yes, of course you know the route, don't you? You guys and Rio. Birds of a feather, right? We don't need to ride in a car with more bombs. Been there, done that. Would like not to do it again. The end."

"They're perfectly safe until I trigger them," LaBrenda says.

Tasha's mouth opens and closes, twice. Somehow she expected, hoped, that LaBrenda would contradict her. That she'd stop toying with the tomato leaf and say, "Bombs? Oh no, this is just an exploratory mission!" Or, "Bombs?! Tasha, we don't actually blow things up!" But they do blow things up; Tasha knows this. She knows it all too well. If LaBrenda is sitting in the backseat, her bombs are in the hatch. They go together: two explosive peas in a pod.

"Think about what you just said," Tasha says, squinting. Frustrated, she wants to be angrier than she is. The pleasant ache in her scalp is thanks to LaBrenda, the neat rows of braids on Tasha's head that she'd admired in the gray mirror before coming up to the roof. Yesterday Tasha's tears had stained LaBrenda's shirt, and LaBrenda had given her comfort.

"I know, I know," LaBrenda says, sighing. She crouches again, the tomato leaf fluttering from her fingers to the ground. She doesn't continue right away, instead looks down at the rows of vegetables. Then, unexpectedly, she digs her hands deep into the soil. The hand that is flesh blends in with soft tones of black and brown earth. In the right light she could be a plant herself, a beautiful black stalk sprouting from the ground. LaBrenda stares at her hands.

"I've been doing this a long time, Tasha," she says. Her voice is soft; it barely carries up to Tasha's ears. "The gardening, not the bombing. When I lost my arm in that prison, I wondered how I'd hold a spade. I wondered how slowly I'd have to pick weeds, plant seeds, with part of me missing. They've been cutting off our arms, our hands, for so long, girl. I got a new arm. I have an opportunity to give us all a new arm. I want to give them an arm that'll last."

Over the stalks of the bed of soil before them, Tasha sees Malakai appear. He's still sleepy, his eyes a little puffy. He's twelve now—too old to cry, he would say; but she wonders if he has. She doesn't know how old he'd been when his father was killed, but she wonders how much sleep he has lost on account of that death; how many dreams became nightmares. She remembers how unafraid he'd been when she first found him on that South Side playground. Same world, new monsters. Somewhere a few hundred miles west of where Tasha stands right now, Amani is walking. Tasha pictures her crouching in their own little garden, her baby hands clutching the weeds her mama points to.

"And you think blowing up all these buildings will give us arms."

"Yes," says LaBrenda without emotion. Tasha can still hear it in her voice though: the bright, trembling coals that burn in her, ready for ignition. "Or at least the chance to use them."

Tasha bends to the tomato plant, fingers the round red orb, green at the stem where it's still becoming what it will be.

"Okay."

They leave an hour later, the dog prancing in the dust outside the Pentagon, excited to get back in Monica Potter's SUV. The goodbyes are brief: they all go down the row shaking hands quickly until Tasha reaches Alexis, who pulls her into a hug. "LaBrenda's my friend," she whispers in Tasha's ear, close enough to make her nape tingle. "You take care of her."

"I will," Tasha whispers, and realizes she means it.

Z and Roger hug but don't kiss, which relieves Tasha. Roger's stiffness tells Tasha he's a little relieved to see them go, though she's not exactly sure why. Probably many reasons.

LaBrenda hugs everyone, quickly. She reaches the end of the line where a silent woman the shape of a pear waits. The woman blends in: Tasha has to check to make sure she's actually seen her before. She hasn't spoken at all during their brief stay at The Pentagon. Tasha wonders if she ever does. The woman reaches behind her and hefts two lumpy backpacks, one larger than the other, hands them to LaBrenda with a look. Tasha averts her eyes, watching Alexis load other bags into the back of the car: potatoes, she says, along with some other vegetables. A dozen large packets of seeds for wherever LaBrenda ends up, to start planting again.

Malakai smiles at everyone. Like the poodle, he's excited to move on: boyish hope, maybe; thinking something good lies ahead. The garden had been pleasant, pleasant enough to soothe him a little, a salve over recent wounds. Maybe he's thinking the next place they stop will be even better; that the worst is behind them.

They hadn't unpacked much, but that which had been removed from the SUV goes back in; the dog ordered into the car and made to sit on the floor when LaBrenda climbs in. Everyone boards, Tasha settling into the driver seat and adjusting the mirror even though she was the last to touch it. What's behind her looks different now: she needs to adjust her view. They wave, especially LaBrenda, and then they're moving: the car starts without trouble and the sky ahead is without clouds. They're going, and it feels different than when they'd packed up outside Dr. Rio's house, the neighborhood gathered to either say goodbye or go themselves. It feels less like a ceremony now, just a matter of course. There are places ahead that need getting to. That simple. Once you've done some leaving, nomadism sinks into the bones; the feet get used to wandering; the eyes grow accustomed to straining for the horizon.

"Keep straight for sixty miles," Z says without looking up from the map, unfolded on her thighs. Tasha keeps straight, following the sun.

CHAPTER 12

They find Bianca's body a hundred miles from the Colorado border. They wouldn't have seen her at all if it weren't for Malakai.

Tasha has become used to steering around bodies. Depending on where in the road they are, sometimes she doesn't even have to slow down. A small turn of the wheel, the SUV becomes a smooth fish in white water, curving around corpses, still and hard like creek bed stones. But sometimes there are obstacles and she is forced to brake: an overturned car, or in this case a giant digital billboard fallen from its perch above the highway, obstructing the way with diagonal wreckage, several cars stopped around it, some smashed. Tasha had braked, the thrumming of wind outside the car changing its pitch. There was a body on the ground, laid on its back, but Tasha paid it no mind. There were always bodies, laid on their backs. Their sides. Sitting up. She tries not to look anymore: they could be trees, construction signs: unremarkable features of the landscape that run together, easily ignored.

She had steered delicately between the ruined signs and the shoulder of the highway. The body was just another thing to avoid. But Malakai looked.

"Wait!" he cries, his voice causing the poodle to yelp. His cry startled Tasha too: she almost thought the yelp was her own. LaBrenda sits bolt upright where she'd been lounging in the back, her face steely.

"What? What?" she says, not quite shouting, but nearly.

Tasha has already slammed on the brakes, the back of the car just having cleared the wreckage of the board.

"Sorry," the boy says, meeting her eyes in the rearview mirror, pulling his lips into his mouth to make a sheepish face.

"What is it?" Ishmael says, his body turned toward his brother. Tasha sees in the rearview that he's already grabbed the Chipotle mace from the floor of the car. It and his bicep flash in the mirror.

"Bianca," Malakai says, pointing through the rear window of the SUV. "She's back there. On…on the road."

"Bianca?" Tasha demands, straining her neck to look back. "From Rio's house? Out there? You mean, dead?"

Malakai nods.

Tasha looks over at Z, whose nostrils are slightly flared. They haven't seen any Minkers, but Tasha knows enough not to assume this means there are none. In any case, she decides with a quick look around that there are none in the immediate vicinity, and throws the car in reverse. She backs up a few feet, then turns off the car.

"Stay in the car," Ishmael says. Tasha assumes he means Malakai and goes on unlocking her seatbelt. As she reaches for the car door she hears Ishmael's voice again. "Tasha."

She glances back at him and then looks again, harder.

"Wait, me? Why?"

"I'm going to check it out."

"What, by yourself?"

"I'm going to check it out," he repeats.

She snorts.

"Nah."

She opens the car door—pausing to fish the Wusthof from her backpack—and steps out onto the dry road, dread making her move slowly. Behind her, before she closes the car door, she hears Z say, "If anything you should stay with Malakai. We'll be right back."

In the end, they all get out of the car, LaBrenda last. She shrugs at Tasha.

"Even the dog got out," she says. "I wasn't going to just sit there alone."

Her shrug draws Tasha's eye to the metal object in her hand. "What's that?"

LaBrenda holds it up for her to see.

It's a trowel, a small handheld shovel with sharp edges and a dangerous-looking point. Tasha purses her lips in approval, nodding.

"But watch this."

LaBrenda moves her thumb, presses some unseen lever or button on the handle of the trowel. Immediately, three prongs snap out of the sides of the tool, halfway down the metal blade. They make a thin, metallic sound that almost makes Tasha jump.

"Another invention of your mom's?" Tasha says, holding out her hand to inspect it. Behind her, Ishmael and Z are making their way over to inspect the thin body on the pavement. Tasha wants to pretend just a moment longer that it's not Bianca.

"No," says LaBrenda, passing Tasha the tool after returning the prongs to their hiding place in the handle with the press of another button. "It's just a trowel. You use it to pull out stubborn roots. Seemed appropriate."

"Indeed," Tasha says, taking it. She stares down at it. Another thing that has been taken away from its purpose to deal with this stupid apocalypse. She holds it alongside her kitchen knife, clutched as always in her other hand. She can barely remember what it had been like to cut chicken breasts with it. Even if LaBrenda is right and blowing up these hubs will kill all the Minkers, this blade will never cut chicken again. How could it, after all this? She presses the lever on the side of LaBrenda's trowel: the prongs spring out. She still jumps at the muted metallic clang.

"It's her," Z calls from Bianca's body.

"I know," Tasha replies, but not loud enough for anyone to hear. Of course it's her. Somehow Tasha had known Bianca would never make it. Maybe she's been avoiding looking at the bodies on the road with that specific fear in mind. She feels a small irrational spark of anger at Malakai: why had he been looking? Why did he have to see? But she knows it's right that he did. Otherwise Bianca would have lain here forever, her body decomposing unnoticed, one of millions of anonymous skeletons. That wouldn't be right.

Tasha finally finds herself standing over Bianca's body. Ishmael goes back to the car to wait with Malakai, distracting him with the dog while Tasha and Z stand with Bianca. LaBrenda waits nearby, appearing to keep watch for Minkers. But Tasha can see she's just trying to give them space.

"How long do you think?" Tasha says to Z. They stare down at Bianca. She's on her back with her shoulders slightly turned. Her eyes are closed, thankfully; her eyebrows slack and relaxed, giving her an expression of being unbothered by the place her body came to rest. Her mouth is slightly open, that's the worst part: her teeth look like a dead person's. Which they are, Tasha thinks. Her lips look like a dead person's lips.

"I don't know," Z says, rubbing the back of her neck. "A day? Two? She doesn't look too bad. But she's starting to…swell, you know."

"Do you think it's different, what happens to dead bodies that had the Chip and those that didn't?"

"We think so," LaBrenda says from where she stands nearby. She's been listening, of course. "We've seen some intel that suggests the Chip fortifies the organs while it's in the body. Even when it's destroyed, its effects preserve the body longer than an unChipped body."

"A happy, healthy, easy life," Z says in a singsong voice, mimicking the old advertisements. Tasha feels a chill travel down her spine.

"How did she die?" LaBrenda says. She's taken a step toward where Z and Tasha stand, but pauses there.

It's not a real question. A real question would be "Did Minkers kill her?" As it is, "how did she die" is a placeholder; a softer phrase for an unpleasant thing: like saying "bathroom" instead of "shithouse." Tasha's not a coroner, and she's already learned there are only two ways to die in this world. By Minker, and by something else.

"Not by Minker," Tasha says. Bianca's body is unbloodied except for the slightest red crust around her right nostril: a soft, rusty tint that never trickled down to her lips. Her clothes are untorn, her hands are relatively clean. She's not murdered. Just dead.

"Heart attack, brain aneurism. Could be anything," Z says. She can be so cold sometimes, Tasha thinks. Her voice is like a hand swiping crumbs from a table. Brisk.

"Why is she alone?" LaBrenda says. She's standing there with them now, looking down at Bianca's body. It suddenly feels strange—hunters looming over the carcass of a deer—and Tasha crouches instead, lays a hand on Bianca's arm. It's warm, but from the sun overhead, not life. Her skin feels like marble, and under its former bronze sheen Tasha thinks there's a tinge of green. The body giving up on itself, she thinks, giving in, becoming soil.

"She wasn't supposed to be," Tasha says. She takes her hand off Bianca's arm, rubs her fingers together, as if death might transfer to her skin, creep up her arm. "She was supposed to be with a caravan from Chicago."

"Is she on route?" LaBrenda says, directing her eyes at Z.

"Yeah. I mean, we are. So I'm assuming the others are taking the same way. It's the route Dr. Rio mapped."

"They're definitely driving, not walking," Tasha says, looking up at the sky. Anywhere but at Bianca. "There's no way they'd still be this far ahead if they weren't."

"Why wouldn't they be driving?" LaBrenda says.

"Rio wanted us to walk."

LaBrenda raises an eyebrow.

"He didn't trust machines," Tasha says, almost apologetically. "It was just…I don't know, the way he was."

"Maybe Bianca was the only one driving," Z says. She crouches down now too, looking at the body more closely. "Maybe the rest of them wanted to walk and she said fuck that."

Tasha smiles at this thought, studying Bianca's face. Bianca wanted to do what she wanted to do. Tasha could easily see her breaking away from the group if she was tired of walking and the rest of the group didn't want to take a car.

Tasha looks at the cluster of cars smashed around the digital board, one of them with four bodies in various poses and stages of decomposition. The doors of most of the cars hang open, bent metal wings on the carcasses of grounded birds. Tasha stands to look at the nearest vehicle, a late-model electric car with both of its two doors closed. There doesn't appear to be any blood splashing the windows inside. It could be idling, waiting for its driver. Tasha goes over to it, peers inside.

She recognizes the backpack as one of Rio's, and opens the door quickly to retrieve it. The air inside the vehicle is hot, stifling. Tasha's arm swims through it to grab the bag, which she pulls out and holds up for Z to see.

"Yep, she was driving. Alone, it looks like." The car doesn't have any other belongings in it. No sign that Bianca had a traveling companion.

LaBrenda goes over to the car, bends down inside, curling her neck to see around the steering wheel. She fiddles with something by the column, and Tasha hears a ding.

"Out of power," LaBrenda calls over her shoulder. "Or at least close. She wouldn't have made it much farther."

Tasha opens Bianca's bag, peers inside. Cans of beans. A few packages of the space food Rio had given them. She doesn't seem to have eaten much from her original supply: maybe she'd been eating at stops along the road instead. Tasha looks at Bianca's body. Thin with age, not with starvation.

"What do we do?" Z says softly. Tasha reaches into the bag, feeling around until her fingers come in contact with the stiff edge of what she knows is a picture frame. Tasha smiles. Rio had told her to throw it away: Tasha had even helped her take the photos out. But here it is, Tasha sees, withdrawing it from the bag. She shields the photo from the glare of the sun, gazing at it. Bianca's face beams up at her, the old woman's thin brown arms draped around the shoulders of two grinning children. Too young to be hers. Grandchildren, perhaps. Their teeth are gapped and white, the sun in their eyes making them squint.

"Bury her?" Z says in the same soft voice. Tasha looks down at Bianca. It seems her skin has gotten greener just since Tasha touched her body. She wonders if maybe her gentle touch started a chain reaction, a release of chemicals that will send Bianca even further from the person she had been. Without meaning to, Tasha thinks of standing at the gates of her parents' kennel in Kentucky, she and Leona each carrying a jar of ashes. The jars weren't labeled: they had no way of knowing which jar contained which parent. Surely they were mixed; perhaps even containing ashes of other people's loved ones—grandmothers, sons, taken too soon. Surely, Tasha thinks, the crematorium

220 OLIVIA A. COLE

didn't bother cleaning the furnace for people as insignificant as those without MINK. Why would they? Either way, Tasha wishes there were a crematory for Bianca. Burying her in the lonely dirt alongside the highway seems wrong.

LaBrenda holds up her trowel.

"It would take a long time with just this, but I'll help if you want, Tasha," she says.

Tasha doesn't look at either of them.

"Maybe we put her back in the car?" Z murmurs.

"No," Tasha says. "No, we'll leave her here. This is where she wanted to be."

"On the road?" Z says, slowly, as if asking Tasha if she understands what that means.

"Under the sky," Tasha says. She turns away. This is where she lay down, she thinks. This is the spot she chose. Who are they to change it?

She bends down and gently places the picture frame on Bianca's chest, letting her hand rest there for a moment. She thinks of Vette, her Snicker bars, and feels a sudden stab of regret for not taking her body back to the stadium. She should have left the food, taken Vette instead. Vette hadn't chosen the corner store, but Bianca chose this spot on the road. Let her keep it.

She hopes Malakai doesn't ask, and he doesn't. They get back in Monica Potter's SUV, leaving behind another dead woman, another woman left under the sky. She'd never had the chance to see her parents' bodies—burned before she and Leona arrived—but since the Change she has seen too many bodies of people she has known, however briefly. For a moment Tasha just sits, staring through the windshield.

"Her car was out of power," she says eventually. No one replies. She presses the ignition key. The car trembles once, its shudder barely noticeable. She looks down at the energy bar on the dash. Still green. At the very bottom before yellow. Yellow isn't bad, she knows. There's still all of yellow and orange to go until the meter slips into red, glaring red that will put a stop to their progress.

"Not even yellow yet," Z says, sounding positive. In her eyes, yellow is enough: maybe not enough to get them to California, but enough to get them somewhere acceptable to stop. Somewhere with other cars, or with power. But suddenly yellow seems like nothing to Tasha. The vast expanse between her and Leona is wider than ever, dry and hot and the sun glaring red overhead like the meter on the car will be all too soon.

"Do we think she separated from the caravan?" Ishmael says.

"Yes," she says.

"They may have passed her without even knowing," he says. "Like we almost did."

"Most likely," Tasha says, still staring at the meter.

"But you have no way of telling whether your people from Chicago are ahead or behind?" LaBrenda says. She's trying to keep up. Tasha doesn't bother helping, not right now.

"My mother's caravan is way ahead," Ishmael says solidly. "They left days before us. Even if they walked they'd be ahead of us still, as many stops as we've made." Tasha thinks she hears a bite in his voice. He wants to be angry at someone. He's afraid now that with all the bodies they've passed on the roads, one of them could have been his mother's or his brother's.

"We could take the SkyDrive," LaBrenda says from the far backseat of the car. She says it innocently enough, but Tasha thinks she must know what she's suggesting. Tasha glances up into the rearview and finds LaBrenda's eyes already on her.

"It's off-route," Tasha says without feeling. At this point she doesn't care about the route, about Rio's rules, but the SkyDrive makes her uneasy. They'd passed close enough to it in Iowa to see the cars zipping along on its tracks, their pods unmanned by anyone living. The SkyDrive is like blood still flowing through the vegetative body of the countryside. The body lies dead and prone, but the vein still pumps with life, transporting mechanical cells along the track toward whatever limb they're borne to. Tasha can see them from here still, though tiny: the specks of vehicles illuminated in blue. An enormous cross-country Volamu. The thought gives her a sudden unexpected pang for Chicago. The SkyDrive had never made it that far: they'd started building in Nevada, hoping to make the country smaller, hoping to defuse the tension in California and reel it in. They hadn't known it was destined to separate itself, a shift as unchangeable as the continental drift. Tasha pictures the SkyDrive as giant glowing sutures stitched across the broken face of the States, an unfinished job as the architectural surgeons were chased from the table.

Californians had destroyed the Los Angeles stop, of course, not long into its construction. It had been on all the web stories that week, President Walker stirring the pot as he raged about the dangers of divisiveness in the face of economic turmoil. It had been just before the secession, the final straw breaking the dromedary back of President Walker.

"They're not interested in unity!" he'd said about "the Western terrorists." "And so we must not be either! We must stand strong in the face of subversive forces that seek to divide us!" It had been an impassioned speech—one of the interns must have been pretty worked up to write it. Then President Walker had bombed California, and the letters from Leona had stopped for awhile. Tasha had feared her dead for two months until the next envelope came, rumpled and smudged.

"It would get us to Phoenix a lot faster," LaBrenda says.

Tasha glances at Z to gauge her reaction to this mention of Phoenix. They haven't talked about it, haven't acknowledged the specter of her brother hanging between them all like a lurking piñata. To her credit, Z doesn't bat an eye, and Tasha doesn't ask. There's no point, she knows, as Z will only lie. Tasha would have lied too, back in Chicago. If someone had asked her if she planned on risking her life to run inside Fetch Fetchers for the possibility of finding her mother's ring, she would have lied. Or maybe not even known the truth yet herself. Z will say she has no intention of setting foot inside the Box when LaBrenda goes to plant bombs and extract intel. But Tasha knows the same way she knows that Z's brother is dead that when they get to what Tasha imagines to be high barbed gates, Z will want to go inside. And why shouldn't she? Her father's unavoidable death left uninvestigated in Chicago. Her sister's fate unknown in distant New York. Dragon is something she can see, maybe even touch—even if the only thing left to touch is a corpse.

"Ish?" Tasha says. He's silent and still in the backseat. She moves her eyes from Z's face to his in the rearview. He's gazing out the window, at nothing.

"I need to catch up with them," he says softly and Tasha grips the steering wheel a little tighter, her throat constricting.

"They're fine, Ish," she says quickly. She lets go of the steering wheel, turns in her seat to face her passengers. The dog stands quickly and aims its pink tongue at her face. She dodges it. "Malakai? They're fine. We're gonna get to California and they'll be there waiting, you'll see."

"Who's this?" says LaBrenda, leaned forward and looking from face to face, searching for the story. She's been trying to put the pieces together on her own and now sees an opportunity to ask.

"My mom and my brother Marcus," Malakai says.

"We're going to catch up," Tasha says.

"The SkyDrive would definitely accomplish that," Z says to no one. "Does it stop in Phoenix?"

LaBrenda nods. Tasha wonders if Z noticed; she's looking out the window. Z's not thinking of Ishmael's mom. Her own blood is on her mind.

"So?" says Z. LaBrenda doesn't say it, but Tasha can feel her thinking it, can feel all their opinions streaming out of their skulls and filling the car with buzzing. Only the dog is without specific desires, gazing at her from between Ishmael and Malakai. Tasha can hear the swishing of her tail. Above, one of the digital billboards still standing around the wreckage of their comrade carries the smiles of two white women who are almost terrifying in their airbrushed state, grinning maniacally with teeth like squared-off tusks. They stare down at Tasha with eyebrows too arched, obliques too pinched and shiny. They make her shift in her seat, staring down at her through the car window. She wishes she could draw drapes closed to block out their eyes. She starts the car.

"So?" says Z again.

"We'll take the SkyDrive," Tasha says. Her backpack is on the floor between her feet, tipped over and blocking the accelerator. She yanks it up onto her lap. Even it seems to have an opinion. "I'm Prada!" it whines. "I shouldn't be on the floor!" She shoves it to her left side, against the car door, hoping that will satisfy it.

"Good," says LaBrenda. Tasha doesn't even look at her. How different is she from Rio, really? She's loaded the backseat of the car with explosives, urging them toward a building she wants to blow up. Yet Tasha can't picture throwing her and her bomb collection out of the car. How could she? She pats her braids, which tingle, puts the car into drive, and steers them toward the SkyDrive.

The drive-on platform to the SkyDrive is empty, as Tasha knew it would be. She had hoped, however, that she'd be wrong: that the portals that will carry Monica Potter's SUV toward Arizona would be clogged with the metallic corpses of cars, cages for their raging drivers. And there are some, Tasha sees: a Minker peers out at her from the back window of a brand-new Honda. The battery on that beauty would last them all the way to California, she notes, and considers suggesting they kill the Minker and take the car—skip the SkyDrive altogether. But LaBrenda speaks before Tasha gets a chance.

"The SkyDrive will charge the car too. By the time we get off in Arizona we'll have plenty of juice to get you all the rest of the way to California."

Tasha hears "you all" and notes the missing "us." She says nothing.

"I didn't know it charges the car too," Z says. It's the voice of someone who wants to sound as if they're being convinced when they never needed convincing to begin with.

"Yep. All we need now are snacks. Like taking the train."

"We have snacks!" Malakai says brightly. "From Whole Foods."

"Once we get onto the track you can go in back and get some," Z says.

So we're doing this, Tasha thinks. *Okay*. She's never liked rides— maybe this is the source of her anxiety. Her dad's grandmother Noni used to tell a story about a girl she'd heard of in Kentucky who'd had her feet chopped off on an amusement-park ride. Tasha feels her ankles give a sympathetic throb.

"It's not as high as I thought it would be," she says. She hasn't edged the car forward into the port yet. She studies the SkyDrive—this is the closest she's ever been. The name "SkyDrive" is actually a bit ambitious, considering how low the structure is to the ground. "Sky" is a definite imaginative stretch. It resembles a squat Golden Gate Bridge, with a framework encasing it, but not enclosed like the subway. She can see pods whistling by, some carrying cars and some not. They could so easily become a different kind of ride, and Tasha mentally gnaws her nails. Bumper cars, perhaps. How close are they to the thirty-day mark since the Change? Could the tracks grind to a halt at any moment, sending cars crashing against each other?

"Ready?" Z says, glancing at Tasha. They're wondering why she's not already driving into the port. She swallows. *Okay*.

She steers the car forward, feeling a slight bump as the tires roll up onto the paddock. The car shudders slightly and so does Tasha. She turns the steering wheel slightly but finds it locked: the SkyDrive has already latched onto the car.

The windshield illuminates, and Tasha jumps a little. It's the same pale blue as the glow of the rest of the structure, and the previously silent speakers of Monica Potter's SUV suddenly breathe a little, a slight change in the kind of silence they emit. When the digital woman appears in the windshield, her voice comes through the speakers.

"Thank you for using SkyDrive," she beams at them. "Please select your direction of travel."

The woman fades a little, and two boxes with gently rounded corners appear in front of her at waist-level, as if she's offering them. One says East, the other says West. When Z leans forward and presses West with her fingertip, the boxes disappear and the woman glows brighter again.

"You are traveling West, thank you. Please select your destination."

She fades again, offering more boxes: Salt Lake City. Denver. Phoenix. Las Vegas.

"Front door service," LaBrenda says from the back.

Z taps Phoenix. Tasha can feel her eagerness, her hope. She hasn't been stupid with her hope in the past, but Tasha thinks that may have changed. Tasha weighs potentially dangerous hope against the fact that the trip will be faster. They've never actually agreed to go on this mission, and yet they hadn't needed to. They were always going to go.

"You are traveling to Phoenix," the woman in the windshield says. She's like a small glowing genie, popping out of a digital box to offer them wishes. "Your fare will be deducted from the account registered with your license plate. You may disengage your seatbelts once on the track. Please enjoy your journey, and thank you for using SkyDrive."

She smiles a seductive smile—no matter what is being sold, the smile is always seductive—and then fades out of the windshield. Tasha glances up at Ishmael in the rearview, but he's still looking out the window.

The car is advancing forward, but not by Tasha's volition. The paddock is moving, carrying them forward to approach the port entrance of the SkyDrive. Pods whiz by in front of them every so often, some carrying cars. But they're moving too fast for Tasha to see if they're occupied. She's been assuming they would be filled with dead people, but now she wonders if maybe there are other survivors like her, being borne east or west to check on relatives.

"What happens now?" says Malakai. He's leaned forward in his seat, seatbelt straining across his small chest. He's eager; excited for the same reason that Tasha is afraid: it's like a ride for him.

Before anyone can answer him, their paddock moves smoothly and swiftly forward, the frame of their carriage being merged onto the track by the vast robotic mechanisms of the SkyDrive. They pause, and then the pod containing their car rises, crossing an invisible bridge over the eastbound track, and lowers again onto the westbound track. Then they're moving. It reminds Tasha of the old dry-cleaning place her grandmother used to take her when she was a little girl, the last of its kind in the city: shirts on a mechanical line being moved quickly back and forth at the whim of the operator. Tasha feels like one of those shirts: whizzing down the line, dangling on a hook. She realizes she's still gripping the steering wheel. As the world zips by them on either side—empty pods zooming by in the opposite direction every now and then—she slowly releases the wheel and lets her hands fall into her lap. She's not driving anymore—the SkyDrive carries them faster than she could ever drive.

"Malakai, how about those snacks?" Z says, and Tasha can hear the smile in her voice.

Malakai glances at Ishmael, who nods, and the boy eagerly whips off his seatbelt and moves to the back of the car, reaching over the far backseat alongside LaBrenda to explore their piles of food from Whole Foods. Tasha thinks it's a bit like a road trip and allows herself to smile too. Not so bad.

Her backpack is still in her lap, pressed against the door, and she opens its flap, reaching past the Wusthof for a granola bar. She's sick of the honey flavor and wishes Dr. Rio had stocked other kinds: oatmeal or raisin or something. But she tears off the yellow wrapper and nibbles it anyway, glancing out the window. She realizes there's a bit of a gap between the eastbound track and the westbound track: she can see the ground blurring beneath them through a break that looks to be a little less than the width of a car. The sight of the ground comforts her. Not too tall. Has she always hated heights? Or, like so many other traumas, had that begun in the Apiary with Dr. Rio?

She finishes her granola bar and stuffs its wrapper back into her backpack, tucking a t-shirt around the blade of her knife before withdrawing her hand. She won't need it for a little while, and if she decided to use the pack as a pillow on the ride she'd rather not impale her skull.

"It's almost like being underwater," says Malakai.

Tasha unbuckles her belt and turns in her seat, pulling one knee up to her chest to rest more comfortably. Malakai has one palm against the glass, gazing out at the blur of the world zooming past. She can see why he'd say underwater. The bluish glow of the SkyDrive gives everything an aquatic quality, the sky beyond the framework not sky but ocean. Looking at Malakai, she sees him as a small Captain Nemo, charting unexplored depths of the ocean in this, his submarine. Will they still be traveling in this pod when night falls? By then he'll be an astronaut borne for the far reaches of the galaxy. Can he still grow up to be anything in this world? Could he ever?

"So, Brenda," says Z. "What's the plan when we get to Phoenix?"

"Did you just call me Brenda?"

Z pauses.

"I mean, yeah. Just a shorter version, you know."

Tasha looks past Malakai at LaBrenda, who is smiling a small smile. One eyebrow, though, is arched a little more than usual, Tasha notes.

"I'd appreciate it if you'd call me LaBrenda," she says. Tasha looks to Z.

"Brenda is in your name though," says Z. She's turned in her seat like Tasha now, seatbelt off. "It's not like I called you, like, Marsha."

LaBrenda laughs, a real laugh.

"Marsha? Is that a name?"

"Yeah, sure. It's a name."

"Well, thank god my name's not Marsha," LaBrenda says. "But it's not Brenda either."

"It's just a nickname," Z says. "Like Z. I'm Azalea and I hate my name, so I go by Z."

"I don't hate my name though."

"But…"

"Z, for god's sake, she wants to be called LaBrenda! That's her name!" Tasha bursts out.

Z turns to look at her with her eyebrows high. Tasha feels her face spark into a burn. She had been a little loud, a little sudden. She shoots a look at Ishmael, who is no longer looking out the window. His eyes are on her. He looks surprised, but she thinks she sees a smile on his lips, somewhere behind the beard that gets thicker every day.

"Anyway," Tasha says, tearing her eyes from his mouth. "Good question, Z. What's the plan?"

She looks at LaBrenda, determined not to notice Z's eyes still fastened on her. Eventually she can feel Z turn to look at the back of the car as well.

"Well…," says LaBrenda. She pulls her legs up into the seat to sit cross-legged. Tasha notices she's taken off her shoes. She has to speak up a little to be heard over the hum of their traveling car. "I have Dr. Rio's Glass. Roger found some data in the files that should help me get inside the Box if everything is still locked up. Security may or may not be high. We're not sure how the staff left the location before the Change, since Rio's intel is a little old. Could be swarmed, could be clean. I really have no idea."

"But if it's not?" says Z. "Swarmed, I mean."

"If it's not, then I'll find my way to the control room, extract some data if possible, and then…um, drop off the package, you know."

Tasha darts her eyes at Malakai, but he's looking out the window, this time up at the impressive framework of the SkyDrive.

"Seems simple," she says to LaBrenda, who grins.

"It ain't gonna be. But…well, that's the plan."

Malakai turns to look toward the front of the car.

"Is a movie going to come on?" he says.

"What?" Tasha looks back at the windshield to find that the illumination has returned to the glass, glowing the way it had in the port when Z had chosen their destination. "Do they have movies on the SkyDrive?" Tasha directs this question at LaBrenda, who shrugs.

"Not sure. That'd be cool."

"It would be weird," Z says, turning to the windshield. "I haven't even thought of movies. Like, at all."

Tasha doesn't say that she has, that since the Change she has thought of movies and actors and storylines almost daily. The vintage movies from the '90's and '00's that she'd planned to make her thesis before dropping out of college; their gaudy soundtracks and their strange, rambling dialogue. Those and newer movies too she's thought of: she's not sure if it's because of her course of study or because the world is now so much like fiction.

A woman appears in the windshield, though not the SkyDrive woman. This woman has Tasha's complexion, but her features are changing before Tasha's eyes. Adjusting, slimming, shading. The face is becoming Tasha's.

"It's an ad," Tasha says, feeling both embarrassed and annoyed. The SkyDrive must come equipped with MMDs, which are now registering her appearance and adapting so that the digital rendering resembles what they perceive to be the consumer.

Some things, however, don't mirror Tasha. Her hair in the windshield is long and straight, not the curly explosion she knows it to be now. Her skin is a few shades lighter, her nose slightly slimmer. Her lips don't look quite as round either.

"Hey, it's you," Malakai laughs. "It's like on the train in Chicago."

"Not quite me," Tasha says, trying to keep the edge out of her voice.

The face has all but finished rendering, though a loading bar appears faintly in the corner of the windshield. Gathering data, she presumes. Searching for extra angles to use to sell her things. Some ad platforms had the ability to collect sensory data—body temperature, heart rate—for even more advanced targeting. Tasha looks for the exit button as the face that is almost her face beams at the car and opens its mouth to speak.

"Enjoying your trip on the SkyDrive?"

The face waits and Tasha almost answers her, rudely, but instead leans forward to peer at the edges of the windshield for the exit button. They always hide it.

"Do you have an appetite? I'm compiling a list of restaurants based on your profile and destination."

"She's like a nicer version of you," Malakai says, still laughing. Tasha ignores him, annoyed. She wonders if this is what Ishmael thinks. If this version of her is someone he would prefer.

"She's not nice, she's brainless," Z sniffs. She's placed her hand on the dashboard, also looking for the exit key.

"Perhaps you would like to see nearby spas and salons," the face beams. The loading bar in the corner of the windshield is nearly full. When it's solid, Tasha knows the ad will have even more things to offer. Tasha would rather smash the windshield than listen to more suggestions from the Wonderland version of herself.

"Shut it off," LaBrenda yawns from the back.

"I'm trying," Tasha says.

The bar is full, and suddenly the face that is almost Tasha is beaming directly at her, her eyes shining and her smile wide.

"Natasha Lockett," she says, her voice cheerful. "I know what you like."

A second or two passes before Tasha realizes the car is slowing down, the blur of the world becoming less blurry, the colors solid, the shapes real. The car is slowing, slowing, then grinding to a halt on the track, like a pea caught in the throat of some massive neck.

Malakai is alert, sitting up in his seat like a soldier, his eyes wide.

"What's going on? Are we supposed to be stopping?"

"No, we're not." Tasha is bobbing her head around the steering wheel, looking for something she might have unintentionally hit to disengage from the SkyDrive. Her heart is hammering in her chest. At least they haven't gone crashing through the framework, but why are they stopping?

"The eastbound track is still working," Z says, her voice tight. As if to confirm her words, a pod across the short gap whizzes by, the wind from its momentum rocking Monica Potter's SUV.

The feeling causes Tasha's stomach to lurch, the sensation of a thousand beetles materializing in her guts.

"I can't tell if pods on our track have stopped too or if it's just us. There's none around," LaBrenda says, peering intently out the back window. "Something must have happened with the power?"

Tasha's hands are shaking. She grips the steering wheel to steady them.

"Please remain in your vehicle," Tasha's almost-face in the windshield beams.

"Shut her up," Tasha snaps.

"I can't find the exit button," Z says, leaning closer to the dashboard.

"It's there," Malakai points. "On her pants. On her belt."

He's right: the slightest "x" outlined in a faint box, right on fake-Tasha's belt buckle. Z presses her finger to it quickly, the woman in the windshield lingering for a brief, awkward moment of starey smiling before disappearing in a blip. Tasha hadn't noticed the buzzing coming from the car's speakers until the advertisement has withdrawn and the sound faded. She expects silence, but doesn't find it.

"What's that sound?" she says, listening hard.

No one speaks, everyone listening. There is the faint hum of the SkyDrive, almost as quiet as the Volamu despite its size, aside from the occasional whoosh and rock of an eastbound pod whizzing by. But there's something else: an occasional muted punctuation in the silence. Ragged, almost like a yell but more like a bark…

"It can't be…" Z breathes.

"Drive, Tasha!" Ishmael says. "Drive!"

"I can't!" Tasha yells. She stomps on the accelerator. No response. The car is in the SkyDrive pod, operating under its command. The lights of the dashboard are illuminated, the ignition area glowing, but the pedals are useless, the steering wheel locked. She slams her palms against the wheel. The pain shoots up her arms and she slams again and again. "Fuck!"

"We need to either get the car unhooked or return power to our pod," says LaBrenda. She's already opening her car door, already moving, already deciding. She's put her shoes back on, Tasha sees, her trowel is in her hand. With its prongs tucked in it's just a shovel, nothing more. She looks so comical it's tragic. A lady off to tend her garden. She throws open the back door, her metal arm shining, and in comes the sound that they hoped they hadn't actually heard. Minkers, barking.

"Where are they?" Z says. She hasn't moved. Only her eyes are in motion, peering and scanning. "Where are they?"

"I don't see them," Tasha says. Z's motionlessness has infected her: deer syndrome, its terror sunk into her skin and holding her bones. Headlights all around, freezing her in place. Where are they?

Tasha's door is thrown open and she screams, scrambling. Her knife is in her backpack, it's fallen to the floor.

But it's LaBrenda, her metal arm reaching in and grabbing Tasha's bicep. Her mother used to grab her there, a sudden bolt of memory. She looks blankly into LaBrenda's face.

"Tasha!" she shouts, so close that a tiny spit droplet lands on Tasha's cheek. She gasps: the idea of someone's spit on her face jerks her consciousness away from the approaching sounds of Minkers and into this moment. Angry, she swipes at the tiny dot of saliva on her cheek.

"Come on!" LaBrenda yells. "Help me!"

Tasha's foot is caught on her backpack. She stumbles out of the car on one leg, reaching back to untangle her ankle. Once free, she swings the backpack onto her back and runs to the front of the car where LaBrenda is bent.

"The track still has power," she says. "The connection has just been fucked with. I don't know how to fix it yet, but I can fucking fix it!"

Tasha had stupidly expected the track of the SkyDrive to be an actual track: a moving tread like a treadmill. Instead, the pod that holds their car connects to the upper framework of the SkyDrive, much like the dry cleaner of Tasha's memory. She turns and gazes westward down the track; she can make out the receding shapes of pods continuing toward the last stop, where she guesses they revolve and then come back east toward Iowa. It's not the track: the power is fine. It's their pod.

"Of course," she says. "Of fucking course."

Before Tasha knows it, LaBrenda is climbing on the hood of Monica Potter's SVU. Not understanding, Tasha nearly climbs after her, the sound of approaching Minkers echoing from somewhere she can't see. LaBrenda turns and points her trowel.

"Stay on the ground! Kill any that come up. It's okay, Tasha! We can be okay."

"But…what are you going to do?"

LaBrenda ignores her and is on the roof of the car in seconds. She's fiddling with the column that connects their pod to the upper framework of the SkyDrive, her trowel held in her teeth like a pirate doing some electrical work.

Tasha turns her back on LaBrenda and the car. She swings her backpack to the front of her body to yank the Wusthof from where she'd wrapped it in a shirt. She steps toward the driver door, intending to toss the backpack into the car, but there's no time: the Minkers have arrived.

Three of them, she sees—coming across the eastbound SkyDrive track. They stumble wildly forward, eyes on her. Their mouths are wide open, eyes squinted angrily, as always. They cross the road like mad chickens, not checking for traffic.

A pod hurtles east, obliterating one of them. Tasha involuntarily throws out her hand like a traffic conductor, her palm forward in a horrified and belated "stop." She has no idea how fast the pods go—must be well over a hundred miles per hour—but the pod had appeared so quickly that she'd barely heard it. There's nothing left of the Minker. She doesn't even see any blood, or pieces. Gone. She looks back eastward, expecting a blur of metal and death bearing down on her like an impossibly fast and massive hawk. There's nothing. But she's not stupid enough to believe that will be true for long.

The surviving Minkers lumber across their track and growl toward her. They pay no mind to gap between the east and westbound tracks, the one Tasha had peered down through to see the ground. It's like an empty river between them, but they are confident in their intentions, their teeth bared with purpose, hands rising as they approach; ready to claw, snatch, grab, choke. Are they going to jump across? Are they capable? She has witnessed their stupidity for weeks, but somehow whenever she faces them, she grants them supernatural abilities. They're almost to the gap. She readies herself just in case.

They fall. They plummet down through the empty space between east and west, their expressions unchanged as they disappear from her sight. It's not as shocking as the Minker being hit by the pod, but the effect is the same: they were there one moment and the next they're gone. Tasha resists the urge to step forward and peer down to the ground: it won't help her acrophobia, for one thing, and she knows they won't be dead anyway. No satisfaction to be had there. She doubts the fall would be enough to kill a regular person, let alone a Minker.

"Tasha!"

The tone whips her head around. It's Z, screaming, the terror exploding from her mouth like a swarm of bees. She's half in and half out of the car, the box cutter clutched in her hand and pointed up at the sky. Even with Z pointing, Tasha looks back instead of up; looking for pods hurtling down the track to obliterate their small dam in the river.

"Tasha!" Z repeats, this time with a tone of *what the fuck are you doing*.

Tasha follows Z's finger this time, and now she sees the Minkers.

They're like human spiders, creeping from the metal roof of a shed. Before she even feels the fear, she wonders at their agility: they come from above, holding on to the metal frame of the SkyDrive with grim determination, sliding down the beams before reaching for another hold. Some of them fall, plummeting down from the framework to the tracks. Then Tasha realizes they're not falling.

"They're jumping," she says breathlessly. Human lemmings mindlessly flooding off the cliff toward their destination, their eyes on Tasha and the car. Where did they come from? Where have they been hanging out, and what dog whistle brought them rushing to this place?

The first one to land on the tracks breaks both legs. Tasha sees them splinter inward and outward at the same time, matchsticks spearing through the denim of his pants. The Chip seems to have difficulty repairing the breaks: the Minker flails there on the ground, barking in frustration, his eyes and arms reaching in Tasha's direction as if he might kill her that way, by glaring.

"LaBrenda!" Tasha wails. There's no way she can kill them all, not without a machine gun or some other weapon that might mow them down. If only LaBrenda were already in Phoenix, raiding the Box. Suddenly the bombs in the trunk seem like precious cargo: LaBrenda on top of the car attempting to jumpstart whatever system has failed them is Noah patching a leak in the ark. Their little ship must carry on.

"Almost!" LaBrenda yells. She's stuffed her trowel into her back pocket, where it pokes out like a spiny tail. She's doing something with her hands, the metal one glowing a little like it's on fire.

"What are you doing?" Tasha screams. One can only scream things in times like these. Everything is electric: words cannot be just words, questions cannot be just questions when Minkers are dropping to the tracks like comets, putting their bones back together so they can pick themselves up and come to kill.

"I'm fixing it!"

"Tasha!" Z has stepped away from the car, her box cutter drawn. Ishmael too, on the other side. Tasha glances at Monica Potter's SUV, the faces of Malakai and the poodle gazing out through the windshield. The poodle, in the driver's seat, looks poised to steer them both away from this madness. Tasha wishes she could.

The Minker with the matchstick legs, repaired now, staggers across the track. With a quick look, Tasha searches for another pod to come barreling down on him, but there's only the long empty track, endless and metal. She turns back to the Minker. She has to do it herself.

Ishmael beats her to it, the Chipotle axe swinging like a shining blur. It sends the Minker spinning to the ground, blood arcing away to disappear onto the tracks. Another smash of the axe and the Minker doesn't move, no black tentacles oozing out to repair the wounds. Another is approaching, nearing Tasha. It trips on the smooth metal of the tracks, falling toward her. She swings the Wusthof like a golf club, cleaving the Minker's throat open. It's not enough, she knows, and she kicks it hard in the stomach, wobbling a little, which brings it down to its hands and knees. She goes for the flashing dot on the neck, gouges it with the tip of the knife.

Behind her comes a mechanical whirring, and her heart nearly explodes, assuming a pod has finally come to sweep them off the track. But it's their own pod: LaBrenda has done something to make it work, something that has brought the blue light of the SkyDrive back into the eye of their pod, the mechanical vital signs spiking to show life. Tasha peers up at LaBrenda as Z shoves a Minker against one of the columns of the pod, hacking at its neck. LaBrenda's index finger is pressed against part of the column like the digit of God poking Adam, glowing somehow. The metal hand is like a welding gun, sparks flying from it in a blue shower that turns white as it falls down over her arm. She doesn't feel it, of course.

Two more Minkers are stumbling across the tracks, their eyes fixed on Tasha.

"Why are you so obsessed with me?" she screams, lunging at one.

"It's like they don't even see me!" Z shouts, intercepting the one on its path toward Tasha. Her razor finds the Chip under its ear efficiently.

The sound of Minkers' bodies striking the tracks as they hurl themselves from above is repetitive and dull, a thudding sound occasionally accompanied by a clang as one of them strikes a rail in just the right way. There are too many now, Tasha knows, stabbing another and putting it down. They're like wasps crawling out of an unseen nest, swarming toward her.

"We have to go!" she says, yelling without meaning to again. The yell comes out all on its own, fear turning her throat into a megaphone.

"One more thing," LaBrenda shouts back. Her glowing finger has become two glowing fingers, her human hand holding the trowel, pulled from her back pocket and now being leveraged as a screwdriver. Nothing is ever just one thing, Tasha thinks. No one is ever just one thing.

"We need to go *now*," she shouts. She hears her mother in her voice, suddenly and without warning. A shadow pours into her throat, filling her body with its gray weight. Her mother is dead. Her father is dead. Now she might die too. The idea of Leona, the last, alone on this planet absent of other Locketts, makes her eyes fill with tears. Or maybe Leona is already dead too. Tasha wants to slap herself, almost does slap herself.

"LaBrenda," she says, begging, but through her tears she sees LaBrenda climbing down from the roof of the car, jumping from the hood and slashing an approaching Minker with the trowel.

"Let's go, Tasha!" she says, almost smiling. Tasha knows the smile. She had worn it when fleeing the Apiary with a bomb ticking behind her. Adrenaline, fear, excitement, invincibility. She blinks back her tears, grips the knife a little tighter, and runs toward the car.

The car is already moving toward her.

"It's moving," Z shouts, sprinting to the passenger side.

"It's going to be moving a lot faster in a second," LaBrenda yells. "It's hooked back to the SkyDrive's power. Hurry!"

Tasha snatches at the door handle of the driver's side. The car is picking up speed and she sidesteps awkwardly to catch it. The car bumps a Minker who has followed her, a middle-aged guy who stands several heads taller than Tasha. She immediately thinks of the Minker who had killed Vette. His neck was too high to get at easily. She doesn't have time for this.

She kicks savagely at his knees, hoping to break one or both of them and give herself time to open the car door. It works, a little: he stumbles, but falls toward her, one hand catching in her hair, the other grabbing her chest. She feels her breath catch. She swings the knife, slashing his face but not his neck, kicking again. He's too close, the car moving too quickly, his body in her way.

"*Move!*" she screams. Z is inside the car scrambling to open the door for her. She shoves open the door and it knocks the Minker sideways, but not enough to make him fall. Tasha chops at him with the knife, using her other hand to open the door wide enough to slide in. The poodle is in her seat now, barking loudly.

"Move, god damn it!" Tasha yells. The car is moving faster; she's jogging to keep up, her backpack jolting around on her back with every pace. Whatever LaBrenda did to their pod, the SkyDrive has it firmly in its clutches again, slowly gaining speed to what will soon be hundreds of miles per hour. She definitely doesn't have time for this.

She feels teeth on her forearm, and for a moment thinks it's the poodle. But it's the tall Minker, his gums bright like

Bubblicious, his teeth mossy and bared. He doesn't have time to sink those teeth in: she punches him hard in the face, enough to loosen a molar, and breaks his grip. He's behind her now that she's chased the car, but it only takes a moment for him to shake off the punch and catch up, trotting and barking. Her arm throbs where he'd started to bite her, more with the memory than with pain. Her head aches with the voices of everyone in the car screaming at her to get in: she can see LaBrenda in the backseat, half-standing, her mouth moving quickly, telling her something she can't hear. The poodle in her face, barking, it too yelling at her to get in. Don't they all know she's fucking trying?

She lunges forward, sideways, forcing her hips into the car and hoping the rest of her follows. One leg in, one arm in, holding onto the steering wheel like it's the fin of a dolphin surging onward in the ocean. A shark is at her back, his teeth raging. In the corner of her eye, just beyond the Minker, she can see the still-comforting colors of the earth beneath the SkyDrive—green in some places, warm constant brown in others. It's all beginning to blur as the pod carrying the SUV picks up speed: the sound of the wind becomes a thing she notices in her ears, her braids flapping behind her like kite tails. She wants to let go of the knife in her left hand, use both hands to grip the steering wheel and drag herself fully into the car, but she can't: the dog is still in her seat, Z screaming at it, trying to drag it backwards. Tasha hears the dog snarl, sees the teeth flash. Or maybe those are the teeth of the Minker, bright and white and coming for her elbow again. His human teeth tear into her skin, the pain flowing up her arm to her brain, where it explodes in bright light. She lets go of the steering wheel, turns to stab, slash, punch.

Then she's floating. A moment of weightlessness, of supreme lightness, before she's falling, her head slamming against the tracks, where she lands with a grunt. The world is turning black, beautiful calming black, when her clouding eyes find the shape of another pod hurtling down the track toward her, a blur of speed and hum far away but not for long. Monica Potter's SUV is gone, Z is gone. Ishmael is gone, thundering off toward Phoenix. Maybe she'll just lie here, be blown apart, a red mist like the Minker before. She almost does. But as the light fades, the feeling of blood oozing from her scalp through her hair and down her forehead, leaving her heavy and empty, she twitches.

Not yet. She twitches, has no energy. Her body isn't hers. The blur of the next pod approaching: she is a fragile branch in its path. She twitches, rolls. Then there is no more metal. Only air. She's falling. Good.

CHAPTER 13

Tasha's mother cracks an egg into the skillet. Tasha hears the oil pop from where she sits at the kitchen table slicing peaches. Leona steals one, stuffs it into her mouth. Tasha glares, brandishing the knife. It's a small blade that has only ever cut food: peaches, potatoes, apples. Its metal is shiny and wet. Tasha wants to lick it but does not. She must be squeezing it too hard: her hand throbs, stings. She lays the knife down, rubs her hands together. Leona grins.

Their mother brings them plates: eggs, potatoes, toast.

"Turkey sausage is almost done," she says, sitting to Tasha's right. Her skin shines, a little sweaty from the heat in the kitchen. Tasha's sweating too: too much to just be sitting and cutting peaches.

"I'm vegan, ma, remember?" Leona says, sliding her eggs onto Tasha's plate, who rolls her eyes. "I don't really need the bread either." She keeps it, though.

"You're gonna starve yourself," Tasha says, chewing.

"Not with all these peaches you cut," Leona says. "We're only making one pie, Tasha, damn."

"With you eating all of them, we'll be lucky if we get to make a tart."

244 OLIVIA A. COLE

"The dogs are barking again," their mother says from by the sink. Tasha hadn't noticed her stand. She's looking out the window. Tasha joins her, then Leona. They stand there together, looking down the green hill at the rows of chain-link pens. Tasha hears them too, their barks and whines rising and carrying up to the house in distant waves.

"There's daddy," Tasha says, pointing. He's there, tall and tan and walking down the empty row at the center of the kennel. He carries a red bucket. Even from this distance she can tell he's looking at the window, at the three of them. He raises a hand to wave.

Tasha waves back, eagerly, squeezing her mother's shoulder with the other hand. The kitchen is so hot, with her mother and sister standing so close, but she wants them nearer still. The dogs bark and bark, greeting her father. She wants to bark too. She squeezes her mother's shoulder, tighter and tighter until the pain in her hand makes her gasp.

The pain is what wakes her. Her hand, but her head too. Her shoulder. Her back. Her arm. It takes her brain a moment to reassemble the last thing she remembers. She's looking around for Z and the others when she remembers Monica Potter's SUV being carried off by the SkyDrive, the screams of those inside it, seeing her left behind on the tracks. With the pain all over her body, she thinks for a moment that she was actually hit by the oncoming pod. But her face is in sparse grass and there's dirt in her mouth. She's on the ground. She fell.

She must still be dreaming. She hears a dog barking. Not a Minker, a dog: shrill, angry barks, the sound only a canine makes. She can't move, not yet. If a dog is going to attack her, there's nothing she can do about it right now. Her hand seems to glow with pain. Her forearm throbs where the Minker on the tracks had bitten her.

The barking dog won't shut up. It goes on and on, and Tasha thinks it sounds a little hoarse. She squeezes her already-shut eyes even more tightly closed. Her skull must have a crater down the front of it. That's the only possible way it could hurt this badly. She groans, but it's barely a groan. It's like a gurgle. Babies gurgle, she thinks. I'm a half-dead baby.

She doesn't really want to be a half-dead baby. She opens her eyes, which is actually just one eye. The other eye is either swollen closed or pressed too tightly into the ground to open all the way. She can't tell. Everything hurts.

The first thing the open eye does see is her bloody hand, her mother's ring glinting wetly. It's the blood that's wet—shiny and almost rude in its redness. At first she thinks her hand has been severed, the way it just lies there inertly. But she can barely summon the energy to feel upset about this. LaBrenda has one hand: she's still hot.

But her hand is not disembodied, she sees. She can make her fingers wiggle, all of them. It's just lacerated, a deep cut along her palm. From what, she's not sure. So her fingers can move. What else can she do?

Slowly, slowly she turns over onto her back, inch by inch, her body screaming with each inch. She finds that it's difficult, as her backpack is still on her shoulders like a hump keeping a camel from rolling over. She settles for lying on her side. Once there, she thinks it's okay to say she's not paralyzed. She might have a crater the size of the Grand Canyon in her skull, but she's not paralyzed. Gathering her strength, she slowly sits up, using all the strength in her wobbly arms to help.

The barking dog, she sees, is the poodle, standing on three legs and snarling at two Minkers nearby who are in worse shape than Tasha. One of them is in two pieces, its body separated neatly into legs and torso, but that doesn't stop it from snarling in Tasha's direction, its eyebrows knitted and its eyes blank. The other one is in one piece but the Chip had repaired its splintered legs badly: one is so crooked it's almost the shape of a lightning bolt. The other leg appears to be backwards.

Tasha wants to mock him but she can't muster the energy that mocking would require. Besides, the poodle is making enough noise for both of them, froth dripping from her mouth in rage and probably thirst.

"Dog," Tasha says weakly. It's really only a squeak at first. She tries again. "Dog. Hey, dog. Andromeda. Whatever your name is."

Hearing her voice, the poodle turns back to look. She won't be diverted so easily. She looks at Tasha with her ears pricked, then back at the Minkers, barking again as if to say, "Do you *see* this shit?"

"Come here, girl," Tasha sighs, closing her eyes. The sun is so bright. Her tank top is wet at the armpits and lower back. It's hot. "Come here."

The dog comes, limping. Her back left paw is held up in a curled way, as if the ground is too hot for that one foot and she doesn't want to burn it.

"Did you fall too?" Tasha says. She manages to hold herself up with one arm and uses the bloody hand to pet the dog's ear gingerly. "How did you get down here?"

The dog pulls her head away to smell Tasha's hand. She gives it a small, sympathetic lick.

"Yeah," Tasha says. "I'm a little worse off than you."

The dog sits down beside her, growling in the direction of the Minkers every now and then. Tasha pulls her legs under her to sit cross-legged, and has little trouble doing so. The pain blooms in her hip but only a bit: in general it's her shoulders and back that seem to have taken most of the punishment. She wonders if she'd hit her head again when she'd landed on the ground, or if the pain is from the tracks alone. She wants to lift her hands to feel her skull, gauge the seriousness of the wound, but she can't bring herself to do it. Who knows what her fingers might find? Not now. Not right now.

She leans back against her backpack, feeling the can opener prod her ribs through the canvas. That's probably what caused some of her injuries, she thinks. Landing on a can of black beans. At least she hadn't landed on her knife.

Her knife.

Where is it?

She feels panic that even the crater in her head hadn't spurred. She's unarmed. She's damn lucky the two damaged Minkers had been unable to reach her, but the luck won't last forever. She's in the middle of nowhere with nothing but a few cans of food and an injured poodle. And with her own injuries, she's sure she won't be able to run. Fuck.

"First things first," she grumbles, and leans forward off the backpack, contorting her shoulders and one arm enough to pull down the straps. She drags the bag around from behind her, and pauses to assess how she feels after that tiny bit of exertion. Fine. Mostly fine. The pain in her head and her hand makes her slow, but she feels okay. While paused, her eyes rest on the backpack. Prada. The label is there like the eye of a familiar friend, comforting. She rubs her thumbs over it. Alone, she doesn't wonder if Ishmael or the others think she's foolish. She remembers Malakai looking bemused in his mother's kitchen: Aren't there cheaper backpacks? Yes, but they wouldn't be this one. She knows this one, and it knows her. She hugs it to her chest for a moment before opening the flap and digging out the single bandage from Dr. Rio's house and her last clean t-shirt. Clean is relative, of course, after being housed in the bag with everything else, but it hasn't been worn so it's her best option. She wraps it around her hand, wincing as the cotton comes into contact with the flesh, and ties it as best as she can. It immediately comes untied, and she grits her teeth. It's hot. The sun watches her attempts at bandaging with keen interest and she inwardly tells it to fuck off and quit being so nosy. She doesn't have the energy to say it out loud.

When the t-shirt finally stays tied around her hand, she uses the bandage to wrap her head. She's glad for her braids, at least, which keep her hair off her forehead. She wraps her head until she runs out of bandage, ties it off, then gets out the canteen of water she'd been given by Dr. Rio. She shakes it, noting the smallness of the resulting slosh. About half full, she thinks.

"Half empty," she says out loud, slowly gathering her strength and pulling herself into a standing position.

The dog stands too, on three legs as before.

"Sorry, dog," she says. "I'm not a vet."

The dog looks up at her, its beautiful, ridiculous hairdo sprinkled with dust. Tasha feels guilty under the stare of those brown eyes. At one time she would have known exactly what to check for on the dog: where to feel for breaks, how to wrap whatever needed wrapping. Where had that knowledge gone? And why does she feel afraid to look for it?

"Sorry," she mumbles again, feeling foolish but not enough to not say it.

She takes a few steps, waiting for the dizziness to seep down her spine from her skull. She feels nothing, only pain. The backpack feels as if it's weighing her shoulders down, stretching them away from her neck and turning her head into a balloon floating on a string. The blood leaking out could be helium, her balloon shrinking and shrinking until there's nothing but string, curled in the dust between the straps of her backpack. It doesn't seem so bad.

The dog growls as they pass the bodies of the Minkers, and Tasha pauses, looking at them. They growl and snap, flailing toward her like salmon on some dry hot bank. The one with the broken legs actually makes some headway, dragging himself awkwardly by the arms, determined to bite her ankles if nothing else. She takes a step sideways, instinctively reaching for her knife. Then she remembers she has no knife, nothing with which to finish off the Minkers.

She peers up at the track above, the sun in her eyes from farther west than it had been when they'd boarded the

SkyDrive. She wonders how long she'd been out, if Z and the others have made it to the next port, or if they're already in Phoenix, breaking into the Box. She can see LaBrenda telling the rest of the group that they have a mission to fulfill, and that Tasha is gone. Z wants to find her brother. Ishmael wants to find his mom. LaBrenda and her one-eyed Rooster. Everything they care about is ahead, not behind. There's no reason they'd turn back, not for her. She feels her eyes well with tears. Left behind.

The Minker with broken legs wiggles closer and she glares down at him. He has ruined everything: he and his kin. Every time she has something, every time she's given anything, MINK takes it away. Her dream swims back to her—her father and the red bucket, her mother cracking eggs, her sister eating peaches. Tasha draws back her leg and kicks the Minker as hard as she can. She wants him to grunt, gasp, something that tells her he's human, but there's nothing. If she's bruised him, the Chip is already erasing the damage, her mark. She kicks him again, in the ribs. She kicks him again, in the stomach, so hard he flips onto his back. She can feel the impact of each kick through her Nikes, but she kicks him again, her breath hot and ragged, her face wet. Tears, sweat, blood: she's not sure which she's tasting in her mouth. She kicks him again, his snarls constant, his body shifting in the dust.

Something's shining under him, and she thinks immediately of the MINK cards she's seen so many of them carry. She wants to smash it. She stoops to reach for it when the Minker in two pieces grabs her ankles from behind. He'd been inching toward her, a path in the dust behind him like the dry trail of a slug. His hands like vices, he yanks, bringing her down hard onto her hip as she swivels to keep from face-planting onto the other Minker. The one behind her has his hands trapped under her and he pulls to free them, his mouth wide open. The broken-leg Minker eagerly scoots over to join the fray from where Tasha had kicked him, his eyes bright and dull at the same time, his mouth a round, sharp hole. Tasha sees two of his teeth are broken, making him look even more like a shark. She kicks at his face as she struggles to stand up. She wants to break more of his teeth. But her head throbs with every movement, making her kicks weak. The three of them wriggle like a wrestling match in a hospital wing. She feels tired, too tired.

A brown blur joins the struggle, with something like a roar and a squeal. The Minker with broken legs snarls louder and struggles against the newcomer, which Tasha realizes is the poodle. The dog is almost screaming: the sound raises goose bumps on Tasha's skin. It's the sound that would send her and Leona running to the kennel with brooms: dogfights, when teeth would fly like white swords and the only way to stop it was to use long wooden handles to separate the beasts.

Tasha has no broom and doesn't want one, of course. But she doesn't have time to watch the poodle attack: the half-Minker snarls at her back, its teeth crushing against her butt through the denim.

"Are you seriously biting my ass?" she pants, struggling away from it now that the dog is distracting the other one. Her foot strikes something in the dust, the metal object she'd been stooping for when Halfsie grabbed her ankles.

The Wusthof.

She almost screams with delight and scrambles to reach it. The brown whirlwind that is the poodle is attacking the Minker only inches away from it, and years of training warn her to not reach for it: the dog might bite her too. But she needs it, and she flounders away from Halfsie while stretching out her feet to reach the blade. She drags the knife toward her with the toe of her Nike, reaching for it with her fingers when it's out of the danger zone. When she finally has it in her grip it's as if one of her hands *had* actually been disembodied and now feels sewn back on. She holds it tight in her right hand and shoves off the ground with her bandaged left, pain lancing up her arm, and staggers to her feet. Once standing, she feels more than a little dizzy and sways, her vision clouding and then clearing. At the center of it all is the upper body of the Minker wiggling closer to her in the dust, its hands sweeping through the dirt searching for ankles.

She stabs him quickly where she knows the Chip is buried. The knife sinking through the flesh slows her heartbeat. She knows this. She's done this. Business as usual.

She doesn't wait for the sparks to stop before turning for the remaining Minker, who is still being harassed by the poodle. The dog's snarls are more fearsome than his, more insistent: every time the Minker attempts to sit up or move—which is over and over—she leaps on his chest in a flurry of teeth, her front paws scrabbling at the Minker's chest. Without lower body strength, the Minker flops back helplessly with each assault.

"Down, girl," Tasha says, standing above the scene. The dog pricks its ears back for an instant before closing its jaws around the Minker's forearm again, previous wounds by the elbow already closing as her teeth leave more punctures. "Down! Dog! Off! Quit!"

One of the words is something the dog has heard before and she reluctantly backs off, her muzzle wet with blood and slobber.

Tasha dispatches the Minker quickly with one slice and it topples back onto the ground for good, a small cloud of dust rising and then settling. She looks around for more— something she should have done sooner—but sees nothing. She wonders where the swarms of them from the SkyDrive went. Still up there, she guesses, gazing upward with a hand over her eyes to shield the sun. She hopes they're roaming the tracks getting smashed by westward pods, one by one. She thinks of Z and Ishmael, pictures them continuing west, Z in the passenger side with the map on her lap as usual. LaBrenda in the drivers seat, perhaps, guiding them toward Phoenix; Tasha and the poodle transformed from friend to anecdote: just one more bloody punctuation mark in the story of their journey west. Not even a period but a comma, a brief pause before the story goes on without her.

She decides to stop picturing this and instead sets her eyes to scanning the horizon to the west. There she finds the shape of buildings, some low and some high, far but not too distant. A few miles, maybe, nothing but flat land between her and them.

She hears snarling and turns to her left, alarmed. She'd put her knife through the necks of both Minkers: if they were animating once more, she had a problem on her hands. But it's not the Minkers: it's the poodle, her teeth bared at the two—three, depending on how you viewed Halfsie—bodies in the dust. She curls her lips back to reveal her beautiful white fangs, her glamorous head fur quivering a little. Tasha laughs.

"They're dead, warrior princess. Don't worry."

Saying it, something like a light bulb flickers alight in her mind. A memory of an old, old movie. A show perhaps? Remakes upon remakes. A warrior princess: as pretty and tough and absurd as Tasha's (only) companion.

"Xena," she says at the dog's blinking eyes. "That's what I'm going to call you."

She thinks Malakai would approve, but the thought of the boy makes her throat tighten, a feeling like homesickness overtaking her chest. So she settles her gaze back on the horizon and slowly begins to walk.

"Come on, Xena."

CHAPTER 14

She ends up having to carry Xena, the dog's limp becoming more and more pronounced with each mile. Eventually she had begun to yelp with every step, lagging far behind, until Tasha turned, feeling guilty, and bent to examine her paw.

The dog winces at Tasha's inspection, and shows her teeth a little before flattening her ears apologetically. Tasha's careful fingers explore the bones beneath the dusty brown fur, searching gently for breaks. She finds not a full break, thankfully, but a minor fracture, her hands charged with memory when she discovers it. It had been her father who'd taught her about dogs—her mother was the business brain behind the kennel—and in a flash of something like light and something like a slap, she remembers her dad holding her hand as a child, guiding it through the forest of a sheepdog's fur, showing her fingers the break buried there. Xena needs bandages and anti-inflammatories. So does Tasha, she thinks, looking down at her own paw.

"Sorry, girl," Tasha croons into the velvet ear. "I'm sorry."

She turns to look at the buildings they've been trekking toward. Another mile, maybe a little less. They've already walked at least five, the sun on Tasha's chest dampening her entire shirt with sweat. She looks down at Xena again and sighs, stowing the Wusthof in her backpack before bending down to scoop her up. The dog doesn't wriggle—she seems too tired to protest. Tasha carries her a few steps, stops to readjust, and then walks some more. By the time she's walked a half-mile she's drenched in perspiration, beads of it running down into her eyes from her scalp. The dog has settled into a limp tote draped across Tasha's arms. She whimpers every now and then but is mostly silent. They both pant, from heat and from pain and from thirst. Tasha wants to stop for water but that would mean putting Xena down and she might not be able to force herself to pick her up again. So she staggers onward, the buildings ahead looming closer too slowly.

Approaching what is revealed to be a town, Tasha sees that she's been walking parallel to a road, which curves toward her now that their paths to meet the town. Like the town, the road is small and dusty. Neither of them is actually road or town, really, but pale versions of each; either forgotten or only half-dreamed, the things that might make them real either missing or not fully formed. Pavement, in the case of the road; storefronts, in the case of the town. There are no cars except two: one appears to be missing its tires; the other's front sits on top of a fire hydrant. The hydrant is broken but there's no evidence that water had ever gushed from it: no mud, just the endless dust. The wide, silent street looks to Tasha like the empty Western settings she's seen in so many films: quiet and yet sinister in some unobservable way. It's for this reason that she walks a block or so down the street, nearly staggering with the dog, and checks the windows of the stores for lurking Minkers. She finds none—she finds nothing, actually. The stores are empty, of wreckage and of normalcy. They're empty. Is she hallucinating?

She tries to put Xena down carefully, but her knees buckle as she squats and the poodle topples a little, dumped onto the sidewalk unceremoniously. Tasha expects her to yelp but she's quiet, panting softly, her ribs rising and falling quickly as she slides down on her side to rest. She's in pain. Tasha feels the same way, sighing shakily as she reaches behind her to swing her backpack off her shoulders. Her neck feels bruised by its weight, but it can't be. She's walked much farther with it on her back and with more items inside it. The pain in her head makes everything worse. She plants her butt on the sidewalk next to Xena with a thump that almost hurts. She digs the knife out of her bag, just to have it with her, and then she and the poodle just sit there, silent except for the panting of the dog.

Eventually she fishes out the canteen from the backpack and drinks, one long swallow followed by another. She knows they're not in the desert, but the sun feels different here. She wishes she had a compass, but only Z, in her assigned role of navigator, had been given one of those by Dr. Rio. She does, however, have a map, which she hasn't looked at since they left Chicago, as Z had hers out constantly. But she doesn't really need either: at one point her sense of direction had been pathetic, but now she feels the west calling to her bones like a sparrow, migrating to a new land. California had seemed so much closer when she'd been in the car with Z and the others: her fear of the SkyDrive aside, it had been an arrow connecting two dots she desperately wanted to bridge. Now she's floating somewhere in between, Nebraska—probably Colorado at this point—spread out around her like the edges of a vast green gown she'd rather not be wearing. The town she's found herself in is alone for miles as far as she can tell, aside from the glowing line of the SkyDrive running there a few miles away. If the SkyDrive is a conveyor belt, the town is a box that fell off on the way to its destination, happened to remain intact, and then has merely sat unopened until Tasha came along. Its emptiness soothes her and unsettles her simultaneously—she briefly imagines claiming it as Lockettville and never leaving. She and the poodle, growing old and gray together, sitting on this curb in silence. She would put the knife on a mantel someplace where she would allow it to collect dust as a symbol of the bygone need for stabbing things. She sighs, and places her hand gently on Xena's hip, which twitches slightly as if Tasha's hand might be a fly. The dog whines softly.

"Your dog's bleedin'," says a voice nearby, a gentle voice like a toddler. Xena's head jerks up, the motion of which surprises Tasha more than the voice itself. Her hand snatches up the Wusthof, of course, but her heart's rhythm doesn't accelerate. She's not afraid and she's not sure why. Perhaps she's too tired. Perhaps her head hurts too much to allow her to be distracted by fear.

The voice comes from a woman younger than Tasha: a girl, really. She's fat and brunette, freckles sprinkling her nose like a dusting of brown sugar. Brown eyes, skin slightly red at the cheeks and nose with apparent sunburn. She's beautiful, Tasha decides, with a shyness that gives her a disarming quality. She nods at Tasha.

"You're bleedin' too."

Tasha shrugs, not taking her eyes off the girl.

"I thought I might be. You always sneak up on bleeding people?"

The girl looks bashful, smiles and looks away, across the street. Tasha looks too, in case someone's there. There's no one. The girl shrugs with one shoulder.

"I coughed when I came up. You didn't hear me, I guess. You were thinkin'."

"Yes, I was thinking."

"Did you get in a car accident?"

"Something like that."

"Is your dog okay?"

"She's not my dog," Tasha says, and then feels guilty, glancing at Xena to look for hurt feelings. "She's nobody's dog. We're just…hanging out."

"Do you need help?"

Tasha looks at this girl, eighteen at most, her eyes squinting but only because of the sun. It must be around two in the afternoon. Maybe later. The light has just passed the irritating stage of starkness that characterizes twelve to one. The girl stands alone, not leaning, not hiding, but still somehow not showing her full self. At one point Tasha might have chalked it up to shyness and shyness alone—now she searches the girl's face for malice, for the streak of lunacy she's seen in those like Amy, and even before the Change in people like Cara. She doesn't find it in the girl's round face, just curiosity.

"Where are all the Minkers?" Tasha asks. The town's ghostly silence is beginning to make her anxious. The SkyDrive had been crawling with them. Had this little burb been their home base?

"You mean the crazy people," the girl says. She doesn't look afraid. "There was only one person here who went nuts. We locked 'em up."

"We?"

"Yeah. Me and my friends."

"Where are your friends?"

"At the dorm. They sent me over to check you out. Since we're both girls."

"Oh. Um, okay."

The girl looks around awkwardly.

"I can take you over there if you want."

"Where is it?" Tasha says. She feels wary but also stupid for feeling wary: the girl is so shy it's like flinching from a butterfly. The idea of carrying Xena another mile makes her feel lightheaded. Her forehead feels wet: she hasn't reached up to touch the bandage but the girl had noted blood and the idea makes Tasha nauseated. Her hand throbs too: the t-shirt wrap does nothing for it. She wonders if the bite on her arm is bad. She realizes she hasn't looked.

"At the end of the street and then over a little," the girl says. She crosses her arms over her pudgy belly, chews on her lip. "We have medicine," she says at last.

Tasha doesn't look at her, her elbows on her knees and her head hanging between. If this is bait on an awkwardly laid trap, she's almost willing to walk into the box where the carrot waits on a hook. She shows the girl her knife.

"I have no problem using this," she says, and she means to add a threat to the end: *if you try anything!* But she can't quite form the words: it feels silly and cinematic. The girl doesn't reply. Tasha thinks she sees her turn to look over her shoulder, back toward where the dorm must be.

"What are you doing here?" Tasha asks after a moment.

"They sent me over to talk to you."

"No, I mean here. In this town."

"Do you need help getting up?"

Tasha squeezes her eyes shut, blocking out the concrete, her feet planted there as if they'll never move.

"Yes," she says.

They walk slowly down the street, the girl carrying Tasha's backpack and Tasha carrying Xena. She's put the knife carefully into her back pocket and it pokes her a little with every step, but not too hard if she takes short strides. The dog doesn't feel as unbearably heavy as she had before, but Tasha's glad they don't have far to go. The girl carries the backpack in one hand, glancing down to admire it.

"Is this real Prada?" she says softly as they walk along.

"Yeah."

"Where'd you get it?"

Tasha feels her nostrils flare slightly.

"At Prada."

"Oh."

"Why is this town so weird?" Tasha says, renewing her question as they pass more empty stores. "Is this even an actual town?"

"Sort of. It was actually a film set."

For a big production, Tasha learns, a remake of something that the girl hadn't even known was a remake until Tasha tells her. The studio had built the town as both a set and a camp for the crew to facilitate a yearlong shoot; when the film wrapped, everything was left as is. Water and electricity shut off, but the buildings still standing, empty and dry.

"So you worked on the set?" Tasha says, she and the dog both panting.

The girl giggles a little, looking at the ground.

"No, I came with my boyfriend, and some friends. We call it Camp Hollywood."

"What does that mean? You guys just came and started living here after the set closed?"

"Pretty much. His friend Rick was a sound engineer's assistant and when Rick saw they were just gonna leave it, we came to check it out. We were just going to stay for a couple weeks. Party and stuff, you know. But then Rick went crazy and we had to lock him up. Me and my boyfriend went to a real town for a doctor and that's when we realized it wasn't just Rick."

"So you came back here."

"Yeah, we came back here. This is the dorm," the girl says, pointing.

Like the other buildings on the silent street, the dorm is a sandy brown color with large windows like a department store. Unlike the other buildings, though, the dorm's windows are shaded with heavy maroon curtains. They remind Tasha of the curtains at the Pentagon where she met LaBrenda, and she can't help but feel a little anxious at the sight of them. What do they hide? She's afraid of what's beyond them.

But she doesn't have to wonder for long. The glass door between the two large windows swings open and two skinny white boys come out, one shirtless and the other wearing a red tank top. On the chest of the shirt is a skull with roses for eyes, leaves and diamonds on its face, and the words "Phuk Phuket." Tasha has no idea what it means.

"Is this her?" Skull Boy says, gesturing at Tasha, and she sees him right away, sees not just the skull on his shirt but his own skull and what's inside it.

"I'm her," Tasha says, squatting slowly to put the poodle down carefully. The knife almost falls out of her pocket as she bends, but she reaches around to grab it before it does. "Who else would I be?" At one point she might have thought this and not said it out loud, but the pain in her head removes a lot of filters, along with every drop of patience.

The boy in the skull shirt looks at her then, his face showing the insecurity of his youth and, too, the arrogance of a young man who has recently found himself to be in charge and enjoys it. He looks at her for only a moment before returning his eyes to the girl.

"Is that her backpack?"

"Yes," Tasha says.

The girl shifts her eyes from him to her, looking uncomfortable.

"What's in it?" he says roughly.

"None of your fucking business," Tasha snaps.

"Empty it out," he says, pointing at the ground.

Tasha steps forward then, pointing her knife at the girl, the tip unwavering and aimed at her face.

"I'll take that back now."

The girl hands it to her quickly, not looking at the boy, whose expression seems to wilt. He twists his mouth sideways with a look that might be nervousness. His eyes dart up to her forehead.

"What happened to your head?" He sounds more like a teenager now, backing away from whatever pulpit he was testing out before.

"I fell," Tasha says. She stares at him coldly, in case he should start feeling like a big man again.

"Must have been a bad fall," the other boy, the shirtless one, says. His tone is the verbal equivalent of surrender. Skull Boy looks at him, and Tasha thinks maybe he'll say something sharp, but he doesn't. When he looks back at Tasha, he has fully returned to seventeen.

"We have bandages," he says, addressing the pavement. "And stuff."

He turns awkwardly, one arm jerking as if it wanted to motion her to follow but changed its mind halfway. The shirtless boy gives Tasha something between a smile and a shrug and follows his friend inside. The girl joins them. Tasha hesitates for a moment, and then she and Xena slowly enter the dusty building.

The room inside is shallow: the back wall is only thirty feet or so ahead, the sunlight from the large front windows barely reaching back even that far. A flimsy-looking staircase fills the left side of the room, its rails draped in t-shirts and a few towels. There's no furniture to speak of except for three or four folding chairs, the plastic dull and green, one of them leaning drunkenly to the side. The floor is littered with bottles and trash. They'd come here to party, the girl had said, and they'd done just that. The smell of sweat and dust kindles a sneeze in Tasha's nostrils that doesn't fully form.

"Hold on," the boy with the skull shirt says. He retreats to the back of the building, where Tasha sees wooden crates, the sides of which are lettered with red ink. Left behind from the film set, most likely. The boy flips the lid off one crate; its clatter is jarring in the emptiness of the room. The echo seems to needle its way into Tasha's head wound, making her temples throb. His pale arms disappear into the mouth of the box, to reemerge clutching a hefty black case.

"I don't know what's in here," he grumbles as he rejoins them at the front of the room. He blinks, stepping back into the sun. He's begrudgingly helping her, as if his will to do so is steered by an upbringing he can't quite shrug off.

"She doesn't need much," the girl offers.

"Shut up, Claire." He frowns into the case that now lies open on the floor. Tasha can see rows of syringes, packets of bandages, and plastic cylinders full of pills. Her heart palpitates a little at the sight of it—hope in the form of gauze and painkillers. The boy darts a look up at the windows. "Bennington is gonna have something to say about this."

Neither Claire nor the other boy reply. They too glance at the windows, and Tasha does the same, expecting to see some demigod striding in through the glass doors, striking fear into the hearts of mortals. But there's only the dusty street, the glare of the windows across the way. Tasha turns her eyes down to Xena, who has sunk down to the floor by Tasha's feet. She licks her paw slowly, methodically, her tongue a thick pink eel.

"Let's see what we've got," Tasha says, and moves toward the medical case.

The boy in the skull shirt seems to consider blocking her access, but steps back instead. Without looking at his eyes, she feels him regarding the knife. None of them appear to have any weapons. Regardless, she holds the Wusthof firmly as she picks through the contents of the case with the hand she'd already bandaged, badly, by the SkyDrive.

The bag holds an impressive variety of medical supplies—everything from bandages to tiny surgical scissors and sutures. She hopes she doesn't need those, and wishes she had a mirror to finally take a look at her wounds. She thinks back to the day she'd first met Z, Z bandaging Tasha's bitten bicep. Her heart constricts, a small python of sadness squeezing it in her chest.

Whatever, she thinks, pushing the snake away. Now it is she who will do the bandaging.

She can feel the sandy grit from outdoors coating her face in a rough film—walking the miles from the SkyDrive to this place had transformed her skin from flesh to scales. She tries not to think about walking again when she leaves the Hollywood town. First things first.

"I'm assuming you have a bathroom?" Tasha says, directing the question at Claire.

The girl nods.

"Does it have a mirror?"

The girl shakes her head, looking apologetic.

"No, not really. I got a compact though. You want to use it?"

"Yes. Please."

The girl moves toward the staircase and pauses, looking over her shoulder at the window again for an instant, before turning and disappearing up the steps. Tasha can hear her moving around upstairs, every step accompanied by a creak. A tiny puff of downward dust tracks her path. Tasha lowers her eyes from the ceiling and finds the boy in the skull shirt watching her.

"How old are you?" he says.

It's a teenage thing to ask. He has realized she is pretty, despite her knife, and senses she might be too old for him.

"Older than you," she says, continuing to sift through the medical case. Ointment and disinfectant. Antibiotics. Claire comes back down the stairs, her hand outstretched to offer Tasha the mirror. Tasha accepts it, nodding her thanks, but the girl says nothing, staring.

Tasha holds the mirror up to her forehead, clenching her teeth to prepare herself for whatever her eyes might find. She's not afraid of red, she's afraid of white—she's afraid that through the blood she can feel caked around her flesh she'll find the hard bright white of her skull, leering out from the pulp like the pit of a weird plum. She holds her breath.

It's not as bad as she thought. And really, she should have known. If it had been anywhere near the horrors she imagined, Claire and her companions would have been staring at her forehead and not the knife. What she finds when she peers in the mirror is an ugly bruise with swelling nearly the size of an egg. The egg nearly hatched, a cut across the center of it like the work of a single tiger's claw.

She's hot. The building is stifling; sitting in the sun near the window with no breeze brings the sweat pouring from her pores again. The three teenagers stand staring at her, each of their faces saying something different. The shirtless boy looks wistful, as if there are questions he wants to ask but can't. Skull Boy's expression is stormy; he glares at her with a malice that seems uncalled for. Claire's eyes are fixed on Tasha's face, occasionally traveling down over her body, as if trying to crack a code that's written on Tasha's skin. Her stare eventually rests on Tasha's backpack, eyeing the Prada label. Tasha thinks maybe some of the malice from Skull Boy has crept into the girl's eyes.

Tasha pours a bit of the disinfectant over her forehead and it stings like lightning when it finds the wound.

"Fuck," she growls, squeezing her eyes shut as the liquid drips down her nose. She blows it off her lips. Claire and the other two just watch. She thought maybe one of them would offer to help, but the shirtless boy looks as shy as the other two look unwilling.

"Where are your parents?" Tasha asks them as she attempts to bandage her head with one hand, holding the mirror in her other. "None of them had anything to say about you guys leaving and partying for weeks?"

"It doesn't matter anymore," Skull Boy says. He's even angrier now—she's triggered something. He glares at her. "Are you done yet?"

"No," Tasha says, staring at him hard. "I'm not."

After she bandages her arm and head, she turns to Xena. The dog cowers, a low whine in her throat.

"Dude," the skull boy cries. "Your dog just peed on our floor!"

Tasha looks. Yes, she had, Tasha sees. Afraid. In pain. She suddenly thinks of her parents, her dream, and clenches her fist to feel her mother's ring.

"I'm sorry, girl," Tasha says to Xena, low in her ear.

"Your dog peed on our floor," the boy repeats, as if he wants an apology.

"It's probably not the worst thing on this floor," Tasha snaps. "I'll take her outside. Get the case for me."

She doesn't look to see his reaction. She picks up the knife, tucking it dangerously under her arm, then awkwardly picks up the poodle, who struggles a little. Tasha feels something damp on her leg. Xena peed again. She can't even bring herself to feel disgusted. No one moves to open the door for her, so she pushes it with her hip, the glass sending triangles of light dancing over the sidewalk. She steps back out onto the pavement and lowers Xena slowly to the ground. The dog slumps, gazing up at Tasha with a dull expression. Tasha unslings the backpack, sets it down on the pavement. Several feet behind her, Skull Boy emerges from the doors with the case.

Tasha hears an engine, coming toward them down the street. Her heart leaps, absurdly expecting to see Monica Potter's SUV rolling toward her with Z waving from the window. But the hope is dashed quickly: zipping toward them, churning up dust, the car is yellow and small. As it nears where they all stand, Tasha waves the dust out of her face, looking. The car stops just ahead of her in the street, a convertible, looking bizarre in this dry empty town: a single yellow wasp separated from its hive. The door opens before the dust clears and a small man gets out.

"Brownsbury is completely deserted," he says to Skull Boy. "I got us a bunch of shit. I don't know why you were being such a bitch about going."

Tasha realizes this must be Bennington. He stands in the open door of the yellow car. He's dressed extremely well and extremely inappropriately for the heat, Tasha notices. He looks like he stepped out of Vogue's fall edition, with trousers and a sweater. He leans down to wipe some dust off his loafers. He looks ridiculous.

"It was a shorter drive than I thought it would be. Still plenty of charge in the car. Tomorrow I'm taking you over there with me. You're going to stop being such a cervix about all this shit, Jimmy."

He glances at Tasha and her dog as if seeing them for the first time, gives Tasha the up and down before looking back at the skull-shirted boy, who Tasha now knows as Jimmy.

"Who the fuck is this?"

"Some chick," Jimmy grumbles.

"She was just passing through," Claire says.

Bennington looks at the shirtless boy, who is farthest back on the sidewalk, closest to the windows.

"Todd?"

Todd shrugs. Bennington squints at Tasha.

"If she's just passing through," he says nastily. He's looking at Tasha but not addressing her. "Then what's she doing with our shit?"

"She just needed some bandages," Todd says. His voice is deeper than Tasha expected for such a skinny guy. His bass does nothing for him, though. He's clearly cowed by the 5'3" Bennington. The absurdly dressed man is noticeably older than the three kids Tasha's been dealing with so far. What kind of grown man comes to an abandoned town—dressed like that— to party with a bunch of teenagers? Tasha says nothing. She's still deciding how dangerous he is.

"Not for free," Bennington says, almost a laugh. "She might have needed some bandages but she's not getting them for free. She needs to give *us* something if she wants a single fucking Band-Aid. That's how this works."

Tasha feels unease stir in her stomach. She reads his meaning immediately: an open book written in red, lecherous ink. Bennington is the kind of guy who has been waiting for the apocalypse all his life.

"We were going to make her trade," Jimmy says. His voice is thin with the lie. Tasha wonders if Bennington hears it.

"Trade for what, Jimmy?" Bennington sneers. He still stands by the open door of the car, and now he turns to address Tasha. "What do you got to trade, little girl? What do you got in that little backpack?"

Tasha wants to look around, check for escape routes, but Bennington is like a snake reared up on its tail: she's afraid that if she takes her eyes off him, he'll slither away behind her, wrap his coils around her throat. She swallows. Her mouth is dry. Bennington stares somewhere right above her head: he wants to look at her without seeing her.

He turns and makes his way toward Todd and the windows. His toes point too far out to either side when he walks. He will have waddled for most of his young life, Tasha thinks, a gait that he eventually converted into a swagger, which he has spent his adult years convincing others is natural. Looking at him here in the sun, in the town he has claimed like a miniature Columbus, Tasha thinks she can see his whole life spread out behind him; a series of slights and privileges that shrank and grew, shrank and grew, until his journey brought him here. She wants to slap him. But instead, she shifts her weight from one foot to the other and settles her gaze on him like a laser, ready for whatever he does next.

"So what's in the backpack?" he says again, turning back to her when he's deeper in the shade. "You've taken gauze already.

Disinfectant, it looks like. That's valuable stuff. So what are you going to give *us* for it?"

For the first time since arriving here, Tasha actually feels nervous. She doesn't have much to trade. Her knife isn't an option. Inside her backpack are just some cans of food, broken sunglasses, and a can opener. Her sister's letter. The map, which is valuable to her but useless to them. She slowly swings the backpack from her shoulders and begins to rummage through it with the bandaged hand, crouching. Next to her, Xena sighs in the way only dogs can.

No surprises appear in the backpack. No sudden lump of gold she'd forgotten about that is magically just what she needs. LaBrenda held on to Dr. Rio's Glass, so she doesn't even have that. She takes out each item—the can opener, her sister's letter, the map—and lays them on the ground, pinning the letter with the can opener.

"I have food," she says, keeping her eyes on the backpack. That's the only thing left that she's not willing to trade.

"Do we look like we need food?" Bennington says immediately, as if he had known this is all she has. "I mean, does Claire look like she needs to eat any more?"

Claire's round cheeks burn red and Tasha's desire to slap him increases exponentially.

"Fuck your food," Bennington says sharply. "What else?"

Tasha stares blankly at him. Crouching as she is, she feels like a woodland creature gazing up at the glare of a horned owl. She hadn't been afraid of Jimmy and the others. Their hostility was fragile. But Bennington she fears. She tries to take in his body without looking away from his eyes. Does he have something that he could use to kill her under that well-made sweater? Tasha thinks maybe he wouldn't need anything other than his hands.

"Do we really need anything?" Todd says in a mouse voice unsuited to his bass. "You said you got a bunch of stuff from Brownsbury, right…"

Bennington wheels on him, one of his fists balled.

"Did I fucking ask you, Todd? Did you hear me say anything to you? Did the word *Todd* come out of my fucking mouth?"

Todd doesn't physically cringe, but his energy quails. He can't be more than eighteen. He's just a kid, and Tasha's stomach sinks for him: out here in the middle of nowhere, trapped with this psychopath in loafers.

"Her bag," Claire pipes up, her voice shrill as a sparrow. "How 'bout that? It's Prada. That's worth a lot."

Tasha jolts at the suggestion. She gapes at Claire in disbelief that she would propose such a thing, but Claire's not looking at her: her eyes are on the backpack. Her want has overshadowed Tasha's need.

Bennington stares fixedly at Todd for a second longer, as if making up his mind about beating him. Then he drags his eyes to Tasha, he and Claire both eyeballing her. Tasha feels her hand clench around the lip of the backpack without asking it to, her fear of losing it almost primal.

"What the fuck would we do with a Prada bag…," Bennington starts, and Tasha's relief must have bloomed on her face, a tiny flower of hope, because he stops. Before he even speaks again, she knows he'll stoop to pick the flower. "Prada, huh? Yeah, why not? Hand it over, sister."

Tasha's stomach smolders, not just at the word "sister" but at the way Bennington looks at her: a combination of mirth and rage that seems to fill his eyes with poison. Tasha can't bring herself to look at Claire. She might go kill her, she might close the few feet between them and slash her across the neck. Her fists tighten around the backpack and the knife.

"Let's go," Bennington says. He leans forward on his toes, claps his hands three slow times. "If you want the bandages then I need the bag. We can figure out what else you can trade if you want something for your mutt."

"No," Tasha says. The claps have brought her away from the edge of rage, and she feels the cold coals of obstinacy settle down in her gut.

Bennington squints.

"I said give me the bag, bitch."

"And I said *no*, bitch."

The words feel good. When they leave her mouth, she feels as if she has thrown two stones. By the look on Bennington's face, the words were stones for him too. She sees his wrath growing inside him, the furious wave of a hurricane rising from his feet and filling his body.

He takes two long steps toward her, and she scrambles up, snatching for her knife, ready to fend off whatever attack he envisions. She loses her balance, tips sideways onto her hip. But instead of going for her, Bennington draws back his leg and kicks Xena hard in the back. The poodle gives a high-pitched cry, tries to rise on her injured leg, and stumbles, yelping.

"You motherfucker!" Tasha shrieks. A hurricane rises in *her* now, the insanity of his attack stirring the frothing waters. She lunges forward on the ground, knife raised, and stabs its point directly through the top of one of his loafers and into his foot.

Bennington screams, a long throat-ripping sound that raises the hairs on Tasha's arms.

"Oh shit," Tasha hears Todd rumble, but she doesn't look at him: she sees only the blood that appears on the soft leather of the shoe as she yanks out the knife. Then, too late, she sees his fist.

Bennington's punch smashes into the side of her head. She had the barest opportunity to turn away from it as it came, but the blow still knocks her onto her other side, one of her knees striking the poodle, who cries again. The dog finally stands and stumbles over to the still-open door of the yellow car, cowering.

Bennington comes after her again, blood pouring from his foot now. All his pain has billowed up into blind anger: his eyes are almost red as he bears down on her. She scuttles backwards, slashing upward with her knife. Bennington is almost roaring as he looks for a way to lay hands on her.

Tasha's ears are filled with the sound of Bennington; Xena's frantic barking; Todd's hoarse shouts. Then Claire's screaming is added to the mix, the sound of cursing from all around. Tasha manages a glance between Bennington's legs, at Jimmy, who soundlessly points down the empty street.

But the street is not empty. At the end of the dusty road of their Hollywood town is a group of swaying figures. They move slowly, teetering like drunks. They're not drunks. Tasha feels her throat constrict at the sight of them. Had they followed her here, the Minkers from the SkyDrive—leaping off the tracks and sniffing after her like murderous hounds?

"Are those…?" Bennington starts to say, the red clouds of his rage clearing just enough to let him smell fear.

"Minkers," Tasha says.

They're all screaming. Tasha struggles up from the ground and, as if the sight of her rising triggers his wrath once more, Bennington snatches at her as the Minkers begin to run. The school of sharks arrows toward them, the sound of their snarls rising and carrying down the street toward where Tasha fights against Bennington's grip.

His arms encircle her, pinning her at her elbows. The Wusthof clatters to the ground. She flails away from him, hating the feeling of his hard body against her back. He's as mindless in his attack as the Minkers, and instead of fleeing, his grip tightens as the Minkers race closer. She can actually count them now as they come near: at least four.

"Get the fuck off me!" Tasha screams. She squirms, throwing her head back. By luck, her skull slams against Bennington's nose. His hold on her loosens immediately as he curses in her ear, and she uses her head as a club once more, ignoring the stab of pain it brings her by jolting her previous injury.

Bennington staggers backwards just as the Minkers fall upon Todd. They rip his skin. He doesn't scream. The silence of his mouth, opening and closing as if to shout but never managing it, burns itself into Tasha's mind. She screams for him, drops to the ground scrabbling for her knife. Bennington has crouched, his hand on the blade, trying to make his fear-frozen fingers grip it, his head dizzy from Tasha's blow.

She shoves his hand away as a Minker falls down onto her back, biting at her shoulders. She screeches, the heat of that mad breath searing through her shirt. Her arms give out under her, her chest slamming down to the ground with the Minker scrabbling on top of her. She writhes, half on the sidewalk and half in the dusty street, struggling to get her fingers around the knife. She's afraid to turn over, exposing her throat. She throws an elbow back, catching the Minker in the gut. The blow forces him—or her, she has no idea—backward. She strikes again. If this were a movie, she'd stab it from this position, despite its weight and her weakness. As it is, she can't make her limbs work. All around her is the sound of Minkers barking, and in the door of the car, Xena barking and snarling, one paw held up in pain. Behind her are screams: Claire's or Jimmy's, she doesn't know. A Minker has Bennington's hand in its mouth, blood forced from his body like a set prop.

Tasha throws herself forward against the front tire of the car, the Minker stumbling to stay on top of her. She twists her body left and right, shaking almost like a dog to keep him from getting a hold with his teeth. Using the car as leverage, she hauls herself to her feet, kicking backwards when her chest is over the edge of the convertible. Her head spins, the wound from falling off the SkyDrive pounding and crashing like both drum and cymbal. Arms shaking, she shoves off the car and forces herself to spin, facing her attacker.

The Minker is a teenager. She can't tell if the speckles on his cheeks are freckles or the spray of dried blood. He flings himself at her with arms windmilling, his mouth a furious cavern, an ugly roar emanating from his throat. She almost forgets she has a knife, instead throwing her arms out between them as a shield. He runs into the knife, uselessly, and at the feeling of the flesh, weak, giving underneath the tooth of the blade, she draws it back and hacks at him with it. If only Ishmael were here. The Chipotle axe she'd made for him. She wants the creature's head gone. Off. She stabs wildly, her breath coming in sobs. She can barely see, sweat and probably blood pouring down into her eyes. But somewhere through the blur there's a spark, and the blood-speckled teenager's limbs go loose. He sinks to the ground. She topples backwards against the yellow convertible, almost falling into the driver's seat. She paws at the sweat in her eyes with her free hand, trying not to think of the filth that must coat her fingers.

Cleared of sweat, her eyes fall upon the medical case. Todd lies dead, a bloody mess. Tasha swallows her nausea. Jimmy sinks to his knees by the door to their dormitory, shouting and shouting, two Minkers yawning down at him, his blood already on their tongues. Another Minker lies dead—she doesn't know who killed it. A third, previously focused on Jimmy, turns and sees Tasha still standing. She can almost see its face register annoyance, and it slowly turns toward her, prepared to take her apart.

She sprints toward the case, Xena barking behind her. Even the dog knows it's a stupid idea. Tasha's legs carry her forward, two dying propellers sputtering out of energy. The Minker charges toward her, her approach only seeming to madden it further. She feels like a matador, as if she should be waving a red cape with a flourish. She has only her knife.

She reaches the case and skids to a stop, on sudden impulse feinting to the right. The Minker goes for the fake, lunging past her. She screams as she dodges, the sound ripping out of her throat involuntarily. Something makes a horrible cracking sound: the Minker's leg, she sees. Somehow, with the change in angle, he had broken one of them. The Chip struggles to mend the break. Tasha dives at the Minker, dispatches the Chip frantically. Then she goes for the case again, pouncing on it, scrambling to put in items that have fallen out. She thinks maybe she's screaming but it's Jimmy. He's still fighting, still trying to fend off his two attackers.

Case under her arm, she makes as if to run to the car. But then she stops mid-stride. Her backpack. Where the fuck is it? She frantically looks around on the ground. It had been near her when Bennington attacked. Where did it go? Her eyes find themselves going again to Jimmy, who's finally succumbed to his attackers. They loom over him as if to make sure. Behind them, Tasha sees a face.

Claire. Safely behind the glass door of the dormitory, watching it all. She hugs her arms around herself, watching her friends be torn apart. Her eyes are round, but dry. She sees Tasha looking and squints her eyes. Not until then does Tasha notice that she clutches the Prada backpack to her chest.

From behind Tasha comes a shrill canine bark, and she whirls to find Bennington, bleeding, trying to climb into the yellow car. Blood streams from his arms and his neck. Xena bellows at him and then sinks her teeth into his leg. He curses, but before he can kick her, the Minker he'd managed to shake off leaps onto his back, raking his shoulders with its teeth. Bennington's absurdly thick sweater serves a purpose at last. He whirls in circles trying to shake off the Minker, which eventually stumbles sideways from the momentum. Bennington goes for the car again, ready to hurt Xena, but Tasha leaps on him then, kicking him as hard as she can in the back of the knee. He almost falls but doesn't. He staggers away from the car, takes one look at the recovering Minker, and flees down the dusty street.

Tasha doesn't have time to watch him run. The Minker he'd shaken off lunges at her now, eager for a new target, and she's forced back against the car once more. Ahead, the two Minkers that had finished off Jimmy sway toward Claire, who still stands just behind the glass doors. Tasha sees her standing there gaping before focusing her attention on the Minker taking aim at her own throat.

She manages to get her knee up, forcing it into the gut of the creature snapping its teeth in her face. It heaves itself forward, its breath obscenely foul, and she jabs her elbow into its throat, trying to keep its mouth far from her. She awkwardly angles her other hand, the one gripping the knife, toward the outside of its neck, trying to stab the Chip without also stabbing her own arm.

She kills the Minker just as the glass doors break.

The sound of Claire screaming is all Tasha can hear, even as Xena whines at her feet, even as her own breathing is thunderous in her ears. She stands frozen by the bright yellow car as the two Minkers stagger in through the jagged opening of the doors, their blood tinting the remaining glass. Claire backs away, still clutching Tasha's backpack, shrieking mindlessly, helplessly, as they bear down on her.

Tasha tells herself to move. Tells herself to take her knife and go in to save the girl. But she can't. She's rooted there, staring, as the two Minkers blunder inside, get their grip on Claire, and bring her down. Tasha can't move. She hears the coughing cries and all she can think of is Claire saying, *Take her bag.* She's rooted to the spot, watching the Minkers' backs bend down and down.

Something in her snaps back to life. She doesn't think. She sprints toward the building, leaping over the bodies of Minkers and teenage boys, and dashes through the broken doors, turning her body sideways to avoid the fangs of shattered glass.

One of the Minkers is already rising from Claire's body but hasn't yet turned to see her. Her blood thrumming in her ears, Tasha swings the knife wildly, catching it in the side of the neck where she hopes the Chip will be. She stabs three or four more times, praying with ragged breath that the blade finds the implant. It does, the Minker jolting and falling sideways against its companion, sending them both crashing to the floor. Tasha springs onto the survivor before it can regain its footing. Something must have broken in the fall—the Chip's light pulses red, and she buries the point of the knife in its center, the electric pop loud and clear.

She stumbles backward, panting. There should be only two bodies: the Minkers. But there are three. Tasha knows there are three. One is Claire, her body limp and bloodied, her face turned away from where Tasha stands, as if even in death she can't bring herself to face her. The lump in Tasha's throat expands like a sponge, soaking up everything she's feeling and growing larger, choking her. She wants to go over to the body, to look. But she can't. The backpack is on Claire's chest, as if she'd tried to use it as a shield. And failed. To take that shield now feels evil. It feels wrong.

Tasha turns away and walks back through the broken glass doors. The hot sun feels like it might turn her into ashes, and she can't find it in herself to care. She squeezes her eyes closed and angles her face up at the sun, willing herself to become dust under its glare. But when she opens her eyes again, all she finds of herself is flesh, and Xena's brown eyes watching her mournfully from the shade of the car.

Tasha walks over to the car, stopping to pick up her can opener, her letter, her map. They seem like stupid things to have. She tosses them into the passenger seat before bending to get the medical case that she'd left by the car. In it goes. Then comes the task of coaxing Xena to get into the car, and she ends up having to pick her up and place her in the backseat.

The keycard is still in its slot. She presses it, as Ishmael had showed her. The car vibrates. When she finally begins to drive, she stares at the road ahead and nothing else. Not back. Never back.

Eventually, when she's driven far enough to render the Hollywood town invisible—no sign of Bennington, who had fled without a trace—she pulls over. She needs to see to Xena's injuries, and the ones her own she hadn't had a chance to tend.

The Minker bite by her elbow is a pattern of puncture wounds similar to the one on her bicep at the Web in Chicago. She dresses it easily, if awkwardly. Her hand is another issue. She must have cut it on her knife when she fell: as soon as she removes the t-shirt from around it, the flesh opens and blood seeps out like lava from a crack in the earth. Her stomach turns, not at the blood but at the idea of her body being open, at risk. She quickly pours disinfectant over it, gritting her teeth and writhing in the driver seat as it burns. She reaches over to the passenger side for more gauze from the case and sees packets of thread and curved needles for putting stitches in flesh. Her hand pauses over one of the packets for an instant, wondering. She leaves them in the case, of course. With her lack of skill she'd end up piercing a major artery. For now, a bandage will have to do. She wraps the hand firmly with gauze, tying it with the assistance of her teeth before turning to Xena.

She locates the spot on Xena's leg where she'd found the slight fracture and also discovers a small laceration, her fingers coming out of the poodle's soft fur wet and red. She grits her teeth a little. More blood. She pushes thoughts of Claire's blood aside.

"You've got a cut in there, girl," she murmurs, reaching for the disinfectant.

Xena squirms when the liquid finds the cut, but a few whispered words from Tasha calm her. When she goes to extract bandages from the case, she finds a white package that contains a wrist brace. For a human sprain, of course, but what's the difference? When the leg is wrapped—gauze around the wound and the wrist brace around Xena's leg—Tasha opens a packet of ibuprofen.

"You're not going to like this," she says, and hears her dad in her voice as she says it, pictures him crouched in a pen, young Tasha standing by the gate watching carefully. She mimics his movements now, holding Xena's long brown muzzle gently but firmly, prying the jaws open. She forces the ibuprofen tablets into the back of the dog's mouth, the thick pink tongue convulsing against her wrist. It's been a long time since she's done this, but the memory comes back to her fingers easily. She closes Xena's mouth, holding it, massaging her throat, forcing her to swallow the pills. Xena coughs but doesn't spit them up, and Tasha wipes off the saliva on her jeans.

They stare at each other then, Tasha remembering walking down the line of kennels with her father, looking at the chart for which dogs needed medicine. The sun would be setting and the dogs barking gleefully to greet them, Tasha talking to each one they passed, reciting to her dad the name of each breed. She reaches over to run her hand through the poodle's dusty fur, tears in her eyes.

"Damn, Xena," she says. "Damn."

The dog gazes back at her, looking placid. She's had a hell of a month, Tasha thinks. She needs to rest. At least she doesn't have to drive.

Tasha looks around. Where to? She notices, with a feeling like the slow wilting of a plant, that this feels a lot like Chicago. Alone again. Except this time *she's* the dead friend left behind. For some reason this makes her feel better, closer to Dinah and Vette, so far behind. The feeling is like pressing a bruise, the pain a dull tribute that she has paid to some cruel gatekeeper. Might as well pass through.

She starts the car again, surrounded by nothing. It's not until she's put the car into drive that she sees the sign ahead where the actual highway begins, which is mostly unkempt and unused since the completion of the SkyDrive. She drives close enough to read the sign, hoping that it tells her something about upcoming

THE ROOSTER'S GARDEN 279

towns. A "Minker population of…" addendum would be nice, she thinks. But instead the sign says "North Platte Memorial State Mall. 30 Miles."

A mall. She can't quite work up a smile, but Tasha aims the nose of the car straight ahead. 60 miles. Maybe there's a god after all.

CHAPTER 15

At first she thinks they're soldiers, the long line of people streaming out of the North Platte Memorial State Mall. She wishes she had binoculars, although from the way she's crouching behind a bush atop this hill overlooking the building, she feels plenty SWAT-like without them. Her heart beats faster, imagining that the military has come to start clearing the area of these mindless killers, mile by mile. It takes her a few moments to notice the way the marchers sway. The truth slows her pulse. They're Minkers.

Tasha watches them sway out the north end of the mall in a long line, the same way she and Ishmael had seen them walking in Chicago. She hadn't understood then and she doesn't understand now, not fully. But Ishmael's likening of this activity to a dog's response to an unheard whistle seems apt. She wonders if they've been at the mall all along, or if something brought them here from elsewhere and now they're off to the next stop on their bloodthirsty tour. Either way, it's good news for her. The head of the line is miles away now: the mall is emptying and they don't show any sign of turning back.

Tasha returns to the car to wait for awhile—she has no intention of going down to the mall until the last Minker is out

THE ROOSTER'S GARDEN 281

of sight. As Tasha sinks into the driver seat, Xena thumps her tail in greeting from where she sits on the passenger side.

"How's it going?" Tasha says, regarding her companion. "Holding up? Being a trooper?"

The dog stares back, less weary than she'd been before. The ibuprofen must have kicked in—it has for Tasha. She wonders if Xena understands that Tasha had stolen a car from a group of corpses—had caused one of their deaths—and if she's judging her for it.

"Oh!" she says, surprising herself and Xena. "The stuff!"

Bennington, the psycho *Vogue* model, had been on a supply run before he returned with what he had called "a bunch of shit." He'd been in Brownsbury, he said…foraging for what? Porn, she thinks immediately. Almost certainly porn. And drugs, probably. Porn and drugs.

There's nothing in the backseat except the medical case she'd thrown in, so she hops out of the car and goes to the trunk. It's small, like the rest of the car, but Bennington had managed to stuff it almost entirely full with paper bags. She pulls one out.

Porn. And weed. She laughs. She barely glances at the porn—digital, the typical barely-adult women with faces contorted into a violent virgin's idea of orgasm. She tosses the porn over her shoulder into the dust, instead examining the weed, velvety green and encased in a transparent canister. She hasn't smoked since college, where she'd attempted to get high with Gina on multiple occasions, never feeling anything but a headache and a scratchy throat. She tosses the weed back in the trunk. Maybe she can trade it later now that she's on her own.

In the other sacks she finds multiple bags of Quesitos, one of which she opens immediately. Munching the fake-cheese chips, she checks the expiration date, which is next year, so they must be at least forty years old. Whatever. They're fine. There are also a few cans of tuna and some vacuum-sealed pasta, neither of which looks appetizing and some of which is expired. Canned tuna? This crap was what Bennington thought of as appetizing? She's even more disgusted with him than she had been before.

The contents of the bags toward the back of the trunk are boring but valuable: a flashlight, batteries, plastic trash bags, two ponchos. A box cutter. Syringes. All the makings of a survival kit. There's also a smaller bag full of cash—two thick stacks held by a wide black band. She doesn't count it, even though she sort of wants to. Useless, but she doesn't throw it to join the porn. Who knows—it might come in handy. In the same bag as the cash, inexplicably, are a few bottles of nail polish. Tasha's eyes light up at the sight of them. They must have been for Claire, she thinks, a tiny gift of some sort. Or perhaps Bennington had equal taste in loafers and nail polish. The bottles are of one of the more upscale brands, colors ranging from pink to black. She leaves those in the trunk too. Besides the porn and the cash, the car is a gold mine. She moves one of the last bags—full of condoms and vitamins—and her eye falls on something shining at the very back of the trunk.

It's an axe—a simple thing with a wooden handle and a polished iron head. She stares at it, thinking of Ishmael. He'd carried his in such a way that his bicep was continuously flexed, ready to raise his weapon at a moment's notice. She reaches in and pulls it out of the trunk, the sun glinting off its blade. She stares at it, almost expecting to see his face looking out of the reflection like a magic mirror. She lets it hang by her side for a moment, sighing with her eyes closed. Damn.

The contents of the trunk returned and the lid closed, she gets back in the car. Xena opens her eyes, thumping her tail once in greeting.

"Ready to roll?" Tasha says.

She starts the car and steers it over to the edge of the road, looking over the hill. The last of the Minkers are disappearing around a curving road far to the north, their smallness now giving them the appearance of ants. As she starts down the hill toward the mall below, she wishes she had a giant can of Raid.

Strange place for a mall, she thinks: almost nothing around it other than the highway. She wonders if it's one of those malls she's heard of that gets its labor from private prisons, with one wing of the building serving as a holding area, disguised from shoppers with friendly signs that say *Employees Only* in bright nonthreatening colors. Nearing the mall now, she doesn't see anything with barred windows that might suggest its inhabitants were once literal retail slaves, but who knows. She knew of the existence of such places only through Leona, her letters describing the atrocities of private prisons in slanting capital letters. Tasha is glad she has her sister's one letter, even if it is short. Even if she never sees her again, Tasha will have this one artifact of Leona's unmatched dissatisfaction with the world.

Xena is standing up in the passenger seat now, even with her injured leg.

"Sit," Tasha says, glancing at her as they roll slowly into the parking lot. The dog whines a low whine and doesn't sit. For a moment, Tasha's gut clenches, wondering if perhaps Xena senses some danger in the area; something Tasha can't see. But when she stops the car, the dog hops easily out of the convertible, landing awkwardly on three legs. She then crouches to pee. No danger—just a full bladder.

The parking lot, or what had been a parking lot, is empty. Not even a scooter in sight. Weeds taller than Tasha's knee sprout from cracks in the pavement, which, unless they have been fertilized, have been untended since well before the Change. She considers with an embarrassing feeling of disappointment that perhaps the mall is closed, dead: her oasis a crumbling mirage fading into the emptiness around it. But the Minkers, oddly, give her hope. Whether they were seekers or keepers—a moment of gloom at the thought of Ishmael's terms—they were here for a reason. Might as well look inside. She gets a few feet from the car before she thinks of the flashlight in the trunk and turns back for it. She stuffs it into her back pocket, reaching for another bag of Quesitos. Finally, she reaches in the bag of cash and withdraws a bottle of nail polish, which she stows in her bra. With the knife in one hand and the chips in the other, she moves toward the mall.

The entranceway is already wide open, the yawning doors resembling the mouth of a cave. She pauses for a moment, munching a handful of chips. If there had been any seekers roaming inside, they would have streamed out with the others on the north side of the mall. Even if a few of them remain, she can't imagine that there are many Minkers left inside, considering the number that just departed. She'll just have to be on her guard.

The power is out inside; the mercantile tomb is silent even of the soft hum of air conditioning. Quiet and empty, as she'd hoped, but with the same ghostly quality as everything else in the post-Change world. Not as dark as it could be, luckily: the glass ceilings keep it from being too dim; sunshine streams in to illuminate the dated green marble floors, the squat wooden benches with artificial plants on either side. She's never heard of a mall not being connected to a power grid of some kind, she thinks, walking slowly past empty stores. What kind of mall is this, anyway? She doesn't even recognize any of the store names: Belinda's Baubles, Mastafari. A pretzel stand called Salt and Twist that she dearly wishes were still functioning. It's all strange, no familiar logos of Gucci and Fendi. Still, she breathes it in: the comforting smell of plastic and ceramic, glass and synthetic cloth. Xena seems to enjoy it too, stopping and sniffing each false tree with ears perked.

She sees the first Minker through the glass of a store called Ronaldo's. He wears a white dress shirt tucked into black slacks, standing motionless between racks of clothes and staring blankly at the floor. Tasha wonders if he might be Ronaldo himself, as there are no other employees in the store. Ronaldo looks like he hasn't seen much action since the Change: his white shirt is spotless, his face clean, if scruffy from his weeks-old beard. Tasha wonders if a second edition of the Chip could have been programmed to keep facial hair at bay, or even body hair. *Things we'll never know*, she thinks. First edition soured the market, to say the least.

She pauses at the doorway of Ronaldo's, reluctant to just walk by without worry. Xena has already passed, ignoring Tasha's whispers to wait, and the frozen Minker hasn't moved, but maybe it will react differently to a human. She has only her knife, and she thinks of this sadly: no backpack filled with canned goods to weigh her down. She grips the handle a little tighter and slowly walks in front of the entrance, moving slowly.

Her caution is a waste of effort. Ronaldo, or whoever, doesn't blink, doesn't twitch. He's a bona fide keeper, guarding his hoard stubbornly and without distraction. She knows that if she steps past the threshold into the store, he will snap into action immediately, a theory she had tested in Chicago. She peers into the store. Its merchandise is all men's clothes: cheapish shirts and slacks and a small rack of suits. The inventory looks like interview clothes for college students. No need to disturb Ronaldo for such a selection, so she passes by; his gaze remains blank and bland.

At one point in her life Tasha would have seen an empty mall as a dream come true. And it still is, to an extent: free retail and no crowds is what heaven must be made of. But with no electricity, the light streaming in from the glass ceiling gives the place a feeling like an abandoned library or a museum. Nothing is coated in thick dust just yet, but it will be. With the power off, this place is already a tomb. Perhaps that makes her Lara Croft, she thinks, but it doesn't make her smile. In any case, the first tomb she needs to raid is the food court.

She spies the mall directory ahead, where the entrance corridor opens up into the rest of the mall. It's an actual physical directory, a testament to the age of the building, and she scans its neat white words for food. Unlike the Apiary, which had an entire floor dedicated to restaurants, the North Platte Memorial State Mall has only a small cluster of options, barely a court at all—more like a pod. With the power out, she doesn't know what there will be that's still edible, but she intends to explore it.

Her steps echo as she walks, quiet moderate steps that might be creepy if someone else overheard them. But there's no one to freak out except Xena, who stays ten meters ahead, sniffing everything. She seems unbothered—Tasha wonders if she remembers the Apiary, if somewhere in her doggy brain she remembers that she almost died in a place like this. But it wasn't really like this, Tasha thinks, looking around at the old architecture, the signs to stores that she doesn't recognize; knock-off brands and dollar stores. She's finding that this strange mall makes her sad: a place that was small and dark before the power ever went out. This was supposed to be her haven, a roost for the tired, sad chicken that is her spirit in this moment. But maybe a chicken needs a flock to feel truly at home.

Xena is already in the food court when Tasha gets there. It's a small borough of the mall, dimmer than the rest of the building due to the ceiling having several smaller skylights rather than an entire glass roof. But it's as deathly quiet as the rest of the place, and she approaches the restaurants cautiously, skipping the pizza place and going straight to Tiny Taco.

She puts down her bag of chips to explore, but keeps hold of the Wusthof. She doesn't bother opening the refrigerators. Chilled or not, the weeks won't have been kind to any produce stored inside. The smell of the prep line is foul enough on its own, the buzz of insects on the waste so loud that she'd mistaken it for electricity at first. After poking around, she settles on a 48-ounce can of black beans, her only real choice. She'd left her own can opener in the convertible, so she uses the huge mechanism on the prep counter to open it—pausing to look around when the clunk of its fang into the metal lid is louder than expected—and then carries the can to a table in the court. Taking the flashlight out of her pocket and placing it on the table, she drains the liquid on top of the beans into the planter of a large artificial tree next to her table. Then she uses a plastic spoon to dip into the beans. The feast is pathetic, and for a moment she only stares at it.

Eventually Xena appears next to her, poking her long nose around on Tasha's lap, sniffing. Tasha pours a pile of beans onto the ground for the dog and together they eat, the silence of the mall feeling fuzzy in her ears, as if it's not silent at all but emitting sounds at a higher octave than her ears can detect. The pink plastic of all the food court chairs, the nauseating fuchsia trim of the décor—all of it numbs her. The memory of sitting with Z in the Web, eating fat turkey subs, wilts her spirit still more. She glares down at the giant can of beans in her lap, and the sight of them shining wetly up at her in the dull light from the ceiling suddenly makes her want to vomit.

"Fuck!" she says, too loudly. She throws the can, harder than she'd intended, and it strikes a table nearby with a bang that echoes up to the skylights. Xena jumps and skitters several feet away, looking around in bewilderment.

"Sorry," Tasha groans, looking around to see if any Minkers had been drawn to the sound. She's almost disappointed when none of them appear, the food court as empty and silent as ever.

Xena must forgive her, because she goes over to where the beans now splatter the ground and slurps them with gusto.

"Enjoy," Tasha says, her own appetite gone. She needs to change clothes. Maybe after she finds something new to wear she'll return for another can of beans. Maybe she'll get fancy and find some jarred salsa to eat with them. *Living large*, she thinks.

She's almost out of the food court when she sees it: graffiti. The first glimpse of the red letters grabs her stomach in a tight fist, her mind immediately going to the dripping red paint of the Bean in Chicago, the woman in pearls tracing the word *Cybraknew* with her bony finger. But this is something else, someone else. And though Tasha may not know exactly who left the graffiti, she has a pretty general idea based on the words.

"The Rooster crows," she reads out loud.

Xena's sudden flurry of barking jolts Tasha and makes her spin around to see what alarmed the dog. Two Minkers, both nearly eighty years old, are wobbling their way toward Tasha from the direction of Macy's. Tasha lights up when she sees the store name: finally, a name she recognizes! Podunk mall or not, she's sure she can find some tank tops and underwear there.

The old Minkers are dressed in what seem to be exercise outfits, even if the styles are ancient. Loose jersey fabric from head to toe, matching sweatbands. Their shirts each have the same image on them: a screen-printed photo of two women in their thirties kissing at the finish line of what looks to be a marathon. Not until the Minkers are close enough that Tasha needs to start getting away does she realize the photo is of them: marathoners in love turned mall-walkers in love. Their matching wedding rings rest on their wrinkled fingers, just another identical element of their ensemble.

"Aww," Tasha says as she jogs away, looking back over her shoulder to take them in. They'd probably purchased the Chip to ensure that they could stay active together forever. It's seems so unfair that this is the end result for them.

The two little old ladies growl after her, their aging arms outstretched, as if they still might be running a marathon. They're not as quick as other Minkers: Chip or not, they're over eighty and probably need some oil in their tin-woman joints to pose a real threat. Even so, Tasha doesn't let them get too close; Xena keeps her distance too, growling and looking wary.

As she places a table between the ladies and herself, Tasha realizes that she doesn't want to kill them. She thinks about it as they gape toward her, their wrinkled brows wrinkled further with Chip-induced rage. Maybe it's because they're in love, she thinks, abandoning the table as one comes around each side. Or maybe she's just tired of killing people for the moment. Maybe she just wants to relax today. She's already killed Claire, barely an adult. Killing an old couple in matching mall-walker t-shirts just seems like too much.

She looks around, keeping some distance between them and her, and her eye falls on the pizza place she'd skipped while foraging. It has a counter that, when lifted, admits entry to the food prep area. She jogs toward it, Wusthof in one hand and flashlight in the other, talking to her pursuers.

"Come on, ladies," she says, gesturing. "Come on. Time to retire."

She lifts the counter easily and darts through the opening, entering the prep area reluctantly. This would ordinarily be a terrible idea, a route only a white woman in a horror movie would take: dead-ended and claustrophobic. But she hurries inside, pausing at the end of the food counter and calling to the marathoners, who are already hustling into the entrance she'd made for them.

"That's right, come on in."

They're two feet from Tasha when she quickly hops up on the end of the counter, spinning on her butt so that her feet end up on the outer edge, and then hops down again on the other side. She races the few feet to the part of the counter she'd lifted and deftly slams it down into place, neatly corralling the old couple behind the counter of Patricia's Pizza. If the Chip enabled brain functions other than "kill," they could crouch and crawl under the liftable part of the counter, but as it is they just smack their hands against the food prep area with its rotted cheese and toppings and glare at her over the glass.

She thinks suddenly of the Minkers on the SkyDrive—how did they get so adroit? Maybe there's a category other than seekers and keepers.

"Sorry, girls," Tasha says, turning her attention to the two women, and feels a little stupid for actually being sorry. It makes her sad to see them cooped up there: they've been running all their lives.

The mall is growing dimmer, the light from the sun outside fading to sunset and turning the edges of the glass skylights orange. If she still wants to get new underwear tonight, she needs to hurry. She turns away from the marathoners and clicks her tongue at Xena, calling her softly. They move on toward Macy's.

This Macy's is certainly *the* worst department store she's ever been in, Taha concludes, but the entire mall is such a relic that she curbs her criticism and focuses her attention on the fact that there are actually some brands that she recognizes. She sifts her fingers through racks of garments, the sight of them like the familiarity but strangeness of a family reunion. The names on the tags aren't what she would normally buy at the Apiary, but something about knowing the names makes her feel that she's among distant relatives. Without meaning to, she thinks of the closet she left behind in Chicago: the rows of hanging cousins she'd turned into a shrine. Saying goodbye to that room of cotton and satin had been like cutting off her arm, wrapping it in Hermes, and then leaving it to rot in open air. But it doesn't feel like that now, she notes, walking through the clusters of apparel, looking for underwear. If she cut off her arm in Chicago, it had grown back like the tail of a gecko bent on survival. She let whatever beast that had preyed on her keep the arm, and now she has a new one. Maybe something like LaBrenda's mechanical limb, though probably not as impressive. Entering the women's lingerie department, she wonders if escaping the past always means a pound of flesh, or if anyone ever gets away from anything whole.

The lingerie section is less disappointing than the rest of the store: shockingly so. Matching bra and panty sets, garters, thigh-high stockings. The mannequins sprawl here and there like sexy crash dummies, though once or twice she jumps to find something humanoid in her peripheral vision. Xena trails after Tasha quietly, sniffing here and there but mostly just being a shopping buddy, which Tasha appreciates. There's something nice about having a companion who doesn't have a thousand opinions about what you're picking out. Perhaps it's because of Xena's silence that Tasha ends up with an armful of lingerie: red and black and leopard spots, lace and satin, ruffles and smooth. She doesn't even feel ridiculous as she moves toward the fitting room. She's alone. Who cares?

The fitting room is dim but not dark, though the individual rooms are too gloomy to use. Instead she changes in the open in front of the large central mirror, plopping her selections on a padded bench. Xena lies by the entrance, watching half-interestedly as Tasha undresses. The nail polish escapes from her bra and thuds to the floor. The little black bottle sits there waiting like a beetle as she considers it. Later. She places it by her knife and turns to the lingerie.

She tries on the red set first, complete with garters and thigh-highs. The bra is a little too big, and she wonders if it's the brand or if she's lost weight. Staring at herself in the long mirror, she can't tell. Her thighs actually seem bigger, perhaps from all the involuntary sprinting. The dim light reminds her of a boudoir spread in a magazine and she strikes a pose, pushing one hip out and lifting the hang-time of her braids with one arm, the other arm—bandages and all—draped across her stomach. Standing like this, she studies herself. Does she look ridiculous? She can't tell. Is there a place for poses like this in the world of now? With no new editions of fashion magazines rolling out, is there a reason to ever stand this way again? She lets her arms fall to her sides, relaxes her hip. Is there even a reason to wear lingerie?

"With boobs like this, hell yes," she says to herself, smirking, and Xena perks an ear, raising her head. "No, no, not you, Xena. Chill."

The leopard set is next but she doesn't like it as much: it shoves her breasts together so much they look fake. Besides, she hadn't seen matching garters out there, and she found that she liked the look with the first set. So she puts on the black, which has some classic lace around the butt and back of the bra, and stands looking at herself again.

The room has become still darker, so she retrieves the flashlight from her jeans. The light illuminates the mirror like a small sun, and in the reflection it's almost as if the light is shining directly from her body. Shadows obscure her feet, but Tasha is suddenly intensely aware of them as she stands staring at herself. Her feet have carried her all this way; whether she sees them or not, here she stands.

She turns to look at her butt, the lace stretched across it in a lovely delicate pattern. In magazines, underwear like this had always seemed to be covering the thing the magazine really wanted you to stare at: an inconvenient, albeit pretty, barrier to an onlooker's gaze. But here in the near-dark, she feels as if she has gifted her ass with some much-deserved decoration—the lace for it and for her and no one else. She thinks maybe she's been thinking about lingerie wrong her whole life.

She admires herself until the darkness allows her to see only one body part at a time under the eye of the flashlight, and the spell is broken. She points the light in the direction she knows Xena to be, and the dog blinks into the glare sleepily.

Tasha is tired too. She shines the light onto the floor for the knife and the nail polish, retrieves them both, and then starts down the row of fitting rooms, peering into each one. The family-sized fitting room is at the back and, like all the others, is filled with clothes that shoppers had tried on and discarded rather than hanging on the rack at the front.

"Assholes," she says cheerfully.

She makes a nest of all the clothes, fetching garments from the other fitting rooms as well: piling them all up into a large mound. She pats her thigh for Xena, who joins her in the small room, and then closes the door after them both, pressing in the small circular lock. She realizes then that she's still wearing the black lingerie set, shoots the beam of the flashlight at the mirror to catch a glimpse of part of herself, trying to decide how lazy she is. Lazy enough to not bother getting dressed? *Yes,* she concludes, and plops down onto the nest she's built. She lays the knife carefully on the bench, point facing away from her, and places the flashlight next to it before switching it off.

The room is small and close, Xena's breathing coming from nearby like a slow train rumbling on a faraway track. They're alone. Except for the marathoners far off in the food court, they're alone. She wriggles a little, sinking deeper into the cocoon of clothes. Tonight, she already feels like a butterfly. She wonders what she'll be in the morning.

CHAPTER 16

She hasn't felt a tongue on her body in over a year and she wakes up pissed that it belongs to the poodle.

Xena licks Tasha's ankle slowly, carefully, as if she only has a finite number of licks available and needs to be sure Tasha wakes up before she runs out.

It's too dark to see: only a narrow line of light creeps in under the fitting-room door. As she'd lain in the nest of merchandise the night before, Tasha had told herself that there was no way she would actually fall asleep in the retail hobbit hole, the sound of the poodle's breath filling the cell with a sound and a smell like autumn leaves rustling. But she had slept, and she'd slept hard. She raises her hand slowly, the collar of a faux fur cropped vest sticking to the corner of her mouth. She brushes it away and sits up.

She rises slowly, stiff. Her wrapped hand aches more than her head now that the ibuprofen has worn off. Over the creak of her bones, she listens for anything outside her dark burrow that might indicate that she shouldn't open the door. But beyond its thin barrier, the mall seems to be as silent as it had been the night before. She wonders if the marathon couple had ever piped down or if they're still barking like sea lions behind the counter of Patricia's Pizza.

She carefully locates the knife in the darkness and then slowly, slowly inches the door open, peering out. Xena isn't as cautious: she shoves through the crack, sending the door smacking into Tasha's mouth.

"Jesus!" she says, clapping her empty hand to her lip. "Xena!"

The dog pauses at the entrance to the fitting rooms, looking back innocently.

Tasha's so pleased that the dog recognized the name that she forgets about her mouth and follows Xena out into Macy's.

The poodle disappears through the racks of clothes. Tasha assumes she's going somewhere to pee. The idea of the dog doing her business inside disgusts her, but she decides she cares too little to actually do something about it. She sighs, looking down, and is almost surprised to see the black lingerie, the lacy garters still holding stockings in place on her thighs. She almost laughs: she'd mostly forgotten about playing dress-up and realizes she hadn't found what she's actually come for: clean clothes and (functional) underwear. And, she remembers somberly, a new bag for carrying it all. She pulls a robe off a clearance rack, snaps off the tag, and slips it on. She wanders a few feet, gazing around half-interestedly at the sea of apparel, and becomes aware of the soft slapping of her bare feet against the floor. She directs them to the shoe department.

Xena rejoins her there, where Tasha has found a large display of slippers made to look like dinosaur feet. She finds a purple pair, complete with plush yellow claws, and pulls them on. Xena sniffs them judgmentally but Tasha likes them. The robe and the lingerie, with the addition of dinosaur feet and a knife, make her look as bizarre as she feels, out here alone in the middle of the country with a dog. She looks like a divorced Tyrannosaurus wife. Hell hath no fury like a dinosaur scorned. With Xena at her reptilian heel, Tasha wanders through the retail wilderness.

Roaming the Web with Z, trying on dresses and killing Minkers floor by floor, seems like an eternity ago. The light inside the Macy's reminds her of those few days: it's brighter than she expected—it might be close to noon, based on the sunshine filtering in through the glass ceiling. How long had she slept? Her wounds throb slightly. Her body needed time to repair. No wonder Xena was so eager to get out. Tasha doesn't share her eagerness. The thought of Z, their shared memories, drains her. She might have been hungry when she woke up, but the desire for food has evaporated, floating up toward the transparent roof above. A lot of her seems to float.

Her feet carry her out of Macy's and back into the rest of the mall, brighter still than the department store. To her right is a men's accessories store, the kind that caters to seniors. She'd passed it yesterday with only a glance at its keeper once it was established that he'd be staying inside the store. Now Tasha pauses outside, gazing in at the tables of glossy fabrics clearly geared toward men over fifty: not a logo in sight, just stripes and checks, bright colors that didn't necessarily go together. Her grandparents' generation had thought they were so edgy, breaking the rules. But they'd still worn ties.

The keeper stands motionless in the middle of the store, not even behind the counter. He's younger than Tasha would have thought, maybe in his thirties. His blank eyes gaze past her, a wax statue of himself, doomed to guard merchandise he had no stock in other than to stock shelves. But like all Minkers, he is resolute in his glare. He doesn't—can't—see Tasha, but he exists only to keep her from this store and everything in it. He is one of millions of gatekeepers. At the Web, Tasha and Z would have handled him in a heartbeat. But there is no Z now. Only Tasha.

She decides to go in.

As soon as she crosses the threshold of the store, her presence registers on his dull face. As if she'd walked across a tripwire, he focuses his eyes on her figure and staggers forward. Chip or not, she imagines his limbs have to be asleep after just standing there for so long. Her heart pounding, her jaw set, she resists the flaming urge to retreat back out into the safety of the mall. Instead, she waits there by the door, knees slightly bent, anticipating his attack. He stumbles on his own feet as he gets closer but doesn't fall. Instead he thrusts out his arms, ready to grab her, his fingers flexing like fleshy ant mandibles. She takes a half step backwards, her legs almost betraying her plan, and steps on Xena's foot. The dog doesn't yelp, instead yanks her paw away and lowers her head, growling at the approaching Minker. It gives Tasha courage.

It occurs to her as the Minker snarls toward her throat that she should've checked for a sportswear store. Football pads would be wise for this sort of activity. The keeper attempts to grip her in a bear hug, his mouth wide open and his eyes filled with murder. Ready for him, she fends him off with a hefty shove, which she realizes immediately isn't a good idea, the pain in her left hand lancing up her arm. He bounces back quickly, lunging forward again before she's prepared. She yelps in sudden terror, shuffling backwards to get out of his territory, put him back to sleep. But his arms are freakishly long, it seems, and the fingers of his right hand catch in the belt of the robe. Like the jaws of a crocodile, the Minker's fingers snap closed around the sash, thinking he's grasped some piece of Tasha. She swipes with the knife, regretting this stupid plan, staggering backwards. The sash is around the Minker's wrist. Xena, still snarling, rushes in as if to help, but instead gets under Tasha's feet and she feels her blood turn to ice as her weight tips backwards. She air-skates for a moment, and then she's falling, toppling backwards with the Minker crashing down on top of her.

Tasha lands hard on her butt, the Minker scrabbling at her belly. The knife is somewhere on the ground nearby, but not close enough. Tasha scrambles backwards, unintentionally dragging the Minker with her. His snarling and snapping is ferocious, over-zealous, as if he's aware he hasn't seen any action since the Change and wants to make up for lost time. Tasha tries frantically to push him off, looking in every direction for the knife, when suddenly the manic weight on top of her goes limp. His heaviness is so abrupt that she gasps, the entirety of him weighing on her abdomen. She thinks of Brian, her doorman back in Chicago, but this time she hadn't stabbed him. With a heavy breath of air like a sob, she shoves the Minker sideways and onto the floor, struggling up and away. Seeing the knife just out of her reach, she pounces to snatch it, standing and aiming its point at the Minker, ready for his assault to begin again.

But it doesn't. The Minker just lies there, Xena nearby growling low in her throat. Eventually Tasha's heartbeat slows to its normal thump and she takes a tentative step toward the Minker, who slumps facedown on the mall floor. Their struggle has taken them outside his store, Tasha notes: past the threshold he was programmed to guard. Surely that's not enough to kill him?

Grasping her knife firmly, Tasha grabs the Minker by the shoulder and flops him onto his back, springing backwards in case he's playing possum. He's not dead, but he's certainly not in attack mode. His body is rigid, but his face twitches, his lips trembling and going from an expressionless slackness to a snarl and then back again. His eyelids flutter, the crease between the brows deepening and then disappearing, deepening and then disappearing—a mask being pulled repetitively on and off, like a mime playing face games on the street. The inhuman sight sends a chill through Tasha's body, the sight of this undecided face on the floor, held prisoner by the Chip. She can't quite bring herself to stab him, though. It would be too much like shooting a fish trapped in a barrel. She moves on, wishing Z were here to see it. In this moment she misses her Glass more than she has since the Change. To be able to pick up her device and see Z's face floating there, ready to tell her exactly where she is…

To Tasha's right is a jewelry store, the kind that targets juveniles with no income of their own. Tasha gazes in at the shelves filled with bracelets and earrings made of the same material as paperclips. The store's keeper is just inside the entrance, the same blank expression, the same slight furrow on her forehead. The same programming. Tasha suddenly feels crushed under the enormity of this army: an endless expanse of expressionless soldiers, from one end of the country to the other. LaBrenda may never get to the Neovison nest. Even if she does, it may not matter. But Tasha's here. Just Tasha. She steps inside the jewelry store.

The Minker doesn't have time to launch an attack. She's only beginning to snarl when Tasha grabs her by the front of her pink vest and hauls her outside the store. As soon as the woman crosses the threshold, she goes rigid, just like the first guy. Her eyelids flutter, her jaws flex. Tasha thinks it must be the Chip, the coding befuddled by the subject's removal from the hundred square feet it was programmed to guard. With that in mind, the fluttering eyelids look like the malfunctioning lens of a camera. A mall full of people like this. A nation full of them. And Tasha.

She moves through the mall in this way, Xena limping behind like a shadow. Eventually the dog stops snarling when Tasha enters each store to lure the keeper closer to the door, standing just outside with legs stiff and tail still. One by one, Tasha clears each store; never setting her knife to the side, but not using it once. In some stores, when the keeper is stationed far in the back, she steps in to lure them closer and then steps out again, waiting for her prey to draw closer and closer to the entrance before she hauls them out. Some stores have two or more Minkers. After one risky encounter, she skips those places, focusing on the single-staffed boutiques. The Change had been so early in the day—just a manager here or a menial there to open the register and raise the gates. Her lonely work suits their lonely lives, and when she reaches the end of the mall—one level, like the relic it is—it's late in the afternoon. The hours have blurred by, bloodlessly bleeding into one another. She looks down and realizes her hands are shaking. She hasn't eaten or rested. Whenever the pilfered robe sways against her body, it sticks to her sweat. The dinosaur slippers are dusty from the tomb-like tiles.

Tasha looks up from the latest Minker at her feet, hearing rustling. It's Xena, her muzzle buried in a discarded bag of Quesitos. When Tasha whistles, the dog withdraws her nose, orange with fine crumbs.

"You're hungry, huh?"

The dog stares back blankly, licking her lips. Tasha knows she should eat, but can't quite make herself interested in food. This mall, these Minkers…eating subs with Z had seemed so long ago. But it could have been right here. The soft light from the glass ceiling could be Chicago's light. Tasha could be with her friends and not alone. Later still, she could be driving Monica Potter's SUV, looking in the rearview mirror to meet Ishmael's eyes…

She shakes her head hard, her braids swinging around and slapping her in the face.

"Nope," she says to herself, Xena cocking her head. "Nope. Stop."

There's no point. Loneliness is like a Trojan horse prowling through her mind. Memories let it in. Best to block them off. She's been alone before. She's been alone for years. Her apartment in Chicago had been her chamber of solace. Her parents dead, her sister gone. She's been alone before—she can be alone again. She made it alone in Chicago. She can make it alone to California.

She tries to eat. The food court is no longer peaceful since she corralled the mall-walkers behind the pizza joint's counter. She sits with another can of beans, trying to ignore them as they bark and slap at the countertop. Their impotent rage echoes off her eardrums as she slouches at an obnoxious pink table, dropping spoonful after spoonful of beans onto the floor for Xena. The dog snarfs them up eagerly each time, raising her head quickly to look for more. Tasha feeds her mindlessly, numbly. Each motion of the spoon is mechanical and empty. Before she realizes it, she's scooped out every bean in the can, Xena eventually just sniffing at what Tasha drops. She's full, and Tasha had eaten only two or three spoonfuls. But she can't find hunger in her body, and the sunshine is turning an orangey red, the sun sinking and leaving the mall to the shadows. Where had the hours gone? She'd awakened without a plan of departure, but she certainly hadn't meant to stay here all day. But why not, she thinks. One more day in an endless stream of days. Does it matter?

She wanders past the squalling Minkers, barely looking at them. Her knife hangs from her hand. She hasn't used it all day, which is miraculous in itself, but somehow its uselessness makes the weight on her shoulders even heavier. By the time the dinosaur slippers lead her back to Macy's, she's exhausted, as if she's been dragging an anchor since dawn. Her head aches but she can't bring herself to rewrap it.

Like a lone bear in the wilderness, she returns to the cave of the fitting room. The bed she made of discarded merchandise remains, undisturbed. She stands in the doorway of the little cell for a moment before going in, searching for the strength to go outside and get in the yellow convertible, continue her journey west. But her bones are empty of it, and the fading light outside is almost a meter of Tasha's own energy.

She sinks down onto the clothes, letting Xena follow her in and pausing before closing the door. Near her fingers sits the bottle of black nail polish, forgotten from the night before. She takes it in her hand, a lustrous glass thing in the shape of a genie's lamp. Its darkness is comforting, and she finds herself opening it, drawing the dainty brush down each of her nails like a smooth black tongue. She's good at this—always has been.

Three coats, her nail beds hidden by a dark, perfect sheath. She lies there blowing on them, eventually closing the fitting room door with her foot, sinking the room into a comforting shadow. She stays like that, awake, for hours. When she does sleep, she notices the dullness creeping gradually over her consciousness. And for a moment she hopes maybe she's dying instead.

CHAPTER 17

She sleeps until she can't sleep anymore. And even when she can't sleep anymore, she lies still on the pile of clothes, listening to Xena's nearby breathing, occasional whines punctuating the rhythm. Like Tasha, she's awake, but Tasha's gloom is a bubble that even the dog knows not to puncture. Tasha rubs her arms in the dark, almost expecting to feel a coat of dust on her skin—she might have been in this heap for years. But they're bare, the robe lost in the night somehow, twisted off in the midst of twisting dreams.

When she does sit up, she reaches for the door handle in the dark, cracking it open. A stripe of light spills in, illuminating the fur vest she'd found stuck to her mouth the morning before. Maybe she'll take it when she leaves. She needs new clothes, a new toothbrush. New soap. A new bag to put it all in. It's the first time she's really focused on the loss of the Prada backpack, and the truth of its absence makes her squeeze her eyes shut. The loss weighs on her chest like a small blue elephant, heavy and sad. But is it the backpack she mourns, or the thought of Claire? She needs air.

"Come on, Xena. Outside."

All English-speaking dogs know the meaning of "outside," and Xena barks once, happily, jumping up and streaming out into the fitting-room hall. Slowly Tasha rises, retrieves her knife from the floor beside the mirror, and follows her, shuffling in her dinosaur slippers.

Since the tornado in Iowa, she's always partially ready to open the door onto a world that has been torn from what it was when she went to sleep. Well, since the Change, now that she thinks about it. But the Macy's remains as placid and unremarkable as it had been the day before, red clearance signs dotting the retail landscape meaninglessly. Tasha moves toward where she'd picked up the slippers yesterday; the shoe department had been close to the door.

The door is broken, she finds, and partially open: most likely one of the exit points for the army of Minkers she'd seen when she arrived. They could have come right back in and murdered her as she slept—she hadn't even bothered to check the entrances to the store. She glances down at herself before sidling through. Without the robe she's a comical figure in lingerie and dinosaur feet. Xena pushes past her in a huff, as if to say, "Who's around to see, singleton?" Tasha follows the dog.

The parking lot is empty. The always-present fear in her had expected the army of Minkers to be returning, the horde of them streaming like ants to swarm her and her strange dinosaur-lingerie picnic. But aside from trash and—she squints—what looks to be a few dead bodies out farther away from the mall, it's all clear. Xena trots around, looking for grass she won't find, and Tasha stands there on the sidewalk, half Tyrannosaurus and half supermodel, gazing off toward where the sun is climbing in the east. She should be smoking a cigarette, she thinks. She needs sunglasses. But she has none, their shattered frames just another broken thing she left behind.

Looking eastward, far down at the other entrance to the mall, she can see the bright yellow of the convertible where she'd left it. It looks unbothered, as stupidly colorful as ever. She reminds herself that the key card for it is in the back pocket of her discarded jeans. She'll need to get that when she's scavenged what she needs and forced herself to leave. She wonders how much juice the car has: if she drove straight through to the end of its charge, how close could she get to California?

Hearing Xena yelp, Tasha jerks her head to look for her, scanning the mostly empty parking lot. Had she hurt her leg again? She might need to rewrap it. She should have yesterday, but yesterday was…not good. She almost doesn't see the dog in the wasteland of the parking lot. Then her eyes find Xena and her heart leaps. One of the bodies on the ground that Tasha had assumed to be corpses has latched onto the dog's back legs and is towing her toward its open mouth.

Tasha runs—the knife cutting the air and the dinosaur slippers slapping against the pavement. The lingerie doesn't do an admirable job of supporting her breasts and she clutches them with her empty hand, fear forcing her legs to pump faster and faster. The wound on her head seems to reactivate—she feels cloudy. But she runs—Xena crying and snarling, trying to reach backwards to bite the person clutching her.

Tasha skids up to where Xena is writhing on the ground and quickly crouches to stab the Minker woman gripping the poodle's legs. The woman's face bears a spider tattoo that gives her the impression of a superhero, but her eyes are what makes Tasha gasp: there's clarity, a human expression of confusion as the woman gurgles, "Dog…perro…"

But then the woman's eyes go angry and she makes the sound that Tasha knows too well: the half yell, half bark that no human should make. Her mouth is bloody and wide. Then the eyes go human again.

"Dog…dog…come."

Tasha grasps frantically at the hands gripping Xena's paws. Does she stab this person? A Minker speaking a human language throws a wrench into the easy routine of skewering the Chip. She looks for an implant and finds the area on the woman's neck where it should be a mass of disgusting sores and discoloration. The flesh is so purple and mottled that Tasha can't see where to stab.

"Perro…perro. Dog."

"Let go!" Tasha screams. "Just let go!"

Does she kill her? Is the woman with the spider tattoo a person or is she a Minker? The eyes go angry and glazed, the brow furrows. The teeth snap, the hands release Xena's paws and reach for Tasha instead.

Tasha jerks back as Xena scrambles to get away, stabbing the purple neck viciously, once and then twice. Nothing happens: she can't even see the red light flashing to improve her aim. She stabs again frantically, knowing she needs to kill her before the eyes go soft again, before she says *dog*.

There's no spark, but the woman's body suddenly goes limp, the eyes open and without expression, human or otherwise. Tasha falls back onto her butt, the gravel scratching the bare skin of her butt, breathing hard. Had she killed a woman or a Minker? It's a question she can't answer and it makes her heart pound, sending tears surging to her eyes. Is there a difference? Has there ever been?

Tasha thinks it's Xena barking, but she's wrong. She scrambles up from the pavement and sees them: at least six Minkers stumbling out from behind a dumpster nearby. They see her and are already coming her way, their chorus rising in a confirmation of their plan: attack.

"Oh shit oh shit oh shit. Xena, come!"

She stumbles, gauging the distance before she takes off in a sprint. She needs to fly.

"Xena, *come!*"

They run, Xena limping, taking off toward the mall. She can only pray that this is just a straggler group and not scouts for the whole damn army returning from deployment. Her legs feel wobbly but she puts everything she has into her strides. As her blood pounds, she can feel her wounds throbbing under their bandages. If she can just get inside… But the doors won't close, she remembers, terror spreading like poison through her veins. Even if she gets into the mall, they will follow.

Screeching tires, a car barreling toward her from the direction of the yellow Mustang. The car roars in her ears, chorusing with the Minkers' barks. *Bennington*, she thinks. *Oh my god.* He found her. He's tracked her down, determined to get the convertible and the contents of its trunk. His weed. His money. She puts on an extra burst of speed. Two predators, one quarry. If she can just make it to the mall, maybe she can hide: lose them in the labyrinth of clearance racks. Sic them on each other like in the Hollywood town. Faster. Run faster.

The car zooms ever closer to her, the Minkers behind showing none of the feebleness of the old ladies in the food court. She can hear them, too close, barking, can hear their ragged breath. Xena races next to her, stiff-legged from the makeshift splint. Tasha's guts churn. She thinks she'll probably die, either by Minker or Bennington. One of them will kill her. If she can just make it to the mall…

The black car is mere yards away, aimed straight for her. She had almost been hit by a Pumapod in Chicago once, when she'd come up in the Lift from underground. That would have been an accident, but this will be murder, black steel barreling down on her with the intent to break her body. Bennington's foot must be heavily on the gas: there's no way she can outrun it. He's going to hit her. She feels a scream rip from her throat as the car bears down.

The car drives straight into the crowd of Minkers, a mere two yards behind her. She shrieks again, keeps running: she can see the Minkers scatter like bowling pins in the reflection of the mall doors ahead. They won't stay down for long, she knows. She's almost to the doors. *Don't stop. You can make it. Hide.*

Three people leap from the black car—she can see them in the glass. Bennington and his new cronies, she knows, her heart pounding, her heart crashing. This is it. She's going to die. She may even be tortured. But...Bennington didn't have black hair. Even if Jimmy wasn't dead, he didn't have skin the color of a mahogany tree. None of them had an arm made of smooth black metal...

She collapses against the mall doors, her back against the glass, tears running down into her mouth. Z, Ishmael, and LaBrenda dispatch the crowd of Minkers quickly, one by one. A smaller person gets out of the car—which isn't a car, Tasha secs now, but a black SUV—a boy whose hair is growing into a tight curly Afro.

"Tasha!" says Malakai, running to her. He closes the gap between them quickly, falls onto his knees next to her, pressing his hair into her face. She clutches him, breathing in the smell of him, her mouth salty and wet with tears.

Z approaches, bending to wipe her box cutter on her jeans.

"Nice outfit," she says, nodding, tears already spilling from the corners of her eyes. "Is there a Victoria's Secret/Jurassic Park runway show I don't know about?"

Tasha stares at her, still clutching Malakai, still unable to speak. Her knife lies discarded on the pavement. For this moment, she doesn't need it.

CHAPTER 18

Eventually Tasha stops crying and puts on pants.

Instead of jeans, she chooses a pair of cargo shorts from the men's section, a decision Z and LaBrenda initially mocked and then imitated.

"We're going west, baby!" Z says when she finds a pair that fit her. "No more freezing-ass Chicago! Plus, the cooch needs some breathing room."

LaBrenda, in the fitting room next to Tasha, squawks with laughter.

"Why do you think I've been wearing leggings?" she calls. "I don't know how you two have dealt with jeans this whole time. How do you even run?"

Tasha remembers running down Lakeshore Drive in only jeans and a bra, and now across a parking lot in lingerie and slippers. She can run in anything, when it's important. But shorts are a better idea. Still, she laughs. They're high, all of them, with the thrill of reunion, the reality of what had seemed impossible flooding them and filling them with silliness.

The three women parade out of the fitting room, catwalk-style, to where Ishmael and Malakai wait.

"Where's the rest of your shirt?" Ishmael says, looking at Tasha's white tank top, which stops two inches from the top of her shorts.

"Don't worry about my shirt," she says, but she finds herself holding his eye, seeing the light there and swallowing it. He's shining for her: she sees it coming out of the small smile on his lips.

"You guys look cool," says Malakai, surveying their attire and nodding. "Like a band."

Tasha throws back her head and laughs, enjoying the feeling of her braids swinging against her shoulders. She doesn't think she's ever been this happy, as happy as she is in this moment. She's walked the earth with a hole in her heart for years, and the idea of losing these people had scooped her out wholly. With them here, Z smiling and Ishmael shining and Malakai a child, she feels as if her hands had been open and a golden egg dropped into her palms. She clutches it tightly—she doesn't think she'll ever let go. She feels the stupid tears again and busies herself packing her new backpack.

In the hunt for cargo shorts and other necessities, Tasha had found a brown backpack that she doesn't hate. It's no Prada, but it's a pleasing canvas material with the same kind of flap and buckle as her old one—plus it can hold a lot more stuff. She shoves her new shirts, underwear, and socks inside, plus a sports bra and a pair of leggings. Finally, on top, a self-foaming toothbrush, the bottle of black nail polish, and a new pair of sunglasses. With a case this time. A loose end of her head bandage flops into her face just as she starts to straighten up.

"You did your nails!" Z says, grabbing Tasha's hand and admiring the black polish.

Tasha pulls her hand away, embarrassed.

"Yeah...I just...yeah."

"Cute. So what happened to your head?" says Z, squinching her face at Tasha's bandages. Tasha reaches up to touch it gingerly.

"From when we got separated. When I fell off the tracks."

She tells them all that happened, glossing over the events in the Hollywood town. She'll share that with Z and Ishmael later when Malakai is asleep—he doesn't need to hear about it. But she does tell them that she grabbed the car and drove until she saw this place. She doesn't mention the lingerie and no one asks, though she knows Z will rib her about it later. She tells them about the army of Minkers exiting the building, sway-marching off north, at least a hundred of them.

"Oh!" she interrupts herself, remembering. She turns to LaBrenda. "That reminds me. Your secret boss or whatever, One-Eyed Rooster—someone left a message about him in the food court."

LaBrenda's face is suddenly iron-hard.

"What? What did it say?"

"I'll show you," she says.

As they walk down the length of the mall, LaBrenda is the first to note the intermittent bodies of Minkers stretched out in front of their stores.

"What happened here?" she says, nodding.

"Keepers kind of short out if you drag them outside their territory," Tasha says a little awkwardly. To another's eyes, the outstretched bodies might resemble rodents left on the porch of a cat's beloved master. Offerings. To her own eyes, they are manifestations of grief.

"Interesting," LaBrenda says, and sounds like she means it. Tasha would give anything to see inside her mind. She imagines it to be an endless blackboard, infinite notes in formulas whose logic only she knows.

"You did all these?" Ishmael says, eyebrows raised. In another life he could be talking about a collection of portraits, paintings. *The artist's blue period*, Tasha thinks. But "yeah" is all she says.

As they continue their walk toward the food court, Z talks, illustrating her words by waving the box cutter.

"We couldn't get off the SkyDrive until the next port," she says. "We thought it might take us all the way to Phoenix since that was our first selection, but it let us change our destination once we reached top speed. We got off at some town north of Denver—thank god we didn't stop in Denver: you just know it's swarmed—and then came straight back toward you."

"Well, not *straight* back," says Ishmael. His voice carries something rough in it, the words wrapped in sandpaper. Tasha looks at him with a question on her face, but LaBrenda jumps in.

"He's referring to me," she says hastily, frowning. "I...I suggested that we keep going."

Ishmael looks away, ahead, his expression stormy.

"I was overruled," LaBrenda continues.

"Of course you were overruled," Ishmael says.

"She just wanted to get to Phoenix," Malakai says, sounding pained.

"I thought it was likely you were dead," LaBrenda says. Tasha can't tell if it's her version of an apology or not.

"I knew you weren't dead," Z says, stopping their progress and turning to Tasha. "And if you were...well, I needed to see for myself."

Tasha bites her lip, feeling like she might cry. Again. She looks up at the glass ceiling of the mall.

"I can't believe you came back," she says finally.

"We never left!" says Malakai. He comes over and throws his arms around her waist, leaning his head against her shoulder. "I mean, not because we wanted to. The stupid SkyDrive..."

"Oh my god, I'm going to cry again," Tasha wails.

"That's okay," the boy says, and she kisses the top of his head. It shocks her, this: Leona had done it to her when they were girls, the quick sisterly peck. It's been so long, Tasha doesn't know where it came from. As they start walking again, Malakai stays by her side and she drapes an arm around his shoulders.

"How did you even find me?" she says as they pass a toy store Tasha hadn't noticed when she'd been sweeping the mall yesterday. She'd been single-minded in her pursuit and had stopped noticing what the stores even offered. In the display window is a huge robot who walks in small anxious circles. Either its motor is still running or it's a Minker in costume.

"We got off the SkyDrive and started driving straight back east. Well, after our discussion with LaBrenda." Z shoots a look at LaBrenda, who doesn't look her way. Tasha wonders if they'd fought. The tension rises like a fin from the water. Z continues. "We drove as long as we could before it got dark. Driving is so much slower than the SkyDrive, you know. We slept in the car. Did it again the next day."

Z pauses, smiling a small smile.

"I thought, if Tasha is alive and looking for a place to hole up, where would she go? The mall is, like, your mothership, right? I figured we'd at least stop by: see if maybe somehow you made it this far. When I saw the convertible, I knew for sure. I don't know how you would have gotten it, but I just knew."

"She did," LaBrenda agrees, and Z manages to look pleased. "She called it."

"Then we saw you," says Ishmael, his eyes straight ahead. "I didn't want to get my hopes up, but then we saw you."

"Just in time too," Malakai says, and Tasha laughs, the sound echoing in the empty mall. She squeezes his shoulder.

"Yes, just in time."

Xena begins to growl as they reach the food court. Her hackles rise and she aims her nose at the marathoners, still barricaded in Patricia's Pizza.

"Shh, Xena, it's okay," Tasha says softly, and the dog looks over her shoulder, wagging her tail hesitantly as if to ask if Tasha is sure.

"Xena? You named her?" Malakai says, smiling.

"Yes, it just…came to me."

"Xena. I like it."

"Yeah, I think it suits her."

"Xena, come here," he says, patting his knees. The dog comes eagerly, still limping on the injured leg. "I can't believe we found both of you!"

"We thought the dog was a goner for sure," Z nods.

LaBrenda is already over by the graffiti, studying it. Tasha joins her.

"So? What's it mean?"

"It means Red Rooster has sent an order for this building to be blown."

"That's pretty much what I figured," Tasha says. The message wasn't exactly cryptic—not that Minkers can read either way. She mentions again the departing army of them to LaBrenda.

LaBrenda frowns, not taking her eyes off the wall.

"Hmm. I wonder what drew them away. It could have been anything, I guess."

"Maybe when we get to California, you can tell Rooster that he shouldn't waste the bombs."

LaBrenda shakes her head.

"No. This building still needs to be blown," she says. "If Red Rooster has sent the order, that means it's a hub. Just like the Apiary and the Mall of America—it can call them anytime. And that means when we blow it up, any Minkers nearby will be fried."

"They might be out of range by the time your bomber buddies get here to blow it up. Maybe that's why those Minkers left—to beat the bomb."

LaBrenda crinkles her eyebrows, turning to survey the food court, bright with noon sun.

"But how could they have known?" she says. "You didn't see anyone with them? Anyone normal?"

"I mean, they weren't getting herded, if that's what you mean. They were just walking in a line. No one but them."

LaBrenda's frown deepens and Tasha looks away. Not her concern. Z is walking over anyway, gesturing toward Patricia's Pizza.

"Check out the two old ladies," she says. "If they weren't Minkers they'd be adorable. Matching shirts. Oh my god."

Tasha doesn't tell Z that she'd put them there: she'd have to explain why killing them had seemed impossible yesterday, why, still, the idea of killing more Minkers makes her feel tired. This morning she'd killed a woman whose Chip was clearly malfunctioning—had she been Minker or human? Or what if the effects of her Chip had been wearing off and she was becoming normal again? Had Tasha killed her right before she was cured? The idea makes her want to throw her knife far from her and never pick it up again. She turns, starting to tell LaBrenda about the woman with the spider tattoo, but Malakai is coming over to where the three women stand and she'd rather not put anything in his head that will make all of this worse.

"So are your Red Rooster friends on their way to blow up the mall?" he says. He's been listening—she's glad she hadn't mentioned the spider-tattooed woman.

"Something like that," says LaBrenda. She smiles a gentle smile at him and even though she'd tried to persuade her friends to leave Tasha behind, Tasha still likes her. "We should probably go, actually. If someone else is supposed to be handling this site, we shouldn't be here when they get here. They may see us and abort the mission."

"Why would they abort?" Tasha says as they move toward the exit.

"Red Rooster isn't really about human casualties. You remember the stories about drones blowing up California camps during the secession? That's the kinda shit we hate."

"Dr. Rio didn't seem to have a problem with the idea of us as human casualties," Tasha can't stop herself from saying. She knows Malakai heard it and winces. LaBrenda does too.

"Yeah...I think he sort of...lost it a little bit."

"A little bit?" Z snorts, clicking the blade of her box cutter in and out. "The dude was full-blown psycho. Remember his hand, Tash?" She curls her hand—her whole body, really—and opens and closes her fingers, her face distorted into a leer.

Malakai bursts out laughing and Tasha can't help but join him.

"Yes, he went over the edge," LaBrenda smiles as they near the still-open doors of the mall. They're at the south entrance, where Tasha had parked the Mustang. Good, she thinks. She needs to retrieve the contents of the medical kit. But there's one more thing she has to do.

"Hold on a second," she says, turning and jogging back down the corridor toward the food court. "I'll meet you by the car."

"Where are you going?" Z says, taking a step after her. The joke has leaked out of her voice, caution replacing it.

"I'll be right back, go outside," Tasha calls over her shoulder.

She jogs all the way to the food court and up to Patricia's Pizza. The two Minker women in their matching marathon shirts are still there, of course, swaying close together. Tasha pauses several feet away, before they see her and start barking. She exhales. Her parents could have lived to be this old. Maybe they would have worn matching t-shirts too. Under the counter Tasha can see the ladies' matching Asics walking shoes, one pair green and one purple. They've been running forever.

She jogs up to Patricia's Pizza, steeling herself against the barks she knows are coming. They see her and immediately start in, snarling and growling across the counter, slapping the surface with wrinkled hands, beating their matching wedding rings. Tasha comes in low to avoid the top of the counter and shoves the section that lifts from the bottom. It rises easily and she shoves it up and over, the door to the small corral freeing the two old horses inside. Tasha sprints away, dodging hideous pink chairs. She knows they won't catch her: they've barely realized they're free yet. She looks over her shoulder one more time before she leaves the food court for good.

Tasha and the others pile into the convertible, Xena riding on Malakai's lap, and they drive through the parking lot to where Z had parked Monica Potter's SUV.

"There's some stuff in the trunk that we should take too," Tasha says, getting out and opening it. "Though I don't think anyone wants this nasty-ass canned tuna." She makes a face.

"What? I love tuna!" Z exclaims, coming over to grab the can.

"You're sick," Tasha says. "And you're not allowed to eat it in the car. It will stink up everything."

"I'm going to eat it over your face while you're sleeping."

"I will kill you."

They laugh, unloading the medical kit and bags of food and supplies into the hatch of their SUV. Tasha sees their stacks of supplies from Whole Foods and feels like crying again. She won't have to eat Jimmy's disgusting pasta and tuna. Thank god. She sees the backpacks from the Pentagon, still filled with bombs, still sitting there in the back like patient slugs. She ignores them.

She returns to the trunk of the Mustang and her eye falls on the axe, which she'd forgotten. She doesn't know why Bennington got it, but she knows what she's going to do with it.

"I got you a present," she says to Ishmael, who is leaning against the back of the SUV and keeping an eye on the parking lot. At the sound of her voice, he looks over, as if he'd known the words were for him.

"For me?" he says, and she smiles at his expression. It reminds her of the day she and Z had found Malakai on top of the slide. *Who, me?*

"Yes, you," she says, feeling bashful now that his eyes are on her.

He pushes off the SUV and comes over, slowly, looking curious. She leans into the trunk to grab the axe and pulls it out for him to see before he reaches the car.

"An axe," he says. His other hand still grips the mace they'd pieced together in Chipotle. Holding them both, he looks like some kind of strange, smiling warrior. She can't take her eyes off him in this moment: the sun is on his face, glinting off his teeth and his weapons. His skin seems to swallow the sun and shine from within, bright black with a chestnut red under it all. He's the most beautiful thing she's ever seen.

"You're like the huntsman," she says softly. "From the fairy tale, you know. A huntsman needs an axe, and I took yours in the Apiary…"

"But you gave me another one in Chipotle."

She shrugs.

"Not a real one. This is a real one."

He stares at her, and she almost sees herself in his eyes, almost sees herself as he sees her all the time.

"The huntsman, huh?" he says. "I think I remember that one. Wasn't he with Snow White?"

"Yeah."

He looks down at the two axes in his hands, then back up at her, raising his eyebrow.

"Snow White ain't got shit on you."

He places both axes in the trunk, then gently takes the knife from her hand and does the same with it. Then he wraps his arms around her. He embraces her like one embraces something precious, and when she tightens her arms around his back, she thinks she feels something inside her grow, a tight vine uncurling, breaking through the shell of the pod and stretching out its leaves.

"And over here we have what must be one of the oldest Macys on the continent," Z says, her arms over the shoulders of LaBrenda and Malakai, steering them around the SUV and away from the convertible.

"Wing woman," says Ishmael into Tasha's ear.

She smiles, a forest growing inside her.

"That's right."

CHAPTER 19

They can see Denver burning from a hundred miles away. Tasha had insisted on driving—she's come to enjoy it—and Z directs her on Rio's red route, circumventing the city easily: south of Aurora, and angling even farther south now with their new goal of arriving in Phoenix. Tasha doesn't even notice the signs of fire until Malakai points it out.

"Is that smoke?"

They all look, Tasha slowing the car. No one says anything for a moment, and then LaBrenda says definitively from the backseat, "Yes."

Tasha assumes LaBrenda is the resident expert in things that are burning. It's far enough that the flames aren't quite visible. Tasha knows that if they were driving at night the sky over Denver would be a watercolor of orange and red. The smoke now hangs over the city like a shadow, a mountain range descending from above.

"What do you think happened?" Tasha says. "Lightning?"

She thinks of the superstorms that have swept across the nation since she was a child. She was always told that they were bad in Chicago but worse farther west—she'd certainly seen some of that with the tornado in Iowa.

"Maybe," says LaBrenda. "Or maybe Rooster gave an order there too."

She doesn't say it ominously: there's no sense of self-importance that could easily have been present. Tasha imagines that it takes a certain level of smugness to go around anonymously blowing things up. Even so, Tasha can't help but feel annoyed by her. It's all so straightforward with LaBrenda. She talks of people giving the order to blow up entire buildings with the same tone that one would use about standing in line at the Post.

"So, is Red Rooster just going to blow up every mall in the States?" she says, angling her eyes in the rearview mirror at LaBrenda.

"No," LaBrenda says, her eyes still on Denver. "Just the ones that he has intel on. The ones that are hubs."

"Which could be all of them."

LaBrenda looks back at her then.

"Could be. Unlikely, but yes."

Tasha rolls her eyes back at the road, just as a rabbit crosses ahead, a blur of white and gray. It pauses on the other side for half a second before disappearing into the brush.

"Hey, there was a rabbit!" she says. "Did you see it?"

Z looks up from the map, glancing around with vague interest.

Tasha points.

"It was there. It ran into the bushes."

Z shrugs and goes back to the map, gazing at the route she's stared at over and over. Tasha keeps her eyes fixed on the road, hoping for more rabbits. She hasn't seen one since she was a child, living in Kentucky with her parents—even squirrels were hard to come by in Chicago. She wonders if there are rabbits in California, if Leona has to shield her vegetables from them. She wonders if it rains.

"Does it rain in California?" she asks anyone who's listening as they round a bend.

"Of course it rains," Z says, still staring at the map.

"But I mean, like, regularly. I thought it was the driest part of the country. Even more than Arizona."

"It used to be," says LaBrenda. "But there was a huge earthquake in '45. Opened up a bunch of ground water. So even if it doesn't rain, they have water."

"Who told you that?"

"My granddad. He was born and raised there. Gone before the secession."

"Everybody left, right? I mean, almost everybody."

"Well, my granddad was sent to a private prison in Arkansas. So he didn't exactly leave because he wanted to."

"Oh."

Tasha had always wondered if her sister would end up in prison. From the snippets that Tasha saw on the webnews, being a mother wouldn't protect her. Armed forces had raided California towns multiple times prior to the secession—and probably after, but the webnews never mentioned it—snatching as many people as they could to break up what they called "rebel camps." It was well before then that, sensing trouble, Hollywood relocated to Nevada, the upper classes fleeing to Denver and Seattle and Portland. "Leave it for the dogs," Tasha had heard a web anchor say. She wonders if Leona knew that they considered her a dog.

"Was your granddad part of the secession groups?" she says over her shoulder now that she's thought about it.

"Kind of," LaBrenda says, a little softly. It's a voice that's hollow with memories. "He was a little too old. But he vocally supported an independent state. He said the States were like an abusive spouse: they kill you eventually if you stay, they'll try to kill you immediately if you leave. He was right either way: he died in that prison."

Tasha thinks about this. The route has taken them up onto a road that curls around a small mountain. She slows the car as she takes the curves, wishing she could look out at the world below. She hopes Malakai is taking it all in. He'd never even seen the sky before they went up in the Apiary with Rio. Now the sky is as readily available as air. She wants him to inhale it, to fill his lungs with it so it carries him above all this other shit.

"We're going to be going off route soon," says Z without looking up from the map. Tasha glances at her. Her eyebrows are crinkled, her lips curving downward into a focused frown.

"We knew we'd have to eventually, right? If we were going to go to Phoenix?"

"Yeah..." Z's frown deepens, her mouth twisting a little to the side. The map has been her solid ground, Tasha knows. Even before they'd left Chicago, standing around in Rio's cluttered living room, she'd kept her eyes on the map pinned to the wall. Tasha had uprooted her from the sanctuary of the Web and she had found a kind of stability in the solid red line that would lead to California. Going off-route means risk, uncertainty. *That's what this world is made of,* Tasha thinks, but doesn't say it out loud. Instead she says, "We'll be okay, Z. We'll keep angling south and eventually we'll see signs for Phoenix. LaBrenda, do you know where to go once we get there?"

"Yes. Dr. Rio left a nice trail of breadcrumbs in the Glass."

"See?" Tasha says, a verbal shoulder nudge. "We'll get there and then...and then we'll figure it out from there." She doesn't mention Z's brother. She knows the odds of finding him unChipped—let alone alive—are abysmally low. Nonexistent. Somewhere inside herself she thinks Z knows this, that more than anything she just wants confirmation.

Z shrugs, staring at the map. Slowly, as if she's putting away a letter from a dead lover, she folds the map, holding it there on her lap for a moment before stowing it away in her backpack. She's silent, studying the road ahead as if any moment the ground will split open and send them careening to the fiery core of the earth. Tasha doesn't quite know what to say: she wants to comfort Z, but giving comfort has never been her strong suit. She wishes she could sync her Glass—or anyone's—with the car's audio and play some music to distract everyone from the uncertain route ahead.

"Z," she says, "have you checked the console? Does Monica Potter have any music?"

"Who?"

"The person who owned this car. The lady in the parking lot at Whole Foods. Check the console to see if she had any music. A Glass or anything. Maybe it still has some power."

Glad for something to do, Z digs into the console.

"Gum…a cigar…self-foaming toothbrush…antibiotic wipes…baby wipes…sanitizer…"

"A germophobe who smokes," says LaBrenda from the backseat. "What an oxymoron."

They're coming down from the small mountain, miles of flat road ahead. Tasha's heart sinks slightly at the sight of it: more dead towns, dead cars, dead bodies.

"She had suckers too," Z says, holding them up.

"Is that one cherry? I want the cherry one," says Malakai. Z tosses it to him and Xena gets up to sniff it, trying to decide if it's something she wants.

"No music though?" says Tasha, glancing down into the console.

"None," says Z, snapping the lid closed again. "I could sing for you if you wanted."

Tasha grins.

"Oh lord."

Z clears her throat dramatically, pounding her chest with her fist. Tasha looks at her, still smiling, but then Z's face changes, the joke fading, her chest falling. She opens her mouth and sings.

"This lonely road
I've traveled long
Enough to know
How the dawn never comes.
The blue of the sky
Will never meet the green
Of the grass and I
Wait in between, sad and small."

Goosebumps rise along Tasha's arms, her neck prickling. She hasn't heard a sound like this since before the Change. Sweet, sad, simple, Z's voice rising and falling like a frail instrument.

"If I'm given the chance, love,
I'll meet you in the valley.
Plant me a garden, wait for me.
An ocean between us, I will swim it alone
And follow the trail of your whispering."

She stops abruptly, pulling in her lips and staring out the window ahead. The notes still hang in the air: even Xena had stopped snuffling at the sound of Z's voice.

"I didn't know you could sing," Tasha says quietly after a moment of silence.

"I can't," she says bluntly. "Not like my dad. I only know it in English. I...I can't remember the Korean words."

No one says anything—Tasha can still hear the words of the song in her mind, Z's voice quavering on the last note. Tasha wonders if there's more to the song or if she'd finished it. She's about to ask when Z turns toward her door, curling her shoulder.

"I think I'm going to take a nap," she says.

"Okay."

The car remains silent, everyone's breath hushed. Tasha knows how they feel: a glass balloon has floated into their midst, and speaking might shatter it. Tasha steers the car gently around the occasional bodies in the road, hoping none of them belong to people she had known, however briefly, before fleeing Chicago toward what Dr. Rio had painted as the end of the line, the golden land. They're off-route now, she reminds herself: anyone they pass will be a stranger. But she gives them a wide berth, careful with the graves they hadn't chosen. She hopes Z isn't dreaming of tombs. Tasha tries to imagine Leona in her garden, baby on her hip, always looking east for the possibility of Tasha's shadow.

"I'm coming," she thinks, so intensely that she almost says it out loud. "I'm coming."

CHAPTER 20

They've been driving for hours, the car silent except for the repetitive thrum of the tires. Tasha feels as if she's racing the sun: both of them barreling west where they both hope to find some rest. She tells herself that the next time they stop she'll fish her new sunglasses out of her bag; she's grateful for her brown eyes, the pigment like a pretty shield protecting her precious retinas. Still, driving straight into the sun is giving her a headache. Maybe it will blind her eventually, she thinks. Then someone else will have to drive, forcing the steering wheel out of her grip. She grips it even tighter. As long as it's her foot on the accelerator, Leona feels closer and closer.

"Let's stop there," comes a voice from the backseat, thick with sleep. It's Malakai, looking a little dazed, squinting at her in the rearview. She'd assumed everyone else had been asleep too, but now she sees that Ishmael and LaBrenda are also awake, each of them lost in thought. Z is still curled against the passenger-side door; Tasha can't tell if she's sleeping or not.

"Where?" Tasha says, craning her neck to see which digital board he's noticed. The sides of the road are crowded with the advertisements, as they have been for miles. The road itself is empty, without even the few dead cars they had seen when they were still near Aurora. She imagines that the SkyDrive dramatically lessened the traffic on these lonely stretches of road. No wonder everyone moved to the city: the SkyDrive definitely made the nation smaller, but only by connecting those places with jobs and traffic by more direct routes than before.

Malakai sits forward in his seat, pointing.

"There."

She sees it: a digiboard ahead, lit up in orange and white lights. The animation is an anthropomorphized golf ball curling in its limbs and rolling, then hopping up on two legs and waving. Nutter Putter Miniature Golf.

"You want to play mini-golf?" she says, almost laughing.

He leans back into his seat with a shrug, as if remembering he's now twelve. She sees manhood settle across his brow in a reluctant hood and she says quickly, "You read my mind. I fuc…I mean, I freaking *love* miniature golf. Z? Mini-golf?"

Z sits up slowly, blinking. She hasn't been asleep, Tasha can tell. She thinks maybe she shouldn't have said anything— maybe her friend prefers to languish in her gloom for awhile longer. Sometimes it's like that. But Z turns to Tasha with her face flat and earnest.

"I honestly think I might die if I don't play miniature golf right now."

Tasha laughs, as much with hilarity as with relief. The orange rolling ball-man's signs indicate that Nutter Putter is the next exit and Tasha finds herself pressing on the accelerator, wanting to get them there as soon as possible. She hopes it's still in working order; she hopes there aren't too many dead bodies strewn across the putting greens. Although, she thinks pragmatically, getting a hole in one while dodging a corpse would be something of an extra honor for the winner.

The exit is bumpy, not quite gravel but rough nonetheless: asphalt forgotten and neglected by road crews. She wonders if people live here. She hasn't seen anything remotely residential for hours, and they'll be leaving Colorado for New Mexico in a hundred miles or so. She's seen signs for everything from skin clubs to amusement parks, but no apartments, no homes.

The road off the exit is the same rough pavement. A few restaurants she's never heard of, the obligatory skin club, the Nutter Putter, which she turns the car toward, and, mysteriously, dozens of huge white tents.

"What are those?" Malakai says, arching his neck to see them through the window.

"I'm not sure," says Ishmael, looking concerned. Tasha had caught sight of his smile in the rearview when they'd decided on miniature golf, but it's gone now, the wrinkles appearing on his forehead like a worried bloodhound, his brown eyes searching the landscape for danger. But there's nothing: no cars, no dead bodies even. Just road, the few buildings, and the many white tents.

"I think the tops are transparent," Z says, looking. "And they round off at the top."

She's right: the tents are almost like cylinders lying on their sides. As Tasha pulls into the empty lot beside the Nutter Putter, she sees that the tents are also longer than she had thought: over a hundred meters, if she had to guess.

"Weird," she says.

"I hope it's not some kind of creepy UFO site," Z says. "Maybe this is where the government hides all the aliens."

Malakai chuckles at that and Tasha is glad. Ishmael hasn't expressed any misgivings about continuing their miniature golf adventure, so she opens her car door. Xena tries to climb over the console.

"No, Xena!" she says sharply. "Malakai, hold her for a second. She needs to learn to wait for you to open your door."

She closes her door in the poodle's face, but the minute Malakai is out of the car Xena leaps out behind him, bad paw and all, sniffing. Tasha stretches, looking at her braids and her bandage in the side mirror. They've been driving for hours without pause. She doesn't have to pee and knows this means she's not drinking enough water. She reaches for her canteen in the car, patting an itch out of her scalp.

Ishmael appears beside her, new axe in hand. It looks so natural in his grip. She imagines him chopping trees and not necks with it. Maybe they'll build a cabin in California. Could they build a cabin? They could figure it out...

"What are you thinking about?" he says, his eyes fastened on her face with a shadow of a smile, as if he already knows and is teasing her.

"Um...just...you know, ready to play some golf."

"I appreciate you doing this for Kai," he says.

"Kids don't have enough time to be kids," she replies.

They stand there looking at each other a moment, exchanging shy smiles, before turning to take in the Nutter Putter, which hasn't been renovated in what must be twenty years. The ads, however, are digital, the anthropomorphized golf ball from the highway's board here too, his bright white teeth glinting as he tucks and rolls back and forth across the entrance signage, which looks ancient in comparison. After the dim skeleton of the North Platte Memorial State Mall, the dazzling fluorescent colors almost offend Tasha's eyes. She remembers these colors flashing all around her on any given street in Chicago, even on the walk to the train. Everything was ad space, from the Volamu to the few trees, ani-paper plastered to their trunks. She looks away from the manic golf ball, thinking that even with corpses at every turn since the Change, her heart rate might still be a little lower without all the ads.

Just as she's turning away, something leaps from the shadowed entranceway of Nutter Putter, a whizzing blur of barking and snarling.

"Fuck!" Tasha yells, turning with her knife, readying herself for the attack.

But the barking figure races past her, running instead in a direct line to Xena. Not until Tasha turns fully around does she see that the figure isn't a Minker but a dog.

The snarling dissolves into whimpers, its tail wagging furiously, its belly meeting the ground. Xena stands over the strange dog looking bewildered by this sudden onslaught turned immediate surrender. She wags her tail uncertainly, her teeth going from bared to sheathed to bared again.

"I don't think she's mean," Malakai says of the new dog—a spaniel mixed breed, Tasha guesses. Medium-length white hair with reddish patches, a speckled face. She's never been a fan of spaniels: neurotic, difficult to train. Their owners had never seemed to notice, only threw their arms open when returning from a trip to pick up their pet. There must be something to love, she thinks, even if all spaniels do end up having the same kind of names: Lady. Maggie. Daisy.

"Sadie, come! Quit botherin' these people."

Sadie, Tasha thinks. Spaniel name. But then she looks quickly for the speaker of the words, her heart belatedly starting to pound.

It's a middle-aged guy wearing shorts and an orange shirt with a floppy fishing hat, his belly poking out the front of the shirt but his arms hanging thin and scrawny. His neck, too, is skinny, with skin dangling too loosely for someone his age. His eyes are wide and frank, owlish behind a pair of white-framed glasses. He has the deep reddish-brown skin of a white guy who's spent most of his years outdoors without sunscreen, large brown spots covering him and giving him a pattern like a newt.

"You folks looking to play some golf?" he says. "We're running a special."

Tasha blinks, turning to gaze at Ishmael for confirmation. The spaniel, Sadie, brushes against Tasha's leg as she trots over to the guy in the orange shirt, her short tail wiggling. Xena starts to follow, but pauses by Tasha, sitting at her heel. She gazes up, questioning, and Tasha looks down at her without answers.

"So...you're open?" Z says, coming over to Tasha's other side, her box cutter in her hand. "Like normal?"

The man blinks at them, scratching his belly.

"That's right. We don't turn away good business. How old are you?" he says, addressing Malakai with a nod. "Kids under ten play for five dollars."

"Uh, I just turned twelve a couple days ago?" Malakai says. He sounds as cautious as Tasha feels. It feels like the "Twilight Zone"—like maybe someone in a suit will show up with a body cam to broadcast her surprise to the Internet when he reveals that everything that's happened since she killed her doorman has been part of an elaborate reality show and they're finally wrapping it up here in Colorado.

"Just turned thirteen," the man repeats, then cocks his head with a shrug. "Eh, good enough. I'm having a good day. We'll pretend you're twelve today."

"Cool," says Malakai, looking at his brother with wide eyes.

"So...you know the world has gone batshit, right?" Z says. She says it a little too loudly, letting her arms flop.

The man crouches and buries his hands in the fur around his dog's ears. He looks at them without a hint of surprise or confusion.

"What's new, young lady? They'll figure it all out. Now, three adults and one kid, or is your friend in the car going to play as well?"

Tasha turns to look at the car, and finds LaBrenda still in the backseat, seatbelt still across her chest. The side door is open, but she makes no move to get out. When Tasha looks back, LaBrenda motions for her to come over. Xena follows Tasha over to the car.

"What's up?" Tasha says, leaning on the SUV. "You staying here or what?"

"Why are we stopping, Tasha?" LaBrenda says, looking serious. Her eyes squint slightly, staring directly into Tasha's.

"What do you mean? We've been driving for hours. We need a break."

"Then we should take a break and get back on the road. We're wasting a lot of time doing this."

Tasha feels her eyebrows express her annoyance.

"It's not a waste of time. Malakai's a kid. Stuff like this— stuff like this keeps it from being too...bad. We need to do stuff like this."

"It's inefficient," LaBrenda frowns. She darts her eyes over Tasha's shoulder toward the guy in the orange shirt, who continues to pet his dog.

"Look," Tasha says, leaning into the car a little. "We're doing you a favor even going to Phoenix, okay? We're doing this for you."

"And Z," LaBrenda says quickly. "Don't forget: her brother's in there."

"Like you care," Tasha says, lowering her voice to a harsh whisper. She suddenly hears Rio crawling out of LaBrenda's words. "You don't care how much it's going to hurt her— whether she finds him or not. You're selfish: you just want to make sure we take you to the Box. We're going. So chill. "

"Don't act like you're not selfish, Tasha. You don't really care about Z getting hurt. You just want to get to California so you can find your sister."

Tasha jerks her head back as if she's been slapped.

"We were following Dr. Rio's trail—that's *your* buddy. And we're trying to find Ishmael's mom too. It's not just about me. Don't do that shit."

"If you're Z's friend, you will let her find her brother. Whatever that actually means." LaBrenda leans forward in her

334 OLIVIA A. COLE

seat, the seatbelt straining against her chest. "It's important to know what happened to family. If you could know the truth about what happened to yours, you would, right?"

"I know what happened to my family," Tasha says, suddenly feeling frail. The wind that was in her sails drops and leaves her still in the water. "They're dead. I know that."

"But if you didn't," LaBrenda insists, "you'd want to know."

They stare at each other, Tasha's nose tingling around her eyes, tears welling up but unwilling to fall.

"By the way," the guy in the orange shirt calls, standing again. "We have hook-ups if you want to charge your car. We've got a deal running on that too."

Tasha steps away from the car.

"Three adults and one kid," she calls back at him, still looking at LaBrenda. "This one's not going to play."

Tasha gets the money she'd taken from Bennington's survival hoard out of the back of the car. The thick wad of bills feels strange in her hand. She's never held this much cash all at once. It would have easily paid six months of rent. She stares at one of the thick stacks before peeling off a few bills—she hasn't held paper money of any amount since she was a teenager. No one really used it—everyone used their Glass: her bills came from her Glass, her check went to her Glass. The feeling of the paper in her hands is almost surreal: funny how something so flimsy can be worth so much. What she wouldn't have given for this stupid stack of paper when her parents got sick, the mysterious illness creeping through their lungs as doctors stood around shaking their heads until bills could be paid. This stupid stack of paper could have changed Tasha's life.

She stows the rest of the money back in the bag and carries the bills—two fifties—to the guy in the orange shirt who still stands waiting by the entrance to Nutter Putter. Close up, she can read his nametag: Michelangelo.

"Will this cover it?" she says, brandishing the money.

"That'll do," he says. "That'll get you a full charge too."

"Okay. We'll do it after we play."

"Need a place to stay? I've got rooms."

Tasha looks over her shoulder at Ishmael and Z, who both shrug noncommittally.

"Maybe."

Michelangelo pockets the cash and then waves Z and the others to come inside.

"Okay. Let's get you started!" he says cheerily, and Tasha follows him inside.

The air conditioning slaps her bare forehead as she enters the building, neon arcade lights flashing soundlessly around her, Michelangelo's orange back leading her toward another set of glass doors beyond which she can see the green of the golf course.

"You have power," she says. "Solar?"

"Nope, we're on the grid," he says over his shoulder. Tasha hadn't asked if Xena could come inside, but the spaniel had followed her owner, so she says nothing when the poodle trots ahead. Malakai walks between Ishmael and Z behind.

"Oh," says Tasha, crinkling her brow. "A miniature golf course is on a city grid? Which one?"

"Not city. Federal."

"For mini-golf?" she says again, confused.

He pauses before he opens the next door.

"Well, that's not the only thing we do," he says, sounding a little hurt. "We're part of the Greenex growth op. We lose federal approval every now and then as the laws change, but they always change back."

Tasha has no idea what he's talking about, but she gets the feeling that he might discuss it at length, so she decides not to ask more questions.

"Oh," she says.

The first thing Tasha sees when she steps through the doors after Michelangelo is an enormous yellow lion, at least thirty feet high. It sits on its haunches with its mouth open to the sky in a massive silent roar. A red tongue extends all the way out of his mouth and down his belly, all the way to the ground, reaching almost to Tasha's feet. It's a little obscene, she thinks, observing it; she doesn't realize the tongue bears a tube until Michelangelo presses a button on a nearby glass-encased panel and says, "Let's just get your equipment."

Tasha hears a vague mechanical murmuring from the lion's belly, and eventually she notices that a bright blue golf ball is rolling inside the lion's tongue-tube on its way to the ground, followed by three others; yellow, red, and green. The balls click hollowly into a holding area and she stares down at them—these balls like rotund plastic vomit from the bowels of the beast. She wonders how long they've been sitting in the dark holding tank of its cavernous gut. She can't imagine that mini-golf has been in high demand since the Change. Then again, here she is.

"I'm green," says Malakai, stooping. She feels a momentary reflex that wants to stop him—clean the balls first from any mildew or spider eggs that might be lingering. She's always hated spider eggs: only something truly evil could look the way it looks with babies involved. But she decides that stopping him would be too motherly, and he has one of those—not her. So she says nothing and accepts the blue ball that Malakai holds out to her, taking it between two fingers.

"Why do I have to be blue?" she says, in a voice of mock complaint.

"You always seem blue to me," he says frankly, walking over to Z to give her the red ball. "Not sad. Just deep."

"Oh," she laughs and feels strangely flattered. She doubts anyone has ever thought of her as deep before—being fashionable and female usually rules that out for most people.

It doesn't mean she doesn't consider herself that way, but if no one else does, does it really matter?

"And why am I red?" Z says, accepting her ball from Malakai and her club from Michelangelo, who also extends one to Tasha.

"Because you're mad all the time," Malakai says simply, passing the yellow ball to Ishmael.

"I am not," Z says with a frown.

Ishmael doesn't ask why he got the yellow ball. He holds it in the palm of his hand for a moment before tossing it up in the air where it seems to hang for a moment like a tiny sparkling sun before becoming a comet plummeting back to his hand.

"You start at the panda," says Michelangelo, pointing to his left. Tasha looks, her eyes finding a panda about half as tall as the lion, its head lowered and its mouth open, the first tunnel for players' golf balls. Tasha assumes, wrinkling her nose, that this means the ball will emerge out of its plastic panda butt on the other side.

"The order after that is numbered," Michelangelo continues. "When you get to the flamingos you're halfway done. If you get a hole in one on the walrus you get a prize."

"Cool," says Malakai, already walking toward the panda.

"Thanks," Tasha says and Michelangelo nods.

"No problem," he says. "I'll be in the office if you have any questions."

He starts to walk away then pauses, turning back.

"Do you mind if I leave Sadie out here with you folks and your dog?" He nods toward where Xena and the spaniel sniff the feet of the lion. "She hasn't had much company lately…"

"Sure," Tasha shrugs. "That's fine."

"Thanks."

Then he's gone, back into the air-conditioned office to do who knows what. Maybe he'll go talk to LaBrenda, convince her to play. At the thought of LaBrenda alone in the car, Tasha is glad she brought the key card with her. Although, she realizes, frowning, with LaBrenda's arm and its special electric fingers, she could probably start the thing on her own. *She wouldn't do that*, Tasha thinks—*she needs us*. Maybe. Tasha puts the thought out of her mind and follows Malakai over to the panda, where he's placed his ball and is setting up to putt.

"Have you ever done this before?" Tasha asks, smiling at his stiff legs and rigid stance.

"Not in real life. Only on Xbox."

"How different can it be?" she laughs, hoping he doesn't hit it out of the fence that surrounds the golf zoo. Miraculously, the ball arrows straight ahead into the panda's mouth and Malakai whoops.

"Nice!" says Z, stepping up to high-five him. She places her red ball. "But look out, the angry golfer with her angry red ball is here and she's going to kick your ass."

"Language!" Ishmael calls, still tossing the yellow ball.

"Yeah, yeah."

Malakai chuckles.

They play, not keeping score but noting obvious winners and losers. Malakai's Xbox training had prepared him well; he never spends more than five strokes per hole. Tasha, on the other hand, is terrible, better only than Ishmael, who ends up quitting and just carrying his ball and club, attempting to toss one and spin the other, his axe pinned under the crook of his arm. It's not until they reach the flamingoes—halfway around the course—that Tasha notices the feeling of being watched.

She looks first at Xena, wanting to see if she's noticed anything, if her hackles are raised in silent alarm. She's busy with Sadie, though, and doesn't betray any notable suspicion. Tasha dearly wishes she had a dog's nose—not the physical nose, obviously: that would be hideous—but the strength of that sensitive smell. Maybe that wouldn't help either at the moment, though, she thinks. What she needs right now is a sixth sense: something that will carry her eyes and ears on the wind, lift them up to scan the area, pry into shadows. As of now she sees nothing, hears nothing. Maybe Michelangelo is watching them on security cameras. The thought sends her mind back to the Lincoln Park Zoo in Chicago, to when she'd watched Minkers swaying around flesh and blood animals on her own set of security cameras. These golf animals can't hurt her, but the idea of the unseen Minkers unleashed on her from an unseen cage makes her nervous.

"I got it in two that time," says Malakai, grinning. He scoops up his ball from the hole, situated between two ceramic bear cubs, one with its paw in front of the goal to make the game more difficult.

"I'm going to steal your ball," Tasha says. She forces a smile. "Clearly it's lucky."

"Green is gold!" he says, cupping his ball against his chest as if to protect it from her.

Xena comes with her nose pointed at him, wanting to smell the ball. She's probably hungry, Tasha thinks. They'd fed her when they left the North Platte Memorial State Mall, but that was hours ago. Tasha's hungry too—she'd had a granola bar after they'd seen Denver burning, but nothing since.

"How long does Xena have to wear the cast thing?" Malakai says, letting the dog smell the ball to prove it's not food.

"Not for very long. I'll check it tonight when we decide where to sleep. I'd give it a few weeks."

"I think she hates it," he says, studying the dog.

"I'm sure she does. I hate wearing this stupid bandage on my head too."

It's Tasha's turn. She sets her knife down, looking about her as she places her golf ball, as she has at every hole. She hates letting her knife out of her grasp when they're out in the open. She vows, as she has many times, to stop at a sporting goods store eventually for a sheath. She scans the fence line, clogged with weeds, checking for anyone who might try to bum-rush her as she tests her golf skills against the family of grizzly bears. She sees flamingoes. Zebras. A shark, half-out of murky water you had to chip your ball over—the scene of Ishmael's surrender. A hippo. And a face.

Tasha gasps, almost dropping her club. But the face is gone, pulled back into the shrubbery like a tortoise head yanked back into its shell.

"You okay?" says Ishmael. He clutches the yellow ball, not tossing it.

"I saw someone," she says. "There."

Ishmael immediately drops the yellow ball and grabs his axe from where he'd leaned it against the mama bear.

"Where? A Minker?"

"I...I don't think so." She scans the line of weeds cluttering the fence surrounding the course. She sees nothing: no face, no squinted eyes. She doesn't even see a break in the vegetation where a face could have been. The sun shines golden across a few wide leaves, shadows flecking their browns and greens with black. A Minker wouldn't have the sense to hide. And if it was someone like Bennington they'd already have made their move.

"Maybe it was something else," she says slowly. She glances at Malakai, whose pleasure is shrinking, his eyes troubled where they had been playful. "I don't see it now. Maybe it was nothing. I'll tell you if I see it again."

Ishmael looks at her for a long pause before nodding and moving on toward the next hole, where a pack of wolves guards the hole with their heads lowered into territorial poses. The wolf pack creeps Tasha out somehow. But Ishmael walks toward them with a straight back, still gripping his axe. The yellow ball remains on the green at Tasha's feet. She stares at it before walking after him.

"That tiger looks so real," Malakai says a few holes later. He's eased back into enjoying the game and Tasha is glad. She's been darting her eyes at the fences as surreptitiously as possible, looking for the face peering out of the leaves. Nothing.

"It does," Z agrees. "I'm afraid it's going to rip my arm off. Tasha, were there any tigers at the Zoo when you launched the emancipation?"

Distracted, Tasha doesn't hear.

"Huh?"

"Did you set loose any tigers in Lincoln Park when you were there?"

"Oh. No. A panther though." She remembers the animal's great amber eyes on her face, stripping her of her flesh and staring at her heart. The memory calms her. She is not prey— the panther had decided it. She stiffens against the idea of lurkers in the bushes. They can try, she thinks.

Malakai sets up to putt. Watching his focus on aiming between the tiger's widespread paws, Tasha is almost surprised when Ishmael appears by her side, his mouth close by her ear. Her flesh explodes in goosebumps until she realizes what he's whispering.

"There are people watching us," he says, the breath from his lips transforming her ear into something infinitely more alive. She shivers. "Don't look. There's at least ten of them. Not Minkers."

She doesn't look, swallowing to control her heartbeat. Her fear of the unknown watchers is almost as great as the anxiety that Ishmael will notice that she's staring at his mouth. She wants him to go on whispering in her ear, even if it is a warning, but once he reports he steps away again, looking at Malakai and not around at what might be a horde closing in. Not Minkers, he said. Then who?

She moseys toward the putting square, knife in one hand, ball and club in the other. Placing the ball on the square, she wraps her hands around both knife and club handle.

"I'm going to try to hit it over the tiger," she calls to Malakai, who's waiting on the other side of the tiger by the hole where he's already sunk his ball.

"No way!" he calls back.

She swings, entirely too hard, sending her little blue ball sailing high over the tiger, high over the elephant ahead, disappearing into the bushes up near the entrance. Malakai pokes his head around the tiger.

"Well, you lose!" he laughs, shaking his head.

"I guess I do," she says, making herself laugh. She needed to get rid of the ball so she could focus entirely on the matter at hand. She needed to do this without making Malakai afraid or tipping off the threat. She walks with only knife and club in hand. Not a bad second weapon, she thinks.

"Did you tell Z?" she murmurs to Ishmael as they make their way past the tiger, Malakai waiting on the other side.

"She's the one who told me," he says softly.

"How close are we to being done?" she says. "Maybe we can get out of here without freaking out Malakai."

"The dude said the flamingoes were the halfway point. We passed them a couple holes ago. The walrus is last—maybe three more holes?"

"Okay."

Malakai is putting at the elephant, Z standing nearby with her club over her shoulder. Her box cutter bulges out of her back pocket, her free hand tapping her thigh. She's nervous.

"You see them?" she says quietly to Tasha, keeping her eyes on Malakai.

"I haven't looked, not yet."

Tasha stretches, looking up at the sky. As she brings her gaze down to Z, she allows her eyes to sweep over the perimeter of the golf course. She sees them without actually seeing them—an impression of faces, some standing in pairs, barely attempting to hide as they gaze out of the shrubbery. One is so tall he stands head and shoulders above the line of plants, in plain sight. He doesn't duck as Tasha's eyes point in his direction. His brazenness increases her anxiety, but she tries to keep her body language neutral.

"Yeah, I see them."

"I wonder what they want," Z says.

"I almost got a hole in one!" Malakai calls.

"Better get it together, we're almost to the walrus!" Tasha shouts. She wants them to hear her, these faceless monitors at the fence line. They're close enough to see that the group has weapons, so maybe they're planning a move. But if they don't know that the golfers have seen them, maybe Tasha can turn the element of surprise they think they have against them. But she has no idea how. No crystal bee statue to smash, no diversion that will distract them so easily.

"What do we do?" Z says, placing her ball casually and setting up to putt. She misses the ball entirely with her first try, and hits it poorly with her second.

"You're getting worse," Malakai laughs.

"I don't know," says Tasha, her eyes on Z.

"Wait to see what they do? They haven't tried anything yet."

"So we just pretend we don't see them?" says Ishmael.

Malakai goes on to the next hole, impatient with the rest of the group's sluggishness.

"We should hurry," she says to Z. "Putt."

Z finishes with the elephant and follows Malakai, who is just at the start of the meerkat obstacle course. Players have to time their putt just right, as meerkats pop out of their burrows between the tee and the hole. Malakai takes careful aim and then gives his ball a solid stroke that sends it zipping down the lane directly toward the hole. It's nearly a hole in one, but the very last meerkat in the row pops up just as his ball passes by, knocking it just enough to send it edging off to the right.

"Aw man, so close!" he groans.

"So close!" Tasha echoes, forcing herself not to look around. She doesn't see any movement in her peripheral vision, but she imagines the faceless watchers at the fence slithering over the golf course, slipping between the legs of large ceramic animals in a silent sneak attack.

Malakai doesn't seem to notice that the other three people in his party are no longer playing: he is single-minded in his pursuit of a hole in one. He sinks his ball into the meerkat hole, then strides ahead toward the final course, the walrus.

Tasha hurries after him once his back is turned. She doesn't need to look to know that the uneasy peace won't last much longer. She grips the club and the knife so tightly that her bandaged hand aches a little. She's ready when the watchers try something, she tells herself. Not if, but when. She can feel their intent closing around her like fog, the feeling of lasers following her steps, watching her group's every move. She looks for Xena and finds the dog up by the walrus already, trailing Sadie, who trots around the course like she owns the place. Which in a way she does, Tasha thinks. Shouldn't Sadie have noticed the figures at the fence? Dogs always notice these things, don't they? The realization that the dog may be familiar with the people is what sets Tasha's pulse into overdrive: this is a trap. This is Michelangelo's game: lure passers-by into his little setup with miniature golf and a car charge, then murder them with the help of his support staff. She'll die beaten to death with miniature golf clubs; the last thing she'll see is a golf ball falling out of a ceramic panda's butt. She opens her mouth to call for Malakai to run, but he says, "I've got this. I can feel it."

He's set up at the walrus hole, which is difficult. A hole in one will require putting the ball up a steep slope and into a hole that rests between the opening and closing flippers of a mechanical walrus with very convincing whiskers. The animal appears to clap at a moderate rhythm, meaning the player must time the stroke just right. Malakai waits, watches, swallows. Tasha closes her mouth: even with her sudden terror she doesn't dare break a golfer's concentration, especially at a moment as important as this. The boy squints, then slowly brings back his club, waits, and then swings.

With a small *crack*, the ball speeds up the slope, on a perfect line toward the hole. The walrus seems to stare down its snubbed muzzle at the approaching green orb, slowly closing his flippers to keep the ball from going in. Tasha holds her breath despite herself. But Malakai's little ball chugs steadily ahead toward the closing flippers. They close, touching, and Tasha looks for where the ball had been deflected. But she doesn't see it.

"Hole in one!" Malakai shouts, leaping.

"Are you serious?" Ishmael yells.

"Hole in one!" Malakai says again, laughing and running up the slope toward the walrus, who is already opening its flippers again to block the attempt of the next player.

Tasha and Z walk quickly after him, Tasha smiling even as her heart pounds. Xena barks from where she stands a few yards away, excited by the shouting.

"The ball is gone," Malakai says, leaning to peer down between the walrus's flippers. "It's like a tube underneath."

"Probably lets the office know you've finished," Ishmael says.

"He said I get a prize, right?" Malakai grins, turning to look at them. "What do you think I get?"

Then he gasps, his eyes wide. The look of surprise immediately injects the terror back into Tasha's veins: he stares behind them, the golf club hanging forgotten in his hand. Tasha whirls, her knife raised, ready to attack, ready to fend off whatever onslaught the fence-stalkers have launched.

At first she sees no one, nothing near enough to prompt Malakai's reaction. But then she looks down, where a tiny girl stands with Ishmael's discarded yellow ball in both hands, extending it up to him with large serious eyes.

"Oh," Tasha says, lowering the knife quickly.

"Oh," says Ishmael. He sounds how she feels: like a roar had died in his throat as a beast appearing from the bushes turns out to be a fawn.

"Hola," the little girl says, barely a word, half gurgle. She can't be more than three. "Pelota. Pelota."

"Hi, honey," says Ishmael, his axe lowered, his arm slack. Tasha looks at him, curious. Her own father had never called her *honey*, only "bunny," which she had insisted on being called in honor of her favorite stuffed animal, a bunny also named Bunny. But *honey* rolls off Ishmael's tongue like a pearl he's been stowing away in the oyster of his mouth, placed there as a grain of sand by someone who loved him, where it has grown and smoothed into that single small word: honey. Tasha suddenly realizes she might love him a little bit, just a little.

Another figure is approaching them, fast, a slight person with loose black hair to their shoulders. It's a girl about Malakai's age, her eyes wide. After her races a third person, a woman, black hair flying behind her as she runs. Tasha tenses again, taking a step back. Is this the attack? A baby sent in like a tiny cooing smoke bomb to blind them? But the girl and the woman both are more focused on the little girl than on Tasha and the others, and they carry no weapons. And rather than curses, or a signal to her army, when the woman speaks, she cries only, "Lourdes! Niña traviesa! Ven acá! Beatriz, you were watching her! What are you doing?"

"I'm sorry, mama!" the older girl wails. She has stopped running now that her mother has joined her on the golf course. Her mother dashes forward and snatches up the baby, who is still clutching the yellow ball.

"Pelota," she giggles.

"Si, pelota! Niña traviesa! Ven acá! I'm sorry," she says, darting her eyes at Tasha and Ishmael, and then back at Z and Malakai. "She is very curious."

"Um, it's okay," Tasha says, relief and confusion fighting a sumo match in her mind. The woman is clearly the mother of the two girls: the same large dark eyes, but it's really the shape of the face that makes it obvious: rounded cheeks and an almost impossibly pointed chin. All three of them have it, the two little ones with skin as smooth as dolls. Their mother had skin like that once, Tasha knows, but it's worn now, though she can't be more than forty. Scars like tiny craters scatter her cheeks. She looks at Tasha shyly, and with a start Tasha realizes how much the woman reminds her of Dinah.

"Have you been watching us?" Z says, coming forward from where she'd been standing closer to the walrus.

"Yes," the woman says frankly, not blinking. "We all were."

"Who is we all?" says Tasha. The answer could be either cryptic or honest, and she's afraid to assume the latter.

"All of us," the woman repeats, looking confused. "You're not from Greenex?"

"Greenex?"

"Yes. You're not corporate? Mrs. Royce office?"

Is Greenex the thing Michelangelo had mentioned? Tasha's not sure.

"I'm sorry," Tasha says. "I have no idea what you're talking about."

The woman seems to deflate, her disappointment latching its talons into the skin around her eyes, pulling it downward. She looks older now, now that whatever hope she thought Tasha and her group represented is dashed.

"Ah," the woman sighs, looking down at her little one, Lourdes. The older daughter stands back, curious but bashful. "We haven't been paid. Months. We thought…we thought you were corporate. Here to pay us."

"Pay you?"

"Mama, necesito…"

"Shh," the woman says.

Someone is calling Tasha's name, from near the entrance where they'd come onto the course with Michelangelo. It's LaBrenda, looking left and right among all the ceramic animals.

"Tasha, there are people—" she calls, but then her eyes fall on them, their little cluster by the walrus. The words sink back down into her throat, muting herself. She's too far away to hear, but Tasha thinks she probably says "oh" as well. Michelangelo comes out after her and sees the group immediately.

"Hey," he says, waving. "You know you're not supposed to be back here." He directs his words at the woman, who is already backing away, returning to the fence. Tasha looks at the fence line now without reservation and this time she sees them clearly: a dozen or so faces among the scarce trees, peering through bushes. She sees, however, that the tall man she'd thought had been standing in plain sight is actually no man but a particularly tall bush with protruding branches. Ah well.

"Perdón," the woman calls. "Perdón! Tuve que ir por mi hija."

"Okay, okay," Michelangelo calls, and makes a sweeping motion with his hand. "Está bien…"

"They're out front too," LaBrenda says, walking over to join Tasha and the others. The woman is already to the fence, helping her older daughter hop over and passing Lourdes to her before climbing over herself.

"Who are they?" Tasha says, her fear shrunk down to curiosity.

"They used to be migrant workers. Now they work for Greenex."

They return to the car, where another three or four people stand nearby, just outside the parking lot closer to where the rows of white tents begin.

"What is Greenex?" Tasha says softly.

"Did you *ever* watch the news before this?" LaBrenda says. Her tone isn't unkind, but Tasha can hear the judgment in it.

She says nothing. "Greenex is the largest marijuana corp in the country, with more federal funding than any other agricultural corp in history. Every now and then they'll make cannabis illegal again, so all the smaller farms get shut down in the meantime and then Greenex buys them and gets even bigger."

"Like what happened to your friend Roger's granddad," Tasha says, the context of his story dawning on her now. "Damn."

"Yep. This is their labor," LaBrenda says, nodding at the group, who shuffle and speak quietly to one another. "Mostly undocumented. Totally exploited. Uninsured. Some as young as nine. Greenex is disgusting."

"The woman on the golf course said they haven't been paid in months," Tasha says dumbly, scanning the crowd for the woman's face. She doesn't see her.

"Wouldn't surprise me," LaBrenda says disdainfully. "The only people who have it worse than migrant workers are prison workers."

A young man has broken away from the group and is walking toward them with his hands outstretched. Tasha wonders if he's showing them he's unarmed because he thinks they're afraid of him, but then she realizes that her group are all carrying weapons. He's afraid of them. She tries to hold her knife in a way that sends signals of "Hey, I may be holding this knife, but we're cool." But she doesn't put it down.

"Hey," the young man says, nodding. Tasha notices he has a beautiful tattoo of a skull on his neck, colorful and seemingly covered with lace and jewels, the eyes like roses. Jimmy had worn a skull like this on his shirt. She wonders if he knew where it came from.

"Hey," says LaBrenda.

"They said you guys aren't Greenex? You're not here to pay?"

"No," says LaBrenda. "Sorry. We're not from Greenex. We're just passing through."

He looks disappointed, but as if he had prepared for this.

"No money," he says, shrugging. "No supplies. Two months."

"I'm sorry," Tasha says, not knowing what else to say. He looks at her as if he knows she's sorry, as if he believes she is sorry and appreciates her for being sorry.

"Trade?" he says. "Can you trade?"

"Trade," says Tasha, turning to look at the others. "We don't have much. Food? Do you guys need food?"

He nods.

"We'll trade. You want marijuana? Weed? We have lots."

Tasha thinks of the weed she already took from the trunk of the Mustang—she hadn't even wanted to smoke that, hadn't even mentioned its presence to Ishmael and the others.

"Vengan," he says, gesturing. "Caminen conmigo. I'll show you."

Tasha exchanges looks with the others. LaBrenda is the first to nod, which Tasha finds funny, as she had been the one who was rushing when they pulled over. Curiosity shines in her eyes like a lamp in a mirror: she wants to know more, wants to see inside the white tents. Tasha does too. They move to follow the guy.

"You coming back?" Michelangelo calls before they get out of the parking lot.

Tasha turns back, almost rolling her neck.

"Yes, we're coming back," she says.

"Want me to give you that charge you paid for?"

"When we come back," she says.

The young Greenex worker's name—Reuben, as it turns out— leads Tasha's group down the old road. His own group falls in behind them, including the ten or so who join them from the fence line around the golf course. Tasha sees the woman and her two daughters. Reuben looks like the conductor of a silent marching band as he leads them all, dust rising underneath their feet. He points at the tents as they approach.

"This is where we grow," he says. "This is where I work. Other tents," he points. "Processing. Other tents, packaging. Then trucks come, take the shipment. We get paid. But not for two months. No truck. No money, no supplies."

"What's that?" LaBrenda says, pointing. Farther down the road is an empty spot in the line of tents, the ground and road around it blackened and burned.

"That's where we burned a tent," he says. "After one month with no money, we burn the tent. We think they'll come— arrest some of us, pay the rest. But no one came."

Tasha is calculating in her head. One month—had the Change happened two months ago? It can't have. One month since the Change, close to it. Why hadn't they been paid in two months if the world hadn't yet gone to hell?

"Their problems started way before Cybranu," LaBrenda murmurs, as if reading her mind.

"Have you seen any sick people?" Z says, joining Reuben at the front of the procession. "Any crazy people?"

"The people on the news," Reuben says, nodding knowingly. "Not here. We saw it before the Internet went down. Now everyone is like us: alone. We saw you and thought it was over."

They've reached the patch of blackened ground, littered with the remains of the burned tent, its metal frame still standing high and skeletal like the bones of a mighty dragon fallen victim to its own flames.

"We have lots of product," Reuben says, continuing on to the next tent. "Mira."

He slides open the door and motions for Tasha and LaBrenda to come near.

"I can already smell it," says Z from behind them.

They peek inside, Ishmael holding Malakai's shoulder as if he might get sucked in by an overwhelming current.

Tasha had expected it to be dark, but the top is clear as Z had observed, and late afternoon light flows in, accompanied by blazing electric lights, hooked, like the Nutter Putter, to the federal grid.

"Wow," says LaBrenda.

The garden on the roof of the Pentagon had taken Tasha's breath away, but this garden makes her hold her breath. The pungent smell of weed seems almost physical as it wafts out of the huge tent and stuffs itself up her nose.

"Jesus," Z says, stepping back.

"It's strong," Reuben nods. "The best. You want to trade?"

"Um…let us talk for a second," Tasha says. "Un momento."

"Okay," he nods.

Tasha and her group huddle to the side of the tent doorway, which remains open, as if to hide from the smell pressing out of it.

"They want to give us weed?" Malakai says, wrinkling his nose.

"They want to trade," Ishmael says.

"*Weed?*"

"They don't really have anything else."

"They need food," Tasha says. She thinks of the stacks of supplies they'd hoarded at Whole Foods: organic ravioli, canned vegetables. There are no more than twenty people here, she estimates. "Even if we gave them everything in the trunk, it would only last them a week or two."

"Why don't they grow something besides weed?" Malakai says.

"That's the only thing they were allowed to grow," LaBrenda says grimly. But then something bright appears on her face, a spark rising from ash. "I have an idea."

She turns quickly to Reuben.

"Seeds," she says. "Semillas. We'll trade you food and seeds for a place to sleep tonight. Le podemos dar comida si nos…uh… da dónde dormir. Tenemos, uh…semillas? Tenemos semillas."

"Si! Tenemos camas! Sleep here. Eat with us. You have seeds?"

"Yes."

Reuben turns to his group and says excitedly, "Tienen semillas! Ya podemos sembrar nuestra propia cosecha!"

There are nods of agreement, smiles. Reuben turns back to LaBrenda.

"Sí, es un trato. Semillas para camas."

There are eighteen of them: workers mostly from Mexico—later Newest Mexico—and Guatemala, Tasha learns from Beatriz, the thirteen-year-old sister of baby Lourdes.

"I've worked here for two years," Beatriz tells Tasha when they're all back in the lodge where the Greenex workers sleep. It's at the end of the long row of white growing tents, where Reuben had led them after Tasha's group had retrieved the agreed-upon seeds from the back of Monica Potter's SUV. With the intention of gathering more at the next store they come across, they had also given the workers nearly every bag of food, including the produce from the Pentagon. The idea of emptying her precious stash had caused Tasha a stab of almost physical discomfort, but when she turned to find Lourdes's mother already feeding the child a peach from a pop-top can, anything sharp in her body went smooth. Now she sits across from the girl on a blanket as Reuben and a woman wearing a purplish red scarf take the food from the Pentagon bags and the Whole Foods baskets. They arrange it all and take stock, pleasure and relief on their faces. They intend to ration it, she hears the woman in the scarf saying. Tasha turns back to Beatriz.

"You work here? For Greenex?"

"Since I was eleven. My parents came after we got in trouble in Mexico. We were in jail for awhile. That's where I learned English," she smiles, looking like a lamb.

"Oh," Tasha says, taking in the girl's face, her skin unlined and unmarked. Whatever jail she'd been in had not yet settled into her. Maybe the world Before had ended just in time for Beatriz.

"Why did you get in trouble in Mexico?" Tasha says. She wonders if she means New Mexico or Newest Mexico, the lazily named acquisition of the States where Dinah had been born. She's almost afraid to ask—who knows what all this child has to tell?

"Picking without a license. It was my grandma's land. We never needed a license before."

Tasha feels the empty space in her mind around this story— there's context she's ignorant of, a missing piece that LaBrenda probably has stowed away in her skull. She will ask her, later, when she has time to sit and listen, and really hear.

"I like your hair," Beatriz says, cocking her head to the size, gazing above Tasha's eyes. "Did you do that yourself?"

"No, my friend helped me," Tasha says. She realizes she had called LaBrenda her friend. She'd seemed like a friend in the gardens of the Pentagon, but her warmth had faded the farther they had traveled, as if pieces of LaBrenda have begun to freeze the closer they get to Neovison.

"It's pretty," Beatriz smiles.

"Thank you."

"Papas!" Reuben says excitedly and Tasha looks up. He and the woman in the scarf have opened the last of the bags, two of which contain potatoes from the Pentagon.

"Potatoes!" LaBrenda says from where she sits with Z. "I forgot all about them."

"Real potatoes?" Beatriz stands up.

"As opposed to fake ones?" Tasha says, laughing.

Beatriz gazes back at her.

"Well, Greenex brought us cans every month and some said potatoes. But nobody really thinks they were potatoes."

Tasha's laugh dies in her throat, and she starts to apologize, but Beatriz is running over to where Reuben is holding up the potatoes for everyone to see and celebrate.

The lodge is long like the tents but wooden, the walls lined with beds. Long tables fill the center with benches on each side; a scattering of what appear to be tin plates and mugs sit on the tables here and there. She doesn't see silverware. Above are globular lights that cast a yellowish hue over it all, accompanying the sunset's orange glow coming in through the entranceway, the door to which remains open. The floor is bare dirt, packed hard and almost smooth by the habitual passing of many feet. Out the back door, Reuben has told them, is an outdoor kitchen, with stoves and a fire pit and one refrigerator. It's covered by a roof but is open on the sides. This is where they live, Tasha thinks, looking around. Live and sleep and work. As far as sleeping goes, she notes that there seem to be a lot more beds than people. She gets up from where she now sits alone and joins the rest of the group where they lounge at one of the long central tables.

"Do you think this is everyone? There's a lot of beds."

"One of the guys told me that people have left to go bring back food or money. No one has come back," Ishmael says, glancing at Malakai, as if looking at a thermometer that will gauge the seriousness of his words. "They haven't heard anything from them. They're afraid that Greenex is…" he pauses. "They're afraid Greenex is killing them for leaving. So the rest of them stayed here to wait for their supplies."

"But they're not, right?" says Malakai seriously, squinting. "Their company isn't killing them, right? Minkers are."

Tasha winces.

"It's hard to say," LaBrenda says. Tasha shoots her a glare. There are questions you should always answer with *no*, Tasha thinks, when it's a kid doing the asking. But Malakai doesn't falter. He just looks thoughtful.

"They'll starve if they stay here," says Z, somewhat unnecessarily.

"That's why we're giving them the seeds from the Pentagon," LaBrenda says. "I had hoped to take them to California and start a new garden there, but they need to grow something here. I'm sure I can find seeds when we get to Junot."

Tasha feels a pang for LaBrenda and her seeds. Until now, she hasn't mentioned what she plans to do after Phoenix. To hear that she has a destination beyond the place she plans to bomb floods Tasha with relief: no suicide plan.

"My sister has vegetables, last I heard," she says quickly. "We'll get you some seeds."

LaBrenda glances at her and Tasha thinks she sees some of the warmth return to her eyes.

"If it makes you feel better," says Z, "these folks are going to have a garden in no time. When we peeked into the growing tent I saw all kinds of super-advanced fertilizer and stuff. It's a federal op, like you said. The stuff they're using is going to make food grow *fast*."

"Yeah," says LaBrenda with a sigh. "But that doesn't mean it's good for them. That lab-grown shit."

"Yeah, well, starving isn't good for them either," says Z, raising her eyebrows and twisting her mouth.

"Papas! Comemos papas!" Lourdes shrieks, running past them. Tasha is almost relieved by the smile that flits across LaBrenda's lips. They watch Lourdes race down the length of the lodge, her mother following closely with her arms half-extended, ready to catch her if she falls. LaBrenda looks back at the group and grins.

"Well, comemos papas. Let's eat."

CHAPTER 21

The sun seems to have sunk into the horizon quickly, the remaining daylight squeezed out of a sponge and absorbed by the ground. The fire that the woman in the scarf has stoked, however, is large and bright, and the outdoor kitchen is well lit. Sitting as part of a lopsided circle around it, Tasha can easily see the faces of everyone present. If the rest of the workers were here, they may not all have fit. But as it is, here they all are. Tasha sits on a brightly colored blanket with Z; others sit on benches. Reuben has buried all the potatoes from the Pentagon in coals and has dumped several cans of vegetables into a heavy black pot, which now hangs over the leaping flames.

Tasha has never gone camping, but she's seen many movies about those who have, and this feels just like what she had pictured. She leans back on her hands, the fabric of the blanket slightly scratchy against her palms, and watches the fire. It doesn't seem to mind that its coals are being used to cook two dozen potatoes. It's more focused on the ceiling of the four-posted cover. Luckily the roof is high, or the smoke would be too stifling. She almost wishes the ceiling weren't there so she could see the sky. She imagines the fire feels the same way.

"Thoughts?" says Z, and Tasha looks at her. Z always manages to catch her in these moments—that's what friends do, she thinks, taking in Z's amused expression: her dark eyes, the wisps of hair sweeping over her forehead. Tasha had wanted hair like that at one point: a curtain of liquid black. But the cornrows LaBrenda had rooted in her scalp seem to root something else in her too: something that was already growing but that needed some help. Z is still looking at her curiously, but instead of talking about roots, Tasha says, "Are you afraid of what we'll find in the Box?"

Z looks surprised, the look of someone aiming a water gun but finding themselves wet instead. She holds Tasha's gaze only for a moment before she's looking back at the fire, considering its flames as Tasha had. Tasha thinks she may not answer, as she chose not to answer about her brother at the Pentagon, but just as Tasha turns to try to understand the conversation happening in Spanish around her, Z says, "Yes."

"Yes?"

"Yes. But…I need to know, Tasha. You know? My sister is in New York, probably dead. My dad I know is…dead, kind of. A Minker. If Dragon is dead, I need to know. When his face came up in the Pentagon…I know that face. You know? That's my brother's face. I need to know what happened to him."

"I understand," says Tasha. And she does. She had hoped Z's convictions were weaker, less sure—maybe then she could have talked her out of it. LaBrenda thinks Tasha's selfish, with only her own family in mind. But she doesn't realize that Z *is* Tasha's family. They'd managed not to be blown apart in the Apiary, but now they're following a new Dr. Rio into a new mission, only this time they actually know there are bombs involved. *How stupid are we?* Tasha thinks.

"Are you guys talking about Phoenix?" LaBrenda says. She's been on the bench next to them and crawls down now to join them on the blanket. Xena, who has been lying on the ground behind them, away from the fire, scoots a little closer now too. *Just us girls*, Tasha thinks.

"Yes," Z tells her, scooching over to make room. She says nothing else, returning her eyes to the fire.

"Tienes hambre?" says Reuben, smiling at Z. He'd removed the long-sleeved gray shirt he'd been wearing, only a thin white t-shirt left to cover his chest. The neck hole is torn, and Tasha can see the top of another tattoo—what appears to be the portrait of an old woman—as he crouches over the coals. He wields a pair of metal tongs, poking at the potatoes where they're nestled in the red coals. He peers at them with a serious expression.

"Están preparadas!" he says finally and Lourdes, across the circle on her mother's lap, claps her hands and squeals.

The woman with the scarf around her neck has retrieved a tall stack of the tin plates from inside the lodge and distributes them quietly, along with some bent forks. Tasha hasn't heard her speak a word, but she doesn't have the face of a shy woman, Tasha thinks as she accepts her plate. The woman's eyes are intense, almost hard, her mouth a tight, focused line. Tasha wonders who she is, what her role here had been before Greenex went dark, leaving these people stranded with nothing.

"So what's with the golf course guy?" Z asks Reuben as he passes out potatoes.

"No lo toque," he warns, nodding at the potato. "It's hot. Michelangelo? He is Michelangelo. Works here for a long time, before Greenex. Good guy. Lonely, maybe."

"He works there by himself?"

"Yes."

Beatriz, who looks longingly at the potato on her plate that's too hot to touch, says, "Mr. Michelangelo signs papers for Mrs. Royce sometimes."

"Oh."

"He builds things in his yard."

"Oh, okay."

Everyone has a potato, some people eating them already despite the heat.

"What have you been eating?" Tasha says, breaking open her potato carefully with the side of her fork to let the steam escape.

"We have canned things that will last a little. Only a few weeks. What you gave us is very needed. Thank you."

Tasha feels some of her anxiety unknot. They're not starving yet. There is time for the crop to grow.

"So you'll plant a garden?" LaBrenda says, blowing on her potato. Tasha wonders if she feels any longing for the Pentagon with the potato on her plate. Although Roger and the others hadn't felt too much like LaBrenda's family: just coworkers of sorts, roommates at a pit stop.

"Yes, we will plant," Reuben grins. "Tomorrow we choose a growing tent and uproot the crop. We'll plant all new."

LaBrenda smiles, and Tasha feels a certain amount of joy, looking at them looking at each other. Two green thumbs, two people with their hearts planted in the soil. Before, Tasha wouldn't have assumed that Reuben loved gardening just because of his employment with Greenex. But she sees it now, a golden way he glows at the idea of new crops, a new way to support this small isolated community.

"Will you stay here?" Tasha asks, hesitant to break the green spell that draws their smiles together, but curious.

Reuben shrugs, looking around the circle, where people are chatting and eating their cooling potatoes.

"Maybe. We have a place to sleep. Maybe we'll build more. We'll grow more food. The lights won't stay forever."

"Do you know how to build?" Tasha says, interested. She's thinking of California, of the cabin she'd imagined. She has no idea what awaits her in Junot. Leona had written fearfully of the bombings, the airstrikes from President Walker's drones. Maybe California has become a wasteland, with water from below that LaBrenda had described but with wreckage surrounding it.

"No, never built anything," he says, shrugging unconcernedly. "People find a way. Everyone finds a way."

They're all silent for awhile, apart from baby Lourdes, who asks for more potato, her mother blowing on it to cool it before feeding her chunks. Sparks rise from the fire, some of them snapping into black quickly and others floating higher before extinguishing themselves. She thinks of the retractable ceiling at the Pentagon and surprises herself by missing it.

"Where do you go?" Reuben says eventually, chewing. He has an open face, Tasha decides: eyes that hide nothing. She imagines he would be the kind of friend who tells hard truths: the person you only ask for advice when you're prepared for something that may not be easy to swallow but gives nutrients.

Tasha doesn't reply, waiting for LaBrenda to answer, assuming she would. But when she hears nothing, she transfers her gaze from Reuben to LaBrenda, and finds LaBrenda looking back. There's a question in her eyes: she's wondering whether their hosts need to know their destination, if it's prudent to tell them. Her caution makes Tasha prickle with annoyance. This is where they're sleeping. Lay the cards out.

"We're going to Arizona," she says, looking back at Reuben. "Phoenix."

A crash makes Tasha fumble her potato, groping for her knife at her feet, expecting to see a Minker staggering into their midst from the darkness, drawn by the crackle of the fire. But when Tasha looks for one, she finds only the woman with the scarf staring back at her, shadows from the flames creeping across her face.

"You can't," she says, her eyes wide. The crash, Tasha sees, was from the woman's aluminum plate, which she had dropped. It lies at her feet, her potato rolled a foot away. Beatriz is already retrieving it for her, juggling it from hand to hand.

"Excuse me?" says Z. Her eyes are wide too, Tasha knows; she can hear it in her voice.

"You cannot go to Phoenix," the woman says. Beatriz extends the potato and the plate but the woman ignores it.

"Why?" says LaBrenda, and Tasha knows her face without looking too. Caution, suspicion. Her mind is a compass whose needle is constantly in motion, the red line of a heart monitor carefully recording the vital signs she needs to make important decisions.

"Phoenix is poison," the woman says, her hand rising and coming to rest on the blue and red scarf wrapped around her throat. Her face floats ashen above the fabric, her eyes fixed on Tasha's face. "I came from Phoenix. Escaped. It is a prison."

"Prison or poison?" Z says, trying to understand. Her own potato lies forgotten on her plate.

"Prison. Poison. Phoenix is not where you go if you want to live. Desea sobrevivir?"

The hand on her scarf tightens, clutching the cloth in a claw that reminds Tasha of Dr. Rio and his curled fist. Despite the warmth of the fire, she shivers.

LaBrenda does not shiver—she steels herself.

"When were you in Phoenix?" she demands. Her mental notebook is open, ready to add intel.

"I don't know how long they kept me," the woman says. She sinks down onto a bench behind her, her eyes looking at LaBrenda over the fire. Beatriz perches next to her, still holding the potato. "A year. Two. They took me from one of their prisons in Mexico. They took many of us. They took us to the weasel place and made us sign papers. I don't read English. I don't know what they said."

"This was a prison?" Z says. No one is eating, everyone listening. Tasha shoots her eyes at Reuben, who looks sad. He knows this story.

"It was a prison. But different. Cells. Tubes. Glass walls. White coats always watching."

The shape of something is rising through murky water in Tasha's mind, jagged and ominous like the head of an alligator. In the deep it could be anything, but as it rises toward the surface, the pieces, together, begin to make sense.

"Who is they?" she asks, already knowing. Lately she's come to realize there is always a *they*. But she wants to hear this particular *they* spoken out loud.

"Neovison," the woman says, her jaw tight and her eyes hard. "The weasel people."

"The Box," LaBrenda says before Tasha can move her lips.

"Cybranu, I mean, Neovison, took you from prison? They put tubes in you?" Tasha says. She tries to remember every face that had been in the never-ending slideshow of Dr. Rio's Glass, the black and brown faces floating blue in the air of the Pentagon. This woman must have been among them.

"Yes. They made me sign papers. I thought I was getting out. They put us in vans."

Ishmael's fist is pressed against his forehead, his eyes on the ground. Malakai sits tight-lipped beside him, holding his potato.

"How did you escape?" says LaBrenda. Tasha looks at her sideways. She can't tell if she's sympathetic or if she's only mining the woman for information.

"I killed a man," she says. "Me and a friend. Glenda. We killed a man, and hurt a woman, and took a van."

Tasha swallows. In movies someone might give a speech telling the woman she did what she had to do. Or a moving soundtrack might rise from the haunted silence to instruct the audience on what they should be feeling in that moment. But with no music and certainly no speech, Tasha feels afraid. This woman had killed someone, had taken a life with who knows what kind of weapon—maybe her bare hands—and escaped an experimental facility, trekking however many miles to end up here, where Tasha now casually eats a potato in her presence. Without the music, Tasha doesn't know how to feel. She feels a laugh beginning to bubble in the bottom of her throat, spiky with its inappropriateness. She holds her breath, thinks she may snort. *Oh god, it's not funny, it's not funny.* She holds her breath again. How did she get here in this world? And how does she get out?

Just as the laugh threatens to overflow into her mouth and spill out into the air, LaBrenda's voice rescues her.

"You got out," she says, her voice firm as the earth, no comforting tones wrapping it: the words themselves are enough. "That's all that matters. By any means necessary."

No speech. Just that, and the woman with the scarf stares resolutely across the fire at LaBrenda, the flames between them like a flare they've created from their intensity, a spell woven from the strength of their combined fury.

"Where is your friend?" Z says quietly. "Glenda."

"Gone," the woman says, her eyes on LaBrenda for a breath longer before transferring to Z. "We separated on the border of New Mexico, near Navajo territory. She went east, Chicago. She was worse. Probably dead."

She says this matter-of-factly, but not without a tinge of sadness. It's the tone of a soldier who lost a comrade in battle.

"Worse?" says Z. Tasha knows she's thinking of her brother: trying to build an idea of what might have happened to him.

"In some ways. Her mind. My body was hurt worse, but I kept my mind. Her mind…her mind was bad. Broken."

"Jesus," says Ishmael. His fist has fallen from his forehead but it remains clenched, frozen in his lap like an anvil.

"What exactly did they do to you?" says Z. She sidesteps the tact of LaBrenda, her question an arrow to the heart of the matter that makes Tasha wince.

"They made us sign papers," the woman says again. "Took blood. Took hair. Took fingernails. Took urine. They put us to sleep, woke us up again. Many times. The last time I went to sleep, I woke up with a collar on my neck. Bandages, too. My hands cuffed to the bed. I couldn't touch my neck. Itching. Burning." Her eyes grow shiny with tears, none of them falling onto her cheeks but glistening there like the surface of two small pools of lava. "Then hours would pass where I remembered nothing. Blackness like sleep but darker. Heavier. I would wake with my body tired. Like I'd been running all night. Fingers bruised, tongue swollen."

She pauses, bringing her fingertips to her cheeks.

"Face aching. Head strange. Like hangover? Hung over. Cuffed to a new bed."

Her hands drop to the scarf around her neck.

"And this," she says, the tears spilling out of her eyes now as her fingers tug at the bright fabric. The scarf unravels slowly, like a purple python uncurling from her throat. But when the wrap is gone, the purple remains: an expanse of mottled bruising that covers the entire right side of her neck like a map of blue and indigo. The even brown of the rest of her skin seems to sink beneath the raised area of scar tissue, a swamp of a wound in the midst of savannah. She squeezes her eyes shut tightly, as if all the eyes on her throat constrict her breath, cause her pain. Tasha averts her eyes from the sight of it, this thing that has been done to this woman that she now wears like a brand.

"They gave you the Chip," Z breathes.

"Yes," the woman says.

"When she reached us," Reuben says, looking at the woman with a troubled cloud over his eyes. "We weren't sure what it meant. But then a month later supplies stopped coming. And then we saw things on the webnews before it went dark: crazy people, people killing without control. We knew. Pamela was one of the first. Practice."

"They gave it to all of the prisoners?" Z says softly.

"No," Pamela says. Tasha almost wishes she had said yes, to squelch whatever hope springs up in Z. "Dozens of us, yes. I saw papers once. But there was one person—maybe more, I don't know—that they did not put the Chip inside. I don't know why."

"Is it still in your neck?" Z says, her eyes darting from Pamela's neck to her eyes.

Pamela begins to wrap the scarf again, hiding the purple flesh, its cloudy scars disappearing beneath the cloth folds.

"I don't know," she says, looking at the ground. "Maybe not. I'm not crazy. When I killed the man in Arizona, I killed him as myself. No one else."

"It's still in your neck," Tasha says, forcing her tongue to shape the words. She can feel Pamela's eyes on her now like two hornets but she can't look her in the face, so she stares at the fire, feeling its light burning in her retinas.

"How do you know this?" Reuben says quickly.

"Because I killed a woman with a scar like that," Tasha says, nodding at Pamela but still unable to look at her. She does, however, look up at LaBrenda now. "At the North Platte Mall where you guys found me in the parking lot. A woman with big scars just like that. She was…she was malfunctioning. She wanted to kill me one second, and then she was normal for a second before going Minker again."

"Minker," says Reuben. "What do you mean, Minker?"

"Crazy," says Z, looking at Tasha. Her eyes are alive with the many things happening in her head. "Sick. One of them."

Reuben looks at Pamela with an expression of tightness, uncertainty pulling him in different directions. Pamela is not uncertain, however. She looks at Tasha until Tasha finally meets her gaze.

"Was this woman white? Did she wear pearls?"

"No," Tasha says. "But I think we met her too. I think Glenda made it to Chicago. Z, remember? By the Bean."

Z nods once, quickly. She's also putting the pieces together. Pamela purses her lips. Tasha can't decide if she looks sad or angry.

"The woman? That you…killed. What did she look like?"

The only thing Tasha can remember is the tattoo.

"She had a tattoo," Tasha says, pointing to her left eye. "A spider that covered one side of her face."

Pamela squeezes her eyes shut.

"Romina," she says. "I knew her. I didn't know she escaped. We were in the van together. I knew her."

The fire snaps, the only sound Tasha hears. Even baby Lourdes is quiet, standing between her mother's knees and staring up at her face, waiting to be noticed but knowing to be silent.

"Why are you going to that place?" Pamela says finally, her voice low but sharp.

"We're going to blow it up," Tasha says. And suddenly she wants very much to blow it up. The weight that LaBrenda carries she now feels heavy on her own shoulders, the urgency injected close to her own heart.

Tasha has seen too many movies, movies where there are speeches with penetrating looks of meaning as music rises. But there is only silence now, and still the crackle of the fire, as Pamela studies her with an expression not of solemnity and understanding but of total confusion.

"Blow it up?" she says, her eyebrows lowering, and Tasha thinks she looks as close to laughing as Tasha had been a moment ago. "You're crazy. Blow it up?"

Tasha feels her face flood with heat. She had meant it to sound dramatic so that maybe a curtain would close around the conversation, setting the scene for whatever came next. But instead she just feels stupid. LaBrenda is better at these things than she is, and Tasha looks to her for help.

"Not crazy," says LaBrenda evenly, giving Tasha a small smile before turning her eyes on Pamela. "But we have our reasons."

Her tone, her delivery, causes Pamela to raise her eyebrows, gravity returning to her face like a creeping shadow. *See*, Tasha thinks. *That.* LaBrenda is good at that.

"What reasons?" Reuben says before Pamela can respond. He's squinting, his open face a little less open now, Tasha notes. She wonders if he's considering whether the seeds they've given him are enough, or if he should kick these people out of the lodge, with all their talk about killing people and blowing things up.

"It's complicated," LaBrenda says. She pauses, as if to search for something more. "It's…complicated."

"No, it's not," says Malakai, and Tasha almost jumps at the sound of his voice. Everyone else around the fire seems to have sunk back into the shadows—Pamela's story about the Neovison center weaving a complicated knot of vines around them, holding them all rapt. Malakai doesn't seem held by that spell or any other, Tasha thinks, looking at him. "It's actually really simple. We need to go to the place where it all started. And maybe that's where it'll all end."

Tasha thinks maybe Malakai has seen too many movies too, and smiles at him, even if he's not looking. LaBrenda is smiling too. Ishmael is not.

"What is *it all*?" Pamela says, shaking her head. Her expression is one of guarded despair. She doesn't want to say what she's about to say to a child. "I was in the white building for a long time. A very long time. Before that, another prison. For nothing. This…disease did not begin with machines in necks. How can it end with them?"

Malakai doesn't answer, but in the firelight Tasha thinks she sees his jaw flexing. He doesn't look afraid: he looks the way Tasha feels, something inside him marching. He wants to blow it all up too. Whatever *all* may be.

"How will you blow this place up?" Reuben says after they've all stared up at the sparks rising to the ceiling long enough. "The white prison. You'll drive up to the gates? Knock?"

"We have information that will help us do what needs to be done," LaBrenda says, rubbing her palms slowly against each other. Tasha wonders if there were other things in Rio's Glass that LaBrenda has found and not yet shared with the group. A woman like LaBrenda is full of surprises.

"You will need a tooth," says Pamela. She's staring across the fire at them, her eyes shifting from face to face. When her gaze falls upon Tasha, Tasha thinks she sees a bit of stone injected into her jaw as well—some of the fear leached out and replaced bit by bit with brick.

"A…a tooth?" LaBrenda says, surprised. Tasha glances at her, takes in her eyebrows cinched together with confusion. "I'm sorry, what do you mean?"

"Wait," Pamela says, and rises so quickly that the person sitting next to her jumps a little. She takes long strides toward the lodge, her scarf billowing out behind her, and disappears inside. Everyone is confused, and Reuben turns all the way around on his bench to peer after her. Tasha thinks she will be gone longer, and Reuben is starting to rise to follow, when Pamela returns suddenly, emerging out of the shadow between lodge and campfire with a strange expression on her face.

"We took this when we left," she says, returning to her spot on the bench, the people around her shuffling to make more room. Suddenly she seems larger, and they all feel it. Once sitting, Tasha can see that Pamela cups something, the fingers of her left hand curled around it protectively. "Glenda. And me. I told you…I told you we killed a man. To escape."

She pauses, looking at her hand. Tasha feels goosebumps rising on her flesh.

"We took this. We thought maybe we would return. To rescue the others. We thought we might need it. So we took it. From his mouth."

"You took…his tooth?" Malakai says, his eyes wide, his head cocked. Tasha remembers him at his mother's house in Chicago, when Ishmael had said he played too much Halo before the Change. Tasha thinks that maybe violent video games are something like a buffer between a kid and this shit.

Pamela opens her hands.

"We took his tooth."

Tasha can't see. The thing in her palm is too small. Pamela starts to pass it around so it can reach their group, but the man sitting next to her doesn't want to touch it. She gives a small understanding shrug and stands again, coming around the fire to lay the object in LaBrenda's waiting palm. Tasha looks.

It's a tooth, yes. But not a white molar with a bloody root as Tasha had queasily expected. It's an incisor, a little too long and sharp to look completely harmless, but its vampiric appearance isn't what makes it most strange. Where the root should be is a glowing bit of blue, shaped like a bullet and patterned with what looks like almost-microscopic digital circuits.

"This is another kind of chip," Pamela says before returning to her seat on the bench. Tasha notices then that a few people have gone inside. Tired, or afraid? Tasha is both. She doesn't blame them.

LaBrenda doesn't pass it around the group, but holds it up for Tasha and the others to see. Tasha doesn't want to touch it, but she peers at it. She's hated the dentist her entire life. The whirring, the dry sound of drill against enamel echoing through her mouth and into her skull. The sight of this tooth puts an ache in her jaw, a ridiculous paranoia that if she went and pulled out every one of her teeth with pliers, the sink would be full of little glowing bullets like this one. She shudders.

"How does it work?" LaBrenda says, eventually closing her hand around the tooth and gazing at Pamela.

"I don't know. Not much. It's like a thumbprint. The doctors and people in white coats would take this out of their mouth when entering a corridor. Some doors needed them too. Like a fingerprint."

Tasha glances at Z, wondering if she remembers slicing off the thumb of the guy at the Web so they could drive his Ferrari. It had seemed like a bit of harmless revenge at the time— revenge for what, exactly, Tasha's not sure. For everything, she guesses. But this tooth is a key to a much bigger door. One she's not even sure she wants to open. Z's eyes are on the fire, her thoughts elsewhere.

"Genetic material plus digital encryption," LaBrenda says, more to herself, holding the tooth up again, gazing at it in the firelight. She looks past it at Pamela. "We may have had a tough time if it weren't for you. Thank you."

"You will have a tough time anyway," Pamela says quickly. "But I'm glad to give it to you. Maybe you can do what we wanted to do. Me and Glenda. Go back. Help the others."

"We will try," LaBrenda says, and Tasha wonders if she means it.

"Was there a guy named Dragon?" Z says. Tasha can hear in her tone that she's been trying to keep herself from asking, but the question is like hot water bubbling out of a geyser. The question has been scalding her throat. It must come out.

"Dragon?" Pamela says, arching an eyebrow.

"Snapdragon," Z says, leaning forward, staring intently. "He looks kind of like me? With a scar on his hand? Shaped like a Y. Did you know him? See him?"

Pamela's arched eyebrow softens as she begins to understand. This isn't a question of intel; it's a question of love. Tasha thinks she sees her searching for gentle words in the garden of her sharpness.

"There were many of us," she says carefully. "Too many. They kept us separate from each other. Long hallways. Separate rooms. Locked doors, opened only by tooth. I'm sorry. I don't know. But I am alive. Your Snapdragon may be too."

Z exhales in a rush, her shoulders slumping back against the bench, as if the thought of the question was the only thing that had been keeping her upright and alert. She looks wrung out, Tasha thinks, and she carefully puts her arm around Z's shoulders.

"This kind of world is not good to families," Pamela says, her eyes sad.

"When was it ever?" Tasha says without thinking, and she feels Ishmael's eyes fasten on her face. She doesn't look up. Suddenly the crackling fire has lost its warmth.

"It's late," Reuben says. "Do you want to sleep?"

"Yes, thank you," says LaBrenda, answering for all of them, and Tasha is grateful.

"I'll show you your beds."

Later, much later, Tasha lies awake. The darkness of the lodge is heavy and thick: Reuben and Pamela had put the electric lights out one by one, rolling shut the sliding doors at each end of the building and barring them securely. The only light comes through the occasional gap in the walls' wooden slats and from the two small windows at either end of the lodge, and Tasha again thinks of building a cabin. But the thought calls Leona to her mind—somewhere west, bouncing Amani on her hip after the baby woke up crying. She wonders if Amani will recognize her as her aunt, if Leona will have shown her photos. She wonders if Morris is nice, if he will see Tasha as a sister, or as just a face with vague stories attached. Will Leona even recognize her? Will Tasha recognize Leona?

Tasha swings her bare feet out of bed, jumps at the feeling of dirt and not stone or wood under her soles. She's wearing the pair of leggings she found at Macy's and takes a moment to appreciate their softness. She's on the bottom bunk, can see the shadow of Z's hand hanging over the edge, motionless in slumber. She's glad she hadn't bumped it with her head. Z would have awakened, asked her what she's doing, why she's awake. How could Tasha tell her that she's awake because part of her is afraid to find her own sister? Just as afraid as Z is about Dragon.

She doesn't decide to get out of bed, but her legs take her anyway. She places her feet cautiously in the denseness of the dark, the little light from the far-away window barely reaching back into the lodge. But she moves toward it—a slow, careful moth winding its way through the night. When she finally reaches the window—running into nothing, waking no one— she hugs her arms around her body, and it's not until then that she realizes she'd left her knife by her bunk, tucked safely under the frame to avoid stepping on it in the morning. She drops her arms, considering fetching it, but the silence of the lodge soothes her, the still night outside the window soothes her. Moonlight illuminates the dirt lane leading between the rows of white tents, making their pale figures seem to glow. A Minker could walk out of one any minute, she knows. They never seem to be far away. But right now, there are none.

Someone else is awake. She can hear stirring from within the darkness, the gentle creak of a bunk bed. A moment later a shadow shifts, and her eyes pry at the gloom until the shadow becomes a shape and the shape becomes a face. Ishmael joins her by the window, his white t-shirt wrinkled and glowing. She's not surprised to see him. She thinks maybe she's been calling to him here from the window.

"What are you doing awake?" she says, her voice just another shadow in the night.

"Thinking. Watching the window. I fell asleep for awhile and when I opened my eyes again I could see someone standing at it. I figured it was you."

"Why?"

He shrugs.

"You think a lot too."

She *hmms* at this but says nothing, still looking at the moonlight on the lane. Greenex had left their workers to fend for themselves even before the Change. Maybe they'd known it was coming and had gone underground, corporate moles tunneling away from the fallout of Cybranu and Neovison. Maybe the ground is filled with countless other corporate tunnelers.

Somewhere in the dark Tasha can hear Xena whine—maybe trying to get in bed with Malakai. The thought of it brings a smile to her lips, a smile she directs at Ishmael, who's watching her.

"What are you looking at?" she whispers.

"You," he says simply. His hand rises from his side and extends toward her in the moonlight. She reaches out to meet him, a shiver running up her arm at the feeling of his skin. It's warm—soft and rough at the same time. He guides her hand to his face and she doesn't resist when he places his lips against her palm. It's barely a kiss. He inhales her. Then he returns her hand to her and they stand looking at each other silently once more.

Her face and chest feel hot. She finds something to say.

"I bet your mom will be so happy to see you and Kai," she whispers.

He smiles and looks at his feet.

"Yeah. I know she's gotta be worried. But I'm glad Marcus is with her."

"You don't talk about him much."

He looks out the window.

"I guess I don't."

"You wanna tell me why?"

He squints out into the dark.

"Do you see that?"

She cocks her head, still staring at him.

"If you don't want to talk about it, that's all you have to say."

"No, Tasha, do you see that?"

She looks, her eyes refocusing as they meet the moonlight. At first that's all she sees: the pale light and the empty lane, the tents as before. But in the shadows of the bushes and trees across from the lodge, she sees slight movement. Her heart lurches and she grips the windowpane, her muscles steeling to send her racing back to her bed for her knife. But Ishmael's hand rests on her bicep, lightly as a butterfly, a soundless signal to wait. She waits, the two of them holding their breath, peering through the glass.

The shadowy leaves shudder and Tasha knows that any moment a Minker—a pack of them—will emerge, their barking rising as they spy Tasha through the window, drawing more of their ilk from all over. But when the bushes part (much lower to the earth than Tasha had expected), it's not a Minker: it's Sadie, the small dog that Xena had befriended when they arrived. Tasha almost laughs.

"It's the fucking dog," she breathes. "Michelangelo's stupid spaniel."

"Jesus," Ishmael says, his hand dropping from her arm, which feels cold after. She puts her palm where his had been. "I thought it was them."

She doesn't reply; she doesn't need to. He didn't even need to say it, really. The fear is always "them." She's considers telling him some version of this when she notices the bushes are still moving. She's holding her breath again, watching, and Ishmael's sudden stiffness tells her he sees it too. She instinctively presses her body to one side of the window; he follows suit.

Michelangelo emerges from the bushes, moving strangely in a half-crouch, his head hunched down awkwardly between his shoulders. He's creeping, Tasha decides. This is his body's idea of creeping. Sadie the spaniel doesn't seem to understand the covertness of whatever their mission is, however, and trots a few feet ahead of him, looking back at him curiously every few steps.

"What the hell is he doing?" Ishmael breathes.

Michelangelo creeps across the lane, quickening his pace when he's out in the moonlight, hurrying to get back into the shadows by the lodge. Tasha drops into a crouch, only her eyes above the sill, and Ishmael quickly does the same.

"He's going to come in here," Tasha whispers, her heart pounding. She wishes she had her knife but isn't sure if she actually needs it. Would she stab Michelangelo? And for what?

"No, he's going off to the side," Ishmael says, pressing his face against the glass in an effort to keep his eyes on the guy and his dog, who have disappeared by the side of the lodge. "He's going to the back. Come on."

She scrambles up from the floor and together they pick their way through the near-dark of the lodge, careful to avoid the potentially noisy wooden benches that surround the long table in the center. They slow down as they pass the bunks against the wall, the sound of many soft breaths of sleep following them like a murmur of breeze. As they pass Tasha's bunk—Z still motionless on top—Tasha crouches and snatches her knife from underneath the frame, then follows Ishmael to the back of the lodge, their steps hurried but muted.

Outside the back window, the fire from that evening is still smoldering, and Tasha's mind races faster at the thought of all that had been said as they sat around it. LaBrenda had gone to bed still clutching the tooth that Pamela had given her, and no doubt it has been placed somewhere safe and secure for the duration of their journey to Phoenix. Phoenix. It waits ahead like a shadow across their path.

Michelangelo creeps out of the darkness into the faint glow provided by the fire's embers. He glances at the window—to the sides of which Ishmael and Tasha are pressed—but seems more concerned about the dark. He perches on the very bench Pamela had sat on, looking around into the shadows. Sadie sits by his feet, wagging her tail in the dust. And there they sit.

"What's he doing?" Ishmael whispers. Tasha notices then that he carries his axe. He must have grabbed it while she was getting her knife. They stand there at the edges of the window, armed for a battle they're not even sure needs fighting. The interloper seems more interested in warming his toes than in gaining entrance to the lodge.

"He's just sitting," Tasha says, annoyed. He could at least be doing something even slightly offensive: stealing crumbs from their dinner, or raising his middle finger to the sleeping lodge. Something that would give them an excuse to throw open the door and yell like maniacs. She feels the urge to yell like that, to let out the pressure that's been building since Pamela told her story. Maybe it won't be released until they get to Neovison and do what needs to be done.

"What do you want to do?" Ishmael says, and Tasha feels her annoyance double. She had finally gotten a chance to be alone with Ishmael—a desire she's felt building within her—and Michelangelo had snatched the opportunity from her. Now he has the nerve to just sit placidly by the fire.

"I'm going to talk to him," she decides, and moves to unlatch the door.

"Whoa now, hold up," Ishmael says, grabbing her hand. "Let's think about this for a second."

"What's to think about?" she says, pulling her hand out of his grip, even if his skin is warm. "He's alone. He's unarmed. You have my back. Right?"

Ishmael looks hesitant.

"This seems stupid as hell," he says finally, shaking his head. "We should wake up LaBrenda. Or Reuben. We should wake up Reuben. This is their place."

Tasha nods at that. It is their place. Opening up their door in the night seems rude—like eating snacks out of your host's fridge without asking.

"They've been through so much already," she says, eyeing Michelangelo through the glass. "I kind of want to handle this without worrying them."

He says nothing, also watching Michelangelo, who no longer looks out into the shadows but hunkers there by the dead fire like a gargoyle. He still wears his orange Nutter Putter shirt.

"I'm going," she says, and he doesn't stop her. She lifts the latch as smoothly and quietly as possible—the silence of the hinge rewards her efforts—and slowly, slowly inches the sliding door open. It rumbles low like a sleeping dog, but that's all. She stops it after a few more inches and squeezes through.

He sees her immediately, and so does Sadie. The dog stands quickly, tail wagging, and Tasha winces at the inevitable bark, but Michelangelo grabs the spaniel, holding her muzzle, with a swiftness that surprises Tasha. He wants quiet too.

"You're here," he says, standing, and she clenches her knife, ready to slash if she needs to. She hears the rumble of the gate behind her and Ishmael appears to her left. They're outside, the door closed behind them.

"What the hell are you doing creeping around out here?" Tasha says.

"I was waiting for you," he says, gently returning Sadie to the ground. The dog sneezes but looks otherwise unoffended at being silenced.

Tasha squints at him. He looks exhausted, as if he has aged several years since she saw him outside Nutter Putter a few hours ago, when he'd asked if they wanted the charge in their car. She has no idea what time it is—somewhere between midnight and dawn, she guesses—but he certainly hasn't slept.

"Nothin' inappropriate," he says, raising his hands. His entire body is a white flag, a disarming posture of surrender. "I just needed to talk to you. I had to."

"Me? Or us?"

"You. You're...you're the one in the video. You're Tasha Lockett."

Every hair on Tasha's body is suddenly quivering on end, and her knife feels slippery in her grasp.

"Who told you my name?"

Michelangelo shifts his weight from foot to foot, and his eyes are on the shadows again. He reminds Tasha of the stray dogs that would pop up at her parents' kennel from time to time—drawn by the sound of their kin and the smell of kibble. Cautious but usually gentle, their eyes a little wide and red from being on the street without protection. Michelangelo has this same look in his eyes now: red-rimmed, haggard, ready to bolt.

"They just sent the clip," he says. "We all have it. They scanned you on the SkyDrive..."

Ishmael drops his axe and in one motion has his hands wrapped in Michelangelo's orange shirt. Tasha gasps, surprised, and Sadie the spaniel whines, her tail wagging. Spaniels are so dumb.

"What are you talking about?" Ishmael demands. The fear in his voice makes the hairs on her body stand up even more electrically—it means her own fear is justified. She steps closer, getting in Michelangelo's face.

"What video?" she snarls. "How do you know my name?"

"Please," the man says, not begging but sounding tired, too tired to struggle. "I will explain. I don't mean you kids any harm."

For a moment they just stand there breathing, Ishmael's jaw clenched tight and the darkness thick around them like a cloak. But eventually Ishmael's grip loosens, the orange t-shirt slipping out of his grasp, and Michelangelo takes a step back, smoothing the material on his chest.

"It's not me," he says. He stares at Tasha seriously, the circles under his eyes drooping, making him look like a much older man. "It's important that you know that. I didn't ask for this job. But business is so bad. Worse every year. They keep my lights on…"

"Who?" Ishmael snaps. His axe still lies on the ground at their (bare) feet, but Tasha has a feeling he'll snatch it up quickly if necessary. She hasn't loosened her grip on her knife. Barefoot or not, she will do what she has to do if it comes down to it.

"Greenex's parent company," he says with a limp shrug. "Neovison."

Tasha squints in the dark.

"Neovison?" she repeats.

"Isn't that…?" Ishmael starts to say.

"Yes," she says.

"They have their fingers in a lot of pies," Michelangelo says almost apologetically.

"What does that have to do with me?" she says. "*Who* is sending videos? I thought the world was over, for fuck's sake!"

"Just ours," Michelangelo says, rubbing his cheek. "Theirs is still…ticking away."

"What video, dude?" Ishmael insists.

"You did something in Chicago that they don't like," Michelangelo says, flinching a little, as if one of them had raised a fist to him. "I don't know what—I guess you probably do. And they've been looking for you. Then you got on the SkyDrive…that's where the video is from. Inside your car on the SkyDrive. The ads…"

It's as if an icicle has penetrated Tasha's spine, the chill spreading through her body and numbing her limbs.

"The ads what?" Tasha says, her tongue feeling thick and clumsy. "The ads what? They…they watch us?"

Michelangelo shrugs, as if this isn't the part she should be concerned about.

"Of course. Neovison funded the SkyDrive, so they have rights to the information they get from the ads."

"Rights," Tasha echoes.

"Yes."

"And they...they saw Tasha?" Ishmael stammers. "They're looking for her? Why?"

Michelangelo sits heavily down on the bench behind him, Sadie eagerly putting her furry front paws on his lap. He cups her round head gently, staring down at her.

"I don't know everything," he says. "But they say you're a terrorist. That's all they said in the video they sent out. Part of Red Rooster or some such."

"Red Rooster," Tasha says. She can't form new words. She can only repeat.

"Tasha," Ishmael says loudly. He's turned to her and grips her shoulders. She looks up at him blankly. "The Apiary. You used your card to get upstairs to Cybranu. Your ID card."

"The Apiary...," she says slowly. He's right. She'd used her card. Rio had asked her to: that was the only reason she went. It had her name and face on it. She'd scanned it. It had registered. She'd thought the world was over. She'd thought there was nothing left to fear except the obvious, endless Minkers. Autopilot beasts. Remove the hubs, remove the monsters. Now this droopy man comes out of the dark to tell her that there are shadow-people at the controls: shapeless watchers who know her name and her face and are following her across the States.

"Fuck," she whispers. And then it settles in. They know her name and her face. There is a *they*—a bigger, scarier they. Louder, "Fuck!"

"Why are you telling us this?" Ishmael turns on Michelangelo again; the man's body droops like the stray dog he resembles more with every moment. "Who the fuck are you, dude?"

"I don't work for them," Michelangelo says softly, shrinking. "I just...work for them. I don't want to see anyone else get hurt."

382 OLIVIA A. COLE

"Do they know where we are?" Ishmael's fists are balled. Tasha thinks he might hit the man, and though she hopes he doesn't, she doesn't have the energy to tell him not to. She floats there, numb.

"Not yet," Michelangelo sighs. Sadie has finally caught on to the tension and stands back, closer to the lodge, her tail not quite between her legs but close. "But it's only a matter of time. They'll be tappin' into cameras and ads everywhere west of Denver soon."

"Where are they?" Tasha asks, still feeling like shouting. "In Phoenix? Are we walking into a shitshow? We thought every fucking thing was abandoned!"

"I have no idea," Michelangelo says, drooping so much he's almost melting. "I don't know. I know they went dark for a few days when everything…happened. Then came back up again."

"Why didn't you tell Reuben and the others?" Tasha snaps angrily. "They were waiting and waiting for Greenex! They had no idea what was going on!"

He says nothing, staring at the ground. She wants to slap him, feels her hand twitch as if she might.

"You need to go," he says, finally raising his eyes to look at her. The orange of his shirt glows in the night. "You need to find somewhere safe. If they find out you were here and I didn't tell them…"

"He's right," Ishmael says. His clenched fist is pressed against his forehead. "We need to get the hell out of here. We need to get to California."

"California?" says Michelangelo, raising an eyebrow, which raises the droop of one eye just a fraction. "Is it true it's safe out in those parts? I saw something on the Web about it once or twice…"

"We don't know," Tasha says. "We don't know."

"Some dangerous folks out there," he adds. "You Rooster folks have…"

"I'm not Rooster!" Tasha snaps. "And not everyone in California is Rooster either!"

He firms his lips into a straight line, not wanting to argue. Behind Tasha, Sadie has her front paws on the hearthstones around the fire.

"Down, girl," Michelangelo says.

"So they just...sent you the video," Tasha says. She wants to find a hole in his story. She wants to find the secret tunnel that produces the white rabbit inside the hat. This must be a trick.

"Not just me," he says mournfully. "There are other stations like mine around the States. Not in every state, but in a lot of 'em. On their grid."

"So you knew about the Change," Tasha demands. "And you did nothing."

He holds up his hands, returning to surrender pose.

"I didn't know until two days after it had already gone down. Out here we didn't know the difference. Out here nobody has those things in their neck. They put the growth center here because it's isolated."

"But they told you."

"They sent us all the same thing: woodchuck. It's a code word. It means disaster and to keep our heads down. That's all I know."

Ishmael groans. Tasha glances at him. She's not sure why he's groaning but doesn't want to ask. There are many reasons to groan; she just doesn't know the current one. He sees her looking at him in the dark and throws up his hands.

"This is insane," he says desperately. She can make out the soft wrinkles on his forehead. "This is just...insane." He glares at Michelangelo. "They told you 'woodchuck', and you haven't heard anything else?'

"That's all," the man says quietly. "That's all. Until the video tonight. Offering a reward for finding you."

Tasha walks away from the barely glowing coals, out from under the roof covering them. Beyond the area cleared around the lodge there are more bushes, scrubby things with branches extending like a wire fence against the moonlight. She looks up at the sky, the smoky clouds drifting between her and eternity. If she could, she would leap out into that blackness, set a course for the empty solace of the moon. But she's too heavy, and she lacks wings. She thinks even if she had them, anger might weigh her down. She breathes deeply, feeling the solidness of her feet on the earth, their bare soles uncomfortable on its cool roughness. Rio had pictured these feet walking all this way. Had he also pictured the shadow people of Cybranu and Neovison catching up with her? Had he known that using her card would put them on her scent? She sighs, sending—if nothing else—her breath up to the stars. She turns back to Ishmael, who stands waiting in the moonlight.

"Let's wake up LaBrenda."

CHAPTER 22

They left without waking anyone but Reuben. Michelangelo led them up the moonlit lane with a slouch in his shoulders, Sadie trotting happily at his heel, while Reuben asked them over and over if they were sure. About what, Tasha didn't ask. Sure about leaving in the middle of the night? Sure about Michelangelo's information? How could they be sure about anything?

When they were reunited with their car, Michelangelo informed them that he had given them the charge they'd paid for. He also had a gift: power cells.

"You don't need to look for a charging station with these," he'd said, tucking them into the mostly-empty hatch—only the bagged explosives remaining—under LaBrenda's supervision. "Just stop and replace the power cell in the engine with one of these. I'm giving you more than you need for…for where you're going."

LaBrenda had examined the cells and told him they were very expensive. He'd nodded. Then: "One more thing."

When he'd gone into Nutter Putter, Tasha had expected him to emerge with a weapon of some kind: a trick Neovison played by putting him in their path. But when he returned to the lot, lit by the vibrant orange of the neon sign, he carried only a large cartoon duck, stuffed, a blue bandana around its neck, extending it to Malakai.

"For your hole in one," he said. "I didn't forget."

Malakai, sleepy, had held the duck for a moment, one finger tracing the shape of a bright plastic eye. Then he'd handed the duck to Reuben.

"Can you give this to baby Lourdes for me? When she wakes up."

"I will."

And they had driven away.

LaBrenda had offered to drive, but Tasha had ignored her, settling in behind the steering wheel without a word. She drives and drives, her eyes so intense on the road ahead that the headlights eventually begin to feel like two lasers beaming straight from the sockets of her skull. Z had stayed awake for awhile, murmuring directions in the otherwise silent shell of the car, but once they got back to the highway, she'd slowly faded into sleep. Tasha can't tell if the rest of the group sleeps or not—even if awake, the quiet seems somehow nonnegotiable. There has always been danger. But now it has a name, and it knows theirs.

Still, the gift of Michelangelo's power cells seems to envelop the car in a protective haze. They may still need to stop for food, but power is theirs. As long as someone is awake—or alive—to drive, the black engine of Monica Potter's SUV will carry them onward like a rocket charted for a new universe. Even if they were all dead, Tasha thinks, the car might just carry on to Phoenix at least, steered by the power of their posthumous desires. Hours pass, or rather Tasha passes them, her palms against the steering wheel sometimes sweating, sometimes clammy, but always tight enough to make her aware of her pulse pressed against the leather. Onward. Onward. The sound of the tires against the highway is the thrum of her blood through her veins. Onward.

"Where are we?" Z's voice is groggy from the passenger seat. Tasha glances over at her, where she sits rubbing her barely-open eyes.

"Go back to sleep," Tasha whispers. She has no idea what time it is. The car clock is wrong—by how much she's not sure, but it's still deeply night. Nutter Putter and the Greenex camp are only a few hours behind them.

"Where are we?" Z repeats, more alert now. She slowly straightens up in her seat. She's been Tasha's co-pilot in multiple cars since their first Ferrari. Thanks to Michelangelo's gift of power cells, maybe it will be the last car they ride in together. Maybe they won't even need cars in California.

"We just passed Las Vegas," Tasha says.

"What? Las Vegas?"

"New Mexico. Las Vegas, New Mexico."

"I didn't know there was a Las Vegas in New Mexico."

"That's what the sign said."

"New Mexico. Nice."

Z reaches for the map, somewhere in the shadows of the floor in front of her seat.

"Leave it," Tasha says, waving her hand. "We don't need it. There are signs at this point."

"I just wanna see how many miles."

She rustles around at her feet. Tasha can hear the crinkle of granola bars; her stomach lurches with hunger. She shouldn't be hungry—it's the middle of the night. But Michelangelo appearing at the lodge has made her hungry. She hasn't stress-eaten since college, though if snacks were more readily available since the Change she certainly would have been munching her way through Minker misery. She's glad to be driving. Something to focus on.

"A little over five hundred miles left," Z says, the map held close to her face in the dark. Tasha reaches over and presses a button on the ceiling, bathing Z's lap in light. "Thanks. We could be there in…eight hours?"

"That sounds about right. Give or take."

"Wow."

They sit in silence, the knowledge settling over them like dew. Tasha can almost feel it sinking into her skin. Eight hours.

"Are you okay?" Z says. Tasha can feel her gazing across the car, knows without looking the concerned angle of her thin eyebrows.

"Yeah."

"They won't catch up," she says, still looking. Tasha keeps her eyes on the road. These words of comfort assume that the enemy is only behind them. Michelangelo said there were posts like his all over the States, and certainly digital advertisements abound. The strip of highway they're currently cruising is almost bare of digiboards, for which Tasha is grateful. Each ad is suddenly like an eye, every animated surface an electronic spy. Logically, she knows not every advertisement is capable of recording. But she has no clue which ones are which. The rest of their journey to California is a digital minefield.

"Eight hours," Z says after awhile, when Tasha doesn't reply. The words fall out in the shape of Z's brother: Tasha can hear him there in her voice as if Z had said his name.

"Yeah."

The sun comes up sooner than she'd expected. At first, heart jolting, she'd seen its glare in her rearview mirror and thought something was catching up to them: some flaming pursuer trailing their car like a hellhound. The glimmer of light in the dark could only be fire. But sanity returns to her in a breath of realization. Sunrise. Day. Another rotation of the earth that brings her closer to her sister, and safety. And ahead, Wal-Mart.

Or at least that's what the signs tell her. Signs, not digital boards. She feels her heartbeat slow.

Z had gone back to sleep many miles before. LaBrenda now wakes, her stretch catching Tasha's eye in the mirror as she glances back at the sunrise once more. Catching her glance, LaBrenda gives her a nod.

Tasha twists her mouth in reply. Not a smile, but a grimace.

"Stopping soon?" LaBrenda says, not really whispering.

"Yeah. I was thinking Wal-Mart." She points at another sign before they whiz by it.

"How fast are we going?"

"Eighty-five."

"Wow."

"What, I'm gonna get pulled over?"

"Nope. Just happy we're making good time."

"We could be there this afternoon if we wanted."

"Let's talk about it when we stop."

Tasha slows to 45 for the turn that will carry them down from the highway to the long congested strip below. The angle slides Z's head—leaned against the car window—farther and farther forward until it slips, waking her. She wipes her mouth and looks around.

"Where are we?"

"Is that always going to be the first thing you say when you wake up?" Tasha laughs.

Z shrugs sleepily.

"Until we get where we're going."

"We're about fifty miles from the Arizona border."

"We're stopping?"

"Yeah. I need to stretch and we need to find some food."

Z nods at another Wal-Mart sign as they reach the bottom of the curve that brought them down to the strip.

"There's a Wal-Mart. We can go there."

Tasha rolls her eyes.

"Yeah, that's where we're going."

The strip looks faded, as if the buildings and the road that runs down the middle of it had all been brushed in lemon juice and left out in the sun. Everything has a crispiness to it, dry and blanched. A strong wind could disintegrate everything. Except for the Wal-Mart, a half-mile farther along. Its neat bricks and clean blue facade look out of place, a newfangled toy plopped down in the midst of antique marionettes. The sunrise has not gathered its full strength yet, dawn still dim around them, and the enormous store's sign casts its white glow out over the parking lot. Somehow it seems like a mirage to Tasha as she steers the car in its direction. False. As if she'll find that all the food on its shelves is wax, for show only. Behind her she hears Xena yawn, the long somewhat screechy sound of an animal who is comfortable in her surroundings. She glances back. Everyone in the car is awake now.

"It's daytime already?" Malakai says.

"Barely," Tasha says. "The sun's just now rising."

"What all are we getting from the store?" Z says, directing the question at Tasha but glancing back for input from the rest of the car.

Tasha shrugs.

"I figure we just grab what looks good that's still good," she says. "We need to restock anyway."

The parking lot is scattered with the usual post-Change debris: trash and bodies, abandoned vehicles—mostly early-model cars and, Tasha notices, the occasional RV. She hasn't seen one since she lived in Kentucky, when customers would drive them up to the kennel to drop off their dogs before a trip. Only the most expensive models were electric, and so it was rare to actually see them on the road. Rich people didn't buy RVs. They bought planes. These RVs aren't those models, though: their design is too bulky; faded and antique like the rest of the strip. They hulk like mammoths imprisoned in tar. When Tasha parks the car and steps out, she thinks she might just sink into the asphalt herself. Even with the sun barely up, the heat is powerful, a radiating presence that almost seems to hum.

"Whew," Z says. "Glad we're not walking."

"Amen to that," Tasha nods. "I really hope the rest of the group has managed to find cars."

"My mom hates being hot," Malakai says, yawning and leaning against the SUV with the poodle at his side. "She'd get her own car if the group didn't want to."

Tasha smiles, but her mind goes to the body of Bianca, outstretched on the lonely pavement just before the SkyDrive. She'd left her group—or her group had left her. Either way, being a lone wolf on this road west doesn't seem like the best idea.

"Marcus would be with her either way," Ishmael says, frowning. He doesn't like the idea of his mother on her own either.

LaBrenda is already walking toward the Wal-Mart, her spade-turned-machete held easily at her side.

"How many miles did you say we are from Phoenix?" she says over her shoulder.

"About three hundred at this point," Z says, following her. Tasha can feel their eagerness, sharp and quick where her own reluctance is dull and heavy. Each step after LaBrenda feels more precarious than the last, as if she's trailing her on a rope strung across a canyon.

LaBrenda turns, stopping before they reach the store.

"We're going to have to be really sneaky with you when we get to Neovison," she says to Tasha.

"What do you mean?" says Z, sounding suspicious.

392 OLIVIA A. COLE

"Cybranu clocked her in Chicago. They've got a solid scan on her or they wouldn't have identified her on the SkyDrive. If she walks right into Neovison, some camera might pick her up before we even get in. I can't risk the whole joint going up before I get in and find what I need."

"Or what I need," Z says, clicking her box cutter in and out. "Well, who."

"That too."

"Why are they looking for Tasha?" says Malakai. He'd been half asleep as they hustled out of the Greenex camp. "Because of what happened at the Apiary? It wasn't even her."

"It was her ID they scanned," LaBrenda says, shrugging. A breeze rolls over them from the east and Tasha's sigh joins its flow. "They must have known Rio was part of Red Rooster at that point, and they're assuming she's affiliated."

"But she's not," Malakai says, his eyebrows crunched low over his Bambi eyes. "She didn't do anything."

"I know. It's bullsh—" LaBrenda catches Ishmael's glare. "Bullcrap."

"It *is* bullshit," Malakai says, pushing off the SUV. Xena stands from where she's been sitting and pricks her ears forward. She hears the same thing in his voice that Tasha hears. Angry helplessness, fear. If she were to speak it might be in her voice too.

"Kai...," Ishmael begins.

"It is!" he insists. "It's not fair. She didn't do shit now they're coming after her. It's Rio's fault!"

"Malakai, watch your mouth," Ishmael snaps. He moves one foot as if to start toward his brother but stops himself.

"It's Rio's fault," Malakai repeats. A week ago he might have been near tears. Tasha thinks with a sinking heart that maybe he's had the tears wrung out of him.

"Either way," LaBrenda says. She's come back toward the group, stands only a few feet from Malakai. "Now we gotta protect each other, right? They're onto her, but that means all of us are in danger, because we're together. They already sent the Minkers on the SkyDrive for her, and it almost got us all killed. That could happen again. So we gotta be smart. Right?"

LaBrenda had intended these words for Malakai, but when he nods, Tasha nods too. The idea of Cybranu, or Neovison, or whatever, trailing after her like a shadowy bloodhound, its muzzle at her heels, has dulled some edge of hers. Gripping the steering wheel, driving endlessly through the night, she had managed to keep the feeling at bay. She was an untouchable comet blazing through the dark. Now, in daylight, on pavement, Wal-Mart ahead of her like a massive ugly Lego, she's here on Earth again, subject to all its rules and violence. Above her, on poles in the parking lot, are cameras. They don't seem to be aimed at her, but any one of them could be a quiet black eyeball, a more obvious watchman than the one that had registered her face. The idea that the thousands—millions—of ads she's walked past and stood in front of her entire life have been eyes watching her and monitoring her face makes her shiver.

"Let's get the food," she says. "And get moving. Who knows if these cameras are working or not? They might be able to hack them and see us."

LaBrenda makes a sound of agreement and they troop up to the entrance of Wal-Mart, Xena swinging out to the left to sniff what appears to be a dead cat. Tasha snaps her fingers and the dog comes wheeling back, prancing.

"A lot of blood here," LaBrenda observes, pausing as they enter the doors. The automatic doors open for her, oblivious to the state of the world. The bright fluorescent lights inside are even brighter than the sunrise.

"God, I hate Wal-Mart," Z sniffs.

LaBrenda laughs at that, leading the group into the blast of AC that sinks into Tasha's eyeballs, immediately making them feel strange and dry.

"Yeah, that makes two of us. Where Wal-Mart comes, gentrification will follow."

The front of the store is clogged with bodies, at least a couple of dozen corpses strewn across one another in tangles of limbs. Tasha expects the stink of rot to assault her nostrils, but the smell of death is weak.

"Did Minkers do this?" Tasha says. She doesn't want to look too closely at the bodies—she's out of the habit of needing to look. But something is different here. The bodies are piled on top of each other, mostly face down. Not the erratic postures of defeat she's seen in so many other victims of Minkers: defensive, horrified, rigid. These people seem to have fallen where they stood, a line of human dominoes who decided this was the place to die. But so many...

"Those are bullet holes," LaBrenda says flatly. "Look."

She gestures at a man in a blue shirt, separate from the others by a few feet, his cheek against the floor and his back pocked with round red stains.

"Bullet holes?" Ishmael says, taking a closer look. "That'd be a big gun..."

Tasha sees the three men before the rest of the group: three men in camouflage, blending into nothing in the stark plastic brightness of the Wal-Mart, two of them with black toboggan caps on their heads. All three of them with guns. Big guns. She sees them and isn't sure they're actually there. Their guns are a joke, a ruse used to scare people they're unsure of. A warning. She opens her mouth to say something to them, to her group, to anyone. Even Xena doesn't notice the armed men, their unhurried progress from the direction of checkout lane 22.

"Guys," she says finally, but the guns are being raised, first one and then the other two. "Guys, shit!"

The sound is thunderous in her ears. Z screams. Xena flees, out the front doors that open for her, gone. Tasha thinks she feels the smallest breeze, but it's a bullet whizzing by her. She hears the clatter and shatter of walls and checkout signs being struck by the hail of bullets. She cowers, scrambling, Ishmael and LaBrenda both snatching her same arm, dragging her toward checkout 1, where Z has already taken cover. How has she not been shot? The pops of the guns are too close; they sound like cannons. She stumbles over corpses, one of her feet tripping on a dead woman's arm. Nearby, inches away, is a handgun, its muzzle under another body's hip.

"Gun!" she screams at LaBrenda, who has let go and allows Ishmael to drag her. LaBrenda pounces on the gun and scrambles behind checkout 1. Ishmael shoves Malakai toward her and LaBrenda yanks the boy down. He's doing the same to Tasha when a bullet sears past her cheek. It makes a soft thudding sound as it buries itself in Ishmael's body. He gasps, a harsh exhalation that sounds like a cough, and topples to the ground, taking Tasha with him. She can hear herself screaming, can hear Malakai screaming. She throws herself on top of Ishmael, ducking more bullets, and buries her fingers in his shirt, dragging him toward checkout 1. He still clutches his axe. *Pop, pop.* LaBrenda has fired the handgun at the three men. Tasha hears them curse, the clatter of the trio diving behind another checkout. She and Z drag Ishmael to cover, blood making their fingers slick, both of them shrieking at the thick red pool gathering on the tile. And above, a security camera. Tasha sees its flashing red light as the neck of the camera slowly turns the lens onto her face.

CHAPTER 23

"Ishmael! Ish!" Tasha sobs, shaking him.

"Don't shake him," LaBrenda snaps. "Put pressure on the shot!"

"With what? With what?"

"Your fucking shirt, I don't know!"

Tasha yanks her shirt off, Malakai hyperventilating.

"What the fuck do we do? What the fuck do we do?" Z stammers. She must have touched her own face in her terror: a streak of Ishmael's blood decorates her cheek.

"Z! Help Malakai!" Tasha cries, and Z immediately throws her arms around the kid, who is shaking so much he looks like he's being electrocuted. His exhalations comes in throaty sobs, he can't catch his breath. He hugs Z back, clinging to her like a cub.

"I can't tell where he got hit!" Tasha shrieks.

LaBrenda, crouching, straightens up and fires a single shot over the top of the checkout. Her hands shake—there's no way she could have hit her target. But whether she hit someone or not, she's rewarded by a curse from one of the three camouflaged men.

"Rip his shirt!" she orders. She's crying, Tasha sees, and it makes Tasha cry harder.

She grasps Ishmael's shirt at the neck and uses all her strength to tear it. It comes apart easily, more easily than she'd expected.

"It's my arm," Ishmael croaks. "My arm."

"Ish," Malakai says in a strangled voice.

"I'm okay. I think I passed out for a second."

"Oh my god. Oh my fucking god," Tasha sobs, hugging him.

"Damn, it hurts!"

"Pressure, Tasha!" LaBrenda barks.

With Ishmael's shirt off, she finds the wound easily. Blood seeps from the outside of his upper arm, almost at his shoulder. As Tasha begins to wrap her shirt around it, LaBrenda peers over the top of her head.

"It's not bad," she says simply and starts to poke her head up over the checkout again. A volley of bullets forces her to drop down quickly. "Fuck!"

"Use my shirt," Ishmael manages through gritted teeth. "Keep yours."

Tasha thinks her heart might explode. Her fingers shake, slippery on Ishmael's bloody skin. The bullet had torn through his outer arm, she sees, the flesh ragged and open like torn fabric. She clumsily wraps his t-shirt tight around it, knotting it firmly.

"Is this okay? LaBrenda, is this okay?"

LaBrenda fires another two shots. Tasha wonders how many bullets the gun holds. LaBrenda looks at Ishmael's arm.

"That's gonna have to do. We need to get the fuck out of here!"

"Ish...," Malakai sobs. Ishmael sits up and grabs his brother's hand, tugging him off of Z. They embrace, tears and blood between them, Wal-Mart's air conditioning like ice packing it all.

"I'm going to shoot at them some more," LaBrenda says, her back against the checkout. She's not crying anymore. Her face is contorted with fear, but her eyes are dry. "When they duck down, we're going to run."

The doors they entered through only moments ago are a mere twenty feet away, but Tasha can't picture herself leaving this small bit of shelter and sprinting out into the open. The deer in her bones is frozen in the headlights of gunfire. She can't move. If only she had been as quick as Xena, fleeing as soon as trouble was evident. She should've warned the group as soon as she saw the three men, but she was frozen, as she is now. She forces herself to put on her t-shirt. She needs to remember that her limbs work.

"Is that Xena? Where's the dog?" LaBrenda says, listening, gripping the pistol in both hands as occasional bullets from the three camouflaged men spatter the top of the checkout. Tasha winces with every impact. Z sits like a statue, Ishmael's blood like a brand on her face.

"Where?" Tasha pants.

"Barking. Did she make it outside?"

"Yes, she did, but…"

It's not Xena. As soon as Tasha hears what LaBrenda hears, she knows it's not Xena. She hears the muted sound of barking, the ragged vocalization that comes from only one kind of throat.

"Holy fucking shit," Z whispers. Tasha barely hears her over the gunfire. In the short pause between shots, LaBrenda jerks up into a standing position and fires off one bullet. Tasha's head snaps up at the sound of a scream.

"Oh my god!" LaBrenda dives back down, her face wide open with disbelief. "I…I shot one of them. I got him!"

She laughs, a strangled sound like a horse neighing. Then she's crying again, hiccupping.

"Oh my god," she repeats. "I shot him right in the head."

"Jesus Christ," Tasha says, grabbing LaBrenda's arm. It's shaking. They're all shaking. The world is shaking.

"Oh my god," LaBrenda says again, but her shock about shooting one of the men has passed momentarily. She's staring at their escape route, the Wal-Mart doors sliding open at the whim of new shoppers entering the building.

The crowd of Minkers now jamming through the doors is at least ten deep, and Tasha knows there must be more. It looks, she thinks momentarily, like a Black Friday sale. She can hear their chorus rising as they enter the supercenter, the sound of a dozen more behind them, a miniature army of former people, blood ringing many of their mouths like bright red wreaths.

"Ishmael…," Malakai whispers, still clinging to his brother.

"We need to run," Tasha says softly. The Minkers haven't seen them yet: a display of beach balls, on sale for the summer, partially blocks their view. But they move their heads back and forth mechanically like robotic watchdogs scanning the perimeter of their programmed territory. Attack is imminent.

"Wait," LaBrenda murmurs. "Come this way. Be *so* fucking quiet."

She's crab-walking along the checkout, keeping her eyes on the Minkers. She's moving away from the front door, Tasha notes with panic, angling her path backwards toward the jewelry department. But they need to find another escape route anyway. The gunfire from the camo guys has paused—no doubt seeing to their fallen comrade. Tasha follows LaBrenda as cautiously as she can, her sneakers sliding a little in blood. Behind her, Z, Malakai, and Ishmael, still shirtless, scoot across the tile, all of them watching the Minkers with eyes like lasers. If only they were lasers, Tasha thinks. That would solve a lot of their problems.

"Your axe," Tasha whispers to Ishmael. It's behind the checkout, its handle in a pool of blood. He grimaces and reaches out with his good arm to clutch it. Tasha hopes he can still swing it. He's going to need to.

The crack of gunshots lights up the air again suddenly, and with increased ferocity. The guy LaBrenda shot must be dead, and his hunting buddies are angry. Tasha hears one of them yell—the first time she's heard actual words: "You fucking cunts are dead!"

And then the remaining two must have caught sight of the Minkers, because next Tasha hears, "Shit, Gary, fuck!"

The Minkers see them too. They stumble forward, and Tasha sees that she was correct: there are far more than ten of them. Where had they come from? They seem to have sprouted out of the tiles.

"Move, move now," LaBrenda utters, and they all slide across the floor on their asses, staying low, Ishmael dragging himself with one arm, Malakai carrying the axe. Tasha keeps her fingers curled under the handle of her knife to keep it from clattering against the floor. Her heart is clattering loudly enough as it is.

They all slide behind a clearance bin of children's shoes as the crowd of Minkers rushes past checkout 1. More gunfire. Unless the remaining two dudes can snipe every Minker's neck very precisely, Tasha thinks, their big-ass guns are useless, as useless as her knife had been against their bullets.

"Can we get outside?" Z whispers. Everyone has stopped crying. *Survive now, cry later,* Tasha thinks.

LaBrenda is still clutching the handgun, this time in one hand, her other holding her spade. They must have looked ridiculous to the camo guys: knives and garden tools against enormous guns. Yet they had fired anyway. Who are they? Why?

"We can try to get…," LaBrenda starts, peering back toward checkout 1. Then her face drains, her eyes widening. "Run! Run!"

Tasha doesn't bother looking to see what they're running from. LaBrenda's face says it all. They take off toward the jewelry department, Tasha zig-zagging in case it's the men in camo behind them. She has no idea whether zig-zagging is actually an effective way to avoid bullets, but she keeps it up all the way to women's wear. Then she realizes the gunshots she still hears aren't right behind her, but at the front of the store. She's running from Minkers, the sound of their harsh barks carrying over the rattle of gunfire. It's almost a comfort—this familiar monster, compared to the sudden onslaught from beasts of the human variety—until she looks back over her shoulder and finds a pack of seven Minkers hot on her trail, their expressions angry and wild. Suddenly she's sobbing for breath, her legs not pumping fast enough. Wal-Mart's bald fluorescence forces its way into her eyes, burning her retinas with its glare: The harsh light and the chill make her feel as if she's already dead, running toward a white light as her body slips into a morgue's freezer.

"Tasha, over here!"

It's Z, with the others, far to the left in the electronics section. Tasha had split too far from the group: even shirtless, bloody Ishmael is with the pack. Tasha is a lone zebra out in front of the jackals; this image causes her to panic even more, tripping over her own feet to angle toward Z. The hollow barking of the Minkers behind her is electricity in her legs. She charges onward; as soon as she's close, Z turns to continue running. Together again.

"Where are we going?" Tasha pants.

"Sporting goods! Those two assholes probably got all the guns, but we might be able to find something."

Z is running out front, her ponytail swinging left and right over her shoulders. Her arms pump at her sides, one hand clutching her box cutter. She's about to leap over the body of a long-dead Wal-Mart shopper laid out across the aisle when the display of wireless headphones just ahead of her explodes under a barrage of bullets. Z screams, falling backwards.

"They shot me! They shot me!" she shrieks. She still grips her box cutter, her other hand clutching her face.

Tasha and the others drop into a crouch, Malakai clutching his brother's good arm and his axe. Tasha sprints forward, dragging Z up by the elbow. Z's face is bleeding a little from her forehead where shards of plastic from the shelves struck her. A sliver still juts from her eyebrow. Tasha plucks it out.

"You're okay, you're okay," she pants.

Another blast of bullets over their heads sends them diving to the ground again. Ten feet behind the Minkers bark, their eagerness intensifying at the sight of their quarries stopped, as if waiting for them.

"This way!" Ishmael shouts, diving past shelves of hover boards and drones and knocking over a display. Tasha yanks Z after her and they follow, LaBrenda bringing up the rear. Tasha sees her pause, turning to fire two shots behind them at the unseen men in camouflage.

"Keep going!" she yells, leaping after Tasha. "Sporting goods! Sporting goods!"

"I can barely see," Z cries, pawing at the blood in her eyes. Tasha runs with her knife in one hand and Z's arm in the other. They pound through the aisles of the enormous Wal-Mart, the grin of the yellow smiley-face at every turn a cheerful grim reaper that reminds them of the fate awaiting them if they slow down.

"I see footballs," Malakai gasps. Another round of gunfire explodes behind them, but Tasha thinks it's aimed at Minkers, because nothing near them shatters.

"We've gotta be close," says Ishmael. His bare chest is bright with sweat.

Tasha sees a bow and arrow at the end of aisle 11 and sprints toward it, Z in tow.

"Here, here!" she cries, forging ahead.

"Tasha!" Z's shriek rips the chilly air as two Minkers lunge out of aisle 10. One of them runs into Tasha's knife, the blade sinking into his shoulder. He pays no mind, of course, yawning toward her neck as the other grasps her bicep, the grip sinking into her arm like robotic claws. These two ignore Z, their glares boring into Tasha as if they hope to kill her with their eyes alone. Z throws herself at the one going for Tasha's neck, box cutter raised, but he's already turning toward Z and bulling her bodily into a rack of self-baiting fishing poles. Tasha hears the air leaving her friend's body in a whoosh, leaving her gasping on the ground as the two Minkers turn back to Tasha.

The hands on her arm quickly pull her closer as if on a mechanical towline. She twists her arm as hard as she can, feeling the burn of the Minker's grip chafing her skin. Panic rises like a sudden storm, flowing outward from her heart. She can't break loose. She can't get him off. She feels her lungs begin to heave, shaking her entire body as she tries desperately to pull free. She's afraid to raise her leg to kick the one who had thrown Z: she feels off balance, overwhelmed.

Ishmael's axe flashes in a silver arc, lopping off one of the arms holding her. The blood spurts out onto her shirt, joining the red splashes from Ishmael's wound. With only one arm to contend with, Tasha uses all her strength to turn her blade on the remaining attacker. The knife severs arteries—more blood—and the grip falls away. Free, she brings her hand all the way back to her ear to wind up for stabbing the Minker's neck: when the blade finds its mark, it buries itself up to the handle. The other Minker falls to Ishmael's axe. She turns to thank him, but finds Malakai there instead, the weapon hefted with less ease than when wielded by his older brother. He uses both hands, looking young and afraid but defiant.

"I was aiming for his neck," he says apologetically. "I got his arm instead."

"It doesn't matter," she says.

"Sporting goods!" LaBrenda yells, their rallying cry. Behind, five aisles down, Tasha sees more Minkers fall to bullets but rise before they've even settled on the floor. She can't tell if they're coming after Tasha or the camo guys as they drag themselves to their feet. Another one or two are emerging from the children's section. Tasha turns to run.

Sporting goods. At the end of the aisle, LaBrenda springs over the top of a glass counter. Tasha feels her muscles gather to do the same, but she doesn't think she can make it over and runs around the side instead. LaBrenda and the others are pawing through the contents of the case, which had already been shattered.

"Only a couple handguns," she says, her mouth tight and grim. "But at least that's something."

"What's the plan?" Ishmael says, clutching the bandage on his arm. Tasha hopes it's tight enough. Did she even do it right? These are the kind of things she would search on the Internet before the Change. "Guns aren't going to do jack against Minkers."

"We just need to hold them off," LaBrenda says, but Tasha can hear uncertainty tingeing the edges of her words. "We need to get the guys with the guns. Take them out. The Minkers we'll have to handle afterwards."

"But there are so many…," Malakai says.

It's as if they heard him and want to prove him right. A rise in barking causes the group to whip their eyes back down the aisle, where a pack of Minkers is gathering. They crowd there as if conversing, their heads snapping left and right, scanning the area like savage pigeons seeking seed. Then, as a unit, their gaze settles on the group behind the glass counter. Tasha feels a chill like ice injected into her arteries. Even from this distance, she knows those eyes are on her. Her friends would just be collateral damage. Whether it was the camera in the parking lot or the one at the front of the store, she can feel in her bones that somewhere in the shadows of what's left of the world, Cybranu or Neovison or whoever they really are had seen her face, and ordered in the beasts. She looks down at Malakai, both of his hands clutching his brother's wounded arm. In Ishmael's left hand is the axe he'd taken back, which he won't be able to swing as effectively for awhile. Z is poised slightly behind LaBrenda, both of them looking terrified. LaBrenda grips two handguns, two pieces of metal that Tasha doesn't even know how to use. Useless in her hands and useless against the Minkers, which are lumbering down the aisle with gathering speed, their mouths open wider and wider to emit the cry of the hunt.

Tasha leaps over the glass counter, knife in hand, hearing Z scream her name behind her.

"Get the camo guys!" Tasha yells over her shoulder. Her Nikes hit the ground with a solid slap, but no sooner is she on the other side of the counter than she sprints away, heading toward the rear of the store. The Minkers rage after her, the whole pack of them flooding down the aisle like a tidal wave of teeth and howls. Tasha glances back to gauge their distance—a woman with blonde French braids pounds after her in the lead, her cheeks red, her eyes furious. Tasha leaps over a dead body in her path and skids around a corner into another aisle. Behind her she hears the clamber of Minkers falling, struggling over each other to remain on her heels.

Farther away Tasha hears the gunfire again. She ducks as she runs, even knowing that it's not aimed at her. Between shots she hears shouting, and grits her teeth at the thought of any of her people getting hurt. They've survived hundreds of miles of Minkers, have survived a bomb a hundred stories in the air— to die by a bullet seems impossibly unfair.

She has no plan. She sprints past the baby care department. A few paces later she smells the stink of rotting meat and produce—she's at the other end of the supercenter now, where the groceries are. She feels a pang of sharp disappointment at the sight of all the lovely cans of food they could have packed into the back of the SUV. Enough to get them to California and enough to sustain them for awhile in case California proves to be a wasteland. Her bag is in the car—even if she wanted to she couldn't stuff something away, and she assumes running away from Minkers while pushing a cart is a sure way to die.

Tasha skids around another corner. Ahead is the second wide entrance, on the other side of the store from where they had entered. Outside, the sunrise is gorgeous; the soft yellow light beckons to her, a gentle alternative to the burning white of Wal-Mart's fluorescence. She runs toward the entrance, thinking maybe she'll dash outside, run to the car, and then steamroll every Minker she meets. As she gets closer, however, she realizes the doorway is blocked by the pull-down gate used to signify the store is closed. The gate for the doorway they had used must have been lifted by the camo guys. She doesn't have time to lift this one now, not with the braided Minker and her crew hot on her heels. She looks desperately around, hoping to find another option, but instead finds another Minker, surprising her from the front, where he explodes from checkout 30.

He's too close: she stumbles backwards to avoid him, but falls right into the arms of the blonde Minker. The woman collapses under Tasha's weight, surprised by her sudden capture. Tasha lands on top of her, scrambles to get off before the teeth find her skin. She feels clumsy, shaky. They're all around her like a swarm of fish, piranha jaws snapping. Tasha slashes at the woman as the Minker from checkout 30 looms down on her. Her blade manages to cut flesh, but she doesn't know what and knows it's not the Chip. She clambers up, slashing when the woman's hand catches in Tasha's braids, her heartbeat in her ears, and throws herself at the standing Minker. Behind her, the rest of the pack closes in.

She lashes out with the knife and happens to catch the guy's throat. Not the Chip, but close. As he falters, the bloody tentacles in his body stitching up the gaping wound, she slashes again, wildly, as she tries to get around him. She catches the Chip, barely, a lucky cut, and the man's neck sparks as Tasha stumbles back away from him. A display of candy bars blocks her way; she shoves it and it falls on top of the Minker woman, who was slowly rising from the floor. The crash echoes in the huge cavern of Wal-Mart. Tasha spins, her ankles almost twisting around each other, as she directs her feet back toward the other end of the store, where the gate isn't a cage door locking her in with a small army of cannibals...

A cage.

The idea rises in her mind like a mushroom cloud. She races along behind the checkout lanes, grabbing every display she sees and shoving it down behind in her wake. She feels like a video game character, dropping shells and bananas to slow her pursuers. Her feet pound onward, and she forces herself to ignore the sharp pain between her ribs. She tries to breathe in through the nose, out through the mouth. She needs to find Ishmael and the others, and listens for gunfire.

Pop, pop, pop. She's rewarded by the sound of shots and zooms onward in the direction she's already heading. She can hear barking toward the back of the store and prays that those Minkers are after one of the camo guys and not speaking in beast-ese about how best to bring Tasha down. She sprints past aisle after aisle, shooting a look down each one as she passes.

"Azalea!" she screams, the sound of gunshots drawing her like a fish on a reel. "LaBrenda!"

"Tasha!" she hears. It sounds like Z. "I'm coming!"

"No! No, don't! Run, get outside! I have an idea!"

"No, I'm coming—"

"GET OUTSIDE!"

The pack of Minkers is fifteen feet behind. If she can make this work...

Far ahead, at the other end of the store, Z and the others burst from menswear, Malakai and Ishmael out front as Z and LaBrenda hop-skip backwards. Z has something in her hands—Tasha can't tell what—and is fumbling with it as LaBrenda fires from two handguns into whatever or whoever follows them. LaBrenda's spade is gone, lost in flight.

Whatever Z is carrying makes a whirring sound; she holds it in front of her, running sideways. She almost collides with a tall display of candy, but mostly misses it except for her hip, which sends boxes exploding in all directions. As Tasha sprints toward her she can see that the object Z carries is a sort of gun as well, but its body is strangely shaped, purple and almost circular. Z pauses, aims, and fires; the mouth of the contraption emits a blur of blue light, which disappears into the racks of clothes Z emerged from. After firing, Z turns and runs after Malakai and Ishmael, fiddling with the machine again to reload it.

"Keep going!" Tasha yells. "I'm coming, just keep going!"

She stops herself from wondering what will happen if she gets to the entrance and there's no gate. She'll just have to keep running. There are at least twenty Minkers behind her and more throughout the store, she can hear—more than she and the group can handle. Her plan has to work.

Tasha has almost reached menswear, where her friends had appeared, when a man in camouflage sprawls out onto the tile ahead. He still clutches a gun, his black toboggan actually a ski mask, pulled down over his face, his lips and eyes visible through round holes in the fabric. He struggles to his feet, slipping and sliding in terror, and fires a shot into the racks behind him. Then he sees Tasha, and even with the mask she sees the moment of indecision in his eyes. He aims the gun at her, holding it firmly in both hands, his legs planted.

She can't stop running. Death ahead and death behind. She can't stop. She continues sprinting straight at him, and it's as if he sees what chases her for the first time. He lowers the gun fast, his mouth wide open and silent behind the mask, and then without a word turns on his heels and tears off toward the exit. Tasha gulps air and follows him, not caring to look if his surviving buddy follows from menswear. She paints a target on his back with her eyes and forces her feet to catch up. If anyone is getting torn apart by the pack of Minkers, it's this asshole.

He beats her through the entrance. She doesn't see Z and the others but she can't think about that now. She tosses her knife out through the entrance and turns, frantically looking up and around. The gate hangs there just a few feet above her, nylon straps dangling teasingly just out of reach. She can pull it down; she just has to reach it…

She leaps, exhaustion making her heavy and clumsy. She barely leaves the ground, her muscles protesting every movement. The Minkers thunder toward her, rending the air with their throaty yowls. Behind them, emerging from menswear, is the last man in camo, unarmed, limping. He sees her, waves erratically. He knows what she's going to do. He wants to be saved. Delusional with fear, he wants her to wait, to band with him against the inhuman snarls that set them apart. She will not wait.

She leaps again, her fingers brushing the nylon strap this time. A Minker pulls ahead of the pack, his blue eyes ablaze. Her heart feels as if it might explode as she leaps again, but her fingers catch the nylon loop. She holds on for dear life, yanking with her whole body, feeling a tendon in her armpit pull too far, a hot stretching pain. She grips the loop with both hands, and finally the gate yields, slowly coming down from its folded uselessness, its metal clinking slowly at first and then more rapidly, like a dog's chain towed behind a charging mastiff.

The gate is still three feet from the floor when the blue-eyed Minker out front slams into it. Tasha is crouched low, pulling the loop, and his knee rams her skull through the links. She falls back on her ass, pain blooming in her head; to her horror the gate starts rising again, losing momentum. She screams involuntarily and scrambles to her feet, leaping high on the gate, her fingers between the links, dragging it down again with her full weight. The other Minkers arrive in a hurry now, their snarls inches from her face, their teeth straining at the links. The gate slinks downward, finally clinking against the floor. She shouts in triumph, yanking it once more as it bounces a little, but then she's struck by intense, blinding pain coursing through her hand, a sudden shock to her entire body that sends her reeling backwards.

The pinky finger on her left hand is gone, blood spurting from where it had been like a small volcano. She shrieks, staring at it in disbelief, uncomprehending. It's only when she sees the blue-eyed Minker, fresh blood pouring down his chin, that she understands. Her finger rolls from his mouth, his teeth striped red, and drops to the floor. Her hand throbs, and the sight of her dead finger—its nail still beautifully polished with black— alone on the tile floor fills her with rage. She screams again, whirls, snatching up her knife in her right hand, and attacks the gate, the blade slicing through the links and lodging in the Minker's blue right eye. It means nothing. She can't reach his Chip, and her blood spilling down her wrist begins to make her dizzy. She stumbles backward, cursing wildly. The Minkers press against the gate obliviously, some of them biting the links like mad dogs. And behind them, the limping camo guy stands in checkout 4, his hands on his head: incredulous, lost, overwhelmed. The Minkers haven't seen him yet, but they will.

Tasha turns her back and flees, out into the early morning sunshine, squinting, screaming for Z and Ishmael. The car is where they left it, right at the curb, but she doesn't see them anywhere in the lot.

"Z!" she yells, her throat feeling like torn paper, rough-edged from shouting. "Ishmael!"

"Tasha."

Z sounds strangled and Tasha whirls to her left, where she finds Z and the others bunched against the wall, LaBrenda with a black eye. The camo guy who had fled ahead of Tasha stands there with a gun in each hand, leveled straight at Tasha's friends.

"He wants the key to the car," Z says. She looks as if she might have been crying, but anger has burned away the tears.

"What the fuck is wrong with you?" Tasha barks at the guy. She curls her left hand inward, cradling the place where her finger had been. The pain is excruciating. "There are tons of cars! Get your own fucking car!"

The camo guy glares at her. He's pulled his ski mask back and it now perches on the crown of his head. His hair is wild and uncombed, bright red through its length and dark brown at the roots. His facial hair was unkempt even before the Change: he now sports a Viking-esque beard and mustache that belongs on a heavier man.

"I don't want my own fucking car," he spits. Literally. Spittle flies from his lips. "I want your fucking car. Now stop fucking around and give me the fucking key!"

Sudden barking interrupts the scene and they all tense to run, even the camo guy. But it's not Minkers, and Tasha can't help but feel disappointed. It's Xena. She crouches at the edge of the Wal-Mart, twigs in her beautiful fur, showing her teeth and snarling. Camo Guy aims one of his guns at her.

"Don't you shoot my fucking dog!" Tasha screams, and launches herself at him.

"Tasha, NO!" Z shrieks, but Tasha and the guy are already struggling, one of the guns dropped to the pavement and the other between them, four hands gripping and pulling as they breathe too close to each other's faces. *I'm about to die*, she thinks, the thought like Morse code rattling through her mind, and when she hears the gunshot she knows she's been killed, a bullet breaking through her skin somewhere, her life seconds from its close.

But she isn't shot, and neither is the camo guy. No one is shot. It's not even their gun that fired. It was a gun aimed at the sky, held by the tallest woman Tasha has ever seen. The woman sits astride a Pumapod, flanked by six other riders with their machines hovering almost silently by Monica Potter's SUV. All of them are dark-haired—except one, who has dyed his hair blue—but with a variety of skin tones and features. The tall woman, like several of the others, wears a thick turquoise necklace, a wide silver band on her wrist. When she sees she has their attention, she slowly lowers the gun, aiming it at all of them, any of them. Tasha thinks she smiles.

"Okay," the woman says, powering off her Pumapod and floating gracefully to Earth. She looks like an angel. "That's about enough of that."

CHAPTER 24

In the long pause that follows, Tasha's finger screams for attention. Its throbbing dulls her other senses, the adrenaline that has carried her, flying, through Wal-Mart shrinking down beside it so all that's left is pain. She's so focused on it that her reflexes are slowed.

Camo Guy yanks the gun from Tasha's grasp, her wounded hand unable to grip it any longer. He fumbles with it, struggling to aim it at the people on the Pumapods; then, as if struck by unseen lightning, he crumples to the ground. Tasha gazes around, bewildered, and finds Z with her strange purple gun still pointing at where he had stood.

"It's a shock gun," she says. Her eyes are wide. "For rapists and stuff."

"They sell that at Wal-Mart?"

"They sell everything at Wal-Mart."

"For fuck's sake," Tasha pants, and bursts out crying.

Z drops the weapon and throws her arms around Tasha.

"Your hand, your hand!" she cries.

"My hand," Tasha sobs.

"Let's take a look," says the tall woman. She's dismounted her Pumapod and strides over to where they cluster by the fallen guy in camouflage.

Tasha shakily extends her hand when the woman approaches, averting her own eyes from the bleeding stump.

"Ouch," the woman says, twisting her lips. She has a beautiful round face that reminds Tasha of her grandmother, if she'd known her grandmother at forty. Deep-set eyes under finely arched black eyebrows, skin like polished cedar. The eyebrows convey a harshness that isn't present in her eyes—instead, Tasha sees laughter there. As if not only is Tasha's missing finger secretly hilarious, but so is the whole world.

"Found the finger," one of her companions says, emerging from the Wal-Mart entrance. Tasha hadn't even noticed him leave the group. "And about thirty dead-heads locked in."

"You came from in there?" the woman says, nodding toward the Wal-Mart.

"Yes," says Z. "We went in for supplies and these dudes…"

The woman waves her hand, letting go of Tasha's.

"I know what they've done. We've been looking for them for two days."

"Whose idea was the gate?" the guy who found Tasha's finger says.

"Me," Tasha says weakly.

"Smart," he says, wiping perspiration from his forehead with a red bandana. It's the first time Tasha has noticed the heat since they emerged from Wal-Mart. The sun still isn't high in the sky, but the heat has bloomed from it like a sweltering blossom. They all stand in its garden, sweating. "Can you reattach her finger?"

"Unfortunately not," the woman says, studying Tasha's face. "I'd need to perform microsurgery to do it right. I can dress it, however. I'll make sure you're okay."

"Were you a doctor?" LaBrenda says.

"I'm still a doctor," the woman says coolly. "Surgeon. Like my mother and my grandmother."

LaBrenda nods.

"Legacy. Cool."

"What doctor did your arm?" the woman says, eyeing LaBrenda's black metal prosthetic. "It's lovely work."

"Not quite a doctor. My mother. She was an engineer."

"Are you an engineer like her?"

Of bombs, Tasha thinks. But she looks to LaBrenda for her reply, curious about how she'll answer.

"No. I'm something else."

"Your mother didn't make you follow her path?" the woman says with the same hint of amusement.

"No. Yours did?"

"It was a path we knew we had to take," the woman says, serious. Her hands jerk, a gesture of inevitability. "Indian Health Services started sterilizing women in the 1970's. We needed our own doctors."

LaBrenda's eyes squint with recognition.

"The same reason I plant my own food," LaBrenda says.

Tasha thinks that the comparison isn't quite apt, but the tall woman seems to see the parallel clearly, her amusement transforming into something like familiarity. She nods at Ishmael, who clutches his bloody arm.

"What happened to him?"

"Shot," Tasha says. "By one of those assholes. I…I wrapped it really bad."

"Where are the others?" another woman on a Pumapod says. Her face is grim, absent of any of the humor the tall woman's face displays.

"Dead," Tasha says. "We shot one and I let the Minkers—the dead-heads—have the other."

The tall woman looks over her shoulder.

"Radmilla, is this him?"

"No," the woman says. She dismounts her Pumapod, the seat of which she shares with a second rider, and walks over to get a closer look at the man in camo, who is sprawled on the ground unconscious, his mouth slightly open. "It's one of them, obviously, but it's not *him*."

"What happened?" LaBrenda says. She's come forward from where she's been standing behind Z and Tasha. The tall woman, still carrying her gun, doesn't look quite as towering with LaBrenda alongside her. "If you don't mind me asking."

"I do," says Radmilla. Her voice is laced with anger, but one look at her face tells Tasha she's grieving: the sadness is like a sheet of marble just behind the eyes. Tasha knows that look. She still sees it in the mirror sometimes.

The woman returns to her Pumapod and digs in her pack, her hands emerging with zip ties. When she binds the camo guy's hands with them, Tasha thinks she sees her fingers shaking. Meanwhile, her own finger throbs.

"You're...you're not going to shoot us, are you?" Tasha says to the tall woman, who observes the zip-tying without comment. At Tasha's words, she looks down at the gun in her left hand and holsters it at her hip. Over her white pants she wears a flowing red shift with a black geometric pattern—Tasha hadn't even noticed the holster.

"No," the tall woman says. "We're not going to shoot you. Is this your car? Do you have medical supplies?"

"Yes, we have some," Tasha says.

"Okay, then I can show you how to patch this up. What's your name?"

"Tasha."

"Just Tasha?"

"Tasha Lockett."

"Nice to meet you, Tasha Lockett. I'm Esther Blackhorse."

Esther cleans and bandages Tasha's wound and instructs her on how to rebandage it later. After Malakai digs a shirt from Ishmael's pack, Esther examines Ishmael's arm too, and wraps it much more meticulously than Tasha had been capable of doing. In the medical supply kit that Tasha had poached from the Hollywood town she'd assumed was a case to hold things like tweezers and scissors, but Esther's expert eye sees it for what it is: a collection of disposable syringes with varying doses of medications. She injects both Tasha and Ishmael with a painkiller.

"Thank you for your help," Tasha says from where she sits on the curb. Looking up at the woman called Esther Blackhorse requires her to tilt her head all the way back.

The woman waves her hand, as if Tasha's graciousness is a cloud of gnats to be swiped away.

"You'll need more of that painkiller over the next few days," she says. "A shame you had to lose that finger. It could've been fixed so easily before all this."

Tasha stares at her hand, the thick white bandage like a club. She feels empty, staring at it. Maybe the knowledge hasn't sunk in. She has only nine fingers now. It should feel more horrifying than it currently does.

"What are you going to do with him?" Ishmael says, nodding at the guy in camo, who's still unconscious, lying zip-tied where they left him. Tasha wonders how strong the shock was. Surely he should be awake by now. He's not dead—she sees his chest rise and fall—but maybe he has brain damage. She notes that she doesn't give a single shit if this is true.

Esther glances at Radmilla, who frowns and stares off across the parking lot. Esther shrugs.

"That remains to be seen. They kill anyone of yours?"

"No," says Ishmael. He puts his arm around Malakai, who has been sitting silently beside him. "Just shot me. If all the bodies in there are were shot by them, though, they killed dozens."

"Why, though?" Z says, slapping her hands on her knees. "Why the fuck would they do that? We did nothing. We were just looking for supplies. I'm assuming the people inside that they killed were doing the same."

"Or they may have been living here," says one of Esther's group. He has a youthful face, partly due to his round cheeks. He plays with a loose thread on his blue t-shirt. "We've seen that a lot. Wal-Marts and Targets being used like campgrounds."

"But why just go in and kill them all?" Z asks again. She springs up from the curb, her box cutter sticking out from her back pocket. She's wiped Ishmael's blood off her cheek, but Tasha can still see a faint rusty smudge. "It makes no fucking sense."

"It's their way," the round-cheeked guy shrugs.

The guy in camo stirs, a groan rising from his throat. Esther stares down at him before looking over at her blue-haired friend.

"Adriano," she says, motioning for him to come help her. "It's time to go."

Tasha and her group watch from the curb as Esther's people try to figure out a way to transport the guy in camo on their Pumapods.

"He can't sit on the back," Radmilla says sourly, eyeing the guy, who is barely conscious. "As soon as he wakes up all the way he'll either try to jump off or choke the driver."

"Fair point," says Esther, frowning. "We should have brought one of the trucks."

"We should make him walk," Adriano says. "Our ancestors took the Long Walk. Only fair that he takes it now."

"Tempting," says Esther. She taps her chin. "It would be more fitting if we were taking him to Fort Sumner, though."

"Where are you taking him?" Tasha says. Her hand still aches under the dull blur of painkiller.

"To Window Rock," Esther says, not looking at her.

"Where's that?"

"The capital of the Navajo Nation."

"Where does the Navajo Nation start?"

"You're in it."

"Oh." Tasha pauses, considering this. "Are we...you know... allowed to be here?"

Esther turns and looks at her then.

"Are you Diné? Navajo?"

"Me? Uh...no."

"Well then, not really, no. We're making some new rules now that American jurisdiction is...up in the air."

"Oh."

Tasha stares at her, unsure if she's entirely serious, unsure if Tasha should be slowly backing away, taking the medical kit and disappearing in the SUV.

"We didn't know...," Tasha starts to say.

Esther waves her hand, not smiling but not scowling.

"Do us a favor and we'll consider it water under the bridge."

"A favor?"

Esther nods and points at the camo guy.

"Put this man in your truck and carry him to the New Mexico-Arizona border for us. We left a truck there so we could follow his group more quickly. Once we get there, you can go about your business. What do you say?"

Tasha exchanges a look with LaBrenda. She doesn't like the idea of having this guy in the car with them. Of course, she reasons, if he tries anything Z can just shock him again.

"Are you going to put him in jail?" Malakai says, the first words he's spoken since they escaped the Wal-Mart.

Esther levels her gaze at the boy. For the first time, Tasha doesn't see the spark of merriment in her eyes. Tasha thinks she might say something terrible, and Esther must consider doing just that, because she holds her breath for a moment, thinking.

"Yes," she says when she exhales. "Yes, we are."

They load the guy into the hatch of Monica Potter's SUV, and Tasha wonders what Monica would have thought of this particular use of her vehicle. Radmilla has zip-tied the guy's ankles as well; when LaBrenda and Adriano pick him up between them, he looks like a hog ready for the spit. They stand looking at him for a moment, curled in the back of the SUV, his expression muddled. His eyes are fully open now, but lack comprehension. *Must have been a hell of a shock,* Tasha thinks. She looks behind him, where the bags of explosives from the Pentagon slump. Still there. Still waiting.

"Malakai, you're riding up front," Ishmael says without taking his eyes off the guy. Tasha wonders what he's thinking. He hasn't objected to their transporting this guy, but she can see the concern arranged all over his face in varying creases.

"I'll ride in back with the shock gun," Z says, reaching to close the hatch.

"Me too," says LaBrenda. Together they shut the hatch on him, as if he's just cargo, another thing they carry west.

"Follow us?" says Esther. Radmilla is already mounting her Pumapod. Tasha thinks her expression is a little less sour, with the sweetness of vengeance so near the tongue. Tasha doesn't know if they actually intend to lock him up or not, but with a glance back at the sidewalk, where the guy's massive gun sprawls shiny and black, she still can't quite bring herself to care. Ahead, Esther and the others are boarding their Pumapods. The group of silent floating motorcycles is almost like a herd of strange, otherworldly deer, their silver flanks shimmering in the intensifying sun.

"Yeah, we'll follow you," Tasha says, opening the driver's door. She starts to climb in.

"You sure you can drive with that hand?" Ishmael says.

She pauses, looks down at her bandaged hand. She must look like a ragdoll, she thinks, between this and her other bandages.

"Better than you can with that arm," she says, nodding at his shoulder. Esther has bandaged it well, with a bit of a sling holding it close to his body. The fresh shirt he now wears had still managed to get a little blood on the sleeve.

"True," he frowns. He's worried about her. Despite the pain in her finger, she can't help but feel pleased.

"It's okay," she says.

"No, no," says Esther. She brings her Pumapod floating back to the ground. "You shouldn't be driving just yet. Let that hand rest. One of you should drive," she says, pointing at Z and LaBrenda, who stand by the bumper.

"I can drive," Z shrugs, but Ishmael shakes his head.

"No, two people need to be back there with that dude. I can't do much with this arm and Tasha can't do much with that hand."

Esther purses her lips, shifting impatiently on her Pumapod. She's got plans, Tasha thinks. Like them. They're holding up the show.

"Koltey," she says, turning to look at the woman riding behind Radmilla. "You drive. Tasha, you can ride with Radmilla."

"You mean...on the Pumapod?"

"Yes," says Esther, motioning to Radmilla to settle her vehicle back on the ground. Radmilla and her passenger, Koltey, sink down to earth, and Koltey swings her leg over the side.

"Is the keycard still in there?" she says as she approaches.

"Uh...yeah," says Tasha, a little taken aback. She looks at Z, who shrugs nonchalantly. Tasha feels foolish for her suddenly pounding heart—is she the only one who's never ridden one of these things? Is anyone else wondering whether Radmilla won't point the nose of the Pumapod to some undetermined destination, kidnapping her?

"You good?" Ishmael says in a low voice, before Koltey has reached the car. He fixes her with a soft stare that makes her jaw tremble.

She almost says no. The idea of being separated from the group again releases a net of toads in her belly: slimy and hopping. But when she looks up at Esther, that merriment is back in her eyes. She sees Tasha's indecision and is already teasing her for it. Tasha swallows. If Radmilla goes off course, she'll do what they'd feared of the camo guy: Tasha will grab her neck.

"I'm fine," she tells Ishmael, and strides toward Radmilla as bravely as she can manage. She wraps her knife in a t-shirt and stows it in her backpack, returning it securely to her shoulders. Xena follows her, tail waving.

"Xena," Malakai calls from the front seat of the SUV. He claps his hands. "You can't go with her. Come on."

The dog looks back, confused, and Tasha feels a swell of something sweet and silly. She and the dog had been through something together, she thinks: the fall, the mall, the Hollywood town. Xena sees Tasha as her person.

"It's okay, girl," Tasha says. "I'll see you soon. Go on."

The poodle returns reluctantly to the SUV, hopping in and staring out at Tasha with a bent neck.

"Beautiful dog," Radmilla says.

"She is, isn't she?"

"Do you have sunglasses?"

"Um...yeah. In my bag."

"You should put them on."

Koltey starts the car, and Tasha rises in the air, her arms wrapped tight around Radmilla's waist, the ground below golden through the tint of Tasha's sunglasses.

"Everyone ready?" Esther shouts, but all Tasha can do is nod. It's strange to be sitting here in the air, looking down at the SUV, the faces of her friends peering out at her. Malakai grins widely, his mouth moving. Telling his brother how cool it is, she knows. She tries to think it's cool too, but she can't quite shake the feeling of looking down at herself, like a ghost on the ceiling watching her body die. Her finger is down there somewhere, cast aside like a blown tire. No spare. Just the empty axle of her knuckle. She swallows again, the silence of the Pumapod unnerving. An engine like those in the old motorcycles might've drowned out her worry, soaked it up with noise.

But then they're moving, and the quiet is gone, replaced by wind. It beats in her ears, rushing past in a hurry. Radmilla steers them expertly, angling the Pumapod out of the Wal-Mart parking lot and back onto the crowded strip, back toward the freeway.

"First time on one of these?" Radmilla says, not quite shouting, over her shoulder.

"Yeah," Tasha says, probably too loud. She wonders if she's squeezing the woman's ribs too tightly, prays that if she is, Radmilla lets her go on squeezing, at least for awhile.

"Wait 'til we get on the open road! You'll love it."

Ahead, on the strip, is a small group of Minkers, yawning there in the middle of the road like a flock of aimless pigeons, their heads turning left and right at the sound of the approaching vehicles. Esther, in the lead, swerves tightly around them, close enough to make them reach their arms out to grope, grasping nothing but air. Tasha hears Radmilla laugh, feels her body vibrate with the sound.

"What did those guys do?" Tasha says, hoping her words aren't lost in the wind. "To you guys, I mean?"

"The same thing they've been doing for hundreds of years."

They follow Esther onto the freeway, and Tasha chances a glance over her shoulder, where she sees Monica Potter's SUV following closely. They are a strange herd, this group of faces and machines. Tasha looks ahead again, the road stretching out black and blissfully empty before them, and for a moment the rushing air replaces the breath in her lungs.

"See?" Radmilla yells, the wind louder and louder as they pick up speed. "Don't you feel free?"

Tasha closes her eyes, the wind rushing over her braids. Yes. She does.

CHAPTER 25

"Is this Window Rock?" Tasha climbs off the Pumapod, wobbling. They'd only ridden for a little over three hours, but she feels the way cowboys must have felt, the straight legs passed down from her mother turned bowed in just one ride. Still, she can see the appeal of Pumapods now. You're not hovering: you're flying. She doesn't know why she didn't see it before.

Radmilla dismounts as well. Tasha hadn't noticed when she put on the goggles, but she pulls them back onto the top of her head now, where they protrude from her dark hair like two round ears.

"No," she says, stretching and rubbing her lower back. "It's farther to the north. But that's our truck."

She points to a large white pickup truck parked inside a wide asphalt square, at the center of which is a lumpy gray statue, the figures of which Tasha can't make out right away. The truck carries a strange red rack mounted on its hood, a grid pattern marking its surface.

"What's that?"

"Solar panels."

"On the outside of the truck?"

"Yeah. We call it Redshirt. Years and years ago, a girl designed a solar stove on the rez. This is based on her design. Lasts a lot longer than the cells."

Monica Potter's SUV pulls up and Tasha walks straight over to open Malakai's door. He yawns, just waking up.

"Hey," she says, bumping his shoulder with her fist. "How was the ride?"

He shrugs, rubbing one eye.

"It was okay after awhile. Z had to buzz the guy again."

"What?"

The back door opens to reveal Z, who looks smug.

"It's true," she says. "He started calling us cunts and all that again. At first I took off my shoe and stuck my sock in his mouth, but he spit it out and kept at it. So I shocked him."

"Jesus, Z, you're gonna kill the guy!"

Z moves her eyebrows in a way that communicates her half-apathy about this fact, but shakes her head.

"Nah. He's fine. It's just a little shock. And I turned it down from the setting it was on at Wal-Mart. I had it turned on high while we were in the store because…well, obviously."

Tasha eyes the purple gun in Z's hands.

"I've never even heard of those things."

"A couple of the other guards at the Web had them," she says, hefting it. "After they banned guns in Chicago they had to give security something to keep the tenants happy. Never gave me one, though."

"I see why," Tasha says.

"Shut up."

With Z out of the way, Xena leaps from the car, her tail furious, sniffing Tasha's bare ankles. Her dog nose is cold and wet and sends a shock through Tasha's skin, charged with memory. She buries her hands in the dog's fur as Ishmael and LaBrenda emerge from the car. Ishmael's white bandage is still white—Tasha had been afraid she would find a vibrant red seeping through. He gives her a smile.

"How was the ride?"

"It was…," she inhales, searching for the words, still petting Xena. "I'm glad I did it."

"Me too. I was watching your braids flapping around when we were driving behind you. You looked like a little dragon."

"A dragon?" She laughs, not altogether displeased with this image of herself.

"Dead-heads," Adriano calls. It takes a moment for the word to translate into Tasha's own vocabulary. When it sinks in, the emptiness of her hands suddenly feels like a burn. She rips her new bag from her back and fumbles inside for her knife.

"It's just two," Z says in a soothing voice. The size of the group they find themselves in makes her feel safe, Tasha realizes. With Esther and her group, they're no longer a carful of prey. Together they're nearly a battalion.

Koltey gets out of the driver's side of the SUV, closest to the approaching Minkers. From her thigh she draws a long knife from a leather scabbard.

"I've got it," she calls.

"Kolt…," Adriano warns, but the girl waves him off.

Tasha moves to the front of the SUV to watch. Koltey approaches the two Minkers head-on. They stagger toward her, barking, and at the sound, Xena stands rapt with a growl rumbling in her throat.

"It's okay, girl," Tasha says, in the same voice Z had used on her.

Koltey is short—no more than 5'2"—but she wields her long knife confidently. The first Minker rushes to meet her and she shoves him first, slashes second. Her knife is like a blur, knowing exactly where to find the Chip and slicing across it easily. One stroke is all it takes to fell the first one. Her movements are so deft that Tasha almost doesn't understand what's happened when the second one grips Koltey by the shoulders, pinning her arms. The knife falls to the ground, sending up a puff of dust. Koltey doesn't yell, she just wriggles, kicking out at the Minker's shins. Maybe it would have worked if he weren't a Minker, but he is. He opens his jaws.

"Shit!" Tasha cries, and fumbles again for her knife.

Esther is running forward with Adriano and the others, but Z beats them all. She skids up to where Koltey and the Minker struggle, twists her body to the side, and fires the purple gun. The blue blur of light Tasha had seen at Wal-Mart shoots out of the mouth of the gun and almost instantaneously they hear a loud *pop*, a sound like a circuit breaker being blown in the midst of a storm. Koltey screeches and Tasha feels her blood freeze, thinking she's either been bitten or that Z had missed and shot her instead. But when the Minker falls, Koltey does not: she stands rubbing her arms where the creature's grip had held her.

Adriano reaches her and grabs her by the shoulders.

"Are you okay? Did he bite you?"

"No, no," she says, shaking her head, her short black hair flopping into her face. "He just squeezed me really hard at the end. I thought his fingers were going to go through my skin."

Adriano examines her arms, taking each limb in his hand and inspecting it like a lion inspecting its cub. Esther stands watching a pace away.

"Your sister's a big girl, Adriano," she says. "She's fine."

"This guy isn't," Koltey says, pushing her brother away and peering down at the Minker Z had shot. Z crouches next to his body.

"Come look at this," she calls without raising her eyes.

Tasha and LaBrenda move forward, Tasha with her knife in her hand once more. She can't imagine what can be so interesting about a dead Minker, but when she reaches Z's side she sees. The eyes are wholly black, the whites and pupils completely obscured. It's as if someone injected tar into the eyeball, the entire surface covered by a shadow of ink.

"I've never seen that before," says LaBrenda. Tasha hears the notes being taken in her head, information being collected for the one-eyed head of Red Rooster.

"What is this gun you have?" Esther says, turning to Z.

"A shock gun. For rapists or whatever."

"Makes sense that it would work on Minkers," LaBrenda adds, still staring down at the eyes of the corpse. "The Chip must have some kind of electric communication with the brain. The shock must be powerful enough to fry it. Gonna have to keep that in mind for Phoenix."

"Is that where you're going?" says Koltey. She leans down to pick up her fallen knife, wipes the blade on the dead Minker's blue shorts. Once the blade is clean, she sheaths it at her thigh again.

"Yes," says LaBrenda.

"Where'd you get that sheath thing?" Tasha asks Koltey.

"I made it," Koltey says.

"I could use one of those," Tasha says as Koltey returns to the group.

"I have another on my bike," she says, nodding at the Pumapod Tasha had ridden with Radmilla. "I don't think money will do anybody any good, but maybe we can talk about a trade?"

Behind them, by the car, Tasha hears a thud and scuffling. She whirls, thinking another Minker has appeared and is hustling toward them. At first she sees nothing, but at the back of the SUV, on the ground, she sees movement, and bends to get a better look.

"He's trying to get away!" she cries, straightening like a shot, and runs toward the car. "He opened the hatch!"

430 OLIVIA A. COLE

Ishmael and Malakai had stayed by the front of the car, so they're closest. Ishmael sweeps Malakai to the side and strides to the end of the SUV where the camo guy flops in the dust. Tasha rounds the back of the car and finds him still tied at wrist and ankle, but wriggling to get out of one or the other. Ishmael pauses, then draws his foot back and kicks the guy in the stomach.

"Oh shit," Tasha breathes as the camo guy heaves. Ishmael kicks him again and the guy on the ground lies still.

Ishmael squats down next to him and cocks his head to look into the man's face.

"I don't know what you did to these people," he says. "But you killed a lot of people in that Wal-Mart and you shot me. You're not going anywhere."

The camo guy glares at Ishmael, gasping for breath, and pants something Tasha doesn't hear. Ishmael stands up and looks at Tasha, disbelief on his face.

"Did you hear what he called me?"

"No. What did he say?"

He shakes his head.

"Nothing. I wish we could gag this piece of crap."

Tasha squints down at the camo guy, who glares up at Ishmael. He twists his mouth, ready to hurl more profanity.

"Duct tape!" Tasha says suddenly, as Esther and the others join them by the car. "Do one of you still have yours from Rio's house? I used all mine in Chipotle way back."

"I do," Z says, still hefting the shock gun, which she brandishes at the guy on the ground. He makes a face as if he could tear her to pieces and she gives him the finger before digging around in her backpack. Withdrawing her hand with the roll, she tosses it to Tasha, who slices off a strip with her knife and then approaches the camo guy.

"I'll do that," says Ishmael, taking the tape from her and squatting again. The guy writhes, trying to avoid Ishmael's hands and delivering a stream of curses, but Adriano bends down to hold his head. The duct tape seals his mouth and all that's left is his glaring eyes and lowered eyebrows. With his mouth covered, he looks like a Minker, Tasha realizes.

"Well, that'll do it," Esther says brightly and heads over to the white pickup truck, letting down the tailgate with a clang. "Let's get this show on the road."

Tasha watches as LaBrenda and Adriano again lift Camo Guy from the ground—struggling this time—and dump him in the back of the truck.

"I'll put my bike in the back and ride with him," Adriano says. Tasha notes a different weapon on each of his hips: a pistol and a knife. She eyes his sheath.

"So about that trade," she says to Koltey somewhat awkwardly. She gets the feeling they're about to leave and doesn't want to miss her chance.

"Oh right," Koltey says, taking a step toward the Pumapod Tasha had ridden with Radmilla. "What do you have?"

Tasha's heart sinks, remembering her weak attempts at trading with Bennington before the Minkers invaded the deal. She doesn't have much—not even a Prada backpack to bargain with now—and though she'd acquired Bennington's stash, she doubts Koltey will be eager to trade a sheath for a flashlight. Cash is laughable. Tasha goes to the back of the SUV, still open, and peers into the bags, taking stock.

"I have…um…weed?" she says. Koltey just laughs.

"What else?"

They survey the contents of the hatch. Batteries. Cans of tuna. It's a sad spread. Koltey points.

"What about your ring?" she says. "That's pretty."

"My ring?" Tasha clutches the ring with her four-digit hand. It's so out of the question she hadn't even considered it. "No."

"No?"

"It was my mother's."

"Ah."

Koltey looks at Tasha's hands a moment longer, admiring the ring, and then arches an eyebrow.

"Wait, who did your nails?"

"My nails? Oh," Tasha regards the black nail polish, miraculously unchipped over the last couple days. Three coats will do it. "Me."

"So nice," Koltey says, and Tasha hears a shade of something she recognizes in her tone: the neon flare of fashion, like a blaze of aurora borealis in the night sky.

"I can do your nails," Tasha says. She feels bashful saying it, offering cotton candy in exchange for meat.

Koltey laughs, a high-pitched hiccup that almost startles Tasha. Over by Ishmael, Tasha hears Koltey's brother mock the sound. Koltey shoots him a glare and then returns her gaze to Tasha, looking thoughtful.

"Well, between this and your friend shooting that Minker that grabbed me, I think that's actually a pretty good trade!"

She laughs again, and Tasha finds herself grinning.

"Hold on for a little bit, Esther," Koltey calls. "I need to do something."

The white truck is parked beside what Esther tells Tasha's group is a memorial. It used to resemble four mountains, they learn—the four sacred peaks that mark the traditional boundaries of Dinétah—erected to venerate the many Diné youth who had fought to protect the land. It had recently been vandalized after the Diné won a lawsuit against a corporate mine for the toxic spill that poisoned their water sources. Z chews on a granola bar as they all sit in the shade of the structure while Tasha gives Koltey a manicure.

"When was the spill?" Z asks with her mouth full.

"Over fifty years ago," Esther says, leaning against the memorial. "It took a long, long time."

"Fifty years?" Z says, arching her eyebrows.

"I didn't know the right people even won lawsuits anymore," says LaBrenda, shaking her head.

Esther looks at LaBrenda with a look that could be either sadness or amusement. Tasha can't tell.

From the bed of the trunk comes a vague metallic clunk, and Adriano gets up to peer over the side. He returns, waving his hand.

"He was just turning over. No way he's getting loose."

Tasha uses her nail to scrape a stray bit of polish from Koltey's skin. She can't help but feel a lump in her throat at the sight of Koltey's ten perfect fingers, unbandaged and unbitten. She didn't need her ghost pinky to do this work, but everything feels slightly clumsy without it. Tasha doesn't have a file to shape the woman's nails—it's far away: still in her lobby, sticky with the doorman's blood, most likely—but the polish glides over the oval nails prettily, and soon they have nineteen black digits between them, Koltey waving hers in the air to dry them.

"So cute," Koltey says, admiring them. "I haven't had my nails done in so long."

"They won't last forever," Tasha says, screwing the brush back on the bottle. "But this polish is the good stuff. It shouldn't chip for awhile."

"Thanks," Koltey says, looking pleased.

Esther stands from the concrete ring that circles the memorial and brushes dust off her butt.

"So, Phoenix," she says, rubbing her neck. "What's in Phoenix? You never said."

Tasha continues staring at her bandaged finger stump. The last time she'd attempted to talk about what they planned to do, she'd sounded ridiculous. She thinks she'll leave this to LaBrenda. Instead it's Z who replies.

"We're going to rescue my brother," she says flatly. "He's a prisoner in a Cybranu facility, and we're going to bust him out."

Tasha purses her lips, still not looking up. She wonders if Z has chosen to give this answer to avoid the longer version, or because this is the crux of the mission as she perceives it.

"Cybranu…," repeats Esther, and Tasha can hear the frown in her voice. "Isn't that…?"

"The company with the things," says Koltey, tapping her neck with her fingers splayed awkwardly to avoid smudging the polish.

LaBrenda stands and Tasha looks up, then, to see what her face might say. Her expression is stormy, as if clouds have rolled in at the mention of Cybranu. Sitting here in the shadow of the memorial, painting nails, they're delaying; and now LaBrenda has been reminded of what they need to do. Phoenix and the Box are mere hours away. It waits there in the distance like a lurking white spider.

"They keep prisoners?" Esther frowns. "What kind of place is this?"

Tasha isn't sure if she's referring to the Cybranu facility or the entire country.

"We knew there was something weird about all that," says Koltey. "We lobbied against Indian Health Services even providing it on our land."

"Invasive," Radmilla says simply, shaking her head. Tasha thinks that single word might mean many things.

"Didn't keep the people who got it from coming onto the rez with it in their necks," says Esther. She's looking out across the land as if she expects a crowd of Minkers to appear from a puff of dust.

"I think Neovison thought this all out very carefully," says LaBrenda. "Cybranu and its Chip was just one piece."

"My nails are dry," Koltey says, flapping her hands one last time. "Let me get your sheath."

She goes to the Pumapod and digs into one of the compartments along the back of the bike, withdrawing a sheath like the one already around her thigh. She presents it to Tasha with a smile.

"Here you go. Want me to show you how to put it on?"

"Please."

Koltey bends and helps Tasha put it on. It's different than Koltey's: more of a hip holster than a thigh sheath.

"There," says Koltey, straightening. "Try putting your knife in."

Tasha does, the blade sliding in easily and then resting there.

"Good fit." Koltey nods approvingly.

"Thanks for this," Tasha says. She feels emotional, suddenly, but the roots of the feeling elude her. This is a thing she had needed, and now she has it. She hadn't stolen it. It hadn't come from a shelf. She had provided a service for this thing she needed, and though she will likely never see Koltey again, Tasha will carry her sheath. It's a different kind of exchange than the ones she had participated in at Fetch Fetchers.

"Do you know where we can get some food nearby?" LaBrenda is saying to Esther. They're all moving toward their vehicles now, the doors to the SUV open. Malakai and Xena are already inside, getting settled.

"Are you trying to go straight through to Phoenix? It's only a little over 200 miles from here."

"That's about four hours," Z says.

"We'd rather stop outside the city overnight. Go in in the morning," LaBrenda says. Tasha wants to ask when this decision was made, but keeps it to herself.

"Good plan," says Esther, gazing knowingly back at LaBrenda. Something about her eyes says that she knows they're going to do something crazy. She doesn't even need to ask.

436 OLIVIA A. COLE

"There's the forest preserve down there," says Radmilla, shrugging from where she leans against her Pumapod. She's eager to get back on her bike and ride north, Tasha thinks. Eager to lock up their prisoner. Tasha thinks of all the bodies in Wal-Mart, their corpses riddled with bullet holes. She won't convince herself to care about what happens to him.

"True," says Adriano. He's already put his bike in the back of the truck, along with Esther's, and sits on the tailgate. "There's cabins and stuff where you can stay, and I know their visitor center has food. Used to, anyway."

LaBrenda nods. She likes the plan.

"Be careful down there," Esther says. She stands by the door of the truck, ready to climb in and drive. "A lot of Anglos live by the park and they're bound to be a little crazy with all this"— she makes a circular gesture with her finger— "going on."

"Why?" Tasha says. "It still makes no sense."

Esther gets into the truck, starts it while hanging out the door.

"Because," she says with a smile. "This is their first apocalypse. My people? Yours? We've been here before."

She closes the truck door with a bang that makes Tasha jump. Whatever mechanism is powered by the solar panel hums as Esther puts the truck in gear. She raises her eyebrows, still smiling, and then the truck is moving and Tasha can't see her face anymore. With the Pumapods behind her like a flock of metal geese trailing their mother, the drivers waving, the group moves north, dust tossed up behind them that Tasha swipes from her face. She feels a sadness that she knows lacks foundation: their time together had been too brief, cut short by the pressing needs of each group to do things that must be done. She has no number to dial if she wants to see Esther or Koltey again. The world had once seemed so small—it's almost terrifying now in its immensity.

Tasha hears Monica Potter's SUV start and she turns, startled. Z is in the driver seat, using her hand to make a scooping motion, inviting Tasha to the passenger side.

"I'm driving, Hook," she says.

"Hook?"

"Your hand. You're like a pirate."

"I'm only missing one finger, Z."

"Pinky, then. Here's the map, Pinky."

Tasha gets in the car, map on her lap and knife on her hip. Maybe she *is* a pirate. Beneath the tires is an ocean of red earth, her little ship steering toward a horizon where she hopes she'll find safe land.

CHAPTER 26

Tasha wakes to Malakai's voice.

"It looks like a castle," he says. "A castle made of fire."

"You should be a poet," Z says.

Tasha opens her eyes. Cactuses whiz by her window, scrubby bushes where lizards surely live. And scorpions. Spiny things that like the spiny-ness of the shrubs. Ahead, through the windshield, she sees massive rocks erupting from the earth, their orange and red stone jutting toward the sky. With the late afternoon sun blazing down across its enormity, it does look like it glows from the inside, a colossal oven where the gods decided to hide their fire.

"They're called mesas," Ishmael says.

"I see the visitor center," says Z. Tasha feels the car slowing.

"Already?" Tasha mumbles. She feels as if she's only just gone to sleep.

"You've been asleep for hours. I actually had to drive pretty slow. A lot of debris on the roads."

"Oh."

They're driving slowly now, the SUV rocking slightly as it carries them over uneven terrain, plunging off the main road to wander down what seems little more than a deer path.

"Do you see any cars? Bikes?" says LaBrenda from the very back seat. Tasha wonders if she chooses that spot to babysit her bombs. In the rearview LaBrenda leans forward to peer up at the windshield. Ahead is what Z says is the visitor center.

"None that I can see," says Z. "Oh wait, one."

"A car?"

"It's a truck. I think it's a ranger's or something. There's a seal on the side."

They open their doors with caution and shut them quietly. Tasha instructs Malakai to hold on to Xena before she can go bounding off and making noise.

"Tonto National Forest," says Malakai in a soft voice. He's reading the worn wooden sign staked into the ground off the path. "It's so open. I thought forests were...forests."

"Don't judge a forest by its cover," Z says, peering at the visitor center.

"What?"

"Nothing."

The visitor center is a cabin, made to look much older than it is, the synthetic wood darkened with dyes, unnecessary resin shining at the occasional corner. The knots in the logs form a repetitive pattern, convincing imitations of nature. But the tall cactuses that line the front walk are real, some of them with thick white flowers sprouting out near the top. The rustic sign Malakai read is a little crooked, but the letters spell out: Tonto National Forest Visitor Center and Reservation Office.

"I'll check it out," says LaBrenda. "Z, can I have the shock gun for a sec?"

Z looks reluctant and Tasha almost laughs at her unwillingness to share her new toy. But she hands it over, withdrawing her box cutter from her back pocket, and LaBrenda moves toward the cabin.

440 OLIVIA A. COLE

The rest of them watch cautiously from by the SUV. Even with his arm in a sling, Ishmael hefts the axe in the hand of his good arm, his jaw as tense as Tasha's entire body. What happened in Wal-Mart has wound them all too tight. It hardly seems possible that just a few hours ago Tasha had been ducking bullets in the sporting good aisle. The throbbing in her finger tells her that it is more than possible.

LaBrenda holds the shock gun out in front of her like a fire extinguisher, ready to fire at anything that pops up. From here, Tasha can't see if her hands are shaking, and she wonders if she's thinking about how she killed a man in Wal-Mart. She wonders if she'd do it again.

LaBrenda goes to the window at the front of the cabin, staying low. Straightening slowly, she peeks over the sill, peering inside. She ducks immediately, snapping her head back toward Tasha and the others.

"People!" she whispers fiercely.

"Shit," Z says.

"Malakai, get in the car," says Ishmael, immediately turning back to the SUV. Tasha turns to do the same, her heart suddenly pounding. From the back of her mind comes the sound of gunshots, entering her consciousness so suddenly that she's almost convinced she actually hears them.

"Wait, wait...," comes LaBrenda's voice from the cabin. "Wait. They're Minkers. They're just Minkers."

Tasha leaves her hand on the handle of the car door, but turns back to look.

"You sure? How many?"

"Seven or eight."

"But they're all closed in there?" says Z. She wanders back around the front of the car again.

LaBrenda peers, not crouching anymore.

"Yeah. Looks like there's a back door, but it's closed too. Still electricity," she adds, turning her head this way and that to check out the inside. "Lights are on. Ooh—they have a microwave!"

"A microwave?"

"Yeah. There's a little kitchenette thing."

"Oh shit, a kitchenette," says Z, sounding hopeful.

"Why are we acting like this is a viable option?" Ishmael says loudly. He stands by the SUV; inside Malakai is already packed and seated. He stares out past his big brother with round eyes.

"What do you mean?" Z says, turning. "There's a kitchenette! Esther and them said they probably have food here."

"There are eight Minkers in there," he says, in a voice that asks if she's stupid, if they're all stupid. "There are five of us. Two of us have injuries and one of us is a child. Oh, sorry, there are six of us. And the last one's a dog. Also injured, I might add."

He throws the arm not in a sling out to the side and then lets it drop.

"He's got a point," Tasha says, feeling the need to take his side. But internally she yearns for the kitchenette, for all the hypothetical spoils it might contain. Her stomach gives the tiniest of treasonous growls.

Z twists her mouth to one side, wanting to argue. LaBrenda, still looking over her shoulder at them, turns back to peer into the cabin.

"Maybe they're...what do you call them? Keepers," she says.

"All the more reason not to go in," says Ishmael. "Out here they won't mess with us."

"Or maybe we can do like Tasha did at the North Platte Mall," LaBrenda says, not looking back.

"What?"

"Yank them out. One by one."

"Why?" Ishmael demands. "What's the point?"

When LaBrenda turns back, Tasha recognizes something on her face. She's not sure what it is. Maybe a vestige of what she herself had felt outside the Whole Foods hundreds of miles behind them. LaBrenda wants to go into the cabin, and she may not even know why. It beckons to her.

"Because," she says, throwing her arms out to the side as Ishmael had done, the metal one glinting. "It's a good plan. We're close to Phoenix. We can take our time here tonight and tomorrow just…do it. I mean, we're how many miles from Phoenix?"

She glances at Z, who rolls her eyes up to think for a moment and then says, "About 90."

"90 miles. We can be there in under two hours tomorrow," LaBrenda says. "Let's camp out here tonight. It's a small building, easy to secure. We'll eat some food and then figure out a plan for tomorrow."

Ishmael doesn't say anything. Tasha holds her breath.

"Okay then," says LaBrenda, her eyes glowing. "Z, let's do it."

They don't even need to pluck them out—the shock gun, turned on its highest setting, is a tool they should've had all along. LaBrenda acts as bait, stepping inside the cabin door after creaking it open, and draws the Minkers close. When she springs back out beyond the threshold, they cluster there by the door and Z uses the shock gun to, one by one, turn their eyes inky black. The electricity leaves the barrel with an almost liquid whoosh, the blue of it disappearing as it reaches the target. Tasha, Ishmael, and Malakai watch from the SUV, nearly bored. It's almost too easy. The only anxiety is when they discover that one of the cabin dwellers isn't a keeper, and when it comes lumbering out of the cabin LaBrenda has to skip backwards to avoid the bear hug and yellowed incisors.

"Oh shit," LaBrenda gasps, stumbling. "Z, get him."

"Move," Z cries. "You're in the way!"

They dance for a moment, the Minker barking and lunging at LaBrenda, LaBrenda dodging left and right to stay out of its reach, Z weaving about trying to get a clear shot. Xena leaps forward at the flurry of activity, nipping at the Minker's knees. The dog is confused, her tail waving uncertainly as if she hasn't decided whether or not this is a game. Tasha starts forward, five-fingered hand reaching for the knife at her hip, enjoying the coolness of having a sheath even with the Minker ahead. But Z finds her angle: the *whoomp* of the shock gun sounds and the Minker jolts as if he'd grasped an electric wire. He falls stiffly to the ground and LaBrenda finds her balance. Her fro is a little lopsided from the scuffle but she doesn't seem to notice, instead moving back toward the cabin door and peering inside. Then she goes in, Z following closely. It's understood that Tasha and the others should remain outside.

Somewhere nearby a bird trills from one of the scrawny trees, a hiccupping sound that causes Xena to perk up her ears and tilt her head in its direction. Tasha, on the other hand, tilts her head at the cabin, her ears straining for a sound that might indicate what's happening inside. Waiting by the car, tension seeps from her blood and snares her muscles in a noose. The open door of the cabin shows that the place is indeed lit by electricity—but it still yawns there like the mouth of a cave, Z and LaBrenda swallowed within.

Then she hears a yell.

Tasha and Ishmael lurch forward at the same moment, her hand scrambling at her sheath, the axe already in his grip. Malakai starts to leap from the car, but Ishmael shouts him back, Tasha's own yell of "we're coming" blending in, adrenaline already pumping. But Z appears in the doorway, unbloodied and unbothered.

"They have popcorn!" she grins, holding up a bag, already chewing.

"Jesus Christ, Z!" Tasha snaps. She claps her hands once, sharply, as if the fear Z had injected into her veins is a mosquito to be slapped. "Why did you yell?"

"Oh, that was LaBrenda. She walked through a spider web."

LaBrenda appears behind her, her face twisted with disgust.

"It got in my mouth," she says.

Malakai laughs, the first time since Wal-Mart.

"Quit eating all the popcorn!" he calls.

Tasha knows they're going to stay.

Later, after they've cleared the bodies from the doorway and dumped them behind the cabin, they raid the kitchenette and take an inventory of all it has to offer. Little handwritten signs are posted here and there: "Honor system. Leave money—CASH—in basket."

"Cash? A lot of people would have been straight out of luck," Z says as she pulls out packets of dried add-water soup.

"If they came here to go camping, you'd think they would've been planning on roughing it," LaBrenda says.

"They have pizza," Malakai says, and everyone turns to look at him. He stands in front of the open freezer, his expression somewhat awed, as if he'd wandered up a hill and stumbled upon the stone tablets bearing the Ten Commandments.

"Don't play," LaBrenda says. Her face is serious, intense.

"Eight boxes," Malakai says, tearing his eyes away to look at back at the group.

"Oh my god," Z breathes.

The microwave is industrial, the kind that can defrost a frozen chicken breast in two and a half minutes. The pizzas take 30 seconds each, and Tasha and the others lounge on the brushed velvet furniture by a wide brick fireplace eating and talking. Tasha had expected to find blood somewhere inside, some trace of someone who didn't make it, who had walked in for a cabin reservation on the wrong day. But while the tweed chairs and couches are fairly old, the soft beige fabric faded with age, they're spotless as far as blood and brain matter go.

"This pizza is better than anything I ever had in Chicago," Z says, smacking her lips with every bite.

"You just don't remember now," Tasha says. "This is good… but it's not that good."

Malakai nods seriously.

"Oh yeah. Gio's on 53rd was way better. But this is good. Really good."

He feeds Xena the crust of every piece of pizza he eats. The dog sits glued to his side. She'll turn up her nose at kibble after this, but Tasha says nothing, enjoying their contentment.

Eventually she puts down her pizza to help Ishmael rebandage his arm according to Esther's instructions. The wound is ugly, but it's not bleeding anymore. In a strange way she finds herself grateful for this tear in his skin: an excuse to touch him. She thinks maybe he's seeking the same alibi: he demands to do the same for her finger. He changes the bandage around her head too, and they stare at one another as he fastens the last of the wrap.

"Is that better?" he says. The words are soft, for her alone.

Tasha almost says no. Almost asks him to undo the bandages and wrap it again—the feeling of his fingertips against her exposed scalp sinks into her somehow, like water into dry earth. But she merely nods, staring into his eyes.

"Are we going to sleep on these couches?" Malakai says. Tasha looks at the boy, having barely heard him. She thinks maybe he was addressing her, but he's regarding the cabin. It's all one large room, and as night had fallen they'd turned off all the lights but one small one on a side table near where they sit. The rest of the cabin is obscured by shadows—darker, even, than the Greenex lodge where they'd spent the night. The reserve isn't equipped with light posts: the only glow outside is from the moon, which tonight is mostly hidden by clouds.

"Nope," says LaBrenda, swallowing a bite of pizza. "Upstairs."

"There's an upstairs?"

"Yeah, kind of a loft. The ladder is hidden, but I climbed up and poked my head around. There's cots and stuff."

"What about Xena?"

"What about her?"

"Where's she gonna sleep?"

"She'll be okay down here."

Malakai doesn't respond, but his face folds with worry.

"We should move the car," Z says, reaching for another piece of pizza. She's eaten too many to count. "Pull it around behind the cabin where we put the bodies."

"Why?"

"In case someone passes by," she says, chewing. "If they're looking for someone to rob, a car would be a giveaway that there's someone here to rob in the first place."

"I mean, technically we're robbing the place," Tasha says, teasing.

"You know what I mean."

"I think it's a good idea," says Ishmael, standing. "I'm gonna do it real quick."

"Not by yourself," Tasha says.

"It's fine."

"No, it's not," LaBrenda says, also standing. "I'll come with you."

She picks up the shock gun, Ishmael wielding his axe, and they move to the door. LaBrenda peeks outside briefly, and then they're gone. Tasha feels something inside her sink a little. She wanted to go with him: to stand outside with him alone, the night air on just their faces. She hears the SUV start outside, the crunch of tires on gravel, sees the sweep of the headlights as they pull the car around back. Tomorrow they'll load up the supplies from this cabin, but tonight they need their backpacks—they'd left them in the backseat with the bombs.

Tasha stands up, moving to the door.

"Where are you going?" says Z.

"I'm going to help them bring in the backpacks."

Z gives her a look, arching her eyebrow and smirking.

"Yeah? The backpacks, huh?"

"What? Yes."

"He'll be back, Tasha."

They stare at each other, Tasha's face getting warm. Suddenly she's sweating, Z's smile like a glaring interrogation light. Malakai looks at Tasha, then at Z.

"Who? Ish?"

Tasha makes a face as a reply and Malakai widens his eyes.

"Oh! Wait, do you like my brother?"

Tasha squints at him, cocking her head sharply to the side.

"Can I not just go help them with the backpacks? Dang!"

"You do!" the boy squawks. "I knew you did."

The door opens and Ishmael and LaBrenda reenter the cabin, carrying the backpacks from the back of the truck.

"Got these," LaBrenda says, plopping them all on a chair.

"See, Tash?" Z says, her eyes dancing. "They got 'em."

Tasha narrows her eyes and returns to her spot on the couch, ignoring Malakai's grin. LaBrenda withdraws Z's map from the side pocket of her backpack while Ishmael cleans up the pizza. She stares at it for awhile, saying nothing.

"90 miles," she says.

Tasha watches her, the unblinking line of lashes along her eyes. The fingers that hold the map don't tremble, not even the flesh ones, but Tasha thinks she can feel something else in LaBrenda shaking.

"You okay?" she asks softly.

LaBrenda doesn't look up right away, but when she does, her eyes look tired. She puts down the map and rubs them.

"Yes," she says. "Just...thinking."

"Do you know how we're going to do this tomorrow?" Z asks, perched on a couch like a bird.

LaBrenda shrugs and reclines into her chair.

"Kind of. I have some intel from Rio's Glass, thanks to you guys. I would have been going in completely blind if you hadn't shown up with it."

"Serendipity," says Z. At one point it might have been sarcastic, but there's no angle in her voice now. Without their stop at the Pentagon, and its inhabitants' ability to unlock the Glass, Z would have driven right on to California without ever knowing where her brother might be. Somewhere the stars had aligned, Tasha thinks: a perfect trajectory of love and violence that has led them to this place. And tomorrow it will lead them on to Neovison, the Box, where who knows what evil roosts.

"So what's the plan then?" Tasha says.

LaBrenda looks at the map again, but Tasha knows she's looking for information that doesn't exist.

"Well, Pamela gave us the tooth. So we'll use that to get in. Then, if it's not obvious once we're in, I'll use the blueprints from Rio's Glass to find our way to the control room. It should be on the third or fourth floor. From there I'll extract the locations of the other hubs in the States, then set the bombs, then we...you know, go. We get away."

"After we find my brother," Z says. "You can't set the bombs until we find Dragon."

LaBrenda looks at her, blinking. Tasha clenches her teeth, bracing herself for what could become an argument where she can't choose a side.

"Yes," LaBrenda says slowly, and Tasha's teeth unclench. "After we find your brother."

Ishmael comes over from the kitchen, where the mess from their pizza party has disappeared. The counter of the kitchenette is still covered in the food they'd inventoried.

"We can put the food in the car tomorrow," he says, sitting down next to Tasha on the couch. He sits close to her, in the middle, when he could have taken the other end. Her blood pulses.

"Cool," she says.

"You and Malakai are going to need to stay in the car tomorrow," LaBrenda says. She says it suddenly and almost as if she's out of breath. She's been waiting to say it, afraid of the reaction. "We're gonna be moving fast and with your arm like it is, and with Malakai..." She trails off.

"I can go," Malakai says. "I'm not a kid."

"I know you're not," LaBrenda says, and Tasha admires her tone, absent of condescension. "But your brother is hurt and we can't risk it. Plus we need you to take care of Xena...someone needs to keep an eye on her. We can't leave her outside while we're all inside Neovison.""

"Tasha is hurt," he says. He turns his eyes to Tasha. "Are you going to stay outside with us?"

"I think I'm okay," Tasha says carefully.

Malakai frowns. Xena is at his feet, hopeful for more pizza, and he looks down at her, reaching to pat her head. She thumps her tail twice.

"What if you guys need us?" the boy says eventually, and Tasha feels her heart tighten.

"Then we'll come get you," Z says. "We'll come get you if we need you. But you guys have to be ready to roll, okay? Like, you're the getaway car."

Malakai nods. He's not happy, but he's satisfied.

"That's about as planned as it's going to get," Z says to no one. She knits her fingers behind her head and looks at the ceiling. She doesn't seem afraid, Tasha notes. Her brother dangles on the road ahead of her like a beckoning ball of light. Tasha thinks warily that it might be like looking into the sun.

One by one they climb the narrow ladder to the loft. LaBrenda was right: it's hidden—a door off the kitchenette that looks like a closet, opening straight onto the ladder. Tasha had imagined it being taller, but there are only about four or five rungs and she climbs up easily, hauling her backpack.

"We can't leave Xena down here," Malakai is saying. Everyone but he and the dog are upstairs, crowded around the door looking down.

"She'll be okay, Kai," Ishmael says. "Come on."

"Man, she'll be lonely," the kid says, and Tasha stifles a laugh. "She'll think we left her. I'll sleep down here with her."

"You're not sleeping down there by yourself," Ishmael says, stone seeping into his tone.

"She can't climb the ladder, Kai," Z says, yawning. "She'll be okay, come on."

"I'm fine," Malakai says, sounding a little pissed. "I'm sleeping with her."

Before Ishmael can argue, LaBrenda cuts in.

"Here, here," she climbs down the ladder. "I'll get her up here. Z, help me pull her up."

LaBrenda squats, lifting the dog under her belly. Xena is a statue for a moment, her eyes dark and serious, and then she squirms, her nails raking LaBrenda's arms.

"Ugh, she's scratching me. Here, Z."

Clutching the dog against her chest, LaBrenda steps up two rungs and then pushes Xena up toward the opening in the floor of the loft. Z crouches on her knees, wrapping her arms around Xena and hauling her upwards. After much pulling and squirming, the poodle stands triumphantly in the loft, wagging her tail down at Malakai as if getting up there had been her idea.

"Satisfied?" Ishmael says, shaking his head. "All that for a dog…"

Tasha scratches Xena's neck as Malakai climbs up, a smile on his face. It makes her feel better to have the poodle up here too. Now they're all together.

"Malakai, close the door behind you," she says, and turns to check out the loft.

"This is nice," Z says, sounding impressed, and it is. Large windows on three sides, with no trees obscuring the view. They stand looking out the west-facing window, where the sun would have been if not for the deepening blackness of night. Out there, the mesas are towering shadows. In the dark they are unfinished buildings, a stone city being built around this tiny cabin.

"It's so…," Malakai starts, but doesn't finish, the syllables dissolving into silence. Tasha knows what he means.

"We have cots," LaBrenda says. She's turned away from the window to survey the rest of the room. Empty bed frames— at least eight of them—take up space in one part of the loft, and LaBrenda unrolls the mattresses from where they're rolled along the wall.

"They're either new or just washed," she says, tearing receipts from two of them.

"Lucky us," Z says, following suit. "I wonder if the rangers slept here every night?"

"Not a bad situation," LaBrenda says. Tasha hears the thing in her voice again: the thick blue yearning.

"Have you ever gone camping?" Tasha asks, unrolling a mattress onto the frame she's chosen.

LaBrenda smiles at her hands as she does the same, arranging a blanket taken from a large wicker basket on top of her mattress.

"Yeah, I used to go all the time with my grandparents. They had a cabin kind of like this in Shasta, before my granddad was taken away."

"So you've always been an outdoors girl," Z says in her teasing voice, billowing a blanket and letting it fall onto her bed.

"What do you mean?"

"The gardening in Detroit. The camping in Shasta."

Tasha expects annoyance, but instead LaBrenda smiles before sinking down onto the edge of the cot.

"I guess so. My granddad…he loved nature. He loved dirt and trees and the sky." She frowns, the shadow of some submarine monster drifting into the water of her memories. "I think that's why he didn't…last long in prison."

Tasha stops fiddling with her blanket, fastening her eyes on LaBrenda's face.

"People aren't supposed to be in cages," LaBrenda says. She stares hard at the smooth wooden floor.

"How old were you when he died?" Tasha says, the words coming out soft and cautious.

"I think I was around twenty. Not sure, exactly. Private prisons don't have the obligation to notify families when a prisoner dies. He'd been in solitary for two years. We had no idea."

"Jesus Christ, LaBrenda," Tasha breathes.

LaBrenda looks up, her expression drawn.

"Companies like Neovison are a disease," she says without passion. Her eyes are tired. "They ruined the world a long time before this."

Tasha swallows, not knowing what to say. But LaBrenda doesn't hold her eyes; she stands from her bed and tucks the edges of the cover in around the foot. She's walled off. Tasha can see the cement laying itself brick by brick.

Ishmael is having trouble making his bed with one arm incapacitated and Tasha goes to help him, taking the blanket from his one hand and spreading it for him.

"Thanks," he says. She nods but doesn't look at him, keeping her eyes on the safe woven fibers of the cover. *Thanks* is a single word, but she hears its multitudes in the way his lips form it. This is a bed. They stand over it, and she feels as if they might fall from a towering height.

"No pillows," Z announces.

"We don't need them," Tasha says.

"Did someone turn the light off downstairs?" Z says when they're settled. LaBrenda has sunk into her bed like a ghost. Z turns out the only lamp in the loft. The sudden darkness hushes the breath in the room.

"I did," Malakai says when the moment has passed.

"Good."

When her eyes adjust, the loft isn't as dark as Tasha first thought. The moon, though not round, has risen high and bright, finally unobscured by clouds. From where she lies, her cot between LaBrenda and Z, she has a clear view of its lopsided glow, a beam of moonlight falling across her hand, illuminating her white bandage and her mother's ring. She'd risked the lives of almost everyone in this room to rescue this ring—easily the stupidest thing she's ever done. Now tomorrow they'll risk their lives again, though at least this time they're in charge of the bombs. The loft seems to be full of her companions' worries, rising out of their heads like smoke and swirling toward the ceiling. It makes the air thick, and she breathes it in like a vapor—their dreams and fears gathering together in a haze that turns the world black.

She's not sure if she actually slept. When she's conscious of her eyes being open, the moon is still staring back at her, though not quite from the same angle. But something is different.

When she moves her eyes to the left, she finds Z and LaBrenda standing.

Tasha starts to speak.

"What's…"

Z throws her hand out in the moonlight, one finger raised and sharp like a silent talon. Her face is strained, her eyes urgent. Then she brings the talon to her lips. Slowly Tasha sits up.

Someone is outside.

Now Tasha can hear their voices rising from the path in front of the cabin, and through the south-facing window she makes out the glow of what she thinks are headlights.

"Do…not…move." LaBrenda says the words almost without saying them, her lips virtually motionless with the caution of her whisper.

Malakai stirs and Tasha goes to shush him but he's already alert, she sees. So is Ishmael. She was the last to wake. Even the dog lies vigilant on Malakai's cot. He pets her ears mechanically, his eyes wide, in what he hopes is a hypnotic massage. The loft is silent.

LaBrenda takes two slow, soft steps to the window, crouching low. She pauses there, not raising her head above the windowsill. Then she turns to look at the rest of them, her expression grim.

"They're coming inside. They have guns."

Tasha hears the door downstairs creak open, the squeak of steps on floorboards and the hush of lowered voices, one deep and rumbling. Her heart jackhammers at her ribcage, her hand slowly creeping down to the floor, where she'd placed her knife in its new sheath.

"Tasha Lockett!"

Tasha claps a hand over her mouth at the sound of her name, shouted from downstairs.

"Oh my god," Tasha hears Z whisper, the words like mice, soft and scurrying.

The intruders turn on a lamp, the crack of the door leading to the loft suddenly yellow with light. Tasha squeezes the handle of her knife so hard it makes her pulse pound.

"Tasha Lockett!" It's the deeper of the two voices, bouncing off the wooden walls of the room below and squeezing up the ladder. Xena growls low in her throat, and Malakai thrusts his mouth next to the dog's ear, whispering something.

"It's empty," says the other voice, a woman's.

"I can see that."

"Doesn't mean it was always empty."

"Someone was definitely here. The food is all out on the counter."

"Doesn't mean it was her."

"No."

Z finds Tasha's eyes in the moonlight and holds them. Tasha feels a drop of sweat bead from her armpit and slide down her side before being absorbed by her bra. Her fear melts her from the inside.

"Tasha Lockett!" the voice shouts again.

"She's not here," the other voice says, sounding annoyed.

"Maybe she knew we were coming. Left the food and lit out."

"Maybe."

"You act like you don't want to find her. Do you want the reward or not?"

"I'm just tired. We drove four hours to get here because they said she was headed this way, but she could be four hours away by now. She could already be with the Roosters."

"Christ, Vicky. It's a lot of money if we catch her."

"Don't *Christ* me. If you really want to find her we're wasting time."

The floorboards creak. Tasha forces herself to keep breathing. They're talking about her. About catching her. She could be a butterfly; they walk with nets.

"Do you want to just stay here?" the deep voice says. "If you're tired we can take a breather. There's food."

The person named Vicky doesn't answer. More creaking floorboards—she's checking the place out. Tasha thinks she hears Z curse under her breath but the words are too soft to hear. After what feels like an eternity: "It stinks in here. Like someone died."

"Well, shit, somebody probably did, Vicky."

"Then where's the body?"

"I don't know. Maybe in this closet."

Tasha bites her tongue so hard her eyes well with tears. The floorboards creak just down the ladder. If they open the door and climb the ladder, Tasha will have about five seconds to reach the opening to attack. Her muscles tremble.

"Well, Christ, Bill, don't open it!" She pauses. "There might be...one of them in there. The Minkys don't know we're on their side, for god's sake."

Tasha looks at Z, who mouths "Minkys?" and rolls her eyes.

"Do you want to stay here or not?" Bill says.

"No."

"Then where are we going to sleep, Vicky?"

The creaking withdraws from the loft door, receding to the front door of the cabin. Bill says something Tasha can't hear that makes Vicky laugh. A moment of silence and then the bang of the front door closing. Their muffled voices rise again from outside.

"Are they gone?" Malakai breathes.

No one answers, not until there's the audible sound of their car starting.

"Wait," LaBrenda says and creeps like a spider back to the window. She edges one eye up over the sill, then the top of her head, slowly.

"Are they gone?" Tasha says. Or tries to say. Her teeth are clicking together, chattering as the adrenaline dies in her veins.

"Yes," says LaBrenda. "They're gone."

"Fucking hell," says Z, flopping down onto her cot again. "Thank god we moved the car around back."

"They had guns," LaBrenda repeats to no one in particular.

Ishmael, elbows on his knees, covers his face with his hands.

"Who were they?" he says when he looks up.

"No idea. I couldn't see what they were wearing. Someone like Michelangelo, I guess. Random people who work for Neovison on some level."

"Did they say there's a reward for you?" Malakai says to Tasha. The poodle has crawled off the boy's cot and snaked over to her, nudging her palm with her cold black nose.

"Miss Popular," Z says, but the joke has no wings and it sinks, gray and heavy.

"An ad must have clocked us somewhere on the road," LaBrenda says. She too sinks back onto her cot. They don't dare turn on the light, and crouch there in the dark like huddled vampires.

"How the hell are we supposed to get all the way to California with all this facial recognition bullshit everywhere?" Tasha cries. She throws her sheathed knife onto her cot. "There's no way we can get to Phoenix with people like Bill and fucking Vicky running around!"

"You could ride in the trunk," Z says. Tasha sucks her teeth.

"You could wear this," Malakai says. He has something in his hand.

"What's that?" Tasha says. She gets up and goes to him in the dark.

It's a black ski mask.

"Where did you get this?" she says, shocked.

"From Wal-Mart. It fell off the guy's head when Z shocked him and I took it."

"I'm gonna wear a ski mask all the way to Phoenix?" Tasha says.

"It's not a bad idea," LaBrenda shrugs. She leans back on her elbows on the cot. "Who knows how many people like those two are out there. At least no ads or cameras could get your face."

"They might already have the make of the car too, though," Ishmael says, sounding grim.

LaBrenda blinks and nods slowly. Nothing to be done about that.

"Jesus Christ," Tasha mutters, falling onto her back.

"You guys should try to get some sleep," LaBrenda says, rising. She has the shock gun in her hands again, but Tasha isn't sure when she picked it up. Maybe she'd been sleeping with it. "I'm going to keep watch at the window."

"What if they come back?" Malakai says.

LaBrenda looks at him, then looks out the window.

"Then I'll wake you up."

CHAPTER 27

Tasha rides in the passenger seat with the ski mask over her face. At first she had felt ridiculous, the length of her braids poking out from the back and the eyeholes obscuring her eyebrows. After awhile, though, with the window down, the fabric becomes her face. She looks at herself in the side mirror. She could be anyone, someone brave speeding toward what Pamela had called "the weasel place."

When they come around the girth of a mountain, Phoenix sprawls out before them, much smaller than Tasha had anticipated, and lower to the ground. The buildings are shades of brown and gray, the architecture squat and antiquated.

"This is Phoenix?" Z says, arching her eyebrow. She finally takes her foot off the accelerator. She's been blazing up the road like a comet.

"It looks so old," LaBrenda says.

The wreckage here is worse than in any other place they've passed through. They enter the downtown area at a moderate speed, the burned-out carcasses of homes on either side. In front of a destroyed bank, a Minker stands on the concrete, swinging first one arm and then the other, in a manic jerking rhythm.

"Malfunctioning," Tasha says to herself. A thread from the ski mask gets in her mouth and she swipes it away.

"This place sucks," Malakai says, looking out the window.

"I've seen worse after a basketball game," Z sniffs. She steers the car around a throng of what look like bodies. Tasha doesn't want to see why there would be a throng of them.

"Do you think mom and Marcus came through this way?" Malakai asks, and Tasha hopes the question wasn't inspired by the throng.

"No," says Z before Ishmael can answer. "Rio's original route had us going through Utah and down through the bottom of Nevada. They probably missed Phoenix altogether."

Malakai nods, satisfied. It doesn't matter that Utah and Nevada might look just like this. They are something else, somewhere else.

"Check out these guys," LaBrenda says from the backseat.

Tasha turns to see where she's pointing. To the left of the car two Minkers stumble out from the shadow of a dilapidated Walgreens. The sound of the car has roused them and they swipe their hands angrily, giving chase. Z accelerates and they give up a block down the faded gray street. It's only an hour or two past dawn but the heat already bakes the road ahead, the shimmer above the pavement always just beyond the nose of the car.

"How are we going to find this place?" Malakai says. They've found their way into downtown proper—the buildings are slightly taller but just as dusty and outdated as the rest of the city. Tasha hasn't seen a single tree, not even the waxy artificial ones that Chicago had eventually installed along its sidewalks. In the rearview are the mountains they drove through on their way to this place, and Tasha can't help but think they're far more impressive than the man-made landscape that surrounds them.

"I don't think we'll have to search," says Z, pointing north through Tasha's window. "Check that out."

Tasha doesn't immediately see what Z is referring to—just the archaic office-style buildings that populate the area like stiff men in their fathers' suits. Through the gaps between them Tasha can see another mountain, towering to the north like a solemn sentry. But once her eyes settle on its form, she sees there's more to it than crags and ragged bushes. It appears to have windows, great sheets of glass that reflect the sunlight in glinting angles, and there, high in the center of the rock wall, sits a massive white box.

"The Box," LaBrenda says for all of them.

"The white place," Malakai says.

"They weren't trying to be covert, I guess," Ishmael says, frowning out the window.

"Why would they be?" LaBrenda says, her bitterness giving the words barbs. "Most of what they're doing probably isn't even illegal. Especially somewhere like Arizona."

"Taking people from prisons and bringing them here? That can't be legal."

"Maybe not, but I bet a lot more people in power knew about it than you think."

Z has stopped the car on the street. A light breeze carries dust and ash across the windshield. Xena whines from the backseat.

"So I guess we…you know, get to it," Z says.

"Yeah," says Tasha. Her mouth is dry at the sight of the white box on the mountain. It's not what she was expecting: not a towering spire like the Apiary, a white column stretching up into the sky. It's not even an endless warehouse, barbed wire ringing it in ferocious orbits. Instead it looks like a millionaire's über-contemporary mansion, fantasized to the point of absurdity. Z puts the car into drive again and turns the wheel to carry them north toward the white behemoth.

"Here we go," says LaBrenda.

Here we go, Tasha thinks.

At one point there had been a thick metal gate with an access pad, round black cameras on either side. But the gate and one of the cameras are smashed, from the inside by the look of where the gate now slumps toward them.

"Someone came out in a hurry," Z says. "Should we smash the other camera?"

No one says anything for a moment. Then: "Might as well," says LaBrenda.

Ishmael gets out of the car without speaking, stepping over two prone corpses on his way to the remaining black orb. He's just tall enough and, holding the very end of the axe's handle, uses the head to send the camera spinning to the ground, where it smashes open like an over-ripe melon. Ishmael gets back into the car.

Z steers them up the mountainside on a road that seems too narrow for the two trucks they find wrecked along its length. Driving too fast, Tasha guesses, or otherwise they might have trundled down to the gate without incident. One of the windshields is cracked open, the driver's body thrust through it like a test dummy. The door of the other truck is open, blood along its side, but no corpse.

The Change must have been a busy day here, Tasha thinks. Even a three-day weekend wouldn't usually have had people rushing down this road.

The road climbs onward, the enormous glass panes they'd seen from the city below on either side of them. Up close, Tasha sees that they're solar panels, built into the face of the mountain itself, some of them more than three times the length of the car. The idea of all the power they collect being filtered into the white box of Neovison makes Tasha's heart beat faster. No one speaks. The sunlight flashing against the panels is false in its gaiety; its rays are like razors.

The higher the car carries them, the larger the white box above appears. If there were any path other than the one they're on, Tasha might wonder if they're taking the most direct route.

As it is, the only way to go is up, and though she can still see downtown Phoenix easily, Tasha feels as if she's riding the bud of a beanstalk destined for the heaven of giants. Z rounds the next bend, driving slowly, and then brakes suddenly. Ahead is what appears to be a glass tunnel, or the entrance to one. It rears up before them, almost crystalline, an archway six feet higher than the hood of the car, but, surprisingly, only about twice the length of the car. On the other side of the archway, less than a quarter-mile up the road, is the Box.

"What the hell is this?" says Tasha. She yanks on the top of the ski mask, which keeps sliding down, resting on her eyelids.

"I don't know," LaBrenda says. "Hold on."

Tasha looks back to find her scrolling through Rio's Glass. She scrolls and scrolls.

"Well?" says Z after a moment, also turning to stare back at LaBrenda.

"The blueprints aren't exactly easy to understand, okay? It's not like there's a button I can press that will tell me what everything is." She pauses again, studying the Glass. "From what I can tell, this is a security feature. It scans entering vehicles for explosives."

"Well shit," says Z, turning back to the steering wheel. "Well...shit."

Tasha stares through the holes in her mask at the glass archway, feeling sweat beading under her arms again. The transparency of the arch is interrupted throughout with glowing lights like veins, spreading throughout the crystalline surface in nebulous arrays. Each light, she feels, is a thousand microscopic eyes that have the power to see right through her mask and raise a silent alarm, drawing hordes of Minkers to overtake them in the tunnel.

"Can't we just go around?" Malakai says.

"There's no other road," Z sighs, resting her chin on the steering wheel.

"No, I mean, get out and walk around."

Z raises her chin, looking. They all look. On one edge of the archway is the solid mountain wall, but on the other is a little strip of land before the drop-off, clustered with yellow flowers. The cheerful petals blow gently in the breeze, leaning slightly away from the sinister structure of the arch.

"I guess we could," LaBrenda says. She makes a sound of amusement, which Tasha finds herself clinging to. It's a sound that seems devoid of the fear that courses through her own body—a small buoy in the ocean of her dread.

They get out, Xena romping. Malakai calls her before she can get too near the arch. Who knows what it's capable of, after all? Tasha imagines birds winging thoughtlessly through the tunnel and being fried into crispy black ashes, floating to the earth. LaBrenda opens the hatch.

"Who wants to carry the other one?" she says, addressing Z and Tasha. She's referring to the backpacks, the explosive infants she's been babysitting for hundreds of miles. The idea of touching the backpacks makes Tasha feel lightheaded.

"You sure you guys are going to be okay in there by yourselves?" Ishmael looks directly at Tasha when he says it, his eyebrows low. LaBrenda doesn't let Tasha answer.

"It makes more sense for you guys to stay out here. Too many people will complicate things. Besides, we won't be gone long." She hesitates. "Not really long."

Tasha looks at Ishmael through the eyeholes of the mask. It's comforting, being able to stare at him like this. Not quite an invisibility cloak, but a shield.

"You be careful," he says. He's staring back, but he doesn't have a mask, and she can read the furrows in his face like an alphabet of worry.

"I will."

He starts to move toward her, hesitates, and then stops.

"You better," he says, only loud enough for her alone to hear.

"I'll carry the other one," Z says, taking the second backpack from LaBrenda. The vulturous sense of déjà vu swoops down from the sky and snatches at Tasha's eyeballs.

"How are we going to do this again?" she says, turning away from Ishmael and the safety of his forehead's furrows. Her voice doesn't tremble, but only because she's forcing her windpipe to act like an adult.

LaBrenda fixes her with a stare that's a cross between maternal and murderous.

"Let's get this over with," she says.

Worming their way around the glass arch is easier than Tasha had thought it would be. She doesn't want to touch it, lest it sponge up a morsel of her DNA to call in the cavalry, but, following LaBrenda and Z's lead, she manages to walk along the narrow sliver of land at the edge of the road. She picks her way through the drifts of yellow flowers, their brittle branches scraping at her exposed ankles. Halfway past the arch she glances down at the drop-off. She probably wouldn't die if she fell, not from the height alone. But the jagged rocks would make short work of her skull. The ski mask shields her from eyes, not sharp objects.

"This thing can't be the only security point," Z says hopefully. She hopes it's the only security point. She hopes all that lies ahead of them will be nothing like what she's afraid it will be. She hopes that she can walk in, find her brother waiting with his legs crossed in the lobby, shiny and spotless, and walk right back out.

"It won't be," says LaBrenda. Any hopes they might have had were never real hopes. They dissolve and pop like soap bubbles.

"Do you see any cameras?" Tasha manages to say as they near the Box. She looks over her shoulder, where she can see Ishmael, Malakai, and Xena through the tunnel, standing and watching. She almost expects one of them to begin gesturing madly, a soundless warning of some danger she can't see. But they just stand there, close together, waiting.

"Nope," says Z. She clutches her box cutter like a talisman, but her hands don't shake. Tasha realizes her knife is sheathed and draws it.

"Oh, I almost forgot," says LaBrenda. She passes Z the shock gun and pulls her backpack around to her chest. Tasha flinches, almost tells her to be careful, suddenly hyper-aware of the fragility of bombs. LaBrenda withdraws a handgun.

"Where did that come from?" Z says, incredulous.

"Wal-Mart."

She loads it, looking at them.

"Tasha, you okay?"

No, Tasha thinks.

"Yeah," she says.

"I can't see your face with that mask on. It's hard to tell what you're thinking."

"I don't even know what I'm thinking."

There are no doors. The white wall of the Box appears to be seamless, a flat expanse of nothing that stretches to the sky and to either side like the body of a great spaceship. No windows, even toward the top. The only marker on its perfect surface is a bold splash of blood, dried now but still shamelessly red, a handprint that slides away in a long smear. LaBrenda walks toward it.

"There has to be a door on this side," she says, looking left and right. To one side of the Box is the drop off down the mountain and to the other side is the mountain itself. "Somewhere."

They stand by the smear of blood; it looks shockingly out of place on the bright expanse of the building. Tasha feels as if she's in a museum of minimalist art. *Here the artist has demonstrated the fragility of humanity in the space of a wide, white world...*

LaBrenda puts her face very near the wall; for some absurd reason Tasha is afraid she will lick the blood. Her hand jumps to reach for her shoulder, but then LaBrenda is saying, "Here."

She points, then fumbles in her pocket. Z leans close too.

"There's a little dent," Z says to Tasha, who has no intention of putting her face near the bloody wall. "Like a triangle."

"For this," LaBrenda says. In her hand is the tiny tooth that Pamela had given her. Tasha shudders at the sight of it, knowing it had been pried from a dead person's jaw. She'd known this before, but somehow, standing here by a splash of obvious death, the origin of the tooth feels more real.

LaBrenda tucks the handgun under her arm—not good gun safety, Tasha notes—and holds the tooth delicately using fingers from both hands. She extends it slowly toward the wall, aiming it right for the blood. With a gentle magnetic click, the tooth slides into a groove Tasha can't see, and the faintest red circle appears around it.

"How the hell would anyone have found that before?" Z says, her hands on her hips.

"Have to know where to look," LaBrenda says. The red halo of light seems to tremble. Tasha holds her breath. The entire white wall could be one massive surveillance system, watching them like the eye of a monster studying its prey. It already knows they're impostors. Any moment now the alarm will sound.

Instead the halo turns green, a soft shade accompanied by a warm trill that comes from the wall itself. LaBrenda slowly withdraws the tooth, and like the lens of an enormous camera, a circular door rotates open before them. Tasha smells something, something strong: an odor that seeps from the doorway in waves, almost visible in its strength. *Gas*, she thinks, stumbling backwards. Her blade is useless against it, and the stench rolls over her in intoxicating fumes.

CHAPTER 28

"Mmm—lavender," Z says. She hasn't noticed Tasha's reaction, but LaBrenda does.

"Tasha, what's wrong?" Her voice is urgent, afraid. The gun is in her hand again, aimed at the ground but ready to be raised.

Feeling vaguely ridiculous, Tasha realizes that she's not being poisoned. Z looks back at her, alert.

"What happened? Did something happen? God, Tasha, you look so weird with that ski mask on."

"No…I…I…" Tasha pauses. "I…thought the smell was… something else."

"Not everyone likes lavender," Z says, shrugging.

The door remains open, and they peer through. They see a short white tunnel, round as the door but larger. On the other side of the tunnel Tasha can see what looks like a simple white desk and a few chairs.

"It's just a lobby," Z says, craning her neck to look.

"Let's go," LaBrenda says, and Tasha thinks she sounds like she's convincing herself. "The door won't stay open forever."

They enter. The lavender smell is so thick Tasha can taste it. She coughs.

"They kind of overdid it with the lavender," Z admits. "It's in my mouth."

As they enter the lobby, the door closes with a sigh behind them. Tasha looks back, feeling as if she's been swallowed.

"It's nice in here," Z remarks, looking around. Her box cutter is in her back pocket, and she holds the shock gun in both hands, so tight her fingers look whitish.

It doesn't look like an evil secret lab, Tasha thinks. Instead, it looks like a waiting area for an upscale doctor's office. A smooth white desk, white ergonomic chairs. The floor is the same smooth blankness as the Box itself.

"Why have a waiting room?" LaBrenda says. She seems to have deflated in some way that Tasha can't put her finger on. Perhaps she'd expected to start blowing things up the moment she set foot through the door. The abandoned silence of the lobby contains nothing to shoot, nothing to blow up. She spies the residue of a faint trickle of blood, a breadcrumb trail of red spots across the pristine floor leading toward the round entrance. And one of the ergonomic chairs is on its side. But everything else is in its place.

"So...now what?" Z looks at LaBrenda. Fear is settling in. Z's determination to find her brother has propelled her along until this point, but now gravity slowly pulls her back to Earth. The Box is like another planet, its pull even stronger. Tasha feels rooted to this spot.

"Follow the blood," LaBrenda says quietly. The smell of lavender overtakes the senses, almost tricking Tasha into thinking there is sound in the lobby, but there's no sound of any kind. Only white, and blood, and lavender.

A door, closed, is near the trim white desk, but the scant drops of blood trail past it, on through the lobby to another flat wall much like the exterior of the Box. There the trail stops abruptly. LaBrenda pauses, thinks, then leans in close to examine the wall as she had done outside. Out comes the tooth again, her gun tucked under one arm, the red halo of light shining as she locates the groove. Again the halo turns green, but this time the wall slides to the right, opening the path before them.

All three of them jump at the brightness of the blood. It's everywhere. Tasha takes an involuntary step back in sudden shock. In another time the long white hallway before them could have been a pristine porcelain tube. But now it's bathed with the stains of murder, red everywhere: on the walls, on the floor. Some of the splashes reached the ceiling, a spray of red dots above their heads in a pattern like stars. And the bodies... The hallway is a cemetery without soil: corpses crowd the hallway like sandbags. And they have been mutilated, though none of them bear the torn throat that signals death by Minker. These bodies have been destroyed, some of them unrecognizable as human. Tasha sees organs. Bone. She smells a stench of death that leaps out over the scent of lavender like an angry mob.

"Jesus Christ," LaBrenda breathes, almost a sob.

Tasha gags. She turns away, back toward the pristine white lobby. She rips the ski mask off her head and vomits on the seat of an ergonomic chair. She hasn't eaten. It's mostly bile. She heaves, squeezes her eyes shut. What is she doing here?

"You good?" LaBrenda says. She has turned away from the hallway too. She'd rather look at Tasha's vomit than at the scene ahead. Z leans against the wall with her eyes closed.

"Jesus," Tasha breathes, looking at the ceiling. At least the lobby is free of blood. She spits. But the sight of the lobby, its neat white order, chills her. She quickly slips the mask back over her head.

"We have to get it over with," LaBrenda says. "Let's just do it. Let's get it done."

It's a terrible motivational speech, if that's how she meant it. But Tasha knows it was meant for LaBrenda and no one else. She wonders if Red Rooster knows that his bomber is human at her core.

Z steps into the blood-soaked hallway. Tasha knows how it will feel, walking on that floor. The blood is old. It will stick. It will squeak. She swallows another retch and follows her friend.

"Thank god we left Malakai in the car," she says quietly, to herself. "Thank god."

"What happened to them?" Z whispers. Entering the hallway suddenly makes this a place for whispering. The shock gun shakes in her hands.

"I have no idea. Minkers don't do this."

"Maybe they have dogs," Z says. "Like, mutant dogs."

"This isn't a movie," Tasha whispers. Her mouth is still thick with saliva from puking.

"It feels like a movie."

"We need to get to the fourth floor," LaBrenda says from behind them. Tasha glances back. The gun looks unnatural in LaBrenda's hand, even after seeing her use it in Wal-Mart. Her garden spade is somewhere back in that Wal-Mart, forgotten among the racks of poorly made clothes and nameless bodies. Tasha doesn't want to be a nameless body. The elevator is in front of them, but she can't quite bring herself to press the button. The Apiary and its memories breathe hotly on her neck.

Z presses the button instead. She's on a mission to rescue something precious, as Tasha had been, her love stoking her recklessness. What stokes LaBrenda, Tasha wonders as they wait in the red hallway. Duty, the demands of the one-eyed Rooster? Or the memory of her grandfather, languishing in a place that must have been much like this? Love is the only thing Tasha can imagine bringing her here to do this deed. Tasha's love for Z is the only power that moves her forward.

They should have been prepared. Their fears and their reflections hypnotized them, the red horror of the hallway dazed them. So when the Minker staggers out of the elevator, snarling, all three of them scream, the sound reverberating off the bloody walls.

"Fuck!" Tasha yelps, swinging the knife, Z scrambling on her left.

Something is different about this Minker. Until now the methodically savage assault of the creatures has been terrifying but, one on one, somewhat easy to ward off. This one, though, in his blue gown, is frantic, out of control. Angry, deliberate grabs have been replaced with wild windmilling arms, the face enraged, the jaws snapping open and closed like a repetitive mousetrap. He's fast. When Tasha slashes at his throat, he doesn't lumber backwards before heaving himself at her again: he plows forward, raging, the sound ripping from his throat amplified in the hallway and ringing in her ears.

LaBrenda aims the gun and Tasha screams again, ducking. The Minker sinks his teeth into the bandage on her hand. She screeches, flailing, pain flooding up her arm as his jaws find the throbbing vacant spot where her pinky used to be. Z flies at him, her ponytail streaming out behind her, her entire body weight sending him careening sideways.

LaBrenda attacks him from her side, grabbing his throat with her metal hand. Without muscles or tendons to indicate how hard the arm is squeezing, Tasha is shocked when the Minker's skin tears, when LaBrenda rips the side of the neck completely off with her robotic grip. The Chip, somewhere in the mess of flesh, makes a popping noise, the Minker going rigid, then toppling to the floor. LaBrenda throws the handful of his neck, Chip and all, down the hall, disgusted.

"Oh my god," Z heaves. "Holy shit. You...your hand..."

"I need to wash my hands," LaBrenda cries. "Oh my god."

"You ripped his neck off," Tasha says, sheathing her knife, clutching her own hand where the Minker had awakened her wound.

LaBrenda kneels next to the body, frantically using his hospital gown to wipe the gore from her hand. His blood makes her black metal shine.

"I had to," she says. Her voice wobbles, then finds its center. She repeats herself, this time firmly. "I had to. I didn't want to shoot the gun. I might have hit one of you guys."

They're silent. Then Z says, "He was so fast."

"So fucking fast," Tasha breathes. She's still catching her breath.

"He was a patient," LaBrenda says. Everything in her voice that had been trembling has found its feet.

"How many patients are there?"

LaBrenda squints, thinking.

"At least twenty that we saw in the Glass. Maybe twenty-two. There could be more," she says. Tasha pictures the succession of faces in the blue light of the Pentagon, projected from Dr. Rio's Glass. That night the faces had hardly seemed like real people—they were specters of Rio's mysterious origins. Now, looking down at this corpse in his hospital gown, the bottom curve of his buttocks just visible where he slumps on the floor, the reality drips down from the ceiling like drops of blood.

Z stares at the dead Minker. Her eyes are dry but she blinks many times, over and over.

"Z…," Tasha says softly.

"Let's go," Z says. "Fourth floor, right? Come on."

Tasha and LaBrenda exchange looks, then follow Z into the elevator. LaBrenda presses the button for the fourth floor; as they hum silently upwards, Tasha squeezes her eyes shut. She can still hear the dinging of the Apiary's elevator. But four floors isn't one hundred, and the doors slide open before she can prepare herself, catch her breath, get ready.

Carnage.

They're on some kind of research floor, wide and open and white, with windows on all sides that weren't visible from the outside. Somewhere outside one of those windows are Ishmael, Malakai, and Xena, waiting by the car, their hearts pounding, eyes fastened to the door through which Tasha had disappeared. Outside there are cacti and mountains and a blameless blue sky. But here inside is the same heavy, putrid cloud of death that clogged the hallway below, bodies in lab coats slumped and stricken, all of them torn and ravaged.

"Have they been...eating them?" Tasha whispers. The ski mask feels as if it's suffocating her.

Next to her, she hears LaBrenda swallow.

"I think so."

"What the fuck?" Z whispers. "The ones outside don't eat people. They just kill and move on."

"These are the prototypes," LaBrenda says. The three of them stand as if frozen in place just outside the elevator. No one wants to walk farther into this room littered with smashed beakers and broken bodies. "The Chip they got is probably a little different than the one that ended up in the masses."

"Maybe some of them have different chips," Z says, gazing around, her voice wavering. "Maybe they tried different things on different patients."

"Maybe," LaBrenda says.

"Isn't this where the control room is supposed to be?" Tasha says. The room is in various states of destruction, but the lights above are still bright; the interior lighting, combined with the light from the windows, make all corners of the room visible. Aside from the bodies, all she can see are long counters, some with destroyed equipment and others with large still-lit screens. Unlike the tomb-like hallway, this room is not silent. From somewhere she can hear air, wind. She searches for the sound and finds, across the vast room, a shattered window, the blue sky crisper and more vibrant through its jagged hole than through the other windows. Someone's escape path, perhaps. She doesn't want to look.

LaBrenda is moving down one of the aisles between long counters.

"We would know if this were the control room, right?" Tasha continues. "Didn't your friend—Alexis—didn't she say the room is circular? With security or something?"

"Yes," LaBrenda says. She's staring at a screen halfway down the aisle. "This isn't the control room. It looks like this is where they kept the data. Experiment results. Procedure observations."

"Session footage," Z says from behind Tasha. The shock gun dangles at her side.

Tasha turns to look for her and finds her also staring at a screen. Z looks up, her face grim.

"This is fucked up," she says softly.

Both Tasha and LaBrenda go to her side. On the screen is a video feed of what appears to be an examining room, white and square and slightly blurry.

"Is this live?" LaBrenda says quickly.

"No." Z points to the date in the corner of the screen. September, last year.

"I don't see anything," says Tasha. She'd been prepared for another room painted red with blood, but it appears to be empty.

"She's under the camera."

A breath later the subject enters the camera's scope, a small dark-haired woman moving erratically, jerking her head and flapping her arms. There's no audio, but when she turns slightly, facing the camera, her mouth moves in a twisted, vicious way.

"Almost a year ago," Tasha says.

On the screen the door to the room slides open and the erratic woman jerks her body to face it. Tasha's relieved that there's no audio: goosebumps rise at the mere thought of the sound the woman's mouth is making. She races toward the open door, where a man in a white coat waits patiently, his hand folded around a long, thin device that resembles a white sword. He holds it out in front of him as she charges him. When she gets close enough, he raises it and taps the side of her body.

She stops immediately, swaying, but Tasha isn't looking at the Minker anymore, prototype or not. She's not even looking at the strange white sword. She's looking at the man in the white coat, standing calmly inside the door. His high forehead, his wide-legged stance. The rough tanned skin. His hair is in a ponytail, but here on the tape it's actually clean. She knows this face.

"Roger," she says, too surprised to think about what it means.

"What?" says LaBrenda, looking at Tasha instead of at the screen.

"Roger." Tasha points, her finger resting on the chest of his white coat.

LaBrenda's lips form the word once, soundlessly, before she repeats it out loud.

"Roger...?"

There's a sound across the room, a muted shuffle. They all look, Tasha tearing her eyes from the screen where the figure of Roger takes various biometric readings from the dark-haired woman. To their left, across from where they'd entered from the elevator, is a woman. Youngish with red hair, a white mask over her nose and mouth. She carries a bin under her left arm, her right still extended to retrieve a piece of equipment from one of the long tables. Over the mask, her eyes are wide. A rabbit who entered the meadow to munch clover and happened upon what her eyes tell her are foxes. They all stare at each other for a beat. Two. Then the woman says something, muffled by the mask.

"Oh shit."

She drops the bin and turns to scurry back the way she came, toward what appears to be a white wall. She fumbles, her hands fluttering around her face. Tasha is dumbfounded, but LaBrenda is already sprinting across the room toward her,

her backpack slipped off her shoulders onto the floor a few feet from Tasha. Z snatches it up and takes off after her.

LaBrenda grabs the back of the woman's neck just as the hidden door in the wall slides open. The woman lets out a squeal as she's snatched backwards, away from the entrance. Tasha arrives at the wall as LaBrenda yanks her onto her back. The door slides shut again.

"My tooth!" the woman cries. The digital tooth she'd used as a key bounces out of its groove and disappears somewhere across the white floor.

"Fuck your tooth!" LaBrenda shouts. "What are you doing here?"

"I *work* here," the woman snarls. "How did you get in here? You weren't supposed to get inside! He said…"

She stops, and her eyes squint at them, the rest of her face hidden behind the white mask.

"What? *What?*" LaBrenda growls, shaking her. The woman's lab coat is torn and it rips further with every shake.

"Get off me!" the woman wriggles, but LaBrenda's metal grip is unbreakable. Now she points the gun at the woman's chest.

"*What?*" she says again.

"He told us you were coming. But how did you get inside?"

"Who? Who the fuck told you that?"

"You're not supposed to be up here!!" the woman barks, a mixture of fear and anger sharpening her eyes. "What are you doing up here?"

"I said who told you this shit?" LaBrenda yells.

The woman squints stubbornly. LaBrenda cocks the gun.

"Oh, it doesn't matter," the woman snaps. "Don't be so stupid. You had to have had some idea."

"Tell me what you're talking about or I will shoot you, I swear to god."

"Dr. Michaels," the woman sneers. Tasha can't see her lips—only her flashing eyes—and suddenly it makes her angry. She reaches out and snatches off the white mask. The woman gasps, whether from Tasha's action or from the sudden stench of death, Tasha's not sure.

"Who the hell is Dr. Michaels?" LaBrenda snaps, shaking the woman again.

"You might know him as Roger," she says.

"What the fuck do you know about Roger?" LaBrenda demands. "What do you know about Roger? Why is he on that screen?"

"He *works* here," the woman says. She's still trying to shake off LaBrenda's grip. Her eyes scan the floor, looking for her tooth key.

"What are you talking about?" LaBrenda grabs the woman's face, forcing her to make eye contact. "Roger doesn't work here. How the fuck could he work here?"

"He's been in the field for a year," the woman spits, jerking her face out of LaBrenda's grasp. "He told us you were stupid enough to come here, but how did you get inside? You idiots!"

"Roger talked to you?" LaBrenda screams with rage and disbelief.

"Did you bring the girl?" the woman says. She looks at Tasha's mask, her face bizarrely near laughter. "Is that her? You idiots…"

Z slaps her. Tasha gasps as if the slap had struck her own face. The woman yelps and holds her face, wide-eyed. Z winds up and slaps her again.

"Where is my brother?" She demands, her voice grating, tears starting to flow. Tasha thinks she's been waiting for the first available person she could ask, because now she's screaming: "Where is my brother, you piece of shit? Dragon Jang-Mi. Snapdragon. Where the fuck is he?"

The woman reaches out her hands as if to grab Z, and LaBrenda shakes her again.

"I don't know what you're talking about! I don't know who that is!" the woman shrieks, furious. "Let me go! Let me—"

From somewhere inside the Box comes the sound of a metallic lurch, the grinding of some unseen gear. It draws Tasha's eye across the vast research room, but when she sees nothing she turns back to the redheaded woman. Her face, previously pink with outrage, is now chalk-white.

"Oh my god," she says. "He knows you're here. He opened the floor."

She grabs for the gun. LaBrenda, looking over her shoulder for the sound of the grinding, snaps back, shouting. The redheaded woman jerks madly away, her lab coat tearing through, leaving LaBrenda clutching a piece of it. The gun wobbles, and for a moment Tasha can't distinguish its black metal from LaBrenda's arm. The redheaded woman seems to be burning: she thrashes, shakes, scrabbling to gain control of the weapon—whether to disarm LaBrenda or to take it for herself, Tasha has no idea.

Somehow Tasha knew the gun would fire. The sound is deafening, sends her spine careening back to the aisles of Wal-Mart. She drops into a crouch, hands over her ears; her first thought is whether or not Malakai and Ishmael heard the sound. *Please stay outside,* she prays. *Please stay outside.*

Z is dragging Tasha up from the floor even before the redheaded woman's dead body sinks down next to her. Z's pointing, screaming words that Tasha can't hear over the ringing in her ears. LaBrenda scrambles in her pocket, the gun somewhere on the ground, underneath the woman's body. LaBrenda yanks the tooth from her own pocket, looking frantically over her shoulders as she searches for the groove in the wall. Tasha looks back, the edges of the ski mask giving her tunnel vision.

Three Minkers are stampeding toward them from far across the research room, covered in blood that resembles over-the-top cinema warpaint. Their speed is heart-stopping. She can hear their jaws snapping from across the floor, the sound accompanied by the crashing of equipment that they're knocking to the tiles in their unbridled trajectory toward Tasha. Somewhere in her peripheral vision a green halo of light appears on the wall and the door slides open, LaBrenda toppling through, dragging Z, who drags Tasha. The rampaging Minkers are still ten feet away when the door slides closed, but as the crack closes, edging them out of sight, Tasha's heart gives a final lurch, as if one might squeeze through after all and send her blood in a torrent of red to the floor.

"I didn't mean to shoot her." LaBrenda sinks to the floor, her back against the wall of the new hallway they find themselves in. "I didn't even…"

"It doesn't matter," Z yells. "It doesn't matter! How could you not know about Roger? What does that mean, that he works for Neovison? Oh my god…"

LaBrenda seems to be struggling under the weight of some invisible mass. Her mouth opens and closes; her eyes seem glazed.

"Roger's what? A fucking mole? But he knew about…about everything. What kind of scientist goes undercover?"

"One funded by the government, you fucking idiot!" Z shrieks, waving the shock gun.

Tasha can't shriek. She can't do much of anything. She stands there by the now-invisible door, one hand tight around her knife and the other hand throbbing under its bandage. The wound on her head hasn't bothered her for hours but suddenly it's alive again, a slow pulse that makes the space they're in seem fuzzy and blurred. LaBrenda and Z argue, their panic boiling into rage, but Tasha's eyes sweep the area behind them—a hallway full of doors, bright and empty except for a wheelchair in the center like one of the abandoned cars Tasha has passed so often on the highway. The nape of her neck prickles under the mask, as if the wheelchair contains a ghost that sits watching them before it decides to wheel slowly in their direction. No blood. She looks at the ceiling, searching for a trace of what had bathed the other hallway. No sign of red anywhere. Instead, her eyes fall on the signs above each door. Patient 1. Patient 3. Patient 5. The odd-numbered signs go on and on. Tasha finds herself walking toward the doors they label.

"He knew we were coming," Z is yelling. "How do we know you guys weren't in this together? Oh my god, is this a fucking trap? For whoever's looking for Tasha?"

"In *what* together? I should ask you the same fucking thing! You're the one who had Rio's Glass!"

"Tasha, where are you going? We can't just…"

Tasha ignores her and Z's voice trails off. She's seen the signs. Behind her, Tasha can hear the sound of the backpacks being hoisted from the floor, slow careful footsteps following her.

The first three rooms are empty. With each window they peer through, the emptiness is both a relief and a disappointment. No blood. Just medical equipment, slim white hospital beds with the sheets turned back, some slightly rumpled, as if the patient got up to pee and never came back. None of the rooms have windows: the glass panel on the door would have been the only view for the patients inside.

"We need to go," LaBrenda says. Tasha is following Z now. Door to door, silent salespeople in a suburb of customers who aren't home. Z ignores LaBrenda, moves on to the next room. This is what she had come for. Her backpack swings from side to side as she hurries down the hallway, her urgency increasing with every step.

Patient 7 is in his room. Dead. After the few empty beds, their bright white sheets unmarred, the sight of a body is jarring. Tasha jumps when she peeks through the window. The patient's body is curled like a husk, long black hair hanging to obscure the face from where he lies at the edge of the bed. The

482 OLIVIA A. COLE

once-brown skin is gray, splotchy. Blisters mark the visible flesh with a pattern like hotspots on the sun. Decay.

"They just left them like this," Z says, still staring through the window.

"We don't have time for this," LaBrenda says.

Z turns and runs down the hallway. Patient 9's room is empty. Patient 11's room is empty. Patient 13 contains a body, a man flat on his back, his face unrecognizable. The vomit that had entered Tasha's throat when they arrived rises again. She clenches her teeth. Patient 13's room is empty. Z dashes on, Tasha following her more slowly, saying nothing. She knows this mad rush. Z had followed her into Fetch Fetchers. Tasha follows her now.

Patient 15's room is empty. Odd numbers only. Tasha doesn't want to know where the hallway with even numbers is, or what it contains. Patient 17, empty. Z reaches Patient 19's room, almost passes, does a double-take.

"She's alive," she says, her voice a croak. "Oh my god."

Tasha doesn't want to look, but she does. The woman sits on the edge of the bed, her back to the door, her head moving slowly from side to side. Her hair is shaved, a black layer covering the scalp, gray in places. She's thin, the open back of her hospital gown revealing a slim back with protruding shoulder blades. The room, Tasha notes, is bare of the hospital equipment they'd seen in the other rooms.

"They must be feeding her," LaBrenda says, peering over Tasha's head. "No way that she'd be alive otherwise."

"She doesn't have the Chip, the way she's sitting," Z says. "I don't think the other two did either. One was lying in bed. Minkers don't lie in bed, even if they're dying."

Tasha watches the woman's shaking head, the movement of the vertebrae under the deep brown skin.

"So...what? She's a prisoner? If she doesn't have the Chip, what's she doing here?"

The woman's hands rise from her lap, and outside the door they all inhale involuntarily. Tasha feels like she's at a zoo, gazing in at the single tiger, lonely in her exhibit. The woman examines her fingernails, appears to nibble at a cuticle. Her hands are as thin as her back, long fingers, the knuckles jutting out.

"We need to go," LaBrenda says.

Z ignores her and moves on to the next room—the last in the hallway of odd-numbered doors. Tasha gazes after her. She goes to the window of Patient 21, peers through the glass, and then stays there for a breath before stepping away.

"Empty," she says, her voice thick.

Tasha squeezes her eyes shut, exhaling a short, hard breath.

"Z…"

"I thought he'd be here," Z says. She holds the shock gun loosely. "I really thought he'd be here."

Tasha starts to turn away from Patient 19, toward Z, toward the other end of the hallway that will take them out of this long, ghostly corridor, on toward whatever is left of this impossible, bloody mission. But a movement inside the room—the lone tiger stirring—catches her eye. She looks back as the woman stands up from her bed and turns to gaze at the window.

It takes a moment for Tasha to truly see the face looking out through the glass. Large brown eyes, the eyelids angling up at the outer corners. The bridge of the nose wide and distinctive. The top lip is familiar, a prominent arch that Tasha has seen in mirrors and so many frames. Laugh lines around the mouth from smiles long past. Tasha stares, her skin waking, the flesh prickling from her scalp on down, her tongue suddenly thick and dry. The face stuns her, her brain turning on itself, her heartbeat surrounding logic and crushing it into dust. Then she's fully awake. There is no lie in her eyes. She's hammering the door, her knife clattering against the white floor as she beats the window with her fists.

"Mom!" she screams as the woman steps toward the window. Her fists are already numb. "That's my mother!"

CHAPTER 29

Tasha's mother stands halfway between the bed and the window, swaying. Her eyes are cloudy, as if she's staring through dark fog at a dim light that may be only a trick of her vision. She squints, and Tasha realizes what she must see: a black-masked humanoid beating on the door, shouting. Tasha reaches up and rips the ski mask off her head, flinging it, and stares through the window.

Her mother's eyes grow large. A long breath, and then her lips move, shaping a word that might be Tasha's name.

The sound ripped from Tasha's throat is mythical: the cry of something huge and old. She doesn't know where the sound comes from, only that it's torn from somewhere deep within her—a weeping willow with its leaves on fire, its roots buried in funerals with no bodies, only jars of ashes with names on crooked white labels. A mistake, the hospital told her: a mix-up with funeral arrangements. No bodies. Only ash. The face whose corpse she never got to see stands in front of her, blinking. Alive.

LaBrenda and Z have backed away, against the wall across from the door. Their faces are wide open, naked in their lack of comprehension. Tasha whirls on them.

486 OLIVIA A. COLE

"I never saw their bodies," she sobs. The numbness that has enveloped her since they entered this place of horrors is peeled back like scar tissue, giving old wounds new power to inflict pain. All of her pain is laid bare. "I never saw their bodies."

Her mother is at the window, one slender hand reaching toward the glass.

"Tasha," her mouth says. Tasha can't tell if she actually hears the voice or if it rises from her memory. She spins around to LaBrenda.

"Give me the tooth," she says, trying not to shout.

LaBrenda hesitates, her eyes darting over Tasha's shoulder at the window and then back again. She moves her lips to speak, but stops.

"Tasha…"

"LaBrenda, give me the fucking tooth!"

At first Tasha thinks she's not going to do it. The hand cupping the tooth hovers, as if it might hide the tooth in a pocket instead of releasing it. Z's elbow jerks out from her body, nudging LaBrenda in the ribs.

"LaBrenda, give her the goddamn tooth!"

LaBrenda holds it out, the small bluish-white object pinched between her thumb and finger. Tasha snatches it, whirling back around to face the door. She slides her palm along the face of it until she feels the small triangular groove. She shoves the tooth in, fumbling. Her heart pounds as the green halo appears on the expanse of white.

And then nothing stands between them. The door slides away and now they are two pairs of brown eyes taking each other in. Tasha's vocal cords seem frozen, detached somehow from her body.

"Baby," her mother breathes. The words are cracked, limping into Tasha's ears and sinking there.

"Mom," Tasha cries, and rushes to her, embracing her, scarcely able to breathe. "Mama!"

Her mother's cheek against her neck feels cool, smooth like granite.

"Mama," Tasha says. "What…what…"

There are too many questions, all of them too large and too heavy to fit in Tasha's mouth.

"Mama…where's Daddy? How…?"

And then the grinding in the walls, a metallic sound like the opening and closing of the building's mechanical jaws. The sound reverberates through the floor, through Tasha's feet and up her legs. She freezes, holding her mother's thin body.

"Tasha, we need to move," LaBrenda says. She looks frantically around the hallway, searching for cameras. Either they've seen Tasha unmasked or they've seen LaBrenda kill the redheaded woman. Both probably. Intruders. Whoever captains the helm knows they're here.

"Where? Where are we going?" Z demands.

Tasha can't let go of her mother. Not yet. She might turn into ash. She clutches her, staring at the blank room behind her: the plain white bed. The smooth lineless walls. Tasha had imagined her as dust, spread over their land in Kentucky. She had been here.

"We need to get to the cerebellum," LaBrenda cries. "We need to place the bombs."

"How do we know Roger didn't set us up?" Z snaps, her voice harsh.

"Tasha, come on!"

"Wait," Tasha's mother whispers in her ear.

She lets go of Tasha, slipping out of her grasp, and returns to the white room. Her pale blue pants sweep the floor. She goes to her mattress—Tasha staring after her, poised to run in and get her. But rather than sitting down, her mother grips the mattress in her frail hands and lifts it. There's nothing underneath, but Tasha watches as her fingers brush the edge of the mattress itself, pausing at one spot that looks unremarkable until she begins to pull on what must be a thread, and a seam opens. She reaches in, the hole growing larger to admit her whole hand, and when she withdraws she's clutching a bright metal tool. She stuffs her hand in again, drawing out another one. She stands and returns to the door, carrying two scalpels.

"We'll need these," she says, her voice hoarse.

Tasha scoops up her own knife from the floor.

"This way," LaBrenda says. After following the patient signs, they're almost at the far end of the hallway. Tasha grips her mother's hand and follows, but her mother's step is slow. She seems disoriented.

"Drugs," the older woman rasps.

"Wait," says Z. Turning, she dashes back down the hall toward where they entered. She runs to the abandoned wheelchair, still sitting by one of the doors, and races it back to where the others stand, the wheels thrumming in the empty corridor. "Let's roll."

Tasha pushes her mother down the hall, her knife sheathed, the ski mask forgotten. Her mother's thin hands grip the scalpels in her lap. LaBrenda sprints to the end of the hallway, finds the groove, and inserts the tooth. The door admits them into another hallway, as long and blank as this one but with no doors.

"How did you get a tooth?" Tasha's mother asks.

"Long story, Mrs. Lockett," Z says.

"Stella. Call me Stella, please."

"Elevator," LaBrenda says, and dashes to the right. They follow, Tasha straining her ears for the grinding sound that had preceded the three Minkers' entrance into the research room. Nothing. But the silence of the hallway is not to be trusted. Tasha feels watched from every angle. She should have put the ski mask back on—even if the redhead had seemed to see through it. The Box is a structure swarming with eyes.

"What are we doing, LaBrenda?" Z snaps. "If Roger told them we were coming, then they're waiting for us! This could be a trap!"

"They didn't expect us to get inside!" LaBrenda explodes, turning on her. "I have to do this! I..."

"You're going to get us all killed!" Z screams. She's tipping over into rage: Tasha can hear the red in her voice, blazing so hot that it will soon turn white. "They're probably up there waiting for us!"

"I have to try! Rooster needs those locations!"

"You're doing all this for some dude with one eye?" Z shrieks.

"My granddad died in a place like this!" LaBrenda cries helplessly, her voice quaking. The pieces of her that have been made of stone soften, turn to clay. She struggles to build something with it. "I have to. I have to. He died all alone... because of people like this!"

Z opens her mouth to shout, to spit poison. But no words come out. She stares at LaBrenda emptily, the ghosts of their individual loves swimming in the air between them. Tasha says nothing. One of her own ghosts is before her, still materializing in her mind.

"We're going to die," Z says weakly.

"We have to stop them," says LaBrenda.

As if on cue, the elevator door slides open and a Minker is upon them, a bloody-mouthed jack-in-the-box who attaches himself to LaBrenda's arm and rakes it with his teeth, the sound of bone on metal sharp and strange. Another is behind him, struggling to get around him and attack Z. Tasha curses, yanking the wheelchair backward and attempting to scramble in front to protect her mother.

Z fires the shock gun straight into the back of the Minker attacking LaBrenda, then fumbles with the gun as the second one claws past its fallen comrade. She drops the gun trying to crank it into life again. The Minker trips on the first body, sprawling toward her, and Z snatches at her box cutter. Tasha leaps forward, ready to help, but Z has already pounced, jabbing at the creature's neck with the blade, screaming obscenities.

"Christ!" she shouts, stumbling backwards when the Minker lies dead. "It's like they put them in there on purpose! And why are the ones here so fast?"

"They're not all like that," Tasha's mother says from behind them. She's leaned to the side in the wheelchair.

"How many?" Tasha says, returning to the chair.

Her mother shakes her head, the same slow movement they'd watched from the window.

LaBrenda is in the elevator. Z stares at her for a moment, then leans down to retrieve the shock gun.

"LaBrenda, if we're going to do this, you better hurry the fuck up," Z says. She's crying. Tasha thinks the tears must be hot, spilling from the volcano of her pain. She glances sidelong at Tasha's mother. "Sorry, Mrs. Lockett. Stella."

Tasha's mother waves her hand, the way she always has. Tasha's heart convulses.

"In," LaBrenda says. They get in. She hits three. "Stella, can I borrow one of those scalpels?"

Tasha's mother hands it over.

"Be ready," LaBrenda says. "Z's right. They're probably waiting for us."

Tasha draws her knife, clutching the back of the wheelchair with her other hand. She wishes she could put a bubble around her, a cloak of invisibility. She wishes she could pause the world and ask her mother every question that's swelling in her mind. The doors slide open and Tasha is forced to tear her eyes away from the top of her mother's head and look out at what awaits them.

The room is circular, as Alexis had guessed back at the Pentagon: curving walls, no visible doors except the mouth of the elevator they stand in. The ceiling slopes down from the outer edges toward the middle, where it seamlessly joins a cylinder that marks the center, joining floor and ceiling like the trunk of a smooth white tree. A wide white platform surrounds the central core on all sides, covered in screens and dials. It reminds Tasha of the control room in the Lincoln Park Zoo: views into the enclosures of animals caged against their will. The room is empty aside from this structure, its windowless whiteness almost painful to her eyes. She looks down at her mother's graying hair, lays her hand on top of it.

"You should leave," says a voice.

No one speaks. No one breathes. Tasha can't tell where the voice comes from, scans the room for some hidden speaker, her heart beginning to pound. *Here we go*, she thinks.

The man comes out from the other side of the white trunk. He doesn't wear a lab coat the way the redheaded woman had. Instead, a knit sweater drapes his body, worn over a pair of black slacks. His posture is rigid, as if he'd had a spinal curve corrected by a metal rod. His hands are empty. Tasha had expected a weapon of some kind, a Glass at the very least. Instead he holds his hands in front of him, the left twisting a ring on a finger of the right.

LaBrenda looks uncertain and pauses at the head of the group. She slowly shrugs off her backpack and Z follows suit.

"We're not leaving," LaBrenda says finally. "But we don't have to hurt you. I just need the locations of the other hubs. Can you give me that?"

The man does something with his mouth, as if running his tongue over his teeth.

"No," he says. "I'm afraid I can't."

He looks past LaBrenda, his eyes landing on Tasha's mother in the wheelchair.

"Hello, Stella."

Tasha moves to the side of the chair, looks down at her mother.

"Dr. Lane," Stella says. She looks afraid of him, this slender, empty-handed man.

"If you can't give me the locations, then get out of my way," LaBrenda says. She moves forward, tooth in one hand, scalpel in the other. The man takes a quick step forward.

"Stop," he says. Tasha sees his hand reach toward his pants pocket. "I don't know how you got into this building, but if you take one step closer to these machines I will make sure you all die."

Tasha regards this man warily. Any day before today she would have passed a man like him on the street without a second glance. But this is now.

"He's not the boss," Stella says from the wheelchair. She shakes her head in that wobbly way. "He's just an assistant."

Dr. Lane looks straight at Tasha's mother, his eyes flashing, but even with his straight back Tasha sees the bend in him. Her mother's right. He's not the boss. But he's here, and he's in the way.

"I may not be the boss," he says, raising his chin. His eyes are almost lazy in the way they regard the little group before him, as if his hatred of them takes no effort. "But I don't need to be to kill you. Leave this place."

"Look," LaBrenda says. She has paused halfway to where Dr. Lane stands by the platform. "I'm not leaving until I get the locations of those hubs."

She doesn't mention the fact that she will then bomb the place to hell, Tasha notes.

"It's not my job to convince you to leave," he says, with a tone of more intense warning. "It's just my job to make sure you stay away from these machines."

He's been addressing LaBrenda thus far, but now his gaze sweeps over to Tasha, and his eyes narrow when they find her face.

"This is your idea, I imagine?" he says, his tone sharp and accusing. "You must think you're very brave, doing what you did in Chicago and then waltzing in here. Not on my watch."

Tasha almost snorts.

"What I did in Chicago?" she snaps. "You don't know shit, do you? You really don't know shit."

"You don't know shit," Z adds unnecessarily, but Tasha appreciates the backup.

"I know enough," the man frowns. "Dr. Michaels shared enough with us before we lost communication."

"Roger," LaBrenda says. Tasha can feel LaBrenda's energy stiffen, her muscles flex. If Roger were in this room, her metal hand would be around his throat.

"Dr. Michaels," he says in a nasty voice. "He advised us your little party was headed this way. You weren't supposed to get inside, of course. Where did you get a tooth?"

"There's a lot of people that want you dead," LaBrenda snarls, and takes another step forward.

"Ah," Dr. Lane says sharply, holding his finger out to signal her to stop. "Don't. Think carefully. If you come near me, you all die. Is that really worth what you think you're here to do?"

LaBrenda points a metal finger straight back at him, a black sword.

"I'm willing to risk my life, yes," she says. "If it means burning Neovison to the ground."

"You think this building is Neovison?" he says loudly, in a voice like a bark. "You think if destroy this place, you'll find a cure for what has happened to you?"

"No," says Tasha, low. "We thought that in Chicago. Dr. Rio showed us we were wrong."

"Rio!" the man says with something between a snarl and a laugh. "Rio. What a fool. He couldn't see the wisdom in what Neovison is trying to accomplish. The possibility of a new world…"

He squints at them again, as if he'd been lurking in a shadow and one of them had shined a light in his eyes.

"You're wasting your time," he says after a pause. "You're going to die anyway. All of you. If you leave now, I will wait until you're outside to release the patients."

"The patients," Stella says in a voice cracked and hard as a fossil. "You mean the prisoners."

The man turns his eyes back on her, his expression baleful.

"You shouldn't complain, Stella," he says. "You've been living here rent-free and unharmed."

"I've paid my rent," Stella whispers.

Silence. They all stare at each other, the man's eyes sweeping over their group. Anger and fear rattle there in his pupils like the tails of two poisonous snakes. LaBrenda remains still, as if weighing her options. The round white room feels as if it's orbiting around them: it's as slow and quiet as space. Then LaBrenda makes a *tsk*ing sound with her teeth and starts forward again.

Dr. Lane takes two swift steps backward, his anger lanced with what might be panic. LaBrenda goes for the platform, stopping at one of the screens, and then inserting the tooth into a groove on the platform.

"That tooth doesn't have clearance," Dr. Lane says from where he hovers nearby. Tasha wonders if he's going to shoot LaBrenda with some hidden weapon. "Only two people do, and I know that both of us have our keys."

LaBrenda turns on him slowly. Tasha steps forward, away from the wheelchair, just one pace.

"Well," LaBrenda says quietly. "I guess I know where to get one of them."

If LaBrenda signaled to Z, Tasha didn't see it. Z sprints toward Dr. Lane as LaBrenda moves rapidly to join her. Tasha hears her mother gasp.

"Don't shock him," LaBrenda yells, latching onto Dr. Lane's arm as he yells and flails his other arm. "It might zap his key!"

Z drops the shock gun and leaps at Dr. Lane, but he sees her coming and manages to throw his leg out to block her attack. His foot catches Z squarely in the stomach, sending her backward onto her butt gasping for air.

"What are you going to do?" Tasha shouts, rushing forward to help Z. "Yank it out of his mouth?"

"If I have to."

LaBrenda grapples with the man, who doesn't speak but grunts with the exertion of fending her off.

Pulling Z to her feet from where she'd sprawled, Tasha looks back at where her mother sits. Stella's eyes are filled with tears, the scalpel gripped in her fist and held forward like a sword. She's moved forward to the edge of the wheelchair, as if she might get up and attack the doctor herself if she had the strength.

"Shit," LaBrenda yelps. Dr. Lane's elbow catches her in the nose, and two round drops of blood spot the pristine white floor.

"He has a gun!" Z shouts.

LaBrenda blunders backward, but what Dr. Lane pulls from his pocket isn't a gun. It's a short white club, which he brandishes with a certain desperation. His eyes dart from person to person, and then down to the club. He does something to it with his thumb and it makes a whirring noise before giving off a soft, shrill sound like a teakettle. Then Dr. Lane lunges toward the platform, slamming his palm on one of the dials.

LaBrenda is too slow in trying to stop him, and Tasha doesn't have time to wonder what he just did. She hears it: the grinding in the walls, nearer now than the last time she'd heard it. The redheaded woman's words echo back to her: *He opened the floor.*

"You did this to yourself," Dr. Lane says, panting. His eyes are slits. He looks back and forth between each of their faces. "This was never your world. Neovison always wins."

"Tasha," Stella says. She stretches out to grab Tasha's waistband. Tasha turns and finds her mother's eyes on her face, her expression urgent. "We need to go."

"It's too late for that," Dr. Lane barks. He glances around, as if he's summoned a spirit and waits for it to appear. "You never should have come here."

LaBrenda starts toward him again, Dr. Lane flinching, but then a door appears on the far side of the round room, the blank white wall sliding aside to reveal an entrance that had been nothing a moment before. Two figures appear in the doorway, hesitating, as if the whiteness of the room has blinded them momentarily. Dr. Lane aims the white club in their direction, holding it in both hands, the object still emitting its low squeal.

Then there's another sound. A howl, Tasha thinks, that sears like lightning through her ears. A shrill cry that tears the air and electrifies the entire room.

It's Z. She falls to her knees before Tasha can catch her, screaming as if she's on fire.

"Z!" Tasha cries, grabbing for her.

Z slaps at her hands, shoving her away, falling sideways with the effort. As the Minkers start to stagger forward, Z does the same, crawling toward them on the floor as if she's lost her mind, pulled by some gravity the Minkers exude.

"Dragon!" she wails as she crawls toward the two Minkers, tears making the word nearly incomprehensible. "Dragon!"

It's her brother. Tasha doesn't have time to note the similarity— lessened somewhat by his now-shaved head—because he and his Minker companion storm toward them fast, too fast, their snarls melting together to create a blur of savage noise. Dr. Lane, the white club still held in both hands, scrambles backwards until his back is against the control platform. The Minkers pause for a half breath as they near him, the blood draining from his face as they do so, then rage past him toward LaBrenda.

Dragon leaps on LaBrenda, knocking her backwards with his force and weight. She shoves him hard with her metal arm, raising the scalpel in her other hand.

"LaBrenda, *don't!*" Z screams, the sound of her voice like murder it's so red. "Don't!"

LaBrenda's hand hovers. The other Minker stampedes toward Z, sprawled on the floor, now struggling to gain her feet. Tasha hesitates, her mother cringing and shrunken in her wheelchair, then sprints forward, knife held ready. She clashes with the Minker just as he reaches Z, half-risen, frantically slicing him across the throat. Blood sprays from the wound but no spark of the Chip rewards the cut, and the black tentacles appear, lacing the flesh shut. He hurls himself back at them, still gushing blood, but Z meets him, her box cutter pulled back for stabbing. Beyond him, LaBrenda struggles with Dragon, who has her leaned backwards over the control platform, his jaws snapping, spit flying.

"Tasha!" LaBrenda screams. "Get the dude! His tooth! We need it!"

Dr. Lane is edging away from the platform, his expression wild. Z stabs madly at the Minker. The room that had felt so silent and still is now an orb of chaos, the white floors splashed with red, the air rent by screams and snarls. At the doorway yet another Minker appears, heavyset and taking up the whole entrance—Tasha can't tell if another one is behind him. Dr. Lane slides around the back of the platform, still clutching the white club. Somewhere in the uniform whiteness of the circular room is another door—hidden—and he's heading for it.

"Mom!" Tasha shouts over her shoulder. She never thought she'd call someone this again. "Wait—just wait!"

She takes off after Dr. Lane, who has seen her coming and abandons the platform, running toward what looks like a blank wall.

"Fuck no you don't!" Tasha shouts, putting on an extra burst of speed. Behind her she hears Z sobbing at LaBrenda, over and over without pause like a chant.

"LaBrenda please don't LaBrenda please don't LaBrenda please don't!"

Tasha snatches the back of Dr. Lane's sweater, the place where her pinky is missing giving a sudden throb as it buries itself in the fabric. He yelps, the collar of the sweater choking him as she hauls him backwards.

They both fall hard, he still gripping the club as if it's fused to his flesh. Tasha's grip on the knife is not as firm, and it ends up a foot behind her. She draws back her hand and punches him as hard as she can, her fist connecting with his temple with a satisfying *thunk* that makes him yell. She's on top of one of his arms, but the hand still clutching the club springs up and strikes her, the object smashing against the side of her skull and sending her sprawling.

As she reels, he clambers up from the floor just as the thick-bodied Minker from the doorway lumbers over, his jaws snapping. He's slower because of his size but still faster than any of the Minkers outside the Box. He lunges as if to slump down on top of Tasha, but she rolls, catching sight of Dr. Lane scrambling away, the club held out toward the Minker like a cross to ward off demons.

Tasha wriggles away, snatching at the knife with her fingertips; the Minker turns awkwardly to retarget his attack. Knife in hand, she swings at his ankles, thinking vaguely of some tendon that will render him useless for the breath it takes to kill him. The slices produce blood but no stumble, and Tasha crawls madly, forcing her feet underneath her. When she stands, Dr. Lane is moving backwards toward the wall, the white club's whining sharp and distinct. She lunges at him, knife swinging.

The club falls, bounces once, and rolls.

"No!" Dr. Lane shrieks. "Nonono!"

Tasha grabs his arm with her pinky-less hand, ignoring the intense pain, and uses all her strength to swing him. He's already moving, plunging toward the club, and she uses his momentum to send him crashing into the arms of the Minker, whose outstretched hands grab him greedily, the mouth a cave of horribly square human teeth.

"Tasha," her mother yells, a voice cracked and thin, and Tasha's heart turns to ice, thinking she's being attacked. "Get it! Get it!"

It. The club. Dr. Lane is screaming, and Tasha thinks she can hear the sound of his skin tearing, the weak crunch of his neck opening under barely fanged incisors. She springs toward the club where it has rolled several feet away, snatching it up and gripping it firmly. It's molded to fit the grip of a hand, and her fingers settle easily into the grooves.

Dr. Lane is already dead when she turns back, but the Minker tears at his body still, a human beast, rage-hungry, psychotic. She almost can't bring herself to approach him, but adrenaline powers her body with fuel previously lost to terror. She raises the knife, looking for the right spot on his neck, ready for the attack, but none comes. The Minker blinks at the whining sound of the club—she thinks she sees his pupils vibrate when he looks up, his face covered in blood—but goes on tearing at the destroyed body of Dr. Lane.

Tasha stabs him twice in the neck, the pop of the Chip an "amen" at the end of her prayer. She leaps away, clutching the club in one hand, her knife in the other. She dashes around the central trunk once again, just as a Minker sinks its teeth into her mother's arm.

"Mom!" she screams. She is a lion crossing the room, leaping over the body of the Minker Z had killed. Her mother struggles weakly, half out of the wheelchair, her face twisted in pain, stabbing weakly at her attacker's neck with the scalpel in her thin hand.

Tasha's blade sinks so deeply into the Minker's brain that the creature's whole body jolts. Chip or not, the knife damages something crucial and the entire body receives the message. Tasha leaves the knife in the wound, grabbing the Minker by the shoulder and flinging it backward onto the floor.

"Mom, here, here!" She shoves the club into her mother's hands, the scalpel gone, lost, and whirls to finish her work.

The Minker has recovered, risen from the floor with the knife protruding from its head like the accessory of a tacky Halloween costume. Tasha leaps on it, almost too hard, almost tackling it to the floor again. Tasha doesn't want to fight him. She wants to kill him. She grabs for the knife handle and yanks to pull it from the man's skull. It's more difficult than she thought—she yanks again and wrenches it out. Somewhere Z is screaming and Tasha doesn't know why but she stabs the Minker in the neck again and again until it lies still. Tasha shoves off the body to stand, shaky, her hands slick with blood.

"Mom," she says, turning, stumbling on the dead Minker's feet. Her mother has the bottom of her hospital shirt wrapped around her forearm.

"LaBrenda, *don't*!"

The word "don't" starts as a scream but trails off into wordlessness, a sound of human becoming werewolf. Tasha whirls, in time to see LaBrenda bury her scalpel in the neck of Z's brother.

"No!" Z shrieks, flinging herself at LaBrenda.

LaBrenda's stab missed the Chip. Dragon's neck spurts blood but only that pumped by a single, quick heartbeat. The narrow incision healed quickly by the Chip, he lunges forward at LaBrenda's face, his mouth open impossibly wide.

Z tackles LaBrenda, sending the whole group of them careening sideways, into the pools of blood left by the other dead Minker. LaBrenda's nose is still bleeding from its collision with Dr. Lane's elbow, the blood streaming down her face and onto Dragon's, whom she struggles to stay on top of as they stagger, falling.

"Z!" Tasha screams. "Azalea! Stop!"

"He's my brother, LaBrenda!" Z screeches, ignoring her.

Tasha can't tell who's screaming. The sound of Dragon's coughing bark is a ragged tear through any words that are spoken. Dragon's teeth drag along LaBrenda's metal arm, and Z shakes her other arm like it's a neck she's choking. The scalpel rattles from LaBrenda's fingers, disappears under Dragon's body. As she gropes for it, Dragon lurches forward. She loses her balance and ends up on the floor next to him, Dragon fighting to climb on top of her.

LaBrenda manages to curl her leg, placing her foot against Dragon's chest and kicking with a powerful shove that sends him arcing onto his back. No sooner does he hit the floor than he frantically shuffles to rise again, intent on the blood before him. Tasha sees his face then. So much like Z. The eyebrows and the features both angled and open. Their mouths are the same too, even now: both are locked in a snarl.

"LaBrenda, don't you fucking touch him!" Z screams, still clutching LaBrenda's arm as she flails around looking for the scalpel.

"Tasha," Stella says. She's standing in front of the wheelchair behind where Tasha stands transfixed. Tasha looks, frantic. Her mother stares at her, hard.

Tasha races to the shock gun where Z had dropped it before attacking Dr. Lane. It has only two mechanisms: the crank and the trigger. She pants, her mouth dry, and looks desperately at LaBrenda and Z, who fight for control of the scalpel. Dragon rejoins them, snarling, and seizes Z's shoulder in his teeth.

Tasha fires. The blur of blue is like a bit of flame from a gas grill, appearing and then disappearing. It's as if Dragon's body absorbs it, and his lungs make a sputtering sound before he topples, rigid, on top of his sister.

Z's blood runs freely from her arm, but she doesn't notice. She gapes down at the body of her brother, uncomprehending. She gingerly shifts what was Dragon onto his back, struggling under his weight. His head lolls to the side and, from where Tasha stands, still holding the shock gun, she sees his black eyes, the whites lost to oily shadow. Z stares at his face, her mouth moving in trembling, soundless words. Then she looks up, understanding, and sees Tasha with the gun. Watching her face change is like looking out over the sea before a storm, the winds gathering, the clouds darkening. She springs from the floor and launches herself at Tasha, screaming.

"I'm going to kill you!"

CHAPTER 30

Tasha didn't think she would fire. But she does. The sight of Z charging, her eyes full of rage, panics her, and she cranks the gun once before firing at her friend. The bolt of energy catches Z in the belly and she staggers, her expression immediately glazed. Tasha flings the gun away and leaps toward her.

"Z!" she cries. "Oh my god. I'm so sorry. Please…"

Z is unconscious, flopping in Tasha's arms, her chest rising and falling. Her brother lies still behind her, bloodless except for that blood on his lips that belongs to his sister.

LaBrenda has gained her feet, stands panting.

"There will be more," Tasha's mother says. She's sunk back into the wheelchair, her hand over her mouth.

Tasha looks up from Z to LaBrenda.

"Do whatever the fuck it is you need to do."

LaBrenda nods, her chest heaving. She sprints around the platform to where Tasha had left Dr. Lane's body. Tasha is glad she can't see what LaBrenda does, but she returns a second later with the tooth from his mouth and inserts it into the groove on the platform.

"How many more?" Tasha says, straining her neck to look over her shoulder at her mother.

"I don't know exactly," Stella says. "Not all of us were given the Chip. But they will have called more. Only Dr. Lane and Dr. Penny stayed behind, but Neovison will know what's happening right now. They know everything."

"Dr. Penny?"

"She's young. Red hair. She's somewhere in the building."

"We saw her. We already took care of her."

Tasha's mother gazes at her with a look Tasha can't decipher. Tasha looks down at Z, whose head she cradles in her lap. Her eyelids flutter. Tasha wants to sob.

"I've got the files," LaBrenda says, and Tasha looks up.

LaBrenda raises her metal hand and unscrews the tip of her pinky finger. Tasha cocks her head.

"What the hell?"

LaBrenda doesn't look at her. The tip of the finger is like a cap that pulls to the side; behind it, a thin apparatus like a pin. She uses her flesh hand to remove it, and then inserts the pin into the side of the screen she's hunched over.

"LaBrenda?"

"Have to put the files somewhere," she says, still staring at the screen. "Can't exactly email them."

"Your hand is…really talented," Tasha says, thinking of the welding it had done on the SkyDrive.

LaBrenda glances over her shoulder.

"I got it from my mama," she says, and removes the pin from the side of the screen, reinserting it into her finger. She closes the cap and straightens her back. "One more thing and we can get the hell out of here."

She goes for the backpacks. Tasha's heart sinks. The bombs— she'd almost forgotten. They sit there by the elevator where they'd been shrugged off, waiting patiently like two stones. Tasha stays put, clutching Z.

"What's this?" Stella says.

"Bombs, mama," Tasha says with a sigh she can't rein in.

"What did you say?"

"We'll get out in time, Miss Stella," says LaBrenda. She grasps a pack in each hand and carries them over to the platform, kneeling on the floor with them. She opens one and reaches inside.

Tasha holds her breath. Her mind races back to the Apiary, where she'd stood looking at the clouds as Ishmael said slowly, "What's in the bags?" She's been running hundreds of miles and has found herself back in the same place: in a room built by Neovison, surrounded by death. She tries to remember how it felt to be free, the building burning behind her, blazing a path west in the Chevy. She needs that now.

"What the fuck...," LaBrenda says, so softly that Tasha almost doesn't hear her. She whispers something else, inaudible. She stares at the backpack. Then, frantic, she snatches the other pack, dragging it closer and ripping open the zipper.

"What's wrong?" Tasha says. LaBrenda's face is rigid. Tasha feels her heart pounding faster and faster. Maybe the bombs have already been triggered. Just like in the Apiary—Dr. Rio's ghost here to haunt them. "*What's wrong?*"

LaBrenda yanks something out of the bag—a block of what looks like six transparent tubes, with a metal base marked by six round bulbs, only one of which is lit.

"Look at this!" LaBrenda screams, shaking the mechanism at Tasha, who flinches.

"What the fuck, LaBrenda! Is that a bomb? Don't fucking wave a bomb at me!"

"This wouldn't blow up a goddamn doll house!" LaBrenda shouts. She's crying, the tears making the skin under her eyes shine. "Roger...*Roger* did this!"

"What? What happened?"

LaBrenda shoves the bomb toward Tasha, who shrinks away, but looks.

"Do you see this? All six cylinders are supposed to be pink! The reactant is pink. The lights indicate which cylinders are live. All the cylinders on this are dead but one! And *no* cylinders are live in the other pack! Oh my god. Roger did this."

She screams again, grabbing one of the empty backpacks and flinging it away from her. Her whole body shakes.

"We got the other hub locations," Tasha cries. "Can't we just leave with that?"

"Do you know how many Minkers are on their way here right now, Natasha?" LaBrenda screeches. Her voice makes Tasha's blood run cold. "Your mom is right! Neovison will know what's happening here—at least in part! This building is going to be swarmed in minutes! If we can't fry the hub…"

She doesn't finish. She squeezes her eyes shut.

"There's no other way?" Tasha shouts. "We can't just…I don't know…pull the plug?"

"No, Tasha, we cannot just pull the plug! We don't even know where the mainframe is: that's why we use a bomb! To blow it *all* up! With this little-ass bomb I'd have to put it directly on the mainframe, and we have no clue where that is!"

"I do," says Stella. She's sunk back into the wheelchair, her head shaking slowly. Tasha wonders if it will ever stop shaking. "It's on the roof."

LaBrenda gapes at her.

"What?"

"The roof," Tasha's mother repeats. "When we arrived in this place it was by helicopter. We were blindfolded. But that was the day they put it in. I heard them, coming up as we were coming down."

"Mama, where's Daddy?" Tasha says again. The *we* has entered her ear like a poison dart. Stella just stares.

LaBrenda is standing up, moving back toward the elevator, the single bomb in her hand.

"Get Z," she says. "And the shock gun. We're going."

"That was years ago," Tasha cries, still on the floor with Z. "My mom has been gone three years. How do we know it's still there?"

"We don't. But I'm not leaving 'til we look."

Z makes a moaning sound in her throat, twisting her neck against Tasha's knee. Stella is already rising from the wheelchair.

"Put her in the chair," she says, her head still shaking. "And give me the gun."

They ride upward in the elevator like that, Z slumped in the wheelchair, Stella leaning on the back of it, the shock gun tucked under her arm and the still-whining white club in her hand. LaBrenda and Tasha stand on either side, armed, each as antsy as the other. They look at each other over the top of Tasha's mother's head.

"The ski mask made your braids fuzzy," LaBrenda says.

"You can redo them."

LaBrenda attempts a smile.

The door opens not onto daylight as Tasha had expected, but into a short dark hallway, another door two feet ahead. Her mother shivers.

"It smells the same," she whispers.

Tasha inhales. The smell is sour, damp. More like a basement than a structure on a roof, and if it weren't for the daylight streaming under the door ahead she might think they'd gone down instead of up. She tries to picture her mother here, blindfolded and transported from a helicopter into what had been her prison for the last three years. Why?

"Ready?" says LaBrenda. She pauses at the door. It doesn't require a tooth. Instead, there's a bolt that must be lifted. LaBrenda's hand grips it hard, poised for what comes next.

"Yes."

The door flies open and they stand there, blinking in the sun, which has invaded the dark hallway and blinds them. The heat soaks into Tasha's skin—she hadn't realized how cold she was in the Box. No wonder her mother's skin had felt like stone. She looks at Stella, at the tears rolling down her cheeks.

"Mama, where's Dad?"

"Shit," says LaBrenda. "We've got keepers."

Tasha looks. Six Minkers stand around on the wide square roof, their postures slack, their expressions idle. Their arms hang limply by their sides; some of them have tilted their heads back to stare up at the sky. They look like Earthlings over whom a UFO has paused, caught in the tractor beam that will tow them into space.

"It must be up here," LaBrenda says. "They wouldn't have put them up here as keepers if there weren't something to protect."

Tasha hadn't considered this. Her eyes sweep the roof, which at first appears as vast and white as the rest of the Box. But her eye falls on something in the center, something on the ground: a round something that's flat and a slightly different shade of white. She points.

"There," she says. "That's gotta be it. There's nothing else."

LaBrenda studies the roof. The bomb in her hand looks like a toy. A Fisher-Price bomb.

"Let's go."

"Mom, stay here," Tasha says.

"Don't be ridiculous, Natasha. I have Dr. Lane's device. We need to make this quick."

Tasha wants to argue. But the way Stella says "Natasha" and fixes her with a look puts all argument to rest.

"We'll leave your friend," Stella says, looking down at Z in the wheelchair. "Right here."

LaBrenda sets the bomb gently on the ground, and as soon as she steps out onto the roof, the Minkers engage. Like the ones inside the Box, their rage is wilder and more furious than every other one Tasha has encountered since Chicago. They tear across the roof toward where LaBrenda and Tasha are standing and Tasha yelps involuntarily. She almost leaps back into the staircase, but LaBrenda, bounding forward, gives her courage. She grips her knife and prepares for the tall, skinny Minker that reaches her first.

She raises her knife, but the Minker halts, jolts, and topples. Tasha gasps, then sees his black eyes. She turns to find her mother, shock gun poised, already cranking it. Her head still shakes.

"Careful, baby," she says. "He was tall."

LaBrenda swings her metal fist like a club, smashing into the face of a Minker who gets too close. The scalpel's fine blade makes taking out the Chip difficult to do quickly, and Tasha runs to aid her, stabbing the flashing neck savagely before turning on the Minker scrambling at her back. She feels his teeth graze her shoulder through her shirt, the wrong angle to get a bite but enough to make her scream at the closeness. She slashes, cutting nothing but the front of his scrubs. LaBrenda clotheslines another with her arm as she thunders toward the circular structure.

"Oh shit, nice!" Tasha can't help but shout. She finally stabs the neck of the Minker at her back, piercing the Chip with a distinct *pop*. Behind her she hears the almost liquid rush of the shock gun, presumably taking out another Minker. She looks toward the entrance to make sure Z is still okay, and in her moment of distraction a Minker slams into her from the side.

She almost falls, but braces her legs and instead staggers several feet sideways, throwing her elbow wildly at the barking face to keep the teeth from finding her cheek. He's heavy and short, level with her face, and her feet slide on the relatively slick white roof.

"Fuckfuckfuck," she says through gritted teeth. The edge of the roof is getting closer. The roof had seemed so wide, but now it gets smaller and smaller as the Minker bulls her forward, his snarling replacing all other sounds in her ears. She can't swing the knife without slackening her arm and allowing him closer. She screams in frustration.

Her hip bumps the edge of the roof so hard it makes her gasp. She crouches, trying to keep as much of her body below the brink as possible. The Minker bears down on top of her, his hands clawing and grabbing, one of them ripping the neck of her shirt. She hears the tear of the fabric—too much like the tear of skin.

She squats lower. The knife's blade is actually digging into the Minker's stomach, blood pouring from his gut, but it doesn't slow him down. He roars toward the back of her neck; the lower she crouches the more frantically he crawls on top of her. His incisors graze her vertebrae.

She stands up, quickly, powerfully, pushing hard from her heels and shoving with the knife and her empty hand with a shout that tears up through her throat like fire. The Minker is thrown bodily from her shoulders, landing fully on the short wall that surrounds the perimeter of the roof. He squalls, thrashing on his back to get his feet under him and go after Tasha again. Frantic, she shoves him, and he sails off into empty space, plummeting downward to the jagged red and gray rocks of the mountain.

She turns to meet another Minker freight-training toward her. Out of breath, she braces herself and holds the knife weakly, trying to be ready. But her mother cranks the shock gun and fires. Tasha thinks she must have missed—the Minker seems to keep running for another pace until it jerks mid-step, and Tasha sees the eyes go black, the mouth stiffen into its eternal snarl, before the body crashes to the ground.

"Thanks, Mama," Tasha says, gasping for breath. Stella nods weakly.

LaBrenda rips the Chip out of the last Minker with her metal hand, the sparks flying as freely as the blood.

"Christ," Tasha says, still panting.

"Is that it?" LaBrenda says, standing from where she has just put down the Minker she'd smashed in the face. She's panting, her chest heaving.

"I thought it would be...harder," Tasha says. She rubs the back of her neck where the Minker's teeth had hovered.

"That shock gun was a hell of a find," LaBrenda says as she jogs to the circular spot on the roof. She crouches there, her face low to the ground, before digging Dr. Lane's tooth out of her pocket. She carefully plugs it into the waiting groove, and Tasha goes to where LaBrenda had set down the bomb. She doesn't want to touch it, but she lifts it carefully, as if touching something slimy. She carries it to where LaBrenda crouches just as the circular space on the roof rises, rotating upward to knee level.

"There she is," LaBrenda says under her breath, her eyes shining. Before them is a cylinder, hollow, with a glowing red cube resting in its center on four metal prongs.

"Now what?" Tasha says softly, almost a whisper, as if speaking too loudly might awaken the cube.

LaBrenda says nothing. Without taking her eyes off the red cube, she reaches over and takes the bomb from Tasha's hand. She looks down, opens a panel along the back of the device, and does something Tasha can't see that makes a clicking sound. She closes the panel and carefully, gently, places the bomb inside the cylinder alongside the red cube. Then she removes the tooth from the top of the cylinder, and it lowers slowly back down into the roof.

"Now," LaBrenda says, standing quickly, "we run."

The elevator delivers them to is the same hallway they'd first entered from the lobby; just farther down the hall. When the door slides open, the long bloody expanse of the corridor stretches out in front of them like the vein of a gutted beast. After being in the open air of the roof, the stench strikes Tasha like a rotting fist. She gags, but tightens her grip on the handles of the wheelchair and pushes Z out of the elevator. LaBrenda supports Stella, and they limp quickly down the hall. Tasha's sneakers stick in the blood, slipping every few steps. The wheelchair makes a strange tacky sound with each turn of its wheels. Tasha walks a little faster.

"You said the bomb wouldn't blow up a dollhouse," Tasha says as they near their original elevator. "Why do we need to run?"

"Because if it doesn't work," LaBrenda pants. "Then we're seriously fucked."

Tasha doesn't reply—just grits her teeth and quickens her step even more. The silence of the Box crushes inward, as if there's something in the air already that her ears just can't hear. The white club from the cerebellum is on Z's unconscious lap, but its whine is muffled against her leg. Ahead the lobby door is open as they'd left it, and Tasha walks faster and faster, the open doorway beckoning. She suddenly wants to lay eyes on Ishmael very much. Malakai. Xena. She wants to see them, to prove to herself that they aren't a mere mirage out over the Arizona sands.

The smell of lavender hits her nostrils as soon as she reaches the lobby, so heady and vaporous she imagines she sees clouds of it. The lobby is as white and silent as it had been when they'd entered the Box, so when the sharp *ding* rings through the air, Tasha jumps, not sure what caused it. She reaches for her knife at her hip, looking left and right to find the source.

It's behind them: the elevator. She whirls, her back against the wheelchair, Z's head brushing against her hip. LaBrenda stumbles forward, Stella grimacing and trying to take faster steps. She still grasps the shock gun, but weakly. Tasha tightens her grip on her knife, ready for the army that she knows must be queuing to stream from the elevator door. But for a moment the door remains open without a sign of anyone inside—a ghostly invitation to return to the bowels of the Box. Then, over the soft whine of the white club in Z's lap, Tasha hears the shuffle of feet, the low familiar growl bubbling in a mindless throat. The figure sways out from the mouth of the elevator, the pale blue hospital gown and pants wrinkled and baggy on his narrow frame.

"Johnathan," Stella whispers.

Johnathan. Tasha hears the name as it has been spoken so many times in the garden of her memory: over breakfast; whispered low during a film; called from a window over the din of dogs. Johnathan, her father. "John and Stella," the neighbors called them. Johnathan and Stella Lockett. Johnathan. Daddy.

"Dad," Tasha says softly. He can't hear her. His face is not his face: the eyes are not his eyes. His were never this cold, this full of rage. Even as he starts to quicken his pace, the mouth she used to know, the mouth that used to call her "bunny" twisting into a snarl, she stares into his eyes. If somewhere in his brain he's still there—helpless to stop the driver of the missile that his body has become—she wants him to see her face.

Her mother steps forward in the lobby, the shock gun rising, her slender arms flexing, almost out of strength.

"Mama, no!" Tasha says. She doesn't know if she screams it or whispers it. Everything that had been absurd about Z trying to save her brother comes crawling together to form the skeleton of a thing that makes sense.

Johnathon has not yet started to run. His eyes are two lenses that sweep the hallway, searching for his target. Stella turns to Tasha bearing a face streaked with ghosts.

"Tasha..."

She's going to shoot him. Tasha can hear the intent burdening her voice.

"Mama, that's *Daddy!*" In case she doesn't understand. In case she's not seeing the face Tasha is seeing.

"Baby, that hasn't been Daddy for a long, long time." She pauses, a knife in her heart. "I've watched them turn him into… something else."

Tasha's father moves down the hallay toward the lobby, his arms starting to lift, his teeth bared. LaBrenda grips Tasha's bicep, but Tasha doesn't feel it. She wishes it would hurt. She wishes it would burn. Instead she watches the man who used to be her father raging down the hall. All her grief comes climbing from the bones where she'd buried it. It rises up in a cloud of gray dust and sifts into her lungs.

"I love you, John," her mother says, and fires.

The alarm blares before her father's body hits the floor. Tasha doesn't have time to cry. Stella drops the shock gun, her hands shaking, but LaBrenda snatches it up again and drags Stella toward the door.

"Tasha, come on!" she screams. "Bring Z! We need to go!"

Her father's face is hidden by his arm. She feels she would know him by that arm alone, even thin from confinement, even in that blue gown. She tears her eyes away, the numbness seeping from her core to her fingers. She wraps those bloodless fingers around the handles of the wheelchair and shoves Z toward the light, the round open door that LaBrenda stands inside like a beckoning shadow.

Outside the Minkers are like roaches. They swarm up the mountain in droves, the sound of their barking a cacophony of venomous cicadas ringing between the rocks.

"Oh dear fucking sweet Jesus Christ in heaven," LaBrenda cries, with a few more curse words tacked on.

"The bomb didn't work," Tasha whispers.

She blinks in the sun, has to squint to see at all. She feels she's been in the Box for an eternity, on another planet, freezing and far from the sun in a strange, white solar system. But it must be the same world, she thinks: the Minkers are here. Minkers are here and the bomb hadn't worked.

"It may not have gone off yet," LaBrenda cries.

"We…we can't make it," Stella gasps. She's staggering next to LaBrenda, who grips her around the shoulders. "Nowhere to go."

Tasha sees Ishmael. He's by the hood of the car, swinging his axe like a madman at two Minkers who have shown up, his other arm still pinioned in a sling. She doesn't see Malakai or the dog, and what warm blood she has left runs cold.

"Oh my god!" she yells, shoving the wheelchair on. "Malakai!"

LaBrenda sweeps Tasha's mother up off the ground, Stella's bird bones curling up like a collection of slim brown branches.

"Miss Stella," LaBrenda shouts, "we gotta go."

She takes off in a full sprint, Minkers appearing at the edge of the Box, climbing from the jagged rocks below. As Tasha shoves the wheelchair over the uneven road at full speed, she thinks she recognizes the Minker she'd pushed off the roof, his legs repaired, his body working. Figures.

The glass tunnel is just ahead. Tasha can see Monica Potter's SUV straight through it, Ishmael behind the car hacking at the neck of a Minker with his axe. He's already turned the car around, she sees, her heart leaping: the nose points down the mountain.

"We're almost there!" she screams, but Z is slipping in the wheelchair, the chair going too fast. Every muscle screaming her onward, Tasha runs around to the front of the chair and slaps Z once in the face.

Z's eyes flutter open, already with an expression of shock.

"Hold on!" Tasha orders, and flees behind the chair again. She shoves forward, praying Z will do as she says. They cannot stop again. She can't see Z's face—just LaBrenda's back, carrying Tasha's mother like a baby—but she sees Z's fingers curl around the arms of the wheelchair. Tasha grits her teeth, putting on an extra burst of speed.

"We gotta go through the tunnel!" LaBrenda shouts.

She's right. Minkers are crawling up the side of the mountain, nearing the narrow strip with its brittle yellow flowers that Tasha had edged along on their way into the Box. Through the tunnel is the only option. She again pictures a sparrow flapping through that cylinder before being disintegrated into black ash. No big loss, she thinks. She already feels a bit like ash as it is.

LaBrenda and Stella enter first, Tasha close behind with the chair. Immediately a white light glows from nowhere and everywhere, a humming sound accompanying it that drowns out even the symphony of barking that resonates beyond.

"Keep going!" LaBrenda screams, not looking over her shoulder. Tasha's mother's body jolts with every step. Tasha looks nowhere but at Stella's feet where they dangle over LaBrenda's elbow. They seem to run away from Tasha—she strives to keep up. The tunnel's transparent walls will become lasers any moment—fire, a supersonic electric shock that will destroy them atom by atom. The white light takes on a greenish tint and Tasha clenches her teeth, forcing the wheelchair onward.

"Scanning Dr. Lane," a voice says, robotic and British as always. "Scanning Dr. Lane."

The tooth, Tasha thinks. She can't say it out loud. She has no breath for words. LaBrenda sprints onward. Tasha follows her mother's feet. Maybe the tooth will save them from spontaneous combustion. Ahead, just a hundred meters away, she can see Ishmael. He kicks a Minker back over the edge of the mountain, his shoe nearly flying off with it.

The ceiling becomes a face. Not just the ceiling, but the entire inner surface of the arch. The former transparence becomes opaque, colors pooling from nowhere. Where Tasha had seen clouds through the material she now sees eyes. Two blue eyes, enormous in scale, a nose. The mouth forms last, or maybe Tasha doesn't notice it until it moves to speak.

"Your whole family is dead."

The eyes see them. Tasha stumbles, almost stops running. Ahead is the mouth, and it's almost as if she runs straight toward it, giving herself up to be chewed.

"Run!" LaBrenda screams, and Tasha does run, but she can't tear her gaze away from the two blue eyes. They see her seeing them, and burn into her with fury.

"We will find you," the massive mouth says. "We will find you wherever you go. I know your face."

And the eyes are gone. The arch of the tunnel returns to transparency, but the bright white light has turned red; something is whirring, some invisible fire is turning the air hotter and hotter.

LaBrenda heaves herself out of the tunnel with Stella, and Tasha gives the wheelchair a final shove, Z spilling out of it to the ground, Tasha stumbling and nearly joining her, as behind them the archway fills with hissing red light. Steam erupts from the opening.

"What the fuck was that?" Tasha shouts. "What the fuck..."

"Get in the fucking car!" LaBrenda screams. Ishmael is yelling the same thing. Tasha can't breathe. She stumbles again, her hands scratching against the dirt of the road, the bandage on her pinky pulled off, gone somewhere in the dirt. Z struggles to gain her footing, and Tasha grabs her shoulder, yanking.

"Don't you fucking touch me!" Z shrieks, shoving her off and staggering to the car, where LaBrenda is ramming Stella into the open back door. Ishmael starts to run toward Tasha, his face jagged with terror and bloody in the corner of his mouth.

"Come on!" he yells.

"Malakai!" she screams.

"In the car!"

She sprints toward the car as a new chorus of barking rises behind her. Daring to look back, she sees a dozen Minkers emerging from the red mist of the tunnel. They don't have skin; it's been burned off in the tunnel. They loom toward her, a battalion of burned and bloody soldiers, black tentacles all over their bodies trying to restore their flesh where the red mist had melted it. They're flanked by the army advancing up the mountainside. There are so many that their faces blur together. They are a mass of flesh and fang. She turns back, her muscles both on fire and filled with ice. The Minkers coming up the hill are slower, but the bloody-bodied monsters surging from the mouth of the tunnel are from the Box: impossibly fast, loud and furious.

The horde of Minkers reach the car before Tasha can blink, their madness blocking out the pain and fixing their eyes on the only thing that matters: Tasha. LaBrenda is already in the car with the door closed, Malakai enclosed inside like a grain of sand inside a clamshell.

"Keep him safe!" Tasha screams as the Minkers swarm upon her. She swings her knife, hopeless. Ishmael is rushing back around the front of the car, but the Minkers closing in from the edge of the mountain swarm to intercept him. What could be hundreds flock behind them, an angry cloud of bees that exist only to sting.

Tasha feels the first bite on her thigh: one of the throng has fallen under the crowd but is still rabid to claim her blood. The dull pain through the fabric of her shorts lances up through her body to her heart. It's over.

And then somewhere beyond the glass tunnel comes a distant boom, which in another world might have been a car backfiring innocently on the street. Over the heads of the Minkers scrabbling for her throat, a plume of smoke rises from the roof of the Box.

"The bomb," Tasha whispers as teeth flash in her eyes. She can't protect her throat—too many mouths are seeking it. But the mouths are falling away, the electric sting of sparks in her ears, the choked sound of barking dying on countless bloody tongues.

Tasha looks down at her feet, surrounded now by corpses. The place on her thigh where the Minker had found its target is still covered by the fabric of her shorts. Her leg throbs, but neither skin nor material is broken. The world is quiet—she even hears a bird, trilling somewhere in a tree, oblivious to the hundreds of dead that spread across the road, piling down the mountainside. Over the roof of the Box, the plume of smokes rises gray and soundless.

Tasha collapses, her knees spent. Her shoulders slide down the side of Monica Potter's SUV, hot through her t-shirt under the bright Phoenix sun. She can't cry. She merely gapes, drained. The tunnel has returned to its blameless transparency, the red venomous mist faded away.

Behind her the back door of the SUV clicks open. LaBrenda climbs out—her black sneakers stand motionless in the dust. They're all Tasha can see. She stares hard at the shoes. A fleck of blood on the toe. It isn't her father's blood, of course. But maybe it's Z's brother's. In that small drop of red swims endless loss. Tasha squeezes her eyes shut as LaBrenda crouches beside her.

"It worked," she says.

"Yeah," says Tasha, eyes still closed.

A long pause.

"Do you need help getting up?"

"No."

She sits there a moment longer. The side of the car is too hot, but she doesn't pull away. The burn grounds her, wakes her flesh. When she stands, she does so clumsily. She sheaths her knife at her hip, and her hand takes a moment to uncurl, so stiff has it become in clutching the blade's hilt. She stares at the hand. It reminds her of Rio, his tight fist that could never quite unbend itself. She straightens her fingers slowly.

LaBrenda drives. Z curls in the passenger seat. As they drive slowly down the mountain road, Tasha turns to look at Ishmael, who reaches out to touch her face.

"You okay?" he says. Or maybe it was a statement. *You're okay.* She can't be sure. She clutches his fingers a moment, turning her eyes to Malakai, who smiles weakly. Brave boy. Bravest boy.

The car winds slowly down the road. There's no reason to rush. Behind them the Box is a bright white catacomb. The SUV steers between bodies, around the stopped trucks, through the decimated gate, its sightless cameras. Phoenix lurks silently ahead.

Tasha turns in her seat to look at her mother. She wants to stare and stare. But her mother sees only the poodle, her head shaking and shaking, her arm still bloody from the Minker's bite. She pets the dog over and over in a pattern as rhythmic as her shaking head: up the snout, over the head, and around the left ear. Tasha watches her, drinks her in, watering the garden of her heart with the sight of her. When Stella finally looks up, her eyes are filled with tears.

"Your father would have loved this dog."

CHAPTER 31

Tasha hadn't expected signs for Junot, but there are: hand-drawn signs on the backs of torn-down e-boards, with the same red paint she'd seen in the North Platte Mall's graffiti. They could have chosen a different color, she thinks. The red paint doesn't give an impression of welcome and safety. Instead she feels as if she's been driving the five and a half hours from Phoenix toward a haunted house or a colony of serial murderers.

After leaving the Box, they'd driven for hours in silence. Ishmael had moved about the car as much as possible with the medical case, bandaging Tasha's mother's wrist and Z's arm. He re-wraps Tasha's pinky, imitating the technique of Esther Blackhorse, and gives them all ibuprofen. He gives one to LaBrenda too, though she has no real wounds. Her head, she said, was throbbing. Everyone's head was probably throbbing, Tasha thought.

Malakai sits in the far backseat with his brother, his legs curled up, staring out the window. Tasha's mother sleeps. Z sleeps. Tasha tried closing her eyes, but sleep wouldn't come. She still feels as if she must be asleep already: the eerie white Box nestled in the mountain face, the eyes in the tunnel. Her mother. Her father. The grief feels too thick to travel through her veins to her heart. It feels clogged somewhere in her chest—a throbbing gray tumor that can't pass through.

"You thought your parents were dead," LaBrenda says softly, her eyes lifting to look at Stella in the rearview.

Tasha is already twisted around in her seat watching her mother sleep.

"Now my dad actually is," she answers without taking her eyes off Stella.

LaBrenda pauses, swallowing.

"These people have a way of taking everything from you. They'll kill what you love and then kill it again."

Tasha looks at her then.

"What happened to your mom?" Tasha says. "She picked you up from prison with your new arm. And then what?"

"She died in a fire," LaBrenda says flatly. Tasha waits for her to say more, but she never does. The silence stretches and thickens until it's a wall between this moment and the last, barring the topic from conversation. Ahead, another sign: *Junot 10 miles.*

"Ten miles," Tasha says. "I thought Old Los Angeles was farther in from the California border?"

"It was. Junot makes up the entire southern tip of the state now. San Diego. Imperial. All those cities."

"What's north?"

"I don't really know, honestly."

Tasha turns back to stare at her mother. Xena sees her and rises, stretching. The dog moves to the front of the car and rests her chin on Tasha's elbow. It's always amazed Tasha how dogs know how to smile. Xena smiles up at her, her tail wagging slowly.

"She was the one who told us the Minkers were coming," Malakai says.

Tasha didn't know he was awake, and looks up to find his eyes on the dog.

"Ishmael had already turned the car around, but we didn't want to waste the battery. We were standing outside, looking at the building and Xena kept barking and barking and running to the side of the road."

"A real Lassie," Tasha says, petting the dog's long muzzle.

"What's that?"

"Ah. Nothing. She's just a good dog."

Malakai pauses, gazing fondly at the poodle. Tasha watches him, wondering how many pieces his heart is in. He's too young to have seen all this. He looks up, through the dashboard, and squints.

"Is that California?"

Tasha turns to look. Ahead she can see a tall fence, chain link, with what looks like barbed wire along the top in jagged, spiraling curls. There are no signs now. Only the long metal fence, and tall poles far apart, every mile or so, it seems.

"I think so," she says. The fence worries her. She doesn't see a gate yet—only miles and miles of chain link.

The car is slowing. She looks at LaBrenda, who peers at the dashboard.

"Are you kidding me," she mutters. She brings the car to a stop and turns it off.

"What are you doing?" Tasha says. "We're still like a mile away."

"The battery is dead. I need to put in one of the solar cells Michelangelo gave us."

"Jesus," says Tasha. She'd forgotten about the necessity of a solar cell. Not being in the driver seat has removed the existence of such things from her mind. They've just been driving—the car eating the ground and the western horizon seeming a little closer with every mile, even if it's not.

LaBrenda is already under the hood of the car, replacing the solar cell. Tasha can hear the clunking of whatever it is that needs to be done, her view of the metal fence obscured by the hood. She looks back at her mother, still sleeping deeply. Z is awake but looks pointedly out the window. Tasha gazes around them, at the empty road and the dust that surrounds it. On their way from Phoenix they had passed miles of strip malls, a faded amusement park. Power stations, fast food. This road is lonely—only the carcasses of cars and Pumapods dot the landscape. And military vehicles, Tasha notes—some of them burned out. All else is bare, as if developers had seen what California would become and uprooted their businesses, planting them elsewhere. The dust billows across the road, almost obscuring it.

"Z," Tasha says, not looking at her friend but offering her name like a charm. When there is no response, she tries again. "Azalea."

"Don't say my name," Z says. She does not turn her head or body to say it. Tasha's voice is a spirit that Z wards off with neglect. "Don't."

"I had to, Z."

"Stop. Do not talk."

"My dad…"

"*Do not talk.*"

"What's that?" Malakai says. He's turned around in his seat, looking out the back window. Tasha peers in the rearview.

At first all she sees is more dust and sand, the wind blowing it up in swirls. But the swirling brown clouds bear something toward them, some distance back. Tasha squints. It's a truck. A white semi—still two miles away but eating up the distance fast.

She gets out of the car and goes to the front of the SUV. LaBrenda bends over the power modules of the car, mechanical parts in her hands that Tasha can't identify.

"Come here," Tasha says, pulling her arm. LaBrenda, puzzled, comes to the side of the car and looks where Tasha is pointing.

LaBrenda drops the part she was holding.

"Oh shit," she says.

"What is it?" Tasha demands. The panic had begun to rise as soon as she laid eyes on the truck, but now it rears up like a fanged beast, tearing at her heart.

"It's gotta be Neovison," LaBrenda says. She snatches up the part she dropped and tears back to the front of the car. "I'm almost done, I'm almost done."

"We can't run. It's too far," Tasha says, her voice rising and shaking. "My mom can't run a mile."

"None of us can," LaBrenda snaps. "Not from a truck."

Tasha sticks her head back in the car.

"Is it them?" Malakai says quickly. "The Box people?"

"I think so," Tasha says, trying to keep her voice even.

"Fuck," Z whispers. She stares out the back window at the rapidly approaching truck. The single word is both tired and terrified. She's tired of running.

"In!" LaBrenda shouts, leaping back into her seat. Tasha scrambles to follow suit, slamming the door and not bothering with her seatbelt. LaBrenda presses the key card and stomps on the accelerator; with a whine the SUV shoots forward, barreling through the dust toward the chain link fence, the wind blowing the sand in dizzying red-brown patterns that makes the road hard to follow. Tasha hears the thrumming of the tires change their rhythm as they go from road to sand to road again. Behind them the white semi truck grows larger in the rearview.

"They're going to hit us," Z says calmly.

The truck hits them, its flat white face ramming into the back of Monica Potter's SUV. Tasha lurches forward in her seat, smacking her chin on the dashboard. She hears Malakai scream and whirls around in her seat, ignoring the blood in her mouth from her bitten tongue.

526 OLIVIA A. COLE

"Are you okay?" she shouts.

"Drive faster, LaBrenda, Jesus Christ!" Ishmael roars.

"I am! Fuck!"

The SUV is still accelerating, LaBrenda's hands gripping the wheel and her teeth bared in a grimace. The white truck rams them again and LaBrenda yells as the SUV is knocked sideways, spinning, tires sliding on the sand. The car rocks, tilts—Tasha holds her breath—and then topples onto its side, Tasha crashing against the window. LaBrenda is suspended above her by her seatbelt, cursing.

"Fuck!" Tasha screams. Behind her, the dog yelps. It may not have been the dog. It could have been anyone. The white truck rolls past them and screeches to a halt, its half-trailer fishtailing slightly at the sudden stop.

LaBrenda fumbles in the console and yanks out the purple shock gun, reaching up for the door.

"Are you crazy?" Tasha shouts, reaching for her arm. "Don't open the door!"

"They're getting us either way," she screams back, struggling against Tasha's grip. "Maybe…maybe I can hold them up while you guys go!"

"Don't be stupid, LaBrenda!"

Z screams a word Tasha can't decipher, pointing ahead out past the dashboard, the only window they can see through, her words incoherent.

The back of the half-trailer moves mechanically upward, slowly and with a grinding sound Tasha can hear from inside the car. She sees their feet. Then their knees. Then their chests. Then their faces, dozens of Minkers swaying inside the trailer like a cargo of rabid cattle. They pause there for a moment, seemingly unactivated. Then some soundless signal cues them and they're pouring from the back of the truck, some falling, stumbling over each other, swarming the short distance to the car.

"Mom, don't let go of the white thing! Stay close to Malakai!" Tasha screams. LaBrenda is climbing upward out of the car and Tasha struggles to join her, even as the fear erupts from her skin and coats her body in sweat. She wonders if there's a maximum amount of adrenaline that a body can produce— if eventually the gland that makes it dries out like a sponge squeezed too tightly. She feels spent. She feels dry. Empty. She pulls herself up out of LaBrenda's door, her biceps trembling, struggling against the flopping door.

She hears Malakai screaming her name. She closes her ears to it so that all she hears is the barking of the many mouths stampeding toward her. She balances on LaBrenda's seat, LaBrenda standing on top of the flipped car, and shoots her eyes at the fence. It's so near, and the idea of having come so far only to die here in the dust swoops down from the sky and alights on her shoulders like a murder of crows.

The fence has opened. At first glance she thinks she imagined it—a blurring of dust and metal and wire. But the gap is real, a gate she couldn't see before. And through it drive three vans.

"LaBrenda!" Tasha screams, yanking on the leg of her shorts. "Look!"

The Minkers don't stop at the sound of the vans. They tear toward the overturned SUV, their barking reaching a crescendo. Will they climb the car, the way they had scaled the SkyDrive? Tasha considers yanking LaBrenda down into the SUV, closing the door after her like the lid of a submarine.

One of the vans plows through the crowd of Minkers, spitting one of them on the spiked grill affixed to the vehicle's nose.

"Oh my god," LaBrenda cries. Tasha stares with her mouth open, unwilling to believe just yet that these vans might be on their side. They could be more people like the shooters in Wal-Mart: a roving pack of psychos. But they came from beyond the gate…

The second and third vans roll up, smashing through Minkers and squealing to a stop. Two people jump out of each, men and women in various kinds of red clothing: one with a bandana, another wearing a shirt. One woman wears a dress. All of them carry what appear to be long white canes, which they hold out in front of them like swords. The canes look familiar.

"That's what Roger had on the video," LaBrenda says, gripping Tasha's wrist. In her other hand, the shock gun is poised to shoot, even as the Minkers are distracted by the red-clad group.

The newcomers seem to herd the Minkers with the canes, and above the din of the barking Tasha thinks she can hear the low whining ring emitted by Dr. Lane's club. But it doesn't come from the car below. The woman in the red dress carries something—larger than the club—that makes the same sound, and she walks in a circle around the crowds of Minkers, unhurried. The Minkers' barking settles to a low chorus of snarls.

"The truck's a drone," Tasha hears one of the red-wearers shout. She hadn't seen him leave the group, but she sees him returning now, a whining club in his hands as well. "No driver."

"Get us out of here," Ishmael says from below. LaBrenda looks at Tasha and nods.

They pull themselves out one by one, Z lifting the dog up to them first. Xena scrabbles on the side of the car to liberate herself. She jumps down before Tasha can help her, yelping a little and stumbling before turning back to stare. Tasha tries to help Z climb out of the car, but Z yanks her hands from Tasha's grasp.

"Z...," Tasha says, extending a hand.

Z turns on her with eyes so sharp Tasha withdraws her hand as if she's been bitten.

"No," Z says, the words blunt and hard. "Not now."

Tasha's mother comes out last, her head shaking mechanically, just as two of the red-wearers approach the car. Behind them, the rest of their group puts the Minkers down one by one. Tasha's not sure how they do it—they use something small and handheld from their pockets, pressing it against the neck like a barcode scanner, which sends each Minker crumpling into the dust. The woman in the red dress approaches LaBrenda, who has walked out to meet them.

"What are you doing here?" the woman says, eyeing her, eyeing them all.

"We're part of Rio's caravan," LaBrenda says.

The woman raises her eyebrow, but looks beyond the car, back east.

"I don't see no caravan," she says.

"We got separated."

Ishmael is quickly at LaBrenda's side.

"Has another caravan arrived? Is there a woman with them? Monice? With a guy named Marcus? She's my mother. Has she arrived?"

The woman holds up her hand to stop him.

"Who are you? Why was a Neovison drone so hot on y'all's asses?"

"Long story," LaBrenda says, shooting Ishmael a look that tells him to wait. He shoots her a look back that curses her out. "I'm here to see Rooster. I have intel from Chicago…and from Phoenix."

The guy that had walked over with the woman in the dress squints at her, then leans in to whisper in his comrade's ear. Tasha hangs back, one arm around her mother and the other around Malakai. Z stands apart, clutching her box cutter and looking defiant.

"What do you know about Chicago?" the guy says when he's done whispering.

"That information is for Rooster," LaBrenda says quickly.

"You still ain't told us who you are," the woman says.

"My name is LaBrenda Tinsley."

"That don't tell me who you are."

"User name Daisy Shakur," LaBrenda says impatiently.

The woman seems to recognize that and darts her eyes at the guy. He doesn't seem convinced.

"We've had no communication with remote comrades for over a month," he says, squinting. "How did you know to come here?"

"I've had my mission for almost a year," LaBrenda says, raising her voice. "And I finally have what Rooster wanted. Now are you going to take us to him or not?"

Neither of the people in red says anything.

Tasha grits her teeth. Junot is a short jog away. She has crossed hundreds of miles, passed through tornadoes and Wal-Marts to get here. Her finger throbs. Her mother's shoulders shake. Her father's dead. She doesn't have patience for this shit.

"Look," Tasha snaps. "I'm Tasha. Tasha Lockett. I'm one of the people who blew up the Apiary in Chicago. I was there with Rio when he pulled this shit. Now, we've come a long way. And there may be more trucks like that one coming this way. I would like to get my ass behind that fence. Can we talk about this somewhere else? *Anywhere* else?"

The woman raises both eyebrows and exchanges a long look with the man by her side. She uncrosses her arms.

"Put 'em in the van."

They're disarmed and pushed none too gently into the back of one of the vans. One of them gives Malakai a push when the boy pauses at the door, and Ishmael leaps at him.

"Don't you touch my brother," he snarls. "I don't need an axe to end your fucking life if you touch my brother again."

"Chill, man," the red-shirted guy says. He's less concerned about Ishmael than he is about Xena, who sniffs his pant leg. "Call your dog, dude. Hey, call your dog."

Malakai, in the van and sitting very close to Tasha, calls softly for Xena, his voice trembling slightly. Tasha puts her arm around him, hugging him. Ishmael gets in and hugs Malakai from the other side.

"Mama, are you okay?" Tasha says. Stella hasn't said much since the car flipped. She doesn't have any injuries, but Tasha can't help but worry. Her body seems so frail—not the woman she remembers. She rubs her free hand over her mother's knee.

"I know that ring," Stella says in a voice as soft as the fuzz on a peach. She touches Tasha's finger gently with two of her own, stroking the silver metal.

"Yes, mama."

Outside, the sand and dust blow in rhythmic circles as two of the red-clad group stand peering in at the cluster of them. Tasha stares back until someone beyond the doors calls *Ready* and the doors are closed, immersing the back of the van in darkness, the glare of sun and the dull movement of sand only a harsh impression on the back of their eyelids. As the van begins to move, presumably forward through the gates into Junot, Tasha closes her eyes. Finally. She's here. Beyond the fence may be nothing but bones—as bloody and dismal as the rest of the States, as the rest of what Tasha thinks the world must now be. But she's here. And she's alive.

CHAPTER 32

The van's coming to a halt nudges Tasha into wakefulness, gradually remembering where she is. The heat and the motion had rocked her to sleep. And the silence. Z is a stone, and even LaBrenda seems prisoner to her own thoughts. Malakai's head is in Tasha's lap, her mother's head on her shoulder. Tasha feels them stir at the sound of voices outside the van, the slamming of the doors, and somewhere, remarkably, the tolling of a bell.

The doors are yanked open, bathing the back of the van in soft orange light. It's nearing dusk. They must have driven for a few hours; at the realization, Tasha's body suddenly confirms this with stiffness. Her back and legs ache. Her mouth is dry.

"Hope y'all got some of the AC," the woman in the red dress says. "Come on out. You'll need water."

"You didn't give them water?" says another voice. "Rooster will be pissed."

"Shut up. I was rushing."

One by one they climb out of the van, Tasha and LaBrenda helping Stella carefully down to the ground. Not until her mother is steady on her feet does Tasha look around.

"Wow," Malakai says.

They stand in the center of what appears to be a village,

like something colored by the joyful hands of toddlers with unlimited access to crayons. The houses are mostly small; all are painted bright shades that seem brighter still beside the lush green of the trees and bushes that grow around the houses and the square in which they stand. The plants must be cultivated, Tasha thinks—their placement is perfect, their shapes lovely. But the arrangement lacks the organization of a suburb. The trees seem to grow where they want to grow, but grow in exactly the right places.

The woman in the red dress passes Tasha a backpack, a bag Tasha doesn't immediately recognize as her own. But it is: the canvas one she'd scavenged from Macy's.

"Oh," she says, surprised. "You got my bag."

"We got all your bags," the woman says. "Come on. Rooster wants to see y'all."

Tasha finds LaBrenda's eyes. LaBrenda just shrugs. The greenery bedazzles them all. Their journey from Chicago hadn't been all desert, but she feels as if she's been surrounded by grit and sand for a long, long time.

They follow the woman in the dress down a narrow road, her companion following along behind them. Their other cronies seem to have disappeared, and neither of them are armed.

"I wish I had my knife," Tasha murmurs to LaBrenda. The two of them walk on either side of Tasha's mother, supporting her by the arms. "This cute-ass little town makes me nervous."

"Yeah," LaBrenda agrees. "But I haven't seen a single dead body. I don't even smell anything dead. Just flowers. And…I don't know. Air."

Surprised, Tasha inhales through her nose. She hadn't even noticed. Her brain had merely accepted the clean-smelling air as a gift and not considered where it came from. LaBrenda's right. No dead bodies. No Minkers. The road they walk along is dirt, not pavement marred here and there with blood and scorch. Tasha's mother's weight sags.

"Are we almost there?" Tasha calls. "My mother needs to sit down."

"Yes," the man from the back says. "The orange one."

The orange house is on the left, set back slightly from the road. Like the others it's small, with red shutters. *Shutters*, Tasha thinks. Cute little wooden shutters. Where the fuck are they? *This* is Junot?

The woman in the dress knocks once on the door and then opens it, standing aside for the group to file in. Tasha hesitates. This is where Rooster is? She'd expected a bunker. A military base with battalions of rebels at his beck and call—commandeered military equipment dotting a dreary landscape decorated with shell casings and bones. The chain link fence with its garlands of barbed wire had seemed appropriate. Not this.

Inside, the small house is cool and somewhat dim, splashes of gold light from the approaching sunset filtering in through shutter slats. Spare furniture sits in a circular layout: a faded green couch of what looks like worn brushed velvet. A papasan chair. A wooden table decorated with a checkered pattern.

"Rooster?" the woman in the dress calls.

Tasha hears the clink of dishes, around a corner in what feels like it should be a kitchen.

"Out back," a man says, a deep voice that sets her heart racing. She's managed to be calm until this moment. But "out back" in response to "Rooster?" means that Rooster is real. Rooster is out back. Rooster: the one Rio worked for. Who blew up the Mall of America. Who has people like LaBrenda all over the States going on suicide missions, bombs in their trunks like groceries.

"My mother needs to sit down," Tasha says. It's true, but she doesn't want her "out back" with the leader of a terrorist organization.

The woman in the red dress hesitates, then goes to the edge of the room that might be a kitchen.

"I'm going to leave someone here with you, okay? She's hurt."

"Sure," the man's voice says. "Sit her on down."

"I'm not leaving her here by herself," Tasha says sharply as the woman leads Stella to the papasan chair. She hadn't thought this through. Stella sits down gratefully, her head shaking, staring out into space.

"You," the woman says, nodding at Ishmael. "You can stay with her."

Ishmael shoots a look at Tasha. Tasha doesn't want to walk away from him or Stella. But the idea of them together is easier to swallow. She nods, and Ishmael steers Malakai carefully over to where Tasha's mother sits. The woman in red gestures for Tasha to follow.

She leads them through a small dining room with three chairs around a square table, past a tall shelf lined with books, and out the back door, where the smell of earth and air is even stronger than on the street.

"Oh, man," LaBrenda breathes.

The garden is only half the size of the rooftop at the Pentagon, but everything seems to have reached ripeness at once. Tasha takes in the vibrant red of tomatoes, a spectrum of bell peppers, the rich cool shades of eggplant. And everywhere green plants, some sprouting skyward and some creeping across the deep brown soil. Lime trees dot the back wall of the garden, a waist-high red brick barrier that houses homemade bird feeders and flowerpots. Tasha can't help but sigh. Its beauty slows her heartbeat. The red of the peppers is redder and more perfect than blood. The tomatoes help her forget, if only for a moment.

And among all the lush loveliness stands a person, back bent down, plucking at some adventurous weeds that have dared to show their faces by the summer squash. The hands move deftly over the weeds before plucking a cherry tomato from the nearby vine, pausing to examine it.

"Rooster," the woman calls. "They're here."

Rooster turns quickly, the tomato paused on its journey to being eaten. Tasha sees the eye patch first: black and angular and covering the left eye, the strap stretched around a headful of hair, the curls pulled back to the crown in an enormous puff. The woman's cheekbones, high and freckled, jut out from under eyes that are like Stella's: large and curving upward at the corners. Tasha forgets how to breathe. She takes a step forward and then stops. Another, then stops.

"You…you…" She can't find the words.

The tomato falls, lost in the soil. The woman closes the distance between them, wiping her hands hastily on her pants. She reaches for Tasha, holding her face in her palms, the flesh warm and familiar.

"Leona," Tasha says.

"Sister," says Rooster. Her smile is another bright color in her garden, and inside Tasha a vine breaks loose, stretching upward for the sun. "You got my letter."

ACKNOWLEDGMENTS

My deepest and eternal gratitude to my readers, whose passion (and pressure) spurred me onward in the completion of this book. For my husband, who paves a road through all my storms. For my parents, whose love and raised eyebrows make me better. Kwame Alexander, whose vision is like chasing a rainbow. Alysia Carey, for her brilliance and her language(s). Sarah Linkous, Ever Velasquez, and Orlando Grimany Calas, for their willingness. Ari Harris, who is magic. Jenn Jackson and Jasmine Ben: save some perfection for the rest of us. Nicolle Gonzales, for her patience and her truth. Johnnie Jae, for her bright spirit and her deep knowledge. Chris and Jenn Hahn, whose excitement is exciting and whose Facebook threads made this book better. Anna Green, whose imagination is a gift. Jennifer Patiño Cervantes, who could light up the sky with her brain and her fury. Alexis G. Stodghill, who shook my hand once and inspired me forever. And finally, for LaBrenda Garrett-Nelson: without whom, none of this would have been possible.

45726995R00326